First Word

I0777717

Cover Artwork by Martina da Bologna
https://www.deviantart.com/martinadabologna
twitter: @scarlet_artist

Cover Layout by Erica Lynn Evans

Edited by Lily Ingersoll

ISBN: 978-1-963266-10-8

Visit the author on the internet
http://www.therunespring.com

A word on language.

The Earth of First Word is vastly different from the one we know. The Ta'el, the race that were placed on the Earth by the gods after the death of the humans, were over a millennium into the process of developing their own language before they began to read, and understand the left behind languages of the humans. Therefore, they have many of their own language constructs, and I will be placing a glossary at the end of this book to help everyone understand them.

I give gentle suggestion that you have a peak at that glossary before you start reading, if only to pick up on the terms for time. But, if you are feeling brave, feel free to jump in. I hope you enjoy what follows!

~ C.M.

Prologue

"THE STORY"

"Are you ready to tell the story, Little Aya?"

Aya blinked, and the indistinct shape formed of bright crimson mist resolved into an ehta'el. He stood with his paws folded behind his back, his transparent canine tail swaying lightly behind him for balance that he no longer needed. Habits acquired in life that chased him through death and into the Spiritlands.

Aya lifted her sash from the display bar on the wall behind her desk. The band of black leather was wide enough to cover half her chest, yet thin enough to be embroidered with the sigils of her office as a Stone of the Hearth. She slid it over her head and across her body, from shoulder to hip. She turned to the crimson Spirit and held her paws out to either side to ask how she looked.

Her bright sapphire eyes were lidded somewhat from lack of sleep. She nervously smoothed some of the golden fur on her cheeks into place. Aya twitched feline whiskers once to straighten them up, took a deep breath, and then let it out. **They are only cubs,** she reminded herself.

After a long look, Roan grinned and nodded in approval. "I am, Greatfather." Aya adjusted her sash one last time as the Spirit of Greatfather Roan adjusted his own phantasmal counterpart. She had just gotten hers preround, but it was what she had been working towards her entire life. Now she was tasked with telling a group of young cubs the very same story that had kindled her desire to be a Stone of the Hearth. Sashes in place, they departed for the stage together.

The auditorium was an ancient creation of the lost human race. The ta'el had restored the building using both magic and mundane craftsmanship. The seats once held hundreds of humans. Curving, vaulted ceilings were held in stasis by living tree limbs that grew through and supported the superstructure. Where once had been balconies, a wall of branches and greenery now provided seats for those among the ta'el that enjoyed high places.

The seats themselves were sparsely filled with a quadruple fistful of ehta and emta, each barely big enough to climb into them – cubs that were here hoping to find their calling in life. Not all of the little ones in the seats, twenty-one by Aya's count, would become members of the Hearth. However, they were the most likely candidates in the city. Aya closed her eyes, took a calming breath, and then strode out onto the stage.

"Hello, everyone, and welcome. I'm sure that no one told you anything about why you were here niround. They never told us anything when I was your age," Aya started.

A few of the cubs laughed.

"Raise your voice a little more. They won't hear you in the back," Greatfather Roan whispered to her.

"You're here to hear a story." Aya wasn't talking at the top of her lungs, but it was close.

She dropped her voice to a whisper. "I'm gonna go hoarse if I have to shout the whole story like this."

"So ask for help? Eleven turns of training, and you cannot even remember how to amplify your voice?" Roan teased.

She rolled her eyes and then mentally called out to one of the Ancestors. *{Windrider Lalap, if you could attend me invisibly?}* Aya projected her thoughts into the Spiritlands, the parallel realm where the Spirits of the Ancestors resided. A long moment passed before she felt the response as Lalap drew closer.

A moment later, she appeared next to Greatfather Roan, formed of bright azure mist. She had been of avian descent in life, a blue jay, unless Aya missed her guess. Her lack of a personal glow indicated that only Aya would be able to see her.

The high musical tones of an Avian emta'el floated into Aya's mind. *{How may I assist, Little Aya?}* Like most Avians, Lalap's Ta'eltesh was more sung than spoken.

{If you could bear my voice to the ears of the cubs with your power?} Aya asked politely.

{Wouldn't it just be simpler to ask the little ones to gather in close?}

Aya made a face. Her nervousness had clearly interfered with her reason. A silly mistake in front of a room of cubs who had not begun to count their turns yet. *{I apologize, Honored Ancestor. I should have thought of that first.}*

{No need for apologies. I was about to lose my sanity to boredom, anyway. I have not been called upon in ages. Since your first request was a bust, might I suggest that we ask a few other Ancestors to join us so that we may make your story one to truly delight the young ones?}

{I did not want to burden the Ancestors with such a trivial task,} Aya replied.

Lalap lifted her transparent wings in a mantling gesture, the avian equivalent of saying 'don't be silly.' Ta'eltesh was not just a vocal language, and while the vocal parts of it were common to all Ta'el, the body language portions were somewhat species specific. Aya's mother had made sure that she knew all of the ins and outs of the most common species dialects of Ta'eltesh.

{How could influencing the next generation of Hearth Stones be a trivial task?} Lalap asked, drifting closer to Aya and reaching out with her wing. Unlike feral birds, ta'el Avians had some small control over their feathers.

Lalap curled her feathers around Aya's paw and then dissipated into smoke. The smoke enveloped Aya for a moment before vanishing completely.

{I am calling some friends to help us make this a beautiful experience for the cubs. Can you channel them through?} Lalap asked.

Aya hesitated. Channeling a Spirit allowed the living to use their magical abilities, and while many ta'el thought that Aya's skills as a Channeler would be on par with her mother's abilities, they were not. Ayasha the elder, her mother, could Channel more than ten Spirits simultaneously with almost zero effort. She could produce magics of such power that no one had seen the like since the time of the First Ones. Aya was not her mother.

{I can try, but the most I have ever done is six, and it was a terrible strain for me.}

The voice of the Spirit inside of her head sounded perplexed. *{Why would it be a strain?}*

A third voice joined the conversation. *{Our Little Aya has not yet learned to let go of the Ancestors she channels into the Wild,}* Greatfather Roan spoke with gentle reproach.

{Oh, dear. Aya, it is not so difficult,} Lalap said. *{Simply Channel them and then break the connection.}*

{Won't they vanish back to the Spiritlands?}

{Only if you think they will,} Lalap replied.

{Remember, dear emta, much of Channeling is belief. How many times must I repeat this?} Greatfather Roan reminded.

{Apparently once more, Greatfather. I apologize for being such a poor student.} Aya couldn't suppress her tone of sarcastic humor.

{They are here. Are you prepared, Little Aya?} Lalap's sending was slightly urgent.

{What exactly are we doing?}

{You are telling a story, silly emta. We are just going to make it a little more special. Go on and enjoy the show.}

"Hearth Stone?" one of the cubs asked quietly. Even with the extreme acceleration of conversation by thought, Aya had paused too long.

"Yes, sorry, Myrisa." Aya suppressed a nervous giggle. "If everyone could gather in closer. I want you all to be able to hear me."

The cubs all got up from their seats and moved to the front two rows. As they did, a small crowd of Spirits manifested on the stage around her.

Unlike Lalap and Greatfather Roan, these Spirits were each filled with a lambent glow so that everyone could see them. Each Spirit was a different species, and while Aya did not recognize all of them, she saw one that she knew. Wanderer Lane waved to her, his ghostly white glow trailing his paw.

{We all know the story, little Aya,} Lane sent, and they all gathered around.

Aya touched each one, channeling them into her body, allowing them to appear almost fully solid in the real world. Aya immediately felt the drain as her magic fed into them. Aya closed her eyes, and did something only those trained specifically in Channeling learned – she forced all doubt from her mind and believed unequivocally. What she was attempting **would** work. She released the Ancestors into the world, and truly believed that the magic she had given them would sustain them for a time.

{I have no idea what is going on,} Aya said skeptically. The Ancestors were acting entirely of their own volition, without any direction from her.

Greatfather Roan, still standing to one side, lifted a paw from behind his back and made a shooing gesture, urging her to get on with it.

"Seven thousand turns ago, the first ta'el were brought into this world. We were birthed onto a dying world." Aya tried to keep her train of thought as the gathered Spirits did something that Aya had never seen before. They changed their forms.

Aya had seen shapeshifting plenty of times, and even performed the magic herself, but she had never seen Ancestors take on other forms. They had become younger versions of themselves, nearly cubs.

That was far from all they had done. The stage came to life with ghostly images that illustrated the story she was telling, images that Aya had seen before. Behind the Ancestor cubs stood the image of a creature whose beauty stole the breath.

Silver scales of such polish they might have been forged mercury covered every inch of her massive body. Her broad, rounded muzzle split in a contented smile that hinted at dozens of gleaming ivory fangs within. Shimmering blue eyes looked down upon the Ancestors from beneath horned ridged brows. Her sleek, rounded skull was crowned with a half dozen bright silver horns that swept back to frame a face with no visible ears. Each horn was covered in glowing scrollwork that seemed to shift in shape the longer one looked at it. She sat sphinxlike among the Spirits and bowed her lustrous head. Her image began to speak, though no sound issued forth from her maw. Aya spoke for her.

"Though we never saw a human, the Dragons created the Ta'el for the purpose of discovering what the humans had done to leave this world so bereft of magic and life."

The image surrounding the Ancestors changed, and Aya noticed the cubs had edged forward in their seats. She grinned as she continued the story as the image projected across the stage shaped itself into that of a clearing in the woods. Night had descended, and the moon and stars drifted behind the dragon as she leaned down to speak to the ta'el cubs.

"They taught us of magic and Spirits. How our world was damaged. How it needed our care and protection. They taught us that we would all need to work together to make this world our home."

As she spoke, images of Elemental Spirits of Fire and Earth formed within the circle of Ta'el. Channelers among the Ta'el in the image absorbed the Spirits. Each of the small figures raised their up their paws above their heads. A tiny, but breathtaking fireworks display erupted from the image as the figures worked with the Elemental Spirits. The image faded again to a bright summer round with the enormous silver dragon directing the cubs to excavate and repair the remains of a large human structure.

"Some among the ta'el began to restore the human settlements to search for clues to the past, and then to provide shelter and comfort for all."

The image shifted again, revealing a balmy woodland glade ringed in thick old growth monarchs. Dusk had fallen, and only the barest light shone between the trees. A cozy fire had been built at the center of the clearing offering light and warmth to those working within. One side of the clearing was filled by the massive body of the white dragon. Coiled around herself, her body was similar to that of a snake, if a snake happened to grow to the fill the breadth of a subway tunnel. She watched over the cubs, split into two groups.

One group surrounded an injured deer. They carefully cared for its broken hind leg. The other group was crouched beneath the watchful eye of the dragon. They coaxed a skittish looking Forest Spirit out of the brush at one side of the clearing. It emerged a moment later.

"Others dedicated themselves to attempting to restore the Spirits of Nature to improve the health of the Wild." Aya made a gentle gesture towards the image.

The image shifted one last time. This time, though, many of the cubs present were recognizable as figures from their oldest legends. Each of the pawful of cubs had spread themselves about a dilapidated structure, massive in scale. Scattered and covered in debris were massive book shelves.

Many of the ta'el were using ropes attached to block and tackle rigs to lift one of the massive shelves. Just as one of the shelves was lifted, one of the figures hidden by a shimmering grey cloak and cowl lifted a paw. The crumbled remains of the wall behind the bookcase lifted from where they had fallen. The pieces reassembled themselves just as the bookcase came to against the newly repaired wall.

A much smaller number were collecting books. Each book was carefully cleaned, then restored with magic. Afterwards, they were organized on shelves that had been restored on the repaired side of the enormous building.

"But many of us formed the Hearth and dedicated ourselves to fulfilling the command of the Dragons: to discover exactly what the humans had done to leave our world so damaged." As she spoke, the Ancestor Spirits changed.

Aya became a silent observer for a short moment as the Spirits decided to show off a bit. More images showed a myriad of events that those created during those early times had experienced in the process of establishing ta'el society.

"To this very round, we all continue to search for the answers the Dragons asked us to find. Now you can begin to learn how to take up the task of finding those answers," Aya finished the story.

The Ancestors took their bows and waved before fading away, all but Wanderer Lane. The mongoose sauntered over to her before fading from the real world back to his fully spiritual form. The white glow faded from around him, leaving him visible only to Aya's eyes.

{A wonderful first showing, Little Aya. You will be an enormous asset to the Hearth.} Wanderer Lane's sending was suffused with support that made Aya feel warm inside.

{Were you all so bored?} Aya asked.

Lane shook his head and a small smile curled the corners of his muzzle.

{No, Aya, they came for you.}

Aya looked a little dumbfounded.

Lane rolled his eyes. *{You've counted almost twenty-five turns, Aya. You must have noticed by now how much the Spirits like you. Your Mother may be the most powerful Channeler in the last thousand turns, but even she does not share herself with the Ancestors the way you do. Her true passion is for the Elementals and repairing the Wild, but yours, it seems, lies with us.}* Lane disappeared.

Lane was not wrong, and she had known long before she started counting her turns that she didn't want to do what her mother did. Aya looked back to the cubs, who were all watching her. She took a deep breath, put on a toothy grin, and made her way down from the stage. She motioned the children in closer to her.

"We need all the help we can get, and that includes all of you."

The cubs all nodded. Though none of them had reached their full growth yet, they were all ready to decide if they wanted to be a Stone of the Hearth. This would allow training to be arranged for them in the future. One of the cubs approached her. The tiny ehta was born of some big cat species that she did not recognize. Silly as it was, Aya felt slightly ashamed that she did not know immediately despite being born of the Clouded Leopard herself.

"Can we learn how to Channel all those Spirits?" the little ehta asked. After a moment of concentration, his name rose up in her mind.

"The only way to know that, Haran, is to train yourself as a Channeler. As a Stone of the Hearth, we would teach you, but we are not the only way to learn. I would love for you all to join the Hearth, but there are many talented Channelers among the Caretakers of the Wild. There are even a few sages among those of other callings that could teach you as much as any of the Stones. That choice is yours, Haran."

"How long do we have to choose Hearth Stone?" Myrisa, the small Red Panda emta asked.

Aya tapped her gently on the nose. "As long as you need, Myrisa, but if you are anything like me, I suspect none of you will need that long." Aya smiled, remembering how eager she had been at that age. "Now come on, all of you, back to your parents before they wonder if I have stolen you all away."

She shooed them all out into the hallway where their parents were waiting for them, then handled the mandatory shift's worth of questions from every parent about everything that they could expect if their cubs joined the Hearth. When she finally freed herself from their clutches, she went back to her office. The trip home to her apartments took another half shift. She could have gotten there much faster if she had taken the roofways: elevated walkways stretching between the roofs of buildings that permeated the skyline.

Sometimes, though, she liked to walk the street to take in the feeling of the city. Part of the responsibility of the Hearth was to make sure that relations between the Ancestors and the living Ta'el fared well. She paused as she turned onto her street. At the end of the row stood her brownstone that had remained empty most of her life.

The building was a task that she had been assigned when she began her training. Aya had dutifully worked with one of the local Elemental Spirits, spell after spell, to reinforce the building so that it would remain standing until the Naturesmiths could make it livable.

She put her hand against the thick oak trunk that stood as one of the corners of the building. Like all of the other buildings in use on the street, the Heart Tree grew through the walls, reinforced the floors, sealed the roof against the elements, and watched over the ta'el living within. Each surviving building was a crossbreed of mother nature, human made material, and the magic of the ta'el. The marriage might have left the city with the haunting air of a place abandoned were it not for the ta'el who resided within. She patted the tree she had helped the Naturesmiths grow lovingly, and then made her way into the building.

Just as she opened the door to her apartments, her sense of the Spirits disappeared entirely from her awareness. She nearly stumbled, catching the door latch to keep from falling. It was like her entire ability to Channel fled her, and it took her breath away. She gasped for air, near to hyperventilating.

"Greatfather?" She barely recognized her own voice, so strangled as it was with stress.

"A moment please, Aya," Roan responded almost instantly. He floated through the wall into her office. It was decidedly odd behavior for Roan to ignore the rules of reality. Unlike most Ancestors, it always made him uncomfortable to pass through solid objects. That made his behavior stand out as all the more distressing to Aya.

He seated himself in a chair, pulled his legs up into a cross-legged position, and closed his eyes. She stood clutching the door handle, gasping for breath.

Roan's eyes popped open, and such a look formed on his face. Aya had never seen the kind of dread Roan displayed. It was deep, lonely, and unthinking.

"Greatfather?" Aya's voice trembled with anxiety.

"The Elementals are silent, Aya. I cannot gain any sense of the Life Spirit," came Roan's fearful whisper.

Aya finally caught her breath and got her paws beneath her. A pregnant moment passed.

Without warning, her senses flooded with the overwhelming presence of all of the Spirits of the world. She nearly collapsed from relief.

"Greatfather, what in the Seven Sides was that?!" Aya growled.

"I have no idea. However, I think that we must absolutely discover the answer to that question."

Chapter 1

"CONFIRMATION"

Aya stared sullenly at the steak on her plate. There were many ta'el that enjoyed raw meat. Aya was not one of them.

"Why did I chose the Hound as the subject of my Confirmation?"

"Because you are an overachiever who finds it necessary to befriend a nature Spirit in the city. Also, if I remember correctly, you said," a perfect imitation of Aya's voice came from Greatfather Roan's ghostly muzzle, "If I can befriend the Hound, he can help me track down the hidden caches of information in this city."

Aya stared at the raw piece of meat on her plate.

"I'd eat it for you if I could. Don't know why you like it burnt and covered in spices," Roan said.

"Because… it's cold and blood trickles down my throat like I am drinking a copper dust smoothie. How did you find that appetizing?"

Roan shrugged. "I had no trouble befriending the Hound."

"You didn't call the Hound into the city and then challenge him to a contest of wills."

The Hound was the representative Elemental of all canines, possessing magical skills that allowed one to do just about anything a canine could, and then some. It had a godlike ability to track down anything that you could envision. There were certain limitations on its powers, of course. You needed to have a very precise idea of what you were looking for.

That's why you couldn't just tell the Hound to find out what happened to the humans. Many ta'el had tried and failed. Ayasha had a few ideas about how to get the Hound to find things that would lead her to what had happened all those turns ago. Tonight, she hoped she'd find out if those ideas were right.

Ayasha leaned her head back and groaned. "Maybe if I don't look at it I can eat it without upchucking?"

"Pretty sure that your taste buds are not related to your eyesight," Roan said.

"I give up. I can't eat this." She held out her paw towards Roan. "You do it."

Roan made a face. "Must you torture me so?"

"What are you talking about? You helped me last time."

"The last time wasn't your Confirmation. The next time won't be your Confirmation either, but this time, you must do it on your own."

"If I throw up that delicious fish the twins left for me this morning, I swear I'm puking it all over you. You'll be picking white chunks out of your ectoplasm for spells."

"You are a vile, angry child." Roan grinned at her.

"All. Your. Fault."

Ayasha used her claws to cut off a piece of the steak on her plate.

"Hey, if you can find another memory to feed the Hound that it will accept, then you go right ahead and skip the steak. Or, you can possibly not screw up your introduction to an Elemental Spirit that can bite your entire body off while you're fully in its domain."

Aya grimaced. "So, I just have to make him respect me?"

"You haven't studied for this?"

"Of course I've studied for it! I'm nervous, Greatfather. The Hound scares me. The Elementals all scare me. They have since I was five turns old and my Mother was stabilizing the magma flows beneath Yellowstone. You were there. She Channeled the entire power of the volcano. I thought we were going to die. I'm not my Mother, Greatfather. I'm never going to be as strong as she is."

Roan smiled. "Little Aya, you have stood long in her shadow, and you are right. You are not your Mother, nor should you try to be her. Besides, five turns are not so many counted into your training. It was a perfectly normal reaction for one so young," Roan said gently.

Ta'el customarily did not keep track of their age until they were fully grown, until they were, at minimum, eighteen turns old. It was thought best not to burden cubs with the idea of their own mortality. While they were prepared throughout their youth to choose a path for their life, it was at a very slow pace. True training did not begin until they were fully grown. That was long gone for Aya, though. She had been counting twenty-three turns now, but had been a part of the Wild for almost double that time. She had been nineteen turns old when Roan himself had pronounced her grown and old enough to begin counting her turns.

"Why not? Everyone thinks she's amazing."

"It is good to aspire to be like those you admire, Aya, but not to be them. You should be you. Besides, you don't see it yet, but there are things that your Mother admires just as much about you as you do about her."

Aya made a raspberry noise. "Yeah, sure, Greatfather."

Aya plugged her nose with two of her fingers and put the piece of steak in her mouth. She didn't chew, but rather swallowed as quickly as she could. She tore the steak apart and quickly downed the whole of it. When she was done, she made a very unhappy noise.

"Don't do it. You don't have to like it, but if you throw up, the memory will be ruined," Roan warned.

Aya swallowed and got up, rushing into the kitchen. She yanked open the smallest cold drawer near the floor and began touching each of the small ampule bottles inside.

"Aya, what are you doing?" Roan asked.

She shook her head and finally, her finger touched the bottle she wanted. Most of the potions kept in the cold storage drawer were made for specific situations. They were temporary magical effects granted by the Ancestors for occasions when there was no time to properly Channel an Ancestor Spirit. Not everyone could make them, but Aya's father was quite adept at the skill.

Aya had made the potion she was desperately rummaging through the cold drawer for with help from her father, Sahone. Aya was a fair cook, but her father was a bit of a legend when it came to food. He had tried to teach her how to make her favorite dish at least a dozen times, but it was beyond her skill. Her finger touched a purple cork, and the warm sensation of her father's magic rose up through her paw. She yanked out the ampule and snagged the cork in her teeth. She twitched her muzzle and yanked it out.

"Aya, you really shouldn't do that."

The warm, tan liquid inside of the bottle smelled savory. Floating in the liquid was a small, glowing simulacrum of her Father's own Watcher Spirit, Elder Strom. It looked much like a stuffed animal made in his image. It was rather like a slightly transparent green teddy bear and glowed with an emerald light.

"I'm helping myself, thank you very much," Aya said, a little annoyed. She very carefully tilted the bottle up until a single drop of amber liquid gathered on the rounded lip of the bottle.

Greatfather Roan put his paw over his eyes and began to mumble. The drop of liquid fell into Aya's mouth and she quickly put the potion ampule down on the counter before the magic could hit her.

She knew she was using the potion incorrectly, but it was better than upchucking the steak and having to eat another. The flavor of the white fish baked in a red sauce exploded across her senses. It was so overwhelming that it blew away all thoughts of the raw steak she had just eaten. It also blew away her sense of smell and made her tongue go a little numb.

"Augh, Aya! Why did you do that? You're going to smell like fish for a spell! The Hound will not be pleased with that," Roan scolded her.

"Can we go? I just want to get this over with. Maybe I'll get lucky and the Hound will eat me," Aya said dejectedly. She corked the ampule and carefully put it back into the cooling drawer.

Roan rolled his eyes. "Oh, please. As if you have anything to worry about. How many hundreds of Spirits have you befriended?"

"The Hound is different. Elementals are different."

"Yes, because you haven't made a friend out of every tiny Light and Air Spirit as far as the eye can see. Stop being so dramatic. You're a full Stone of the Hearth niround. Hurry up. You'll never make it if you don't take the roofways."

Aya looked at the cloud of white and blue mist floating above the sink in her kitchen. As long as she gave the little Light Spirit living memories of enjoying naps in sunbeams, it would happily show her the rough time of the round by forming a scene of the sky with either the sun or moon visible. The path of the sun or moon told her the time as accurately as she would ever need it.

Roan chuckled a little. "You know your Confirmation is just a formality, right? They're not making a special appointment for you."

"Some formality, and I am not just befriending a Spirit. This is a contest of wills, and…"

"Scales! You really are that same nervous little emta, aren't you?" he teased gently.

"Sometimes."

Aya pulled her sash over her head, belted on her knife and piece pouch, and checked to make sure the right potion vials were in the pouch. She touched the handle of the knife, which sat horizontally on the belt just above her tail. It was within easy reach, though it was unlikely she would need it. She had never taken it out of the sheath in her entire life except to clean it and train with it.

Knife was perhaps too small a word for the large blade. It was almost as long as Aya's forearm, with an edge that curved up to a drop point and a straight, thick spine. Every full-fledged Channeler carried a weapon like this, though they were much rarer among others. Such weapons were a gift given from a master Channeler to their Apprentice when they negotiated the challenge of dealing with their first hostile Spirit. The steel of the knife's blade was invested with magic so that it could cut the flesh of Spirits. It was meant as a last defense against hostile Spirits.

Ayasha headed for the garden and the roofways. She stepped out into the rooftop garden, turning right. Climbing into the sky there was an enormous tree. The Heart tree reinforced the building, keeping it structurally sound. She hopped over the low wall surrounding the roof, and her claws caught in the bark of the tree trunk. She was careful not to let her claws bite too deeply into the bark to keep from damaging the tree.

Aya climbed the tree as easily as she walked down the street. When she reached the top, she walked out onto a limb that stretched across the street and hopped down onto the roofway. Stretching between many of the roofs across the entire city were enormous walkways almost as wide as roads. They were never crowded, though there were always a few ta'el traveling over them, ones that were good climbers or fliers, unafraid of the heights. Outside of flying, the roofways were the fastest way to move through the city.

Many of the most massive buildings of the New York skyline had long since succumbed to the onslaught of time and the ravages of whatever had happened to this world. The ta'el had slowly restored the buildings in hopes that somewhere in the wreckage, they would find some clue to what the humans had done to destroy themselves. As they did, they had made improvements like the roofways.

Ayasha jogged in nearly a straight line to her destination, moving from one roof to another, ignoring the streets below. She sped up to a run, and by the time she reached the Hearth, she was panting a little, fur was soaked with her own sweat, never a pretty state for any ta'el. She had a few extra minutes, though, so she skipped the stairs and jumped straight off the side of the building. She caught the rain gutter there. She dug her claws into the pipe as best she could to slow her descent. It worked, but the horrendous screeching sound left her shivering when her paws hit the ground.

She dashed into the building and immediately took a right, running down the stairs one floor to her office which held a small bathroom and a bath. She stripped off her sash and knife belt, hung them by the door, and practically dove into the small shower stall. She stood in the hot water for only a minute, sluicing off the smell of her sweat, along with a bit of the fish smell of her Father's potion.

She turned off the water and dropped to all fours in the shower and shaking her body violently until the water flew from her fur. She did a quick toweling off just to get the last of the water out, and then pulled on the sash and her knife belt again. When she made it to the door to the gardens, Roan was waiting there.

"Well, at least you don't smell wet anymore," Roan observed.

"You can't smell anyway, smartass."

"Untrue. Smells of the real world are muted, but I can still catch the ass-like smell of wet fur." Roan said it almost completely straight-faced, but even his slight transparency couldn't hide the grin on his stupid muzzle. Aya walked directly through him on her way through the door to the inner gardens. He made a shivering, disgusted noise.

"Must you do that?!"

"Only when you are being an enormous smartass."

The doors opened up onto what looked like portal into a rainforest. Lush gardens maintained by busy ta'el of multiple species filled the massive space. These ta'el were not members of the Hearth, but rather ones with special affinities for plants. Aya stepped onto one of the neatly kept paths of paved stone weaving through the foliage.

"No, it's alright. You may all continue your work. I will not be staying. I just need a place slightly closer to nature."

"Are you sure, Hearth Stone?" a young racoon emta'el asked as the others looked on.

"Yes, please, Erise return to your work. If you could simply keep the noise down to a minimum until I make it to the Spiritlands?"

They all exchanged a look.

"But," Erise started, but Aya grinned.

"No, Erise, I won't be dying niround. With consent and assistance from the Spirits, we can spend limited time in the Spiritlands." Erise looked around. "My escort isn't here yet, but don't be afraid when he shows up," Aya assured them.

"Why would we be afraid?"

"Because a ten foot tall black spirit dog with glowing red murder eyes can be frightening?" Erise swallowed, and Aya grinned to her. "The Hound is quite friendly, even if he does look like he might decide to dine on your liver."

Aya moved down one of the paths, looking for a nice patch of grass, finding one after a couple of bends. She sat down cross-legged in the grass and cupped her paws at her waist, making her fingers into a circle. The posture was one that she had inherited from her Mother. It helped her concentrate on reaching mentally into the Spiritlands.

{I call to The Great Hound, and I request a Trial of Confirmation.}

Aya waited. Roan had warned her that receiving your Confirmation of mastery from any chosen Spirit would not be like meeting any other new Spirit. He had not been lying. She suddenly shivered in an arctic cold that she had not felt a moment before. Her eyes popped open, and she could see only white fields stretching away to tree lines far in the distance. It was dark, and everything she could see had the slight radiant glow of the Spiritlands.

The cold was pervasive, penetrating her fur as if her bones had turned to ice. She began to shiver much more violently after a long moment of looking around. As far as she could see, there was nothing but a flat plane of glowing snow as far as she could see. Frozen grasses that poked up through the fields of snow were the only immediate indication that she was not in a complete wasteland. She got up out of the snow, brushing it out of her fur, and then she mentally reached out for help from the Spirits.

I should be able to call up a Light Elemental to help keep…

Ayasha's thoughts trailed off when she realized that her sense of the Spirits was absolutely silent. This was not even like the previous night, when her senses of the Spirits disappeared. She could feel nothing at all from them. She looked around for Greatfather Roan to ask him, but he was nowhere to be found. That was completely impossible. Roan was tied to her living Spirit quite permanently. The only way he could be severed from her is if she were killed.

She wrapped her arms around herself as she began to shake for reasons other than the cold. She couldn't be dead, though. She wouldn't shiver if she were among the Spirits. She looked around in confusion for a long moment, the light fading over the horizon in the distance. She started moving towards the frozen tree line. She had to get some shelter and a fire going or she wasn't going to last out here.

Her body began to warm as she moved, but she was concerned about the numbness building in her toes. A shift of trudging through the snow allowed her to reach the tree line, but by then, her feet had gone almost completely numb. That was a terrible sign. If she didn't warm them soon, there was going to be a lot of really unpleasant healing in her future. As the light of the sun guttered out, she saw them. In the tree line to her right, a pair of eyes illuminated in red.

Aya froze, her eyes locked onto that spot. She lingered only for a moment, but then her worry reasserted itself. She started to move towards the trees again, and the eyes disappeared back into the forest.

The snow got much thinner beneath the thick canopy of the forest, and in some places, Aya was light enough to walk on top of the icy crust atop the snow. She found a sheltered spot between three large tree trunks, and, ignoring the painful numbness in her paws, she started to scrape away the snow and detritus on the ground.

Within a minute or two, she had scraped away a clear spot. She made a frantic little search of the area, digging with cold-numbed paws through the snow to find dry wood. A few more minutes saw her with a small pile of dried twigs and leaves in the sheltered spot beneath the trees. A reached behind her back and clumsily drew the Heartblade from its sheath. She picked up a small stone and stuck the tip of the blade into the ground at the edge of her pile of kindling.

She scraped the stone against the back of the blade, and sparks showered down over the kindling. Aya blew out a breath she didn't know she'd been holding when the kindling caught. She wiped the blade on her leg to clear the dirt from the tip, and then slid it back into its sheath.

The little fire blazed up merrily after a few minutes of careful work, and she put a few more small pieces of kindling on top of to help it grow. If she was lucky, the fire would attract some light or fire Spirits that she could make friends with. She had found a downed piece of log that was large enough to make a seat for her, plopping down onto it to stick her still numb paws out at the fire. Just as the pain in her thawing paws began to become difficult to stand, she felt the fur on the back of her neck coming to attention.

"Of course. You couldn't wait for my paws to thaw out completely. That would be too much to ask," Aya said with annoyance, but the affectation didn't help her much. She was shivering with fear again. Without her Channeling, she had nothing to defend herself with other than the martial skills Wanderer Lane had taught her and her Heartblade.

{You trespass in my domain, food.}

The low bass growl of the sending pained her, like someone was pushing needles into her temples. Anger pushed Aya to her feet.

"I am no one's prey."

Aya expressed her claws and crouched down into a balanced stance, ready for combat.

{A bold statement for something that squeaks like a mouse. You look like food to me.}

The fear that the voice evoked pushed Aya to turn and flee. The light of her fire seemed to be pushed back by the shadow of the forest as it attempted to swallow her tiny bastion of safety. As she watched, she remembered the first time a Spirit had tested her will with fear. She had run away that time. Afterwards, Roan had told her that it was ok to be afraid. Fear was something that anyone could stand up to, as long as they remembered that it was theirs.

"You are the master of your own feelings, Little Aya, not the other way around. You always decide what you will do."

She would not run away again. Aya turned back to the inky black unknown hiding those burning red eyes. She reached behind her back and drew her Heartblade again. She reversed her grip on it, just like Lane had taught her, the spine of the blade poised along her forearm

"I am no one's prey," Aya repeated.

She spread her feet, digging her claws into the dirt for better grip. Her tail was a perfect arch, allowing her to measure her balance. A black muzzle pushed itself through a wintergreen shrub on her right. Shining red eyes and a massive black furred body followed.

Aya almost took a step back from the force of its presence. The Hound was one of the most ancient of elemental Spirits. The progenitor of all canines. For one brief moment, Aya thought she may have made a mistake attempting to match wills with a Spirit like this one for her confirmation. Then her resolve firmed, and she bared her fangs in warning.

{You are fierce for one so tiny, but you are no match.} The basso growl of the sending rattled around inside Aya's mind like broken glass thrown into a trash can. She narrowed her eyes.

"Test me, then, if you dare."

Aya exposed not a hint of fear in her voice, shoving the stupid voice in her head screaming for her to run away into a locked mental box before it could betray her. Instead, she bristled all of her back fur to make herself look even more menacing.

That was when the beast lunged at her. It flashed over her tiny fire, jaws open wide, straight at her throat. Aya bolted forward as well. She dodged to one side at the last second and brought her knife paw up as the massive spirit flew by. She brought her Heartblade around, the blade springing up from her forearm it sliced into the side of the beast with surprisingly little resistance. She knew the blade was irrationally sharp, but she had expected it to ping off a rib or some other bone.

It seemed though that even as solid as the Hound seemed here in the Spiritlands, he was still a Spirit. Liquid light dripped from a gash down its side when Aya spun to face him across the fire, but his entire body posture had changed from aggressive to friendly. The entire palpable aura of fear that had consumed her just a moment ago burst away from her as if it were sand she were shaking from her fur.

{No hesitation, and even with such overwhelming fear. Your name, little emta'el?} the Hound queried.

"Ayasha."

The Hound came around the fire, his tongue lolling out in a friendly way. He seemed unhindered by the long gash down his side, though she knew it must have pained him. He accepted it.

Aya stood very still, but even though his eyes were still burning red orbs, they were open and friendly. He was eye to eye with her, and he snuffled around her head, taking in her scent. He spoke out loud for the first, and only, time.

"Ayasha. Daughter of Ayasha the Caretaker. Daughter of Sahone the Wildheart. I name thee Ayasha the Speaker, and I confirm thee Channeler Adept." He licked the side of her muzzle affectionately.

She rubbed the side of her face, and then sighed in relief. She scratched the side of his muzzle gently with her free paw. Memories of what she was doing here came flooding back into her mind and she groaned.

"You made me forget what I was here for. How did you do that? I sensed nothing."

{It is your Confirmation, Ayasha the Speaker. You allow us to do whatever we wish to satisfy the conditions of confirming your mettle. The magic is inherent in the request for confirmation.}

"I have a gift for you. I just hope that I have not ruined it with what it cost me to get it," Ayasha said.

{I thank you for your thoughtfulness. It is not often I am called upon for a Confirmation, and especially not one in the confines of a city. You have guts, Ayasha the Speaker.}

Ayasha put her paw on the side of his muzzle and called up the memory of eating the steak before she came. She was careful to limit the memory to only eating the steak and not what came before and after. Memories were often currency among the Spirits. Since they could no longer experience that which they had enjoyed in life in the Spiritlands, it was often their price, that one should experience it for them and then pass along the memory. This allowed them to experience it as if they were alive again. The Hound closed his hellfire eyes and sighed in sheer animal contentment.

"What does my name mean, Honored Ancestor?"

It was a long moment before his eyes slid open, and he answered. *{That was pure joy. Fresh meat on my tongue. It has* *been so long since I was offered a memory like that one. Unfortunately, I do not know. I have never heard its like, though I am not often called upon for Confirmation, as I said. It came to me from the Aether.}*

She had other questions but they were all blown away in Aya's mind by the second thing he had said.

"Wait, Adept?" She swallowed nervously. "Channeler Adept?"

{Indeed. Congratulations to you, Ayasha the Speaker. You may call on me whenever you feel my skills will be suited to your task. I will endeavor to take a less disturbing shape in the future.}

While the Ancestors taking different shapes was an oddity, the Elemental spirits were well known for using various shapes. Still, she had never seen the hound in another shape before.

"I've never seen you take another shape?"

{Have you not? I often assisted your mother in the past. We have met many times.}

Aya's mind flashed back to all of the times she had seen her mother with a canine, not a ta'el. Ta'el sometimes had animal partners, and the remnants of domesticated canines that had made it through whatever had killed the humans often made up those partners. The animals that were not Ta'el made a sort of bridge between Elementals and the Ta'el. They could be very useful in amplifying the potency of one's Channeling, acting as a sort of spiritual support.

"That was you? All those different dogs?"

{I am the progenitor of all canines. With permission, I can embody any canine, whether they be Ta'el or otherwise. Your mother and father have been friends to me when few others would. I often embody a willing canine to assist her with her Channelings.}

Aya realized that the Hound was not often called upon by many people, despite his immensely useful supernatural talents. Forming a bond with him generally required facing him in a contest of wills, and what she had just done was terrifying even for someone as well trained as she.

"I would be happy to fulfill that role as well," Aya said. She would think about finding a canine willing to be her companion to provide a vessel for the Hound to utilize on occasion.

{I know now you do not savor raw meat, so I will think of some other memory that will satisfy me in exchange for my assistance. Perhaps fish would be more to your liking, considering your scent?}

Aya blinked at him. She was still reeling from being confirmed an Adept.

There were several ranks that the Spirits might confer to a ta'el upon completing their training in any given skill. In Channeling, the ranks were generally Apprentice, which one earned near the start of training, Proficient, and Master. Sometimes, the Spirits would convey a higher rank to someone especially gifted. Ayasha had expected to be confirmed as a Master. She did not fit the bill of especially gifted. Apparently, though, the Spirits disagreed with her.

Adept was only one rank below her mother, who was one of the most powerful Channelers in several generations. She had earned the rank of Peerless when she completed her training. It wasn't just about how much personal energy one had to put into Channeling. It was more about how well they learned and used their lessons. Over time, a ta'el could earn a higher rank through experience, but it was uncommon to advance in rank beyond one's confirmation. The Spirits judged rank not only based on who one was right then, but also who they foresaw one would become.

"So, would you be so kind as to get us out of this freezing wasteland before my toes start turning black?"

{Apologies, Speaker.}

Aya's eyes popped open and the garden had returned around her. She was suddenly flooded with warmth as reality reasserted itself.

"What does Wildheart mean?" she asked quietly. Aya had known since she had learned about her Confirmation some turns ago that the Spirits would give her a name. No matter what skill your first Confirmation was for, the Spirits would honor you with a name. She had never heard her Father called by his name, though, until now. The Hound stared at her for a long moment.

{You should ask your father that. It would be somewhat impolite for me to tell you how your Father earned his name.}

"I apologize, Honored Ancestor. Please forgive my impoliteness." Aya patted The Hound on his flank in appreciation.

{Not at all, Ayasha the Speaker. Thank you for your memory. It was a most appropriate gift, considering how hard you had to work for it.}

His massive tongue almost enveloped her hand as he gave her an affectionate lick. Thankfully, the wetness from his tongue faded away just as he did. The ta'el working in the garden were all gathered around her, staring at where The Hound had been standing. Then they looked at her. She smiled.

"Told you he wasn't as scary as he looked," she said a little shakily. Ayasha sat down hard in the grass, yanking her tail out of the way just in time to keep from sitting on it.

"So where did he take you?" Greatfather Roan bent over her, looking over her feet. "Somewhere cold. Extremely cold, considering that some of the flesh on your paw pads has already frozen. Aya, you need healing or you will be in for some serious pain when these thaw."

"I can already feel it. Is my piece pouch around here? I think it fell off my belt when I entered the Spiritlands."

"You can't carry pieces into the Spiritlands. The metal becomes somewhat spiritually heavy because of all the paws that handle it. I've never thought to tell you because you never feel the need to travel through the Spiritlands."

"There is one of the Greatmother Sasu's potions in the pouch."

Roan looked around, and then floated away towards the bushes.

"It fell over here, Aya."

She turned over and crawled across the grass. She pulled the pouch out from beneath the shrub.

"Roan, The Hound named me Ayasha the Speaker. What does it mean?"

Ayasha took the small, round bottle out of her bag. The liquid inside was clear like water, and floating in the water was another teddy bear. This one, though, was bright white in color, and the glow seemed much brighter because the liquid was so clear. She drank down the liquid, which tasted slightly bitter as Greatmother Sasu's potions always did. The taste was immaterial.

As soon as the liquid hit her stomach, a warm feeling spread through her body. Ice scrapes and other small wounds healed up, and the pain coming from her feet faded away. The potions had limitations when it came to more serious wounds, but for her injuries, they did just fine. She looked around for Roan, but when she saw him, his face was a little blank.

"Greatfather?"

"Ayasha, until I can consult with some other Spirits, you should keep your new name a secret."

"You're scaring me, Greatfather."

His ghostly fingers touched the side of her face in a way they could touch nothing else real.

"I know, Little Aya, but this is important. I've never heard anyone named the Speaker. I don't know what your name means. For a keeper like myself to have never heard a name is momentous. At the time of my death, it had only happened seven times in over six hundred turns."

The Spirits never gave someone a name without a reason. It wasn't set in stone, but the names Ta'el earned were related to things the Spirits saw about them in their own living spirit. Some names were common, like the name her mother had earned. Caretaker meant that someone had a passion for repairing the Wild. She had heard a lot of names, even in her short life, and she knew what they all meant. Some, like her martial arts teacher Lane the Wanderer, were quite obvious. Others, like her Father's name, the Wildheart, were much less so. She couldn't imagine what it meant to be a Wildheart. If it had to do with a passion for fixing the Wild why wouldn't he be a Caretaker?

However, what made Aya stare open-mouthed at Roan's statement was that he didn't know what her name meant. When Roan had been alive, one of his titles as a Stone of the Hearth had been Keeper of Names. It was his job to record all

new names and attempt to decipher their meanings. He had
been very good at the job. For him to have no idea what her
name meant was, for Ayasha, chilling.

Chapter 2

"MEANING"

Roan paged frantically through the books scattered about his simple dwelling in the Spiritlands. It was impossible. For four hundred turns, it had been his task to record and memorize every name passed to the Ta'el by the Spirits. That there had been no Speakers during that time was concerning, but the situation was far worse. As a Keeper of Names, he knew when a name was noteworthy. Names such as Aya's were given to only a single ta'el at a time. It did not bode well for Aya's desire for a quiet life of research and cultivating spiritual harmony.

Singular individuals such as those were not forgotten in the history of the Ta'el. He could feel that he was missing something he had once known. Even though he had lost contact with his memories in his passing, some memories held such power that they had followed one even through death.

He flipped through one of the books that contained the memories of his life. These books were the only complete connection he had to that time. Spirits were, to great extent, detached from their memories upon death. However, the power of a connection not quite severed had drawn him here. Something he had seen in life had resonated with Aya's new name.

Roan skipped the pages that concerned his mate. She had outlived him by almost a hundred turns, and she had just recently passed to the Spiritlands. It would be a long time before she would be able to join him. He slowed the riffling pages as his feelings of love turned to mourning. *A long time before I will see her again.* He contented himself with the simple knowledge that she had loved him and would be ready for a new adventure at his side when she passed the Bardo. There was no need to burden his Spirit with the details of what they had left behind.

He was jarred from his revery when the page of memories he had been searching for flicked open at last. It was a small thing, but powerful, something he had never forgotten. He tapped a claw on it. His home disappeared, and his memory played like a movie around him. His living self was sitting at a desk, stylus in paw, scratching a name into one of the genealogical tomes. He got up and walked to the pedestal at the center or the room, where the Tome of All Names was kept.

It had been twenty turns since he had last entered a new name into the Tome of All Names. Roan watched as his living self flipped to the book's beginning. He began his monthly ritual of reading the Tome to ensure he kept them all in his memory. It was the job of every Keeper to keep all the names of the tome in their memory so that new names were instantly recognizable.

He watched himself draw a finger down the page of the magical construct. It shared the names recorded within to each copy of the tome throughout the world. Roan watched as his past self reached a quarter of the way through the book. His living self paused and stared at the book. He knew what he had been thinking at that moment.

He put his finger on the massive page and stared at a name. The name on this line was not the correct one. There should be a name between this name and the previous one. He stared hard at the book and then the names went a little fuzzy in his vision. He remembered this thought too. He had been awake for several rounds without sleep. He shook off his doubts. Roan held up a ghostly paw and the memory froze. He had gone far enough to gain understanding of what had drawn him to these tomes; that he should have listened to those doubts. He stared at the book in utter blank confusion.

He knew how the magic of the Tome of All Names worked. A name being erased was anathema to the very reality of the book. Still, somehow, a name had been removed, or at least had been hidden from him. Some remnant of his mystical senses told him that the missing name was The Speaker. When he tried to focus on that feeling, he felt a deep need to turn his thoughts elsewhere. He knew then that he was right.

Some magic was barring him from trying to explore his instincts on the situation. It was a confirmation, of sorts.

The prospect of this new information coupled with the happenings surrounding the temporary interruption in their connection to the Life Spirit was daunting at best. It was a mystery that should be pursued with all haste. The conclusions he had reached left him with limited options, however. The best of those options was to speak with the White. Only the Dragon herself would have the necessary power to override the Tome of All Names.

He would tell Aya all of this when he returned to her, but he felt disappointed in himself for not being able to be of more help. This development also left him in an unfortunate predicament, as no one had had contact with the White in several hundred turns.

Roan flipped the book in front of him closed and looked up at the simple tile roof of his home. His eyes traced the scrollwork carved into the glowing support beams as he considered the best course of action. Perhaps, there was another option available. The Ta'el that had first recognized that the names the Spirits gave each ta'el were so very important. Like Aya, Olan the Namekeeper had a singular name.

He thought back to his one and only meeting with Olan. Everyone who took up the keeping of Ta'el names met his Spirit or his proxy, Tacal, at least once when they were connected to the magic of the Tomes. While the details were lost to his memory tomes, his feelings of dislike for the ehta came through clearly enough. He felt a meeting with Olan would be a very unpleasant experience for Aya. However, short of the White herself, it might be their only option to get answers.

Tacal was far more pleasant to deal with, but he was also just an intermediary. He only granted access to the magic of the Tome of All Names if Olan was unavailable. There were other options that Roan could think of, but they would be more difficult to utilize. They might have to go that route,

though, since Roan knew that no one had seen Olan in at least
a decade.

Chapter 3

"PATHS"

Aya wended her way through the ta'el crowding the roofways during the afternoon rush. It was not a difficult task because once ta'el saw her sash, they would excuse themselves and open a way for her. Stones of the Hearth were extremely well respected among the ta'el.

She stopped just as she reached the first roof of the housing district. She hopped over the railing surrounding it. Only a moment of freefall passed before her claws caught in the bark of one of the trees that supported the structure of the building. She jumped from branch to branch, all the way down to street level, passing a few other feline ta'el along the way who were using the tree to reach the roofways.

She walked a block down the street to Shop Row. There were several restaurants at the beginning of it, and one of them was having a problem that she had been asked to help with. It was a problem that seemed to repeat itself on a fairly regular basis, considering that the ta'el that had held her position before her had left her notes about the situation. Aya suspected that their notes were somewhat inadequate to the situation. He had been a good Stone, and he had kept this part of the city quiet for almost two hundred turns before joining the Searchers.

He had done his job to the best of his ability, but it wasn't his forte. He had been more of a researcher at heart, and didn't have the same relationship with the Ancestors that Aya was able to cultivate. She was just now starting to work on the little issues he had left behind.

Aya pushed open the thick wooden door, and the smells of roasting meat hit her nose. She had never been in this restaurant before, but she certainly hoped she would again, considering how good it smelled inside. What she had come here to fix, though, might prevent her from following through.

The door swung shut of its own accord, and Aya just barely yanked her tail out of the jamb before it halted and closed very slowly, making her feel like an overreacting idiot. Of course, they wouldn't make a door that would slam on someone's tail.

"Hello! We aren't open yet."

A plump Raccoon emta in a spotless white apron backed out of the swinging doors to the kitchens. She turned around, revealing that she was carrying a large wooden tray covered with stacked white bowls. Her lavender eyes went a little wide, and Aya put her paws over the Raccoon's to make sure that she didn't drop the tray.

"Nothing to be worried over, Hara. I am Aya, your new Stone, and I am just responding to your request for help with your Fire elemental." As soon as she was sure that Hara wasn't going to drop the tray, Aya let go. She did nothing to betray her dual purpose here. She *was* here to help with the Fire elemental, but one of the issues that had been left to her by Eresh involved this particular emta.

"But your sash?" Hara sounded confused, a confusion mirrored in Aya's mind. Hara put the tray down on the bar and touched the sash. "They are sending out Adepts to help with little Fire Elementals that cook our food?"

Aya paused.

"I just received my Confirmation two rounds ago. I am an Adept but I am a very new Adept, and…"

Hara held up a paw. "Okay…" Hara laughed. "Okay, I get it. You are here for experience. Can you help with the Elemental?"

Aya took a breath. "That, I can do."

"I don't know what to do with him. We give him all his favorites to burn, but sometimes he just gets so temperamental. Burns all the food, melts our pots and pans. It's a disaster!"

"I read Eresh's notes. A master of Spiritual Harmony, he was not."

Hara's surprised expression caused an instant realization in Aya. Immediate feelings of stupidity rose up, and Aya looked down at the floor in shame. She started to stammer an apology. Hara began to laugh.

"It's fine, Hearth Stone. Eresh did great for us, but you're not wrong. He didn't think we knew that he would trade out our little Spirit for another each time he came."

"Fire Elementals are really attached to their elements. They like to burn things, but they each come from a source. If you don't give them a little something from their source every once in a while, they get really restless."

Aya dug her fingers into the opening of her piece pouch and stepped past Hara into the kitchen. The opening to the stove was glowing merrily, and she crouched down in front of it to see the small humanoid figure curled up inside. It lifted its tiny head and peered out at her with the burning blue orbs that served as is eyes. Aya crooked her fingers in a tiny wave and the small Spirit stood up and stretched itself. It watched her curiously, now, and the flames dancing on its body became blue and white. The heat coming from the stove became intense.

"Now now, please, Honored Elemental, your heat is going to damage things."

Aya took her other paw out of her piece pouch and held up a small piece of black, charred wood between two fingers. She flicked it through the opening, and the little Elemental caught it. Its fire cooled down to a merry orange blaze again.

"How...?"

"Your particular Spirit came from a small forest fire that was the result of a lightning strike. If you just offer them a little of this, they'll calm down for a few spells. You'll have to enlist a little help from the Caretakers to get you more, but you'll be fine for a while now. Your spirit will be happy for a stint or so."

She held up a small blackened piece of wood smelling strongly of char and pine and held it out to Hara. "If you don't have more before your spirit becomes restless again, give the little one this and it will buy you more time. This is charcoal from a lightning-struck pine. It's the source of their fire. I've already told the Caretakers for the area where your Spirit came from, so they will be looking for more lightning-struck trees for this. It'll help them locate more Fire Elementals for other purposes, as well."

"That was amazing," Hara said.

Aya just shrugged. She dusted off her paws and smiled at the happy little Spirit before standing back up. "Knowing the subject, is all." She stuck a finger into the stove, and the little Elemental caressed her fingertip with a warmth no hotter than a warm bath.

She then headed for the kitchen exit. "Also, there is someone you could have talked to that could have told you this if you had just asked." Hara got a confused look on her face, and then shook her head.

Aya pushed open the swinging doors to reveal a pair of nearly identical Raccoons. One, though, had long grey hair braided into a thick queue.

"Hey, Auntie Hara," the emta of the pair said. She was holding her long grey braid in her paws nervously.

"Why would I ask these two for help?" Hara frowned. "They almost cost me my shop and everything I own."

Aya narrowed her eyes. She had never met Hara or been in her restaurant, but she knew the two cubs very well.

"Because you never picked up anything in your entire life that you didn't mean to," Aya stated with slight sarcasm.

"I certainly never let my tendency to fill my pockets make me pick up an heirloom with a connection to every Ancestor in an entire family's history."

Aya stood up to her full height and stared Hara down with hard eyes. Aya opened her mouth, but the ehta of the pair of twins touched her arm.

"It's all right, Hearth Stone. Auntie Hara is right."

Aya turned back to him and took a calming breath. "Quiet now, Kendal. This is a discussion between myself and your aunt."

"Yes, Hearth Stone," he said, humbled.

Aya turned back to Hara. "Now while I am happy to help you, these two walk past here every round, and this would have been excellent training for a pair of Gadgeteers who must work with fire all the time." Hara opened her mouth, but Aya stared at her so coldly that she snapped her maw shut.

Aya nodded in satisfaction. "It has been four turns since that happened. Your Honored Ancestors and the Ancestors to which that heirloom is linked have all forgiven the twins their trespass. It is time for you to do the same. Besides, the whole city can use their talents and we at the Hearth are tired of attempting to teach them something that we do not have the skills to teach them." Aya shook a clawed finger under Hara's nose.

"No, you are going to put your reputation on the line and speak for them so that they can get the training they need to do what they love. I have even gone so far as to find them a Watcher Spirit that will keep an eye on them and make sure that nothing important ends up in their pockets again," Aya finished.

Hara's mouth fell open. Personal Watcher Spirits were generally something only given to Channelers. It was a lifetime commitment that couldn't be undone. It was somewhat unusual for anyone but a Channeler to have one. They were important to Channelers because of the extra safety they offered when performing magical feats. Though useful to others, Watcher Spirits were in short supply because it was important that the Watcher also have had similar talents to the ta'el to which they were to be tethered.

"Who would ever agree to be their Watcher Spirit?" Hara asked with disbelief.

"Someone who understands." Aya's stern voice caused Hara to flatten her ears in embarrassment.

{Honored Ancestor, would you join us, please?} Aya sent into the aether.

She held out her paw to the Spirit that only she could see. She Channeled the Spirit through the veil between worlds, and a shape began to form next to her in azure mist. A moment later, the glowing outline took on definition, forming an emta'el born of an Otter. She held up a webbed paw and curled her fingers in a little wave. She was smaller than Aya by a few inches. Her spectral eyes were bright with mischief.

She affected an odd leaned-back posture curious to all Otters, as they tended to use their thick tails to balance when standing upright.

"This is Greatmother Auqi, but you probably know her better as Auqi the Metalmind. She was a friend to me when I was a cub, and I used to love Gearworks before I discovered my talent as a Channeler. She has agreed to watch over the twins to make sure that they do not offend anyone's delicate sensibilities with their unwitting thievery."

Hara stared, stunned. Auqi the Metalmind was a bit of a legend. She created some of the greatest Gearworks of the last few centuries, including devices that allowed the Ta'el to access intact human computer systems for information, a feat thought impossible for millennia.

"So, this is going to be the price for your help?" Hara accused.

Aya's muzzle wrinkled in distaste. "If you are asking if I am blackmailing you for my help, don't be stupid. I would assist you even if you idiotically continued to shun your niece and nephew for something that every single ta'el of your species suffers with. I would think you of all ta'el would understand what it feels like to make the mistake they did. But no, if you do not do what a family should for your kin, I will speak for them myself." Aya pointed a clawed finger at Hara's black nose, "but you will have to live with the shame of that for the rest of your rounds. I'll give you four some time to work this out. I have other Spirits to tend in Shop Row. I'll return later to take your decision."

Aya spun on her heel, and found the twins staring at her wide eyed. "And if it is decided that you will be staying, I expect the two of you to mind your Aunt as two respectful ta'el cubs should."

"Yes, Hearth Stone," they both promised.

Aya left then, only to find Greatfather Roan waiting for her just outside of the shop.

"That was neatly done, Little Aya. Sometimes, ta'el need to be made aware of what they are doing wrong before it becomes a real problem."

Aya blew out a breath. "Thought I was going to have a heart attack. Hara is fifty turns my senior. What possessed me to disrespect her like that?"

Roan let out a chuckle. "Give it a moment."

He held up a paw and pulled one finger in, then the second finger, as if counting down. When he curled his third and final finger, he pointed at the door with his other paw. It swung open, revealing Hara as she exited the doorway. Her ears were down, showing her shame, and she didn't look up from the ground for more than a moment. As soon as she saw Aya, she looked down again. She came over to where Aya was standing.

"Hearth Stone?" When she saw she had Aya's attention she went on. "I apologize for my impertinence. I forgot myself. Thank you for reminding me who I'm supposed to be."

"Apology accepted. Just try to help them, please? Your niece and nephew are extremely talented, and they are being wasted on this."

"I'll do my best, Hearth Stone."

Hara went back inside and Greatfather Roan stood next to her, looking entirely too smug.

"I hate you," Aya said.

"I am proud of you, Little Aya. You acted just as a Stone should. Sometimes even ta'el fifty turns your senior need to be told how stupid they are being. It carries even more weight coming from an Adept, no matter how young they might be."

Aya walked away down the street

Roan floated next to her. "I might have a way to find out what your new name means, but you aren't going to like it."

"When do I ever like the actual solutions to things? Is it really that important for me to find out?"

Roan shrugged. "I really don't know. I know that there is a mystery forming here, Aya. A mystery related to what the humans did to damage this world so badly."

Aya slowed down, before finally stopping. "Why would you think that about me? Is my name really that much of a wonder?" Aya asked, confused.

"I think that perhaps it is. It has led me to discover that names are being removed or hidden in the Tome of All Names. We should begin to unravel this mystery with the current Keeper of Names."

"You're scaring me, Greatfather."

"You're a big emta, I think you can handle it. Besides, if you were looking for a safe, quiet life you definitely shouldn't have become a Channeler."

Aya smiled. "Fair point, I suppose, but dealing with Corrupted Spirits, Human things that may or may be attempting to kill us, and trying to figure out how the humans killed themselves doesn't really cover the eventuality of being chosen for some world-changing nonsense by the Spirits."

He just shrugged and kept floating towards their next appointment. "No one really gave you a job description, you know. Hearth Stones do what is necessary to keep ta'el safe and happy."

Aya groaned. "Can I trade in my Channeling for a nice quiet job in the Archives, maybe?" Aya turned a corner and went down one of the side streets. "How many reports came in for me niround?"

"Only these two: Shop Row and this one down in the Paths."

The Paths were a section of the city that had been completely demolished when the Ta'el arrived. Everything there had been razed to the ground with not a tree, bush, or anything else growing there, even though it had not been covered in shattered asphalt like most of the rest of the city. The ta'el had repaired the pathways with paving stones and planted a veritable cornucopia of trees and plants. It was like a tiny forest inside of the city. She had originally been planning to come here, but Roan had said that the Hound would not come to the Paths.

Aya had thought that whatever kept the Ancestors out of the Paths wouldn't have applied to an Elemental, but she had found that any Spirit that had once been alive would not enter the Paths without great need. That meant that even Elementals like The Hound and other ancient and powerful

Spirits who had become avatars of nature would not come into the Paths even for a Confirmation.

"Tell me again why you don't like the Paths?"

Roan shivered visibly. "I wish I could, but something happened here, Aya. None of us have been able to tell what, but I feel a residue of something so awful that it has left its imprint even after several thousand turns. Best guess, a lot of humans died here, and they were not good deaths." Roan used plain words, but the way he said them, the utter black horror in his voice made them sound worse than any grizzly description he could have put forth.

"So, we think someone has upset one of the Elementals that does linger here?"

"The forest spirit that was asked to watch over the bit of nature that we made here does not seem to have the same sense of the evil that was done here, but we have a report that she has been taking Ta'el and molesting them."

"Molesting?"

"No one is really sure. They know that something is happening to them, but they don't remember the time they were missing."

"Has anyone checked them out?"

"Yes, there is no signs that anything has happened to them physically. We aren't sure what is happening, but since no one is being hurt we don't think there is a real problem. Someone probably just damaged one of the trees or something minor and the Spirit is upset, so ta'el get to suffer her pranks."

"She?" Aya asked.

"This particular Spirit is definitely feminine."

"You should wait outside, Greatfather. If the Elemental is upset she is likely more dangerous to you than to me," Aya said.

Roan shook his head.

"Stubborn. Well come on in then."

Aya held out her hand. Roan's Spirit gave her a number of magical abilities. His ability to mimic any sound or voice was useful, but more important was his ability to diffuse any magic cast at her. He had always been good at directing trouble away from himself. They hadn't named him Roan the Trickster for nothing.

The mist slid into her body as she Channeled his magic through herself. He also made her slightly stronger and faster, but that was just a side effect of having two Spirits inside of one body.

"Does she have a den here?"

{She lives inside of one of the big oak trees on the northern edge of the Paths. Could she be possessing them?}

Aya switched to sending. *{Your guess is probably better than mine, Greatfather, but even a Corrupted Spirit should need permission to enter, shouldn't it?}*

{It depends on the situation, but you're not wrong. It's just this side of possible. But I think we are dealing with mischief, here, not Corruption. You would sense a Corrupted One.}

Aya followed the well-maintained cobblestone path through the overgrown woodland. Oak and pine were featured heavily in the tiny forest, and as Aya neared the northern edge of the Paths, the feeling of foreboding began to push forcefully against Aya's mind.

{I don't sense a Corrupted One, but something is definitely wrong here.} Roan's sending was concerned, but not afraid.

{So what am I doing here?} Aya sent back as she walked down the path.

{Let's just try talking to her first. She should be somewhere near her oak.}

{I've never met this Spirit, Greatfather, what am I looking for?}

{She usually looks sort of like a ta'el made of living plants. It's hard to describe. She can remake her body out of plants, but she is usually about your size.}

{Does she...} Aya started to ask if she had a name. That was when the Spirit emerged from the shrubbery alongside the path. It appeared almost exactly as Roan had described her.

She looked much like Aya in shape, but her entire body was made up with layers of leaves and other plants. Her long hair was composed of flowing leaves like a spider plant. She was a little shorter than Aya. Aya thought that under normal circumstances, she would have been very beautiful. Clearly, though, these were not normal circumstances. Her slightly transparent body was colored in unhealthy shades of brown and black. It wasn't corrupted, it was dying. The sickly green orbs shot through with brown that served as the Spirit's eyes spun towards Aya. Aya wanted to ask Roan what could do this, but she already knew.

The Elemental had not been corrupted, but a Corrupted Spirit was attacking and using the Elemental. Aya knelt and held out her paws to the Spirit. It made perfect sense now. Corrupted Spirits were one of the mysteries of their world. Though there was no real evidence, many ta'el thought that they were a result of whatever the Humans had done.

What Aya did know is that Corrupted Spirits often devoured other Spirits. When they attacked other Spirits, those Spirits would sometimes act erratic and do abnormal things with their magic. Typically, Forest Spirits like this one could be mischievous, but as long as they were treated well, their pranks were never harmful. What was happening here was that the Corrupted Spirit was using this little one to drain living energy from the ta'el that came to the Paths. That was why they never remembered what happened to them. The Corrupted Spirit was eating their memories, and using this little Forest Spirit to do it.

{Roan, I need Lishi the Stalker or another Stalker Spirit. Is she nearby?}

There was a pause after Aya's sending. It might take Roan a few minutes to locate the kind of Spirit she needed. Hands of twigs and soft moss filled Aya's paws. The Spirit knelt in front of her, their knees almost touching.

"I'm sorry this has happened to you, Honored Elemental. I will do my best to see you set right."

{No, Aya. None of the Stalker spirits are near enough to contact, but there is another who can help you that is close enough,} Roan offered.

{The Hound. I didn't want to risk another Elemental Spirit being tainted by whatever this Corrupted Spirit is. I can support an Ancestor with my living energy to insure they are protected, but The Hound would be on their own to fight this off until I can engage it directly,} Aya replied.

{The Hound is not just any Elemental, Aya. You were told to call upon them were you to need their help.}

Aya took a deep breath and felt the Forest Spirit shudder in pain. Amber tears bled from the corners of the Spirit's eyes. Aya put her arms around the fading Forest Spirit and pulled her close. "Don't worry, I've got you. Help is coming," Aya said out loud.

{I call to The Hound for aid.} She sent her telepathic call into the Spiritlands as strongly as she could.

The response was immediate. A brisk wind blew through her spotted fur, and then the Hound was there, forming from black mist. A moment later, the towering form of the progenitor of all canines was standing over her.

{How may I assist, Stone?} His growling voice was a little frightening, but not intentionally so. He radiated warmth and friendship to her spiritual senses.

Despite this warmth, Aya still noticed the Hound's blood red eyes darting around warily. Aya caressed the crackling leafy hair of the little Forest Spirit.

"This one is being attacked by a Corrupted One. Will you help me locate the attacker, Honored Elemental?"

The Hound's jaw dropped open in a doggy grin, and he rubbed his muzzle alongside her face. *{It would be my pleasure, Hearth Stone.}*

Aya lifted one paw and placed it against The Hound's side. Instead of Channeling his power into herself as she had done with Greatfather Roan, she Channeled the Hound through the veil and into the real world. She released as much living energy into the Channeling as she thought she could safely spare. The Hound became much more solid. She could feel their fur under her paw now, and the warmth behind it. Blazing red eyes shifted from her and scanned the small forest surrounding them. The Hound's nostrils flared and their head turned sharply to the east.

{The Corrupted One is close, Ayasha the Speaker. I will call to you once I have located this invader. Please support the little one as long as you can.} The Hound disappeared into the trees in one massive leap.

{I will.}

Part of the reason she had invited the Forest Spirit to touch her was so that she could release some of her own living energy into the Spirit to support it. She had to be careful not to release to much all at once. She would need it to face whatever tainted spirit was attacking this one.

{How did it get into this part of the city, Greatfather? It shouldn't have been able to get so far into the heart undetected. The defenses are substantial to protect against this very thing. It's just impossible.}

{I agree, but the obvious solution to the problem pleases me less than not knowing how it could happen.}

{Someone carried the Corrupted One past the defenses.} Ayasha finished Greatfather Roan's very unhappy thought.

"Hearth Stone?" A familiar voice rang out from behind Ayasha and to the left.

"Hayle, you and Kendal need to leave right now." Aya kept her voice calm, though her fear and anger was simmering just below the surface.

"How did you know…" Kendal's voice came out of the trees.

"How many times must I tell you? Your Spirits are connected, and neither of you can go anywhere without the other. Sound familiar? I said it preround, and two rounds before that, and last spell, shall I go on?" Aya's voice was tinged with annoyance.

"Who is that?" Hayle emerged from the trees, twisting her braid nervously in her paws.

"That is none of your concern, young one. You and your brother must leave. Now!" Aya snapped.

"Can't we help?" Kendal asked as he pushed out of the bushes behind Hayle.

Aya turned and narrowed her eyes at them.

"Both of you cubs listen to me right this instant, and I swear, if you do not follow every word that comes out of my muzzle, you will not touch one single Gearwork for the rest of your rounds. You will turn tail right now and run as fast as you can, all the way back to Shop Row. You will tell your Aunt to contact the Hearth and tell them that a Corrupted One has passed the defenses and is in the Paths. You will not stop until you are safely behind her locked door."

The twins exchanged a look for a moment, and then Aya finally lost her temper and roared at them.

"Run!" Tears welled up in Hayle's eyes, and they both turned ringed tail, disappearing into the forest at a dead run.

{Good job. You scared them half to death,} sent Roan.

{I wish I had had the luxury of comforting them right now, Greatfather, but they were vulnerable. I have defenses they don't.}

{I'm sorry, Little Aya. You didn't do wrong. I just wish there had been a better way.}

{There was. I just hadn't thought of it until now. Unfortunately, she didn't see fit to save me until the damage was done, though I fail to see why she didn't stop them herself.}

{You mean Auqi.}

{Yes, Auqi.}

{She wouldn't have come in here. Not yet. The protections of the living do not extend to her yet. She just made a bond with the twins two rounds ago.}

{Well, at least that makes me feel better about scaring the twins.}

Another sending broke into their conversation.

{Speaker, I have found the Corrupted One. I do not think I should face it alone. I sense that this twisted creature has absorbed much living energy, enough to be a danger even to me. Your skills with a Heartblade would be most welcome.}

{Roan, can I leave her in your care? I know this place makes you very uncomfortable, but I feel like this Honored Elemental will need you more than I will. I also feel I may need to Channel a more combat orientated Spirit. I do not yet have enough practical experience for this.}

{You must do your duty, and so must I.}

Roan's spirit left her body, returning to his Coyote shape formed from red mist. He knelt with the Forest Spirit. Thankfully, he was able to hold the little Spirit, since she was also part of the Spiritlands.

"Be careful, Little Aya, and do not sell yourself short. Lane did say you were competent when you left his care. Not a compliment that many ta'el have earned."

Aya seemed confused at how simple competence could be a compliment, but then she shook her head. "Thanks, Greatfather." Aya turned and ran towards the Hound, sending her stripped tail streaming behind her.

Chapter 4

"WORTH"

Aya bolted down the trails as fast as her paws would carry her. She darted around oaks and pines towards the opposite end of the Paths. When the wall surrounding the pits came up, she threaded her way through the door the ta'el had carved through it.

The small section of the Paths had once been a place that humans had kept animals so that they could view them safely. It had also been used for research concerning animals. It didn't make much sense to her when she read the books they had recovered concerning this area of the Paths, an area they had called the pits. The enclosures where the animals had been kept were like pits in the ground with surrounding walls. Some of them even had caves in them where the animals had slept. Not all of the pits had survived through the end of the humans.

It was at one of these pits that she found the Hound. They had hunkered down at an intact section of the wall surrounding the pit. It was not supposed to be a dangerous area of the Paths, and cubs often played in here. There were none in the pits now. They knew that something lurked here and wanted nothing to do with the interloper.

{It is there, Speaker.} The Hound pointed with their nose to the cave on the other side of the pit.

"Have you seen it?" Ayasha whispered.

{No, it has not emerged as of yet, but I can sense its malevolence.}

"I can too." Aya shivered.

{You doubt yourself.} It was not a question.

"I am not a fool, Honored Elemental."

The Hound dropped his jaw in a doggy grin. *{Then you are wiser than most of the Stones that finish their training and think themselves invincible.}*

"How would you advise me to engage this threat?"

{I would suggest that you wait for whatever is in that cave to come out and ambush it.}

"That sounds somewhat mercenary."

{You said something about not being a fool?}

"I just don't feel comfortable with stabbing anything in the back."

The Hound tilted its head and dropped one ear in question. *{How is that better than stabbing them in front? You had no trouble jamming your Heartblade into me when we fought. Such a strange sensibility.}*

Aya rolled her eyes. It wasn't really a ta'el value either. It was admittedly a concept she had found in human books that had appealed to her. Wanderer Lane had told her quite bluntly that she could debate the morality of how she won the fight once she had prevented some nightmare creature from devouring her still-beating heart.

{I think your real trouble is that you are hoping you can save this poor twisted creature from its fate,} The Hound observed.

{Shouldn't I be able to?} Aya asked as she watched the cave.

The Hound sat down beside her. *{No. Whatever made you think that?}* The Hound again had dropped an ear in question.

{Well that is what Hearth Stones are supposed to do, isn't it? Save ta'el and Spirits?}

{I am not truly equipped for such questions, Ayasha the Speaker, but I know this much. Corrupted Ones allowed themselves to despair and be taken by their corruption. Even those forced into a Shadowgap are drawn to it by their own weakness. Now they seek to infect others. They are one of the things that you must protect others from.}

{I want to do better than that.}

{Well, you are the Hearth Stone. There are ways. I am sure you know of them.}

{Not without help. I can't cleanse a Corrupted Spirit that has gained that much power on my own.}

{Ayasha the Speaker, you are a Stone of the Hearth, and an Adept by my own Confirmation. You can never be alone.}

Aya blinked. There was one Spirit she knew for sure could help her. Unfortunately she was likely to be several thousand miles away at this point, but maybe. Aya turned to the Hound.

"Honored Elemental, my Mother's Watcher Spirit is Sasu the Lightmend. Are there any other Ancestors nearby who share her name?"

Aya's sense of the creature within the cave was that it was stirring. It had attempted to force the Forest Spirit to do its bidding, and the Spirit had not responded. It would venture out to find out why. The Hound looked at her with a sly expression.

{Now that is the thought of an Adept. Not nearby, but close enough for your purposes. A simple call will not do to draw her attention. I must fetch her. Can you hold it off until I do, Speaker?}

Aya pulled herself up onto the wall surrounding the pit.

"Guess I'll have to."

{Go for the ambush. I like you, Ayasha the Speaker.}

Aya rolled her eyes and then slid down the other side of the wall until she hit a wide root that had grown through it. She crouched there for a moment, watching the entrance before she ran along the root to the end of the wall. She scaled another collection of roots up the wall of the pit to reach some low hanging tree limbs before pausing again to make sure that she had not been seen. Once she was sure, she scampered along the limbs until she was only a few scant feet over the top of the entrance to the cave.

Aya reached behind her back and wrapped her paw around the hilt of her Heartblade. She crouched on the thick tree limb, carefully digging her claws into the bark to give her more grip. She struggled to remain still as the sense of nearby corruption crawled along her spine.

The Corrupted Spirit stirred. Truthfully, it wasn't any sense of human chivalry that compelled Aya not to kill anything, living or Spirit. That had been an insecure excuse for the benefit of her ego. It was why she didn't like raw meat, because she associated it with the first time she had killed something to eat. It was a lesson that every child of the ta'el that was born of a carnivore had to do at least once. She had complained to her mother that the ancestors helped them grow meat. There was no reason to kill.

Her mother had told her that while that was true, she still needed to know how because as a carnivore she required meat to survive. Even if she never had to do it again for the rest of her long life, she had to know how. She had to know what it felt like. She didn't like it, and she didn't like raw meat because of it.

Aya watched as a blackened snout poked out of the front of the cave. It had three long rends across the top that oozed viscous black blood. It was slightly transparent, but less so than the healthy colored mists that Spirits usually composed themselves of when projecting themselves into the Wild. There was no blacklight glow of a Spirit that composed themselves of black mist.

Then the whispers came to her ears. Aya had never been close enough to a Corrupted One to hear the whispers, but all of her teachers had warned her that she would. And now, she was. The screams of tortured souls as if heard from miles away sounded as whispers to those who came too near to a Corrupted One. There was no description that she had ever heard during her training that had done justice to the sound that lanced her eardrums. She felt as though she would bleed from the ears at any moment. How could anyone possibly get any closer to these things to fight them?

It wasn't just the sound, though, what hit her more was the smell. Spirits did not really give off a smell, but they could affect the smells around them. Their influence raised odors, and also enhanced their vibrancy. This one was different. Aya had smelled an actual rotting corpse. That smell had been effervescent and lovely compared to the putrid reek coming off of this thing. It emerged from the cave, and Aya forced down her bile. The creature was twisted, torn, and broken. Aya got the sense that it had been a lesser elemental at some point, but whatever it had been was long gone now. Now it was something else, something infected.

Aya watched in revulsion as her training came back to her. She could not be distracted by thoughts of how such a creature came to be. It had accepted corruption into itself, and the only response to such an act was to cleanse the corruption by any means necessary.

The creature paused suspiciously, its warped skull turning left and then right. Then it spoke in a ripping bass growl.

"I smell you, Hearth Stone. You cannot hide from me. Your power betrays you, Channeler."

It did not emerge any further from the cave. Tingles of anxious energy flowed down Aya's limbs. If it turned and saw her, the shape of this fight would change. If she could catch it unawares, she might be able to keep it pinned long enough for the Hound to return with help, but she had gotten a glimpse of the size of the Spirit's form. It wasn't much taller than her but it was much wider.

{Hearth Stone, may I offer assistance?}

Aya went rigid as she tried to keep herself perfectly silent. The whispered sending into her mind from the Spiritlands was voiced by someone she recognized.

{I know I am not much good in a fight, but I can at least offer you the additional strength of a second Spirit?} The Spirit was Greatmother Aqui.

{I gratefully accept, Honored Ancestor,} Aya said and opened herself to Aqui. A moment later, she was suffused with the feeling of another Spirit entering her body. The additional physical power was welcome.

{Do you have a plan, Stone?}

{I planned on using my Heartblade to paralyze it, but it smelled me, and now it is suspicious of my ambush.}

{Why not just destroy it? It made its choice.} Aqui was not being vindictive. Her sending was quite sad.

{Because I want to do better, Greatmother.}

{That is an excellent aspiration, Stone.}

The creature emerged a little further and began to turn to look up above the cave. Aya shrank back into the foliage and froze stock still, allowing her dark markings to break up her form.

{Patience, Hearth Stone. There is no need to rush. The prey will come to you if you have patience,} Auqi counseled, her sending quite calm.

Aya would be a stone in truth if she had to. Every moment that passed was another moment she gave the Hound to return with the Spirit that was needed to help her cleanse this abomination. Aya was a little surprised that Auqi had such hunters' instincts.

The sending from Auqi was amused. *{Otters are quite the hunters too, Hearth Stone. You don't have to be a big cat to be a good hunter.}*

{Apologies, Honored Ancestor. I didn't mean to insult you.}

{No insult taken. Pay attention, young one, your prey is becoming impatient. I'll allow you to concentrate.}

Aqui's presence receded into the back of her mind. Aya watched as the Corrupted Spirit bolted out of the cave. She didn't have time to drop on top of it. Instead, she immediately turned and bolted back the way she had come along the tree limb. It was likely the creature would see her, but it was moving very quickly itself. Luckily for her, it didn't look back and ran straight for the wall on the opposite of the pit.

Aya darted back along the wall on the side of the pit. Her increased speed let her pass the Corrupted Spirit. She bolted around the corner of the wall and then leapt into the air, catching an overhanging branch with her left paw, digging her claws into the bark to make her swing sharper. She could have made the swing single-pawed even without Auqi lending her extra strength, but with it, she was able to fling herself fifteen feet into the air. She controlled her swing perfectly, using her increased strength.

She flew above the top of the wall, putting herself squarely above the Corrupted Spirit. It was swinging up the overgrown roots of the trees. Aya drew up her legs and shifted her body so that she was crouching in midair, giving her a moment to look over the creature. It was shaped much like a ta'el, but with exposed cords of blackened, knotted muscle everywhere. She wasn't certain if the vital areas would be the same as in living ta'el, but her training had taught her that it could vary greatly. Wanderer Lane had taught her to trust her instincts. Her instincts told her that she should aim for the spine.

Aya landed on the creature's back and dug the claws of her left paw into its shoulder. It let out a piercing howl, blowing out Aya's left ear drum and leaving her momentarily deafened in the right. She didn't hesitate for even a moment, driving the tip of her Heartblade into its lower back, right over where the spine should be. The creature's screech of rage increased to impossible volumes. It peeled from the wall with Aya still clinging to its back.

The creature flailed its arms wildly back at her, but she crouched down, digging the claws of her feet and paws into the back of its thighs and shoulders. She took a couple of glancing blows to her head and shoulders, leaving her slightly dazed. Aya still managed to twist them both so that she landed on top.

The hilt of her Heartblade punched her in the thigh when they struck the ground, and she was flipped off of the creature's back. Her head struck the stone of the enclosure, filling her vision with stars. She lay there on her back trying to just breathe. Muffled sounds came to her as she tried to shake off the dizziness. After a moment, she realized that Auqi was sending inside of her head.

{Aya...} the sending was just garbled words after that. She pried her eyes open by sheer force of will, but the world looked wobbly and unfocused.

{Hearth Stone, you must rise!}

The telepathic shout jolted Aya awake just in time to see the Corrupted One dragging its body across her legs. She tried to roll over, but she was still too confused to fully realize what was happening. The creature twisted its broken body until it was straddling her. It lifted its blackened nightmare paws to her throat. That was when her addled brain finally regained full consciousness. It was careful not to dig its claws in, Aya realized with some horror, because it meant to enjoy throttling her to death.

Aya arched her back and bucked her body to try to dislodge the horrid thing. It didn't work. The dead weight of its body was too heavy, even for her increased strength. Sickly green eyes the color of diseased snot locked onto her crystal blues. She gasped in as deep a breath as she could take just before it closed its fists and shut off her air. She bashed its elbows, but the oozing black flesh was just too tough, absorbing her blows before they could damage the joints.

"I will devour your Spirit as it leaves your body and discard your carcass like the trash that it is."

The fetid breath of the creature nearly gagged her. Her vision began to darken, and she dug her claws into the creature's wrists. She twisted her paws around them, leaving ruinous gashes behind. It simply growled and continued to choke the life out of her. That was when she caught sight of her Heartblade.

The blade had been dislodged from the Corrupted Spirit's back in the fall and was next to her right foot. Its dead legs were not much good for keeping her own legs trapped, and she took advantage of that. The last of her breath was burning in her lungs when she bucked her body again giving her just enough space to slide her legs out of beneath the legs of the creature. She scraped the claws of her feet across the stone for purchase and spun her body like a top. The Corrupted One just held onto her throat, completely focused on the kill. Her fingers scrabbled against the bone and wood hilt of the knife.

"Why do you persist when there is no hope?"

She could barely hear what it was saying as she writhed like a snake towards her Heartblade. It was amazing how strong the Spirit had become in the Wild. It must have been consuming the energy of the living for spells to have come this far into the living realm. It was no wonder that the Forest Spirit was near death when she found it.

Aya expressed her claws, and they caught on the hilt of the dagger. She closed her fist around the hilt and slashed across both of its arms. The blade severed both wrists with little resistance.

The creature rolled away from her shrieking into the supersonic ranges. Even without its weight on her, Aya did not yet have the strength to do any more. She could only lay where she was and gasp in lungfulls of sweet air. It was long moments before her vision returned to normal, but her slash had been well aimed. It would take a long time for even a Spirit to attempt to knit that wound. It would be even angrier when it found it could not. She was still some ways from being able to move again when The Hound's sending reached her.

{Are you okay, Hearth Stone?} Auqi's sending inside of her mind was concerned.

{I will survive, for now.} Aya continued to gasp and recover. *{Is it getting up yet?}*

{Unfortunately, it is. It looks quite upset, but its paws do not look like they are in any shape to do anything to harm you. Take a moment longer. It seems occupied with attempting to heal itself,} Auqi sent in an oddly clinical voice.

{You sound,}

Auqi interrupted. *{I'm terrified. I have all of a predator's instincts, but none of their fight.}*

{Good thing you aren't, then.}

Aya groaned as she got all four paws under her. She was exhausted, still catching her breath, and petrified in a way she had not been since she was a cub. Her training had taught her how to push aside that fear. She was not going to let this thing hurt anyone else, even if it killed her. She spun her Heartblade so that the blade was hidden behind her arm. She crouched and, with a little effort spent swaying her tail, found her balance.

{Hearth Stone, we are coming.} The sending was a whisper inside of her head, but it meant that the Hound had gotten close enough with whoever he had been fetching that he could reach her again.

{Not a moment too soon. Please hurry, Honored Elemental. I am not doing very well.}

{As quickly as we can, Stone. Run to the north if you must buy time. We are coming from the North.}

{Apologies, Honored Elemental, but I don't have the strength to run over any distance right now. I can play a little keep away for a while but if you do not arrive soon you will likely need to find another Stone to deal with this thing.}

{I am sorry, Ayasha the Speaker. We are still several bouts away. Good luck.}

Aya sighed and spread her feet. She didn't want to do this, but she had done her best to save this Spirit. Now, she had to think about others.

{Auqi, I think I need more help than just a second Spirit. I apologize for the slight, but would it be too much to ask if you could fetch Wanderer Lane for me? You can find him at the House of Contemplation, and be back much more quickly than The Hound will arrive.}

{I am admittedly not a fighter, why would I be offended? But you will lose the strength I am able to pass on.}

{If I haven't killed it by the time you get back, then Lane will be all the help I need.}

{Will he come?} Auqi asked.

It was a serious question. Wanderer Lane was an extremely old, powerful, and extremely busy Spirit. He might already be doing something just as important as saving her hide.

{Unless he is already busy saving someone else's life, he will.}

Lane had taken a shine to Aya, and he would likely come no matter what. Satisfied grunts from the Corrupted One drew Aya's attention back to the creature. Only a few bits had passed during her mental conversation, but the Corrupted Spirit was already mostly healed.

{Lane the Wanderer is one of your Ancestors?}

{No, we are not related in Spirit, but he is close. Please do not approach him if he is engaged in something of equal importance, Honored Ancestor.}

{As you wish, Hearth Stone.} Aqui fled from her mind.

Instantly, Aya's body felt heavier and more exhausted. She gritted her teeth and looked back up, watching in growing dread as the creature managed to begin restoring its paws. If it had not consumed so much energy from the living, it would have been impossible. She couldn't give it any more of a chance to kill her than she already had. She gripped her Heartblade tighter in her fist, and then darted forward.

The creature was caught by surprise, but reacted quickly. It jumped back away from her first slash, and then ducked under the second. It launched itself up at her from its crouch, but Aya was prepared. She had not over extended herself, allowing her to fall backwards into a roll that brought her to her feet with a safe gap between her and the Spirit.

Aya came to her feet fully balanced and prepared. Side-stepping the creature's charge, she took advantage of its failed lunge. With her left paw, she latched onto the creature's left wrist. She planted her feet and twisted her body, yanking the creature off balance. She brought her knife up, and the blade passed cleanly through the creature's forearm, severing its newly healed paw. Spinning away from the screaming creature, she held up its severed paw in her left paw and planted her feet. Holding it gingerly as it leaked disturbing black ectoplasm, she waited until the creature looked back at her, and then tossed it away, and with a taunting grin.

It roared incoherently at her and charged in a rage. Aya sidestepped and cuffed the creature on the back of its head as it went past. It tumbled onto its face, and she took a few steps away. She teetered with exhaustion, and knew that dodging was the only action left to her. It was just a matter of time, now.

{You are in luck, Little Aya.} Wanderer Lane's sending was a breath of relief. He arrived a moment later, his long body forming next to her in bluish white mist. Kind eyes above a conical muzzle traced her from feet to eartips.

{Thank Scales. Might I beg your assistance, Honored Ancestor?}
{As if you even have to ask.}

Lane held out his long-fingered paw and Aya took it. She Channeled his power into her. Her physical stamina and strength increased tenfold and her physical flexibility increased by an order of magnitude. That, however, was the least of what Lane's magic did for her. Lane the Wanderer was one of the most talented martial artists in all of the history of the ta'el. He had been her teacher, but she would need dozens of turns of experience before she could ever even approach his level of skill. Thankfully, his magic gave her something even better than that. Lane was born of the Mongoose, and his magic made her faster, but not physically. It didn't need to do that.

It made her sensory input and reflexes hundreds of times faster than they were without his assistance. She could be missing a paw, both feet, and her tail, and this thing would still be no match for her with Wanderer Lane's assistance. The Corrupted Spirit rushed at her, but it might as well have been moving through molasses for how easily she was able to step out of the way. She slid her Heartblade into the scabbard in the smooth motion. The second portion of Lane's magic gave her some limited access to his experience as a fighter. She took one perfect step backwards, and then curled her paw into a tight fist. She slammed it forward, smashing the creature's elbow joint.

The creature stumbled and crashed into the ground. It would heal quickly from any injury, but not quickly enough. It was clearly not very well versed in having a physical body. She took two quick steps forward, and then slammed the heel of her foot into its knee joint. The leg buckled the wrong way, and there was a sharp snap of breaking bone.

{You're all beat up. Why didn't you send for me sooner?} Lane sent.

{Where were you twenty bouts ago, Honored Ancestor?}

{I was…} Lane began. *{Oh, on the other side of the planet helping Stone Lana finish her lessons.}*

{Precisely. I felt you come through the Tunnel exactly three bouts, and seven bits ago.}

{Apologies, Little Aya. I would have come sooner.}

{I know, Honored Ancestor. That's precisely why I didn't send someone through the portal to fetch you. What you were doing there is important. Further, I would have survived on my own. I was trying not to kill it. I did not forget your lessons simply because you were not here,} she chided.

Lane's laugh sounded inside of her mind, warming her considerably. *{Never thought you would. Far more understandable why you are so beat up. It is much harder to handle someone who is trying to kill you without killing them.}*

{At least when I don't have three hundred twenty turns of practical experience in fancy hurting people.} Aya grinned at the spluttering sound in her head.

The Corrupted Spirit slowly forced itself to its feet. Aya sighed. It turned with a start and flung its paw at her. Something flew at her, and it slowed down in her sight as she stepped back out of the way. Three sharp barbs trailing something black and viscous flew past her. They crashed into the stones of the cave and tinkled to the floor. Aya darted forward, and drew back her fist in a blur. She smashed it into the back of the creature's head. Its body slumped to the ground and she let out a sigh, but she didn't drop her guard.

{We have arrived, Ayasha the Speaker,} The Hound sent.

In but a moment, he was there, forming from black mist next to her. Jumping down from his back was a tiny shape formed of pure white mist. She was much smaller than Aya, tiny indeed.

"Thank you, Honored Elemental." Aya kept an eye on the downed Corrupted Spirit, but it did not stir. "Please introduce me to your companion?"

Aya bowed her head to the white Ancestor Spirit. "Honored Ancestor." The Spirit responded with a bow in kind, and Aya realized she was wearing a very elaborate ankle length dress. It had delicate ribbons piping the long wide sleeves with bows tied at the wrists. There was a wide ribbon around her waist with a large bow tied in the back. The hem of the dress was adorned with a number of tiny bows tied in the drape of lacy ribbon. It flowed about her tiny frame as if floating in water. It was not very often that ta'el wore clothing. Usually only for protection. Then the Spirit spoke into her mind in a very soft voice.

{No need to be so formal, Hearth Stone. I am Kika the Lightmend, but it would please me if you would simply call me Kika.} The soft sending was polite but firm.

"Kika, can you help this poor Corrupted Soul?" At first glance, Aya had not recognized Kika's species, but as the Ancestor Spirit passed her, she saw her long white ears laid down the sides of her head almost hidden in her long white hair. She had been a lop-eared rabbit in life. They were a rare species for a ta'el to choose to be born of because of their heavy domestication by humans. Something about the genetic makeup of many domesticated animals had made them vulnerable to whatever had destroyed the humans. Except for some dogs, most domesticated species of animals had gone extinct the same time humans had. This made them a choice that was rarely available to ta'el. Not as rare as Mythics, but still she was definitely not something you saw every round.

"Please be careful. It has consumed a lot of living energy. It was powerful."

{No need to worry, Hearth Stone. I am less fragile than I appear.} Kika replied with gentle amusement. She put her tiny paw on the side of the Corrupted Spirit and stayed that way for a long moment. Then she straightened and shook her head. *{I can cleanse the Corruption, Hearth Stone, but there is nothing left of the Spirit beneath. It will simply return the energy to the Life Spirit.}*

Ayasha sighed heavily and lashed her tail once in annoyance. "All that work for nothing."

{What did you hope to find, Hearth Stone?}

"Something, I don't know. I realize no Spirit remembers their time once they were corrupted, but it got past the defenses here somehow," Aya complained.

{It would seem obvious that if a Corrupted One passed the city defenses, either there is a gap in the defenses we do not know about, or someone let it pass.}

Kika knelt down again, and Aya watched as her glow intensified as she called on her magic. She held out her tiny paw to Aya. *{If you would, Hearth Stone?}*

Aya padded over next to the Corrupted Spirit. She took Kika's paw and concentrated. She Channeled the cleansing magic into the real world, then touched the side of the Corrupted Spirit. Her paw became suffused with bright white light that soon spread to cover the Corrupted Spirit. She looked away as the magic reacted with the corruption and the light increased to a blinding intensity. When it finally faded, the Corrupted One was gone.

"Thank you, Honored Ancestor." Aya pushed herself to her feet.

Kika smiled up at her. *{If you find yourself in need of my power again, you may call upon me directly, Ayasha the Speaker.}*

"Thank you Kika. May I ask..."

"What species I am?" Kika asked with a knowing smile.

"Oh no, I recognized you. I just wanted to know how far I would be calling you if I did. Where do you hail from?"

{Not far, if we were not coming from the Wild. I am located to the north in the Adirondack mountains at the Shrine of Life. You should come visit, if you ever wish to progress your knowledge of healing.}

"Thank you for the invitation, Kika." Aya had a thought. "Might I ask one more question before you return?"

The rabbit emta nodded. *{By all means ask, Heart Stone.}*

"Do you know what my name means?" Kika's nose twitched, and she tilted her head in thought.

{I do not, but it seems like I should. I have heard many, many names but yours is not familiar. Sorry, Hearth Stone.}

"Not at all. Thank you, Honored Ancestor."

"I assume you have stopped the Corrupted One?" Roan's voice came from the wall above.

Aya looked up to see him standing at the top of the wall. Standing next to him was the Forest Spirit. She still looked wan, but much of the healthy green coloring of her body had returned. Her eyes, which had been dim black orbs before now, appeared as bright blue spheres of what appeared to be glass. She waved a paw of leafy greens and moss-covered twigs. She was back to being slightly transparent, and had a thin but healthy green glowing aura.

"Thank Scales." Aya climbed the wall, and when she reached the top, she was going to release Wanderer Lane.

{Are you sure, Aya? You are still quite exhausted.}

{Thank you for your concern, Honored Ancestor, but I have leaned upon your power more than enough for niround. Roan will assist me if I truly need it. Besides, I'm not that much of a weakling. It was only a little throttling. Nothing is broken, and I feel much better after Channeling Kika's cleansing.}

Lane left her body, and as expected, she felt far more exhausted. She fell to one knee and breathed for a moment as she adjusted to her body actually feeling her injuries. Lane bent over her with concern. Aya held up a paw.

"Honestly, I'm fine. Just needed a moment. I'll get some sleep and be good as new." Aya pushed herself back to her feet.

"Seen that face before." Lane and Roan said at the same time.

Aya laughed a little, and then directed to Lane. "I would like to beg one more favor from you, Honored Ancestor."

Lane gave her a put upon expression. "I suppose I can spare time for yet another favor."

"It's not for me, Lane. It's for her," Aya gestured to the Forest Spirit who was watching the proceedings shyly from behind Roan, "and all the other Spirits who live here. I just want you to contact one of the Stalkers. They might be able to help us find out what happened here. Send them to my home when you have found one?"

"I can do that." Lane nodded and then faded away into the Spiritlands.

Aya turned back to Roan and the Forest Spirit. "Don't worry, little friend. We will protect you." The Spirit nodded to her, and waved in a friendly way before disappearing into the trees. Aya looked around, and noticed that several ta'el were watching her conversation with Roan. "Greatfather, how long have they been here?"

"Not long. Auqi brought them with her when she returned with Lane. They saw just the tail end of what transpired," Roan said, "Just enough to prove your worth to them."

Aya groaned. "Do you do this to all of the new Stones?"

"Yes and no. When an old reliable Stone leaves a post and a new one arrives, we like to assure the ta'el that the new Stone is just as ready for the challenge as the old one was. Some of that happens naturally. Your fight with the Corrupted One, for example, was a natural part. We simply didn't waste the opportunity to show them how capable you really are."

"I almost got myself killed," she said, keeping her voice down as the other ta'el approached.

"No one is perfect, Little Aya. Not even powerful Channelers like you. They can see you fought for them even though it cost you. That's what's important," Roan said.

Aya straightened her sash and tried to brush away some of the stains, and then smoothed a little of her fur self-consciously before realizing most of her hair had come free of her braid. She pulled the green ribbon free, and her long purple locks almost untwisted from the braid on their own. She finished pulling them free, and then pulled her hair back into a ponytail, tying it off with the ribbon. She finally felt more composed as the ta'el approached, even though she was still filthy and her fur was sticking up in directions, she didn't know were actual directions.

One of the ta'el was Hara, and the twins were also there with her, but she wasn't leading the charge, so to speak. In the lead was a face that Aya recognized very well, one of Aya's favorite ta'el, and the only one she had known in Shop Row before niround. His distinct white and black facial markings stood out in the crowd. He was surprisingly jolly, considering his chosen species, though he could be awfully pointy when you caught him in a grump.

"No! Little Aya? Sahone's little emta is our new Hearth Stone?"

The Badger was the owner of the city's enormous denlodge. Everyone who needed lodging in the city who didn't have a permanent home stayed at the Golden Lantern. It had been constructed in the rebuilt remains of a massive building that was, according to the human books, the tallest structure in the human world. It was one of the only structures that remained fully intact in the city when the ta'el had first come here. It was a bit of a hike, but still on the edge of her district.

"Hello, Poro. It's been a long time."

"I haven't seen you in four turns! I knew you were training to be a Stone, but I never imagined you would be our Stone." He came closer and threw his arms around her, nearly lifting her from the ground.

"Uh, Poro, I'm not in great shape, and, I'm, gonna, hurl if you don't, stop squeezing me." Aya tilted her he head one way, then the other. She realized that channeling Kika's cleansing had healed her ear along with some other minor wounds. He quickly set her back on her feet.

"Sorry, Aya, just excited to see you." Poro's grave tones rattled with joy.

"It's nice to see you too."

"They all came to tell you that they are glad you are our new Hearth Stone. I came to ask you if you'll come back to the Lantern for a good meal. I even have a very delicious memory for your Watcher, if he is so inclined."

"Oh Scales, I would love that, Poro, but only if you throw in a few minutes in the bath house so I don't smell like a sewer, and look like one too."

After a round of thanks from the small gathering, Aya and Roan followed Poro back towards the Golden Lantern, Roan was watching her carefully. He whispered to her. "You believe me now," he said. It wasn't a question.

Aya nodded morosely and sighed.

"I felt it too, Greatfather. That Corrupted One was placed there for me, and so soon after my Confirmation?" Aya nodded. "Yes, something is happening, and somehow, I'm a part of it."

Chapter 5

"MYSTERY"

Aya's graceful steps flowed around the masters circle laid out in her personal garden. The perfect circle of blue stained stones in the tiny clearing was a path for the martial art that Wanderer Lane had taught her. Aya's smooth slide from two feet down onto all fours effecting a perfect dodge. She rolled to her feet into a defensive crouch, staying within the circle. The circle was a limit that, when used properly, would teach a ta'el how to move and dodge in such a way that their movements seemed entirely unpredictable. True masters of the art had no rhythm to follow. Each movement was designed to drift effortlessly into the next, regardless of what direction was required to pass the ta'el from danger to safety.

Most ta'el learned the fighting arts, but like with everything, some were better than others. Almost all Hearth Stones practiced daily, with the expectation that they were to be ready to deal with Corrupted Spirits. Sometimes, that was a purely magical effort. However like preround, occasionally they had consumed enough magical energies to give themselves a physical body. Once that happened, a physical fight was almost inevitable.

{Excuse me, Hearth Stone.} The sending came from Wanderer Lane.

Aya's icy blue eyes found him forming from bluish white mist not far away, at the entrance to the small clearing at the center of her garden. "Welcome, Honored Ancestor." Aya mopped sweat from her brow with a towel.

"I have fulfilled your request," he said formally.

A second Spirit formed from an odd mixture of white and black mist beside him. It was the spirit of a ta'el that, like Ayasha, had been born of a big cat. Aya judged her a white tiger, as she was one of the unusual spirits that maintained their living coloration. Idly, she wondered why she had never asked Roan why some Spirits did so. Aya put her paws at her sides and bowed deeply to the spirit.

{Ayasha the Speaker, this is Leylia the Stalker. She is quite talented, and I believe she will be able to help you.} The Spirit bowed in return.

{I am glad to assist you, Hearth Stone. How may I serve?}

"A moment, if you would, Honored Ancestor?"

The Spirit sat down cross legged on the edge of the clearing. *{By all means, finish your exercises, Hearth Stone.}*

{I'll leave you emtas to sort out this problem.}

"Thank you, Lane. Before you go, I have something for you." Ayasha beckoned him closer.

She held out her paw, and he wrapped his ghostly fingers around hers. She recalled a memory from the previous spell, when she jumped off the high street waterfall. The waterfall was two hundred feet high, and it was a seventy foot fall before the first limbs of the tree that overhung the falls. She loved the sensation of falling, and had ever since she was young. She wouldn't remember this particular jump after giving the memory to Lane, but she jumped off of those falls regularly. She couldn't stay away for more than a stint without a good jump. She would definitely make a new memory soon.

Aya opened herself to him so that he could experience the memory as if he had lived it. She gave it all to him, every bit of the experience of flipping through the tree limbs that made a ladder nearly to the bottom of the falls. When it was done, Lane was glowing brightly from the magic of the memory.

{That was lovely, Little Aya. Thank you very much. You care for us so well.}

Aya responded with her sharp smile. "The best I can do."

*{Every Hearth Stone should aspire to do **your** best.}*

Aya blushed beneath her fur at the unexpected compliment, and Lane waved his long-fingered paw, then pointed at her.

{Don't forget to tuck your tail in your roll, and flare it when you come to your feet. You're slightly off balance at the end of your roll in that last movement.}

He grinned when she made a rude gesture at him, because his nitpick had been something she had worked extremely hard to break herself of when learning the arts from him. He faded away into the Spiritlands.

"Jerk," she grumbled, and went back to the edge of the circle to find where she had left off in her practice.

{That one has always been a smooth talker,} Leylia sent, her sending quiet and subtle so as to not break Aya's concentration.

{How long have you known him?} Aya asked as she went through the series of motions.

{Many generations. I knew Lane in life. He was like that from the time he was a cub. Confident, smooth, but never cocky. He's the kind of ehta that everyone likes. Our teacher was very hard on Lane. He didn't much care for Lane's natural talent for the art. He pressed him extremely hard, just like Lane does to you. You must be talented.}

Aya paused for a moment, but then continued her exercises to their conclusion. "I wouldn't say that. When I moved on to my Channeling training, he told me I was competent."

The Stalker blinked, and then grinned. *{Scales, you are young. Surely your Watcher Spirit has told you that Lane does not often call anyone 'competent.' It's certainly never a compliment I have ever earned from him, and I was attributed a master in my time. I believe the best I ever heard from him during a sparring session was, 'Just slightly faster than a sleeping rock.'}*

"I try not to pry into the past of the Honored Ancestors."

Leylia let out a laugh into her sending. *{You have used his magic. How can you not tell what he was like?}*

Aya shrugged as she toweled off. "I just figured his skills were amplified by his transition, as most do when they pass onto the Spiritlands."

The Stalker snorted at that and shook her head.

{Don't be foolish. Lane was nigh unstoppable. I never beat him once, no matter how many times we sparred. I never saw him lose a fight, not even to Wanderer Tak, our master. Not even when he was an untrained runt of a cub. He couldn't beat the master back then, but he didn't lose, either. The master never once pinned him down. It infuriated the master.}

Aya was a little startled by the information. Competent was not a word that she related to excellence even when Greatfather Roan had told her the same thing.

{Frankly, I see him in you. The way you move has that fluidity.}

Aya did not want to be rude, but she found it odd how much Leylia seemed to remember from her life. She almost asked, but decided against it. It was her understanding that a Spirit's memories of life were vague unless they had recently refreshed them. She would ask Roan later, instead.

"Yeah, well, I'm hardly unstoppable. A Corrupted Spirit nearly had me wearing my ass for earmuffs the other round," Aya said with a chuckle.

{You have his fluidity, but not his confidence. It matters.}

"Can't argue with you there. The Corrupted Spirit was why I had Lane ask you here, Honored Ancestor. I can offer you many fine memories in trade for your services, and if I do not have any memories that you desire, simply tell me your preferences and I will do my best to accommodate you."

{You are kind, Hearth Stone, and I am sure we can work something out, but first let us discuss what you require of me.}

"Your task is simply to find out how the Corrupted Spirit that was hunting the Paths made its way into the city."

Aya was about to continue when Greatfather Roan materialized in red mist next to her. The last she'd known was that he had been in the Spiritlands attempting to find out the meaning of her name for some shifts.

"Aya, our theory is no longer a theory. I have spoken to several Wanderer spirits and they have confirmed that there have been multiple instances recently where the elementals that act as our conduit to the Life Spirit have gone temporarily missing, breaking the living connection to the Spiritlands."

"So do you think there is a connection to our problem? It is not totally uncommon for those spirits to be out of contact."

"Definitely. The issue in the Paths started immediately after the first time we were dispelled," Roan affirmed.

"What's being done about it?" Aya wondered.

"Nothing as of yet. The Hearth is researching historical instances and attempting to contact some of the older Spirits beyond the Veil to try to establish precedent to see if there is knowledge of how to correct this issue before we move forward."

"So I'll be getting tasked soon. Good thing I'm already taking steps."

Roan nodded, and then bowed to the Stalker Spirit. "I apologize for my rudeness. We have not been introduced."

{Not at all. I am here to aide in any way I can.}

Aya offered her paw to the Stalker. Leylia took it, and Ayasha Channeled her fully into the real world. While not solid enough to affect the real world, she looked much more solid after the channeling.

"Ah, that's more comfortable. Thank you, Hearth Stone."

"It is the least I can do for your aid. I'm still new at this, so I'm not sure how long this Channeling will keep you in the Wild."

"Thankfully, I am not. You've given me enough to roam the Wild for several rounds. I will find what you have asked of me, Hearth Stone, though I may require more of your assistance if my hunt requires more than the time you have afforded me."

"And you shall have it, Honored Ancestor."

"Then I will be off," Leylia headed for the edge of the roof, dropping to all fours. She leapt over the side and disappeared.

Aya turned back to Roan. "Has anyone else been given my name recently?"

"I had the same thought, but no. There have been a few hundred confirmations in the last two rounds, and no one else has been given the name the Speaker. But Aya, there is a more disturbing mystery to this. I have attempted to speak to the current Keeper of Names. He has no memory of your name, and your name has not been recorded in the Tome of All Names. Some powerful magic is keeping every ta'el not in close proximity to you from remembering anything about your name. I've never seen such vast power."

"What in the seven sides is going on?"

"I wish I knew what to tell you. There is only one thing I can think of to do to get at least the meaning of your name."

"You can't be seriously thinking– "

"Since Olan is nowhere to be found in the Spiritlands, I can only assume he has been reborn. Since I spoke to him no more than ten turns past, he is far too young to be of any use, even if you could track him down," Roan said.

Aya shrugged. "You know that I could."

It was part of the power that let her reach out to Spirits no matter where they were, and trade her body temporarily for a Spirit's use. It was the last major part of the skill. She could always tell what Spirit resided in a body. Even if they were reborn, she could always find a Spirit no matter where it dwelled.

"That leaves us with but one choice. We have to contact one of the Dragons."

"I like not being eaten, Greatfather. I've had enough of being chewed on from the cubs in the last two rounds to last a lifetime."

Roan chuckled and followed Aya into her small home. The apartment was made up of five beautiful rooms that Aya had restored with the help of some of the better builder Spirits in the city. It had taken her the better part of a turn to finish it, but now that it was done, it was a gorgeous place to live. She went into the kitchen, and opened one of the cupboards.

"Don't be silly. The Dragons are much like any other Spirit. Show them the proper respect, and they will assist."

"Alright, fine. How do we get in contact with one of the Dragons?"

"We don't, you do. The only Dragon anyone has seen in thousands of turns is the one known as The White. She is always listening, but I suggest that you be very polite. She is the Dragon that we call the Creator."

Aya bent down to the small glowing window beneath the stovetop where the fire spirit slept. She took a handful of cedar chips out of a bin next to the stove.

"Hello, little one. Could you heat some water for me?"

The tiny spirit made of blue flames stretched like a feline, and then held out its tiny mitten-like hands. Ayasha smiled and gave it one of the cedar chips. It brightened and grew in size until it was heating the top of the stove. Aya set her kettle onto the stove top.

"How long do you think it will take for the White to arrive?"

"Just call to her. If she is willing to assist, she will appear."

In the center of the living room was a shallow pit. The entire floor of the pit was a single spongey cushion of purple moss. Several large pillows sat atop the naturally growing bolster. Aya dropped to all fours in the pit, and went into a languid feline stretch. Cloudy black spots rippled over the golden sky of her pelt as muscles and tendons creaked. She let all of her paws splay out and laid her muzzle down on the comfortable plant life.

"That fast?" Aya's muffled mumble was skeptical.

"The White is not like any other Spirit. Some think of her as a god with good reason," Roan replied.

"Maybe because she is?"

The ghostly rose shape of Greatfather Roan shrugged. "She says not, but you are entitled to believe whatever you like."

"Are not creatures of such unlimited power by definition gods?"

"I'll not debate it with you when I agree, Aya, but you should meet her and judge for yourself. While I suggest you treat her with the utmost respect because I feel she deserves such respect, from what I know of her, she would say that you should think for yourself."

The kettle began a piercing whistle. Aya got up from the pit and bent down in front of the stove. "Thank you, little one." She fed another chip of cedar wood to the little Spirit, and it happily quieted its flames to devour the cedar chip more slowly than the first. Aya took the kettle off the stove and poured its hot water into a mug. The aroma of jasmine filled her kitchen as the tea steeped. When it was ready, she took the mug back into the living area.

The room itself was a simple large square, with sliding double doors on the opposite side that lead out into the rooftop garden that she worked so hard to maintain. Two doors lead off on the wall to the right. The wall to the left was completely hidden from floor to ceiling by bookshelves that had not been constructed but rather grown from the living tree that was the heart of the building.

The immense tree, grown at Aya's request by a minor Forest Spirit that now lived within it, reinforced the structure of the entire building. Many of the apartments within had permanent furniture of living wood that she had personally sculpted with the help of the Forest Spirit. This had been one of the things she had done during her training as part of her service to the ta'el of the city. The building now housed thirty six ta'el families, and she had taken the small top floor apartment for herself so that she could continue to care for the Forest Spirit and tree.

She stared at the bookshelf, and thought about climbing it to take out a book so she could just relax. She was tired, and the thought of calling a Dragon into her home was a little terrifying.

Around the lounging pit were four large comfortable looking chairs upholstered in plush purple velvet. Aya's childhood home had had one of the velvety chairs, and she loved to nap in it. The velvet was exceedingly rare because it was something that humans had made. Ta'el had replicated it, but the materials used to make it were hard to come by. The domesticated animals that produced them had gone extinct. As a result, the materials for making it had to come from the Ta'el themselves. Very few ta'el had chosen to be born of domesticated ungulates like the sheep necessary to produce wool. Aya's velvet had been made from the wool of a close friend of her Mother's, just like the chairs her parents owned.

Each chair had a small table next to it. They were large enough that a ta'el her size could curl up and sleep in one, but not so large that they could seat two ta'el comfortably. It was to one of these chairs that Aya made her way. She put her mug down on the table beside it and climbed into the chair. She arranged her legs in the lotus position, sipped her tea to invite calm, and then set it aside. She closed her eyes and slipped down into the quiet place inside herself where she could feel her Spirit.

Channeling magic in the real world was a combined effort. One part of that magic was using the energy of your own living Spirit to create a channel for magical energy from the called upon Spirits to allow it to flow into the Wild. This was not the only reason to open a Channel into the Spiritlands. Aya mentally stood up walls around her thoughts until she could no longer sense the real world. She floated incorporeal in the upper reaches of her mental landscape.

She could have delved deeper, as she often did when she took the time to come into her mind. Wandering her own mental landscape was absurd and often hilarious, considering how bizarre her own unordered thoughts could be. That was not why she was here. She focused on making a connection with the Spiritlands.

An orb of white light slowly came into view and then brightened until it was almost blinding. She did not have to look away, as she did not have retinas to burn here. She reached out towards the orb and touched it. This was not a process that was normally necessary. She could normally reach into the Spiritlands with a bare thought, but calling to the Spirits was partly relative to distance and partly relative to the Spirit you were trying to call. There were other factors as well, but to be certain she would reach the Spirit she wanted, no matter the distance, she would put some of her living energy into the sending. The little white orb of her own life spirit would seek her intended recipient and deliver the message no matter where they were, even if they had been called into the Wild.

She whispered the sending to the orb. *{I call to The White for aid, and respectfully request your attendance.}*

She released it, and the orb vanished into the Spiritlands. Her eyes popped open, and before she could even reach for her cup, a Spirit appeared in one of the chairs around the pit. She did not fade into view. One moment she was not there, and the next, she was. Aya almost tipped over her tea as she scrambled back over the back of the chair. She hung by her claws for a moment, then pulled herself up to look over the back of the chair with a snarl.

"Forge and Fire, emta'el, I'm lucky I have fur left!" Aya shouted angrily.

The Spirit across from her was only very slightly transparent, and was more real than any Spirit she had ever seen. She was born of a type of vulpine, but Aya could not place it right away. Her own Father was born of the fox, and she had thought that she had seen every variety, but this was one she had only read about in books. After a moment, she recognized the Spirit as the Arctic Fox.

She was also wearing a garment unlike any Aya had seen before. Ta'el didn't wear clothing as a rule. It was just too stifling for most anyone with fur unless you were going into a truly harsh environment, or to a truly special occasion for which such dress was appropriate.

Aya had worn dresses and other clothing for such occasions, but not like what the emta sitting in the other chair grinning at her was wearing. It was too plain to be formal wear. It was simple green cloth that hung at ankle length, belted at the waist with a lighter green ribbon, and Aya thought she spied a simple bow peeking out on either side of the emta's trim waist.

"What are you wearing?"

The Spirit looked down at herself. Then she shrugged. "Looks like a dress. Are you ok?"

Aya pulled herself up over the back of the chair and perched on the top of it. She narrowed her eyes at the Spirit.

"You're doing this on purpose."

"Guilty as charged," the Fox emta admitted. Then she began to snigger. "You should see yourself!" she laughed.

Aya hopped down into the chair and righted herself so that she was sitting with her paws swinging off the edge. Aya's violet eyes locked a glare on the White Fox.

"Oh, stop looking at me like that. Do you know how often someone has the spine to call me for aid? It's been 382 turns since someone requested my presence in the Wild. Do you know how many times I've read every tome of the Heartstone Chronicle?"

Aya sputtered. "That's not a real thing." The Heartstone Chronicle was a legend of the Ta'el - a collection of books that contained the life story of every ta'el who had ever lived.

"Is it not? Am I not the Creator?"

"But, it would be…" Aya's mind boggled at how many books it would take to contain such knowledge.

"Currently, three hundred eight million four hundred sixty-six… " One of the fox's ears fell saying confusion when she paused. "No, five hundred thirty-eight volumes. Seems I will be skimming a few hundred more tomes this evening." The emta seemed to notice that Aya's eyes had gone out of focus. "Oh dear, I see I have gone too far. Ayasha the Speaker?"

Aya shook her head, and seemed to realize someone was speaking to her. "I feel I should refrain from asking you any questions I do not really want the answers to, Creator."

"That would probably be for the best. You may call me White."

"I feel I should offer you something more than your name."

"Most do, but I am not a god as you conceptualize them to be. I have the power to do almost anything you can imagine if I am Channeled into the Wild. However, it is nearly impossible for any Channeler to withstand the requisite power to do so. I gave up my living body because I like this world, and my powers distort local space if I am among the living, but I retain all of my magical strength. So, many think of me as a god, but I am not all knowing. My goals and motivations are much simpler than the kind of overseeing god that the humans thought existed. We Dragons are more caretakers to this universe than gods, so I would appreciate it very much if you would call me White instead of Creator or something more grandiose."

"Very well, White. I apologize for my earlier rudeness. You startled me."

"No need, Ayasha, your reaction was quite understandable. I am not your typical Spirit. I will earn your respect if I would like to have it. None of this, however, is why you called for my aid."

"No, Honored Ancestor and I believe that there is some mystery tied to my name. We are hoping that you can help us to unravel it."

The White looked at her soberly. "I am afraid I cannot tell you much. The meaning of your name is very important, Ayasha, but if the meaning is simply revealed to you, the potential that it indicates will not be fulfilled. You must discover the meaning of your name on your own."

Aya's ears fell and she frowned. "I don't even know where to begin. You were our last idea."

"And a fine idea it was. I will help you on your path, as I have for all of those who have been given your name in the past. They all eventually find themselves in my presence. I simply cannot walk the path for you. Your name is one that is given in times when someone like you is needed."

"Like me?"

The White nodded. "You did not receive your name by accident, Ayasha the Speaker. You were not the only one recently given your name, but all of those who received it have not been able to take the first step to learning the meaning of that name, so they passed the name in exchange for a new one."

It was not unheard of that a ta'el did not find the name they were given to be to their liking. It didn't happen often, but it did happen. It was also not unheard of that a ta'el would have to go on a journey to discover the meaning of their name. The Spirits were usually a lot less mysterious about assisting with that journey.

"So, in what direction shall I be walking, White?" Aya asked.

"Before I tell you where you must go, I wonder if you would indulge me and join in a game?" Aya's left ear fell and the right stood up, a universal expression of confusion among ta'el.

Chapter 6

"A FRIENDLY GAME OF PAHN"

Pahn was a game that all ta'el learned as cubs. It was used in many respects as a teaching tool for peaceful conflict resolution among cubs, but also acted as a primer for interacting with the Spirits. It was the only known way for the living to enter the Spiritlands without enormous mystical effort.

Aya and the White appeared side by side on a flat expanse of grassy field. Each blade of greenery luminesced with the misty energy of the Spiritlands and perfect puffball clouds floated by in an eternally blue sky. Aya did her best not to look askance at the White as she considered the purpose of this game. It was clear that the White was testing her. Aya was not certain she wanted to pass. Perhaps it would be best for her if the mystery of her name remained so.

"Will I be playing Guardian or Rival?" Aya asked.

"Guardian will be your role. Construct your fortress in any configuration you see fit. Choose five Spirits to face me."

Aya nodded, and her eyes lost focus as she considered her lineup. As a cub, she could have chosen any of the millions of Spirits, but as one aged, the number of Spirits you were allowed to choose from was limited to those you had made personal connections with. She closed her eyes and focused more deeply on her possible choices. She concluded that it probably didn't matter because the White was the Creator. Like a cub, she would have connections with every Spirit. Best to choose a group that would work well with her because of their closeness.

"I choose The Hound, Lane the Wanderer, one of the Firescale, the Greyshard, and Elder Windword."

As Aya recited the names, Spirits appeared next to her. The Hound took the form of a basset hound of abnormally large size. His deep crimson eyes remained as ever. Lane looked as he always did, a ta'el born of the Mongoose formed of bluish white mist.

Elder Windword was an ancient Channeler of tremendous power. He was born of the Black Bear, and formed himself of deep green mist. He wiggled rounded ears at her and winked. It was something that always made her smile, and that he had used that as a training tool when she was young and nervous.

The Firescale was an enormous lizard as large as a saltwater crocodile with a long conical tail, wedge-shaped head, and a thick, ovular body with stubby legs. It was formed of bright red mist, and blazing orange flames flickered intermittently across its body.

The last of the party was an enormous spider-like creature. The Greyshard appeared to be made of a collection of slabs of stone. Oddest of all, the parts of the body did not seem to be truly connected by anything. Legs, head, abdomen, and torso seemed to float slightly independent of one another, held together only by an unseen force. Its precognitive abilities would be key if she had any chance of winning this game. Aya noticed the White was watching, her ears perked forward with interest. Her whiskers twitched in a circular motion saying "impressed".

"Well, you certainly show a natural ability to befriend Spirits, just like most of your predecessors."

"Didn't think all of that work was natural ability," Aya groused.

The White chuckled. "Oh, do not think that I am attempting to diminish your hard work. Your spiritual warmth is the only natural part." The White nodded. "I will choose Cat Sith, Hadron the Black, The Grey, a Solarwing, and the Shadow Dancer."

Aya blinked. She only recognized two of the Spirits that appeared next to the White, which was impressive indeed. She had spent most of her life studying Spirits and their appearance. The Grey was, without a doubt, the most impressive of the lot to Aya, but Cat Sith was at least a close second, if not more unbelievable.

The Grey was about the same height as Aya, but far more robustly built, from what she could see of his barrel-chested form beneath the swath of his storm gray cloak. He was a legendary figure among the Ta'el, the first Channeler, and by far, the most powerful of their kind. His eyes shown blindingly blue over a short, powerful muzzle covered in short grey fur with a round black nose.

Cat Sith was not ta'el, but was a feline of enormous size with jet black fur unbroken, save for a patch of white on his chest. His eyes were like black pits of night, shot through with whorls of misty purple light. They seemed fixed on her no matter how she moved and it unnerved her. Though he was not terribly well known, if the remaining human literature was any indication, he must have been an unbelievably powerful Spirit to have been among the fading number of non-elemental Spirits to have survived the death of the humans.

The Solarwing was unlike anything she had ever seen. A raptor made entirely of shades of orange and red light. It was shaped roughly like a falcon, but with a much longer neck and a pair of extremely outsized tailfeathers. She could feel the heat radiating from the bird even at ten paces.

Hadron the Black was much like The Grey, hidden entirely by a cloak, but unlike the Grey, there was no way to tell what was hidden beneath the midnight fabric. The cloak seemed to contain only shadow, and it moved and bent at odd angles that made it seem impossible that it could contain a body.

The last Spirit, the Shadow Dancer, was one that she had heard of, but like every other account, she had considered the Spirit a myth. It was one of the Source Elementals, singular Spirits that were the source of their element. It was the most powerful wielder of shadows in existence.

Aya turned to constructing her fortress. She willed herself into the air, floating high above the playground. A moment later, the White appeared next to her. She had spun herself so her back was facing the playground.

"Why is it that you think you feel so inadequate compared to your Mother?"

The White's conversational tones fooled Aya for one pristine moment and her concentration faltered. Then she took a deep breath and thick white walls of shining stone rose from the verdant field of the playground. A large square took shape as the walls rose. Two hundred feet on a side, it had two massive gaps in the walls, one to the north and one to the south. She did not put doors on the openings per the rules of the game. In the center of the playground, another massive wall appeared. It was circular, and it rose to a height of twenty feet before it was capped with white stone. A second level almost identical to the first rose. The process repeated itself twice more until a four-story tower of polished stone broke the sky. Finally, a dome of stone rose at the top level in a perfect half-sphere. Around the tower on each floor, the stone crumbled to dust and then vanished entirely, forming perfect rectangular windows.

"I have been present for many of her workings, and compared them to mine."

"I think you may be underestimating how much you will mature with age, Ayasha the Speaker."

"My mother's power comes from being older?"

The White shook her head. "Yes and no. Truthfully, in sheer power as a Channeler, your mother has a greater capacity than any other Channeler for a thousand turns. Still, you should know that her greater works were not achieved on sheer power alone. She had help."

Aya blinked and then shrugged. "Why are you telling me this?"

"It isn't complicated. It is quite clear to me that you have deep feelings of inadequacy with regards to your mother."

"No, I just want things to be simple," Aya countered.

The White shook her head. "You want to protect other ta'el or you would not have trained the way you have."

"I don't want to be my mother. I don't want ta'el to stand me on some pedestal. It can be simple." Aya rubbed one arm uncertainly.

"No, Ayasha the Speaker, it cannot. Not everyone has the will to put themselves between danger and others. When one does, admiration is always sure to follow. That is not why we are here, though."

"Why are we here?"

"In every generation, there is a position that we amongst
the Spirits attempt to fill. It requires someone with a very
specific way of thinking. We hoped at first it would be your
Mother, but she proved to be on a different path. When we
gave the criteria to all those Spirits involved with training new
Hearth Stones, Roan insisted that you were the one. Of course,
he was not the only one. There were others whose charges
were promising."

"And why aren't you testing them?" Aya tried to push
down her apprehension.

"Because we already have. None have been the correct
candidate. Now it is your turn."

"I suppose it's pointless to point out that I am the youngest
Stone among the Hearth?" Aya turned back to the White as
she had finished constructing her tower.

"It is not about age or experience, Aya. This is about
finding someone with a mind flexible enough to look for
solutions where others would not. That is why we are playing
this game of Pahn, because I want to see if you are one that has
that sort of flexibility."

"Then let us begin the game."

The White turned back and took a small, quick breath. The
massive tower of white stone was absolutely beautiful. Even
with the unlimited possibilities that Pahn offered to the
Guardian when building their tower, very rarely did someone
build something so stunning as this. Every square inch of the
polished stone surface of the tower was carved in stunning
bas-relief with fanciful animals and forest landscapes. After a
few moments of watching, the floors of the tower spun as if
each floor was a massive disk on the record player of a giant.

"That is among the most beautiful Guardian towers I
believe I have ever seen," The White said honestly.

Aya looked away. She could feel her face heating, and she
was glad that it was impossible to see her blush. She twitched
her whiskers up and back in a way that said "appreciation" for
the compliment.

"It is one of several that I made up after a lifetime of reading books of fantastical things that the humans wrote. The books are a weakness of mine."

Aya waved her Spirits towards the tower, and each of them vanished, presumably to reappear inside.

"Good Luck, White."

"Thank you, Aya, and I wish you the same."

Aya willed herself to appear inside the top room of her tower. There the Hound greeted her warmly by rubbing against her side.

"Hello, Little Aya, it has been some time since we have played a game," Elder Windword said.

"We have to be clever this time, Elder. We are playing against The White, and I think it is very important that we play well."

Elder Windword smiled his quiet smile, and nodded calmly. "I have played against her before. Many of us speculate that she had a guiding paw in designing Pahn."

Aya groaned. "So, we're going to lose," Aya grumbled dismally. She hated losing.

"Without a doubt," Windword cheerfully replied. His ringed tail swayed in delight to emphasize his joke. His head slowly tilted to one side as he watched her. "You are unsure. That is not like you, Little Aya."

"I've wanted to be a Hearth Stone since I was a cub. Now I'm not sure that's what I'll be when this is finished. I don't want to be more, Elder. I just want to be me."

Windword put a paw on her shoulder and a grin split his muzzle. "Perhaps, you should consider that this and what you want to be can be the same thing."

"Thanks, Windword the Caretaker."

"Besides, I've never known anyone stupid enough to stand in your way if you want to do something else with your life," Windword chuckled.

"Well, let's start with the standard defense," Aya suggested.

Lane was well respected as one of the most impressive hand to hand combatants in the histories. It was a major difference in ta'el society. Everyone learned how to defend themselves, without exception. Most ta'el called on a Spirit like Lane to train their cubs in the martial arts. It was one of the few things in her life Aya had felt conflicted over. She never liked hurting anyone.

"I'll take the first level, and I shall take our fiery friend with me." Windword waved to the Firescale. The Firescale was a mythical creature that likely gave rise to the human legends of fire breathing salamanders. Glowing lines ran between the cobblestone scales that covered its body. It went to the old raccoon's side.

"Be careful. I don't know about the rest of the Spirits she has chosen, but Cat Sith is an incredibly powerful creature," Aya warned.

"They are all as powerful as Cat Sith," Wanderer Lane said.

"I've never heard of Hadron the Black."

"Hadron the Black was a ta'el who toppled over a dozen Corrupted Nests in his time. He was known for his ability to appear anywhere he wished to go, no matter how fortified the position." Wanderer Lane explained what little he had learned about the ancient Spirit since his own death. "But Pahn is not about power, Little Aya. You likely do not have the experience to outfox the White, but that is not how the game is played."

"I will let the Hound wander the grounds. He will notify you if anyone bypasses the outer walls. Lane, you can take the Greyshard and engage any threats that get past the first floor," Aya said.

"We will do our best, Aya. To be honest, I have always wanted a chance to test my skills against Hadron. It is rumored that we shared a species, though no one really remembers." Lane's grin was full of sharp teeth. He waited a long moment for the floor to spin, and then he disappeared down the east stairwell. Windword had taken the west stairwell, and that left the Greyshard.

She had made the windows just large enough to permit the Greyshard to pass. It disappeared down the side of the tower. Aya lifted her paw, and waved at the air. Two dozen images appeared in the air like windows into other places. They showed every room of the tower, the grounds surrounding it, and on the right hand side, live images of each of her Spirits. A long, baying howl sounded from the grounds. Aya's eyes darted to the image of the Hound. He was bolting towards the tower with Cat Sith hot on his heels. Aya grunted.

"The Hound is coming in fast toward the east stairwell, Windword, but I think that Cat Sith is a distraction. It is too early in the game to lose a player. Fortify the walls of the tower and leave an opening just large enough for them to pass through. See if you three can defeat him. I have other plans to make." Aya waved at the image of Wanderer Lane and it moved directly in front of her.

"He's coming, Lane. Cat Sith is acting as a distraction. Hadron or The Grey will use this as an opportunity to enter from one of the other gates." He couldn't answer her, but she saw him nod. The Greyshard would be her ace in the hole. It could roam the tower much like the Hound, but with its precognitive abilities, it was a solid match for almost any other spirit. The Hound finally rose through the floor next to her. She grinned.

"Good, think you can find The Grey?" Aya asked.

The Hound barked once and then trotted off towards the west wall of the tower. He disappeared through the stone. It was odd playing a game of Pahn with the Hound now that she had befriended him. When he was called to a game of Pahn, not all of his intelligence came with him. He acted much more canine, and while she knew he understood her, he didn't speak to her here. Many of the most powerful Elemental Spirits were like that when they came into a game of Pahn. They did not lend their full power to the game to keep things fairer, especially when cubs were playing.

She waved her paw, and the image of Elder Windword returned to the forefront. She groaned. The Firescale's form was ephemeral once again, but so too was Cat Sith's.

"The Solarwing and the Shadow Dancer are the concern," Aya said before The Hound's howl echoed through the tower once again. It had found the Grey.

"Windword, I will leave the Grey to you. I am redirecting the Hound to face off against the Shadow Dancer. The Solarwing is going to come in out of nowhere, and if we are going to win, we have to be ready for it. I have to send the Greyshard to help against Hadron, if he hasn't already beaten Lane."

She waved aside the image of Windword and recalled the one of Lane. He was fighting the cloaked figure of Hadron furiously. She had learned long ago how to Channel Spirits like Lane to make herself faster and stronger, but this was a blur of motion that she could barely make out. She had known Lane was fast and strong for his size, but this was beyond preternatural speed and power. He was giving it his all, and it was still not enough. She didn't think Hadron was any faster, but somehow, he was staying one step ahead of Lane. She watched as the Greyshard crept across the ceiling above them. That was when her plan nearly unraveled.

The Greyshard was about to pounce when the Solarwing exploded from beneath Hadron's cloak. Aya finally made the connection between the bird made of light and the Phoenix of human legend due to the fact that it was now made entirely of blazing white fire, but it had appeared a moment too soon. The Greyshard threw itself to the right and trailed a netting of thick web behind it. It fell over the Solarwing and the wet, sticky stuff snuffed the flames. In a blur, the Greyshard had cocooned the Solarwing. The ephemeral form of the bird floated free of the cocoon, and the Greyshard skittered away, disappearing into the darkness.

The fight continued betweenHadron and Lane. Lane could not beat Hadron, but she knew he had wanted to fight him, and the Greyshard would still be there waiting to pounce. She swiped the image of the Greyshard to the forefront.

"Stay with Lane, but let him finish the fight before you attack Hadron," Aya ordered the massive slate spider. Then, her plans actually did unravel. Windword's ephemeral form appeared next to her. He had lost his duel with The Grey.

"I did my best, but the Grey is all he was rumored to be." Windword said.

"That's all I could have asked. Thank you, Honored Ancestor."

Aya held up her paw, and an image of the tower from the outside appeared. She waved her paw through it, and the tower's floors spun. This configuration made a path directly to the top floor from the second, where Lane and Hadron fought. The Greyshard skittered into the path and then she swiped the image of the tower again, floors shifting.

The White watched as the game progressed. She didn't use images to watch the fight as Aya did, her status as a Spirit herself allowed her to simply know all that was happening with her fellow Spirits. The tower was even more impressive than its outer appearance. The White had rarely seen players construct such an intricate defense tower. Her play could have been better, but she was young. She had committed too much too early to disable Cat Sith. Sith was a strong opponent but the Hound was an equally ancient and powerful Spirit. She should have trusted the Hound to defeat Cat Sith on his own. Still, she was depending on Wanderer Lane to be able to defeat Hadron. That showed she could trust others when she needed to.

Both Lane and Hadron were fighters of skill beyond normal measure, and while to the unexperienced eye, it seemed that Hadron had the upper hand, it was simply not true. What most did not know about Lane the Wanderer is that he had spent centuries perfecting techniques that no one else had ever even dreamed of. While Hadron had more practical experience, Lane had specifically studied the nature of fighting and motion.

The Grey had discerned the pattern of movement to the staircases and was making his way up the tower with haste. Still, the shifting pattern of stairwells was slowing him considerably.

{Have a care, her Greyshard is somewhere in those passages, and I am not sure that Hadron can defeat Wanderer Lane. They are both quite something,} she sent to The Grey.

Aya watched the fight between Lane and Hadron as it progressed to its end. They were both peerless fighters, and she realized that she had not given Lane enough credit. Just as the fight drew to a close, The Grey burst into the room where she was commanding the battle. It was an odd creature that Aya did not at all recognize. He appeared to be some sort of canine, but he didn't look quite right. The hood hid too much for her to make a determination.

In that moment, she noticed that the fight between Hadron and Lane had ended in a draw. Both had reverted to their ephemeral forms. So, it all came down to this. The Grey moved cautiously forward. At the center of the room was a pedestal with a large golden crystal, Aya's standard treasure. His eyes darted everywhere. Aya just grinned at him.

He approached carefully, and that was when the floor burst open, the trapdoor thrown aside, the Greyshard springing out at him. It was lightning quick, but The Grey was faster still. His paws came up in a blur, and the net of webbing the Greyshard had thrown at him was blown back across the giant slate spider. It didn't manage to tangle the massive spider, but that didn't matter. Somehow, The Grey had perfectly predicted the Greyshard's movements.

A spear of light appeared between his paws and streaked towards the Greyshard. It speared the spider through the midsection a split second before its legs would have touched the floor. The Spirit of the Greyshard became transparent. It gave a little bow of respect to The Grey before it faded away.

Aya held out her paw in a gesture of permission and The Grey gave a small bow of respect. He lifted the golden crystal and his form faded back to his normal ephemeral being. Aya came forward and bowed to him.

"How?"

"Precognition is an impressive weapon, but once you understand its function, you realize that it has a rather large flaw. If there are too many equally likely options for future events, clairvoyance becomes muddled. My options for dealing with the Greyshard were vast."

The Grey's ready answer made Aya frown a little. "You knew it would be there?"

The Grey responded with a shake of the hooded head. "You nearly had me at the end. If I hadn't been so familiar

with Greyshards, I might not have been prepared for the
webbing."

"I do not wish to be presumptuous, but might I ask if we
could speak again in the future, and if you would perhaps give
me the honor of being a Channel for you in the future?"

He considered Aya's request for a long moment, then he
graced her with a quiet smile, and a graceful nod. "I think that
I would enjoy that, Hearth Stone. You played quite well, and
do pass along my compliments to Elder Windword. I should
dearly like to play against him again. I would also be happy to
be a player for you any time you would like to call on me." He
faded from sight, and her tower followed suit as the game
ended.

Aya willed herself to appear at the ground. The White
appeared next to her a moment later.

"I do not believe that anyone has had the fortitude to
approach The Grey like that for a very long time," The White
said.

"Why the names of colors?" Aya had to ask.

"Oh, two very different reasons. Ta'el called him The Grey
because of his role as a mediator. He was one of the strongest
Channelers to ever exist outside of we dragons, but he was
always a proponent of peaceful resolution of conflicts. He
rarely showed his power unless he had no other choice. He
could Channel a dragon on his own entirely unaided.

Ta'el call me The White because of my propensity for taking
the shapes of ta'el with white coloring. Almost no one can
remember my name these rounds, so it is easier to just let folks
know me as The White. By the time humans came to be, there
were only a half dozen of us left on this planet, so they called
us by our colors. After the humans were gone, the practice
just stuck, even though my brethren have moved on."

Aya sighed. "So how did I do?" Aya's trepidation was
obvious. The Spiritlands faded from sight, and her apartment
reasserted itself.

"You have come as close to defeating me in a game of Pahn
as anyone has in a half dozen generations."

"Has anyone ever beaten you?"

The White grinned. "Once or twice. You have the skills necessary, but the question is, do you have the will?"

Aya picked up her cup of tea, the steam still rising from it. That was one of the best things about playing Pahn. The game happened outside of the normal flow of time. You could spend shifts or even rounds playing a game of Pahn. When you finished, almost no time at all had passed in the real world. She had no idea how it really worked. It was a creation of the dragons. Aya took a deep breath.

"I don't know if I am the ta'el you are looking for."

The White finished her tea and put the cup down on the table. When her fingers came away, a symbol that Aya didn't recognize glowed on the side. No matter how much she stared at the glowing symbol, it remained fuzzy and indistinct.

"When you do, fill this cup with that wonderful tea, and I will return for your answer," The White said.

"I guess I'm just left wondering what you are actually asking me to do."

The White giggled. "Silly me. To find the meaning of your name, you must start in the Below Places. Be on your guard, Ayasha the Speaker. The Below Places as they are now brew a dangerous secret, one that even I have not yet deciphered."

Aya reached for the cup and The White put her snowy paw back on top of it.

"Don't wait too long, Little Aya. Time is growing short, and it is my belief that a Speaker is needed in this world."

The White then faded away, compressing in on herself until only a small point of soft white werelight remained. Then it zipped out of her window, disappearing into the night.

Chapter 7

"LEEWARD"

Aya knelt in the small clearing of her rooftop garden. She had been trying to calm her mind for shifts. The symbol on the side of the tea cup had faded away a few moments after the White had gone, but the memory lingered on in her mind. Not the symbol itself, she could not remember what it looked like beyond that it was both simple and elegant. It was unlike any magic the Spirits had ever given to her.

"Did you see the rune, Greatfather?"

Roan stood unobtrusively to one side of the clearing. His body had brightened to a crimson glow so he could be more easily seen in bright sunlight.

"I did not. I could only see a bright light on the side of the cup."

"It's the key."

"Why would you say that?"

"I was the only one who could see it. I checked with all of the Spirits around the house. They couldn't see it either. Not even the Witness."

A Witness was a Spirit that grew from the presence of living people in a home, a Spirit that observed the home when the occupants were away. They only grew in places that were loved by the ta'el who lived there. The better loved the place, the stronger the Witness Spirit. Her Witness was powerful enough to pierce even the strongest veiling magics. It had seen nothing of the symbol either, nothing but that bright light.

"I don't know what the rune was. I can't hold it in my mind, but while I was looking at it I could see it clearly."

"What do you think that means?"

Aya shook her head, her ears folded back with annoyance. "I think it means we need to find out what the Below Places are."

"Then I guess that means we are headed back to the park. There is only one person who can help with that."

Aya nodded. "The Record."

She rocked herself backwards and came smoothly to her feet, touching the hilt of the Heartblade in its sheath at the small of her back to assure herself it was there. She picked up her piece pouch from the edge of the clearing and slid it onto her belt, and then leapt off the edge of the roof into the trees. Even in her flight, she was careful not to damage the tree as she slid down, using her claws to slow herself. She knew this tree well, and unlike the pampered tree she kept at the center of her garden, this tree enjoyed the feel of a good claw scraping the dead bark off of its trunk.

When she finally landed at street level, she patted the tree and was rewarded with a warm feeling coming up through her paw pads. The tree was happy to help her reach her destination. Roan faded into view next to her as she walked toward the Park.

"Are we in luck niround, Greatfather?"

"Sadly not. The Record is not in the park, but his Watcher Spirit is. Sileas is taking messages for him."

"Sileas? As in Sileas the Player? She is his Watcher Spirit?"

"She is. You got to hear her once, didn't you?"

"When I was a cub. She was extremely old then, but Fire and Forge, I still remember that sound. I didn't realize she had passed the Bardo."

"Well, someone has brought a finely tuned guitar, but no one there is a suitable Channel for her. She needs someone with clever fingers. Also, I may have told everyone that if they waited for you, Sileas could both play _and_ sing."

Aya swallowed. Allowing a Spirit to control your body as if it were their own was dangerous. Some Spirits, once in possession of a body, had a difficult time releasing it to return to the Spiritlands, albeit not purposely. There was very little chance it would happen to Aya, either. She had the proper training to allow a second Spirit to inhabit her body without her own becoming intermingled; the proper training and then some. But those with less training in Channeling had fallen victim to that particularly unpleasant death. The living body cannot permanently house two souls.

"Clever fingers, indeed."

Roan grinned. Aya broke out into a jog. She wouldn't want to disappoint everyone waiting there. When she finally rounded the corner and the park came into view, she stopped dead. Between her and the park were at least a thousand ta'el milling about. She swallowed, and Roan chuckled.

"So, Little Aya, how badly do you want to see Ayrece again?"

"I hate you."

Aya sighed and then she strode forward. Many of the ta'el in the crowd recognized her, but more recognized the embroidered sash. The crowd parted for her with pardons and waves of recognition. It took her only a moment to reach the center of the commotion. It was a large, flat-topped rock at the center of one of the park clearings.

There, sitting atop the rock swinging her feet, was the Spirit of a ta'el of tiny proportions. In life, Sileas had been born of an extinct species of vulpine called a Fennec. Enormous triangular ears twitched in response to every sound around her. She was formed of cream-colored mist, and she looked up just as Aya entered the circle.

Sileas tilted her head, and then a smile split her muzzle when she saw Roan standing next to Aya. She lifted a paw and waved. Aya hopped up, caught the edge of the boulder with her fingertips, and then pulled herself up onto it with little effort. She straightened and then bowed to Sileas.

"Honored Ancestor, my Watcher tells me that I might earn a favor from you if I were to enable you to play a little music for the ta'el."

Sileas nodded but did not speak. Aya's left ear fell in curiosity. Sileas made a gesture with her paws to her throat, and then a more elaborate gesture that Aya recognized as a portion of the Ta'eltesh that she had learned as a child, but was very rusty at using. There were more than a few species of Ta'el who could not actually speak Ta'eltesh. Their vocal cords were not designed for vocal speech. Chiropteran came to mind first. Their voices were so high pitched that they could not form all of the sounds that vocal Ta'eltesh required, so they used pawspeak. It was not very often that Aya had occasion to use it, and she wasn't sure why Sileas would use it now. She had heard Sileas speak and sing in life. Her voice had been beautiful.

I apologize, Hearth Stone, but I am unable to converse in the normal way, the Fennec's tiny paws explained. Aya was about to answer in pawspeak, but Roan interrupted when he saw her concern.

"It is alright, Aya, nothing is amiss. Part of the very special magic Sileas imparts means that she cannot speak vocally in her Spirit form. She will be able to sing again just fine once she is in possession of a living body." Sileas made an affirmative gesture towards Roan.

"Oh?"

"Sileas' magic can allow you to mimic any sound or persons voice that you have ever heard before, but more importantly, she can allow anyone who Channels her to sing away corruption, as well as give a healing sleep to those who are gravely ill. The issue is because her magic has such a direct correlation with the Wild, part of her Spirit remains bound to it. That means when she is not in possession of a living body, she cannot speak."

"Such powerful magic on top of such an amazing voice. Some emta have all the luck," Aya mumbled.

Sileas smiled a sardonic smile. *I think that perhaps I hear the sound of breaking glass?* Sileas' paws formed the words, and Aya looked confused. Her paws moved again. *An old human idiom. Maybe you'll understand one round, may I perform?*

Aya replied in pawspeak. It was considered impolite to speak vocally with someone who required pawspeak as long as you were versed in it. *Of course, Honored Ancestor. I offer you a place in my body for your performance.* Aya had some difficulty forming the correct shapes with her paws.

"Roan, would you be so kind?"

She held out her paw to her Watcher then held out the other to Sileas, who looked at it curiously. Aya grinned at her and wiggled her fingers. When Sileas put her tiny ghostly paw into Aya's, Aya made a pulling gesture, and at the same time, Roan pulled at Aya's paw. Suddenly, Aya was standing beside Roan, looking at her own body. Her body stood frozen, with wide eyes looking back at Aya.

"How? This is no simple Channeling that would allow me to touch something of the Wild." The voice that rolled forth from the muzzle was not Aya's own. It was clearly Sileas'.

Aya's paws formed the words to explain. Taking Sileas' place in the form of a Spirit meant that all of the limitations that Sileas had were now imposed on Aya.

It is part of my personal magic. I began to learn about Channeling at a very young age when compared to other ta'el. It gave me a great deal of time to understand how my Spirit is connected to my body. That lets me trade places for a short time with an Ancestor Spirit. You cannot use your magic, though. It is in my possession now. I cannot use it either, though, since I am not actually attached to the Spiritlands.

Do not worry that you will become trapped. I have complete control. I can return us back to normal at any moment. However, resting control is uncomfortable for you, and I will not do it unless it is absolutely necessary. Come back to me when you are finished playing and we will trade places again.

Aya knew that many of the words were not quite right, as she struggled to remember all of the gestures of the visual language.

All the luck indeed. Sileas replied in pawspeak.

Please feel free to speak vocally.

"All the luck indeed," Sileas said again, testing her voice a little more. "Your pawspeak is very rough, Hearth Stone. I am only really getting three words out of four."

Aya nodded and made a shooing gesture at Sileas, who turned to the crowd. Aya and Roan hopped down from the boulder and moved off to a spot where they could watch the performance.

"Everyone be sure to give thanks for this performance to the Hearth Stone when she regains her body. Now, who had that guitar?" Her voice was resonant and sweet beyond compare. Aya remembered it well, and she was glad she would be able to see the performance.

A moment later, one of the shop keepers from Shop Row came forward. He was born of a lemur, and he owned the only instrument shop in the city. The guitar he was carrying was made of wood that was almost black, and it did not look like it had been constructed. It looked as if it had been grown from a tree. Aya knew better. Irasai had been creating guitars and other instruments for almost a hundred turns, but the instrument he was holding had been made for Sileas by his Greatfather. Aya had seen that guitar on the wall of his shop, and as far as she knew, no one had ever played it. He held it up to Sileas, who bent down and carefully took it from him.

"I had wondered what had become of this after my passing."

"It was given to me by your daughter, Honored Ancestor. I promised to hold it in my care until I or one of my apprentices found someone worthy of playing it again."

Sileas ran her paws over the dark wood. She extended then retracted the claws of Aya's paws a few times, and Aya realized that Sileas was making sure she understood how they functioned.

Will she be able to play with my claws? Aya formed the words for Roan in pawspeak.

"I am not sure. Your paws are very different from hers, but you do have clever fingers. I think she will surprise you."

Sileas put her paws to the strings. She began to play, slowly at first, but then her pace increased steadily as she got used to using Aya's paws. It slowed again as Aya began to recognize the song Sileas was using her body to play. Aya had listened to every song that Sileas had ever composed. What had made Sileas' music so beautiful is that each song stirred some emotion.

The song she played now was one of her oldest. Composed when she was young, it was over eight hundred turns old now. Aya had never met any ta'el that didn't know the song. The guitar began to hum a mellow, repetitive tune. The notes Sileas played were so smooth and rang so pure that they barely sounded like they were played on a guitar. They seemed as if they were unpolluted expressions of the notes themselves.

The number of ta'el gathered in the park began to grow as the song went on. It was a long song, the opening guitar piece alone about three bouts long. Ta'el were humming or whistling along with the piece, and Aya realized why the opening to the piece was so extended compared to some of Sileas' other music. She was making the audience part of the performance. By playing such a compelling piece that you couldn't help but hum, whistle, or tap your paw along with it, the melody reverberated back to her from the crowd.

She so effectively drew in the audience that when she finally started to sing, the melody she had been playing became a background to the same melody being sung back to her by the gathered ta'el. Aya hadn't realized how amazing Sileas had been when she was a cub at all. To turn the entire crowd into an instrument with a single song was almost a magic all its own.

Then Sileas showed why in her paws, a guitar was almost a weapon. She had never in life had claws like Aya's, and yet she began to hook them softly around the strings of the guitar to add humming reverb to the chords she played as if she'd had them all her life. Not only had she made the audience part of the performance, but now even as she sang, she became part of the audience as well. Aya stood in awe of the power of her song. Even a song that everyone knew was brand new in Sileas paws.

Just as Sileas finished the first song, Aya felt the presence of a Spirit that was attempting to get her attention in the Spiritlands. However, her current situation made it impossible for her to use her normal means of communication. She waved a paw at Roan, who had also been entranced by Sileas. She waited until she was sure he was paying attention and formed her words in pawspeak.

Greatfather, someone is attempting to draw my attention on the other side of the Veil. Could you cross and explain the situation to them?

"Of course. I will return in a moment." Roan was as good as his word, and came back within moments. "We may need to hurry this along, Aya. Leylia has returned, and she has found something troubling."

I would rather not, Greatfather. This is not a feat I can perform very often, and this may be once in a lifetime for many of the ta'el gathered here. Aya was straining her memory of pawspeak. She cursed herself for letting her practice with the language lag so badly.

"Half of that was... not actually words, Aya."

She made a gesture that had nothing to do with pawspeak and Roan chuckled.

"But I think I get the gist of it. I will see if I can solve the problem."

Roan faded away and Aya continued to enjoy the performance. Sileas was onto her third song before Roan appeared next to her again.

"Seems we are in luck. I found another Channeler who can get Leylia through the Veil."

Aya narrowed her eyes at the ta'el coming through the crowd, and just folded her paws. She couldn't say anything good about the person who was coming, but they would definitely be able to bring the Leylia through the Veil. She narrowed her eyes at Roan. Aya wished she was skilled enough to make pawspeak with a single paw, but it had been far too long since she had practiced it. She resolved to fix that oversight as soon as time presented itself. She turned away from the approaching feline. Born of the Puma, she was the most infuriating ta'el that Aya had ever met.

Why her?! She unsheathed her claws to put emphasis on the words.

"You see some other Channeler about?" Roan whispered.

But you know what she will ask for in exchange for her help! Aya's gestures were emphatic.

"I suggest you make peace with the idea, even if you will never make peace with Ayria." Aya looked back to the Puma moving through the crowd.

If she sees me like this, she will know about my magic.

Roan rolled his ghostly eyes. "Don't be a dolt. You just showed a thousand ta'el your magic." Roan grinned and Aya deflated.

Fine, but you are the one who is going to end up doing what she wants. You know that, right?

"Yep, I know it. I don't particularly fancy running errands in the Deeps, but I am your Watcher."

Yeah, well not for the next two rounds. You could have found literally anyone else.

"I can only go about two hundred feet from you before I get shoved back into the Spiritlands when you do this." He made an exasperated gesture to her transparent form.

Right. Apologies, Greatfather. I did not mean to seem ungrateful.

"And you were not. Ayria is a gigantic pain in the ass, but she is the only Channeler nearby. Just tell her I will do whatever she likes. If she wants me to trawl the sewer systems so she doesn't have to for a few rounds, at least I can turn off my sense of smell?" Roan grinned at her.

Yes, but I will smell it through you for shifts when you come back, Aya complained.

Roan chuckled. "Here she comes. Remember she's pissed you're an Adept."

Aya flattened transparent ears in annoyance. Ayria stopped in front of Aya, then her eyes went wide.

"Forge and Fire! What happened?"

Aya cringed. *I'm not dead, twit. I switched places with the Ancestor that is using my body to play this concert.*

"Allowing an Ancestor to possess your body is way too dangerous for this." Ayria gestured towards Aya's body playing for the crowd.

Aya sighed even though it made no sound. *Just forget it. It's something I learned when I was little.*

Ayria paused for a moment, as if her brain had experienced a hiccup. Then her standard scowl morphed into a very annoying smile.

"So how can I assist you, Adept?" Ayria's grin was extremely unpleasant, and suddenly Aya knew that Ayria was not going to ask for Greatfather Roan's help.

I simply need you to Channel one of the Stalkers through the veil so that I may speak with her.

"And what do you offer in exchange for my services?" Ayria asked smugly.

Aya really hated Ayria. She was one of the most selfish ta'el that Aya had ever met. She never did anything that was strictly outside of the polite rules of ta'el society, but she was just too prideful about always coming out ahead for Aya to like her at all.

What do you want? Aya already knew what she would ask for.

"You can teach me how you do that." Ayria made a gesture at Aya.

Aya shook her head. *Choose something else. I can't teach this.*

She had learned how to do this particular magic almost by accident. It had not been something she had intended to do when she began to study how her Spirit was attached to her body. To try and teach it to someone would be extremely dangerous and irresponsible. Ayria frowned and lashed her tail once. In the feline dialect, it was an obstinate refusal.

"If you learned it, I can learn it." Aya threw the refusal back at Ayria with a tail lash of her own.

Choose something else. Aya repeated the pawspeak gestures. At the end, she made a chopping gesture with her right paw into her left. It was a gesture of extreme emphasis, like adding an audible growl of warning to her words.

Ayria got a hard look in her eyes. Aya just shrugged. *Or don't help us, and you can tell the Hearth why you allowed a hole in the city defenses to continue to exist because of your selfish nature.*

"You should really brush up on your pawspeak. That was atrocious. Why didn't you just tell me?"

Because I expected you to be you. Aya's paws formed the words slowly. It was uncharitable, but entirely true. Ayria frowned, but held out her paw to one side. A moment later, the spirit of Leylia the Stalker appeared in the Wild.

"I suppose that is fair," Ayria finally said. "The usual, then. If your Watcher Spirit can patrol the spillways for the next couple of nights, I would consider our debt settled."

Aya suddenly felt somewhat guilty and annoyed at the same time. She looked to Roan, but for now, he wouldn't be able to hear her thoughts. He didn't need that, though. He could tell what she was thinking just by looking at her. He shook his head.

The skill to safely allow an Ancestor Spirit to possess your body was incredibly useful for maintaining good relationships with the Spirits. Aya had always done her best not to exercise the power too freely, because she was not lying when she said it was extremely dangerous to learn. She couldn't just run about teaching it to everyone, no matter how well it would improve things for the Spirits. The only reason she had survived her stupidity was because of her mother's teachings combined with her own personal knowledge. It would take turns of study to impart that knowledge to anyone else.

Aya finally snapped out of her own thoughts when a transparent black paw waved in front of her face. Ayria was already turning to head back into the crowd. Aya reached out towards her, and Ayria turned back. Aya concentrated on getting the pawspeak words right.

Each morning, take the Tunnel to the Earthen Shrine in the Adirondack Mountains. Meditate in the garden there and attempt to connect your Spirit with mine through the Spiritlands. If you can actually reach me without assistance from an Ancestor Spirit, I will teach you how to allow Ancestors to use your body.

"But that's impossible."

If you think that, then I can't ever teach you. It wouldn't be safe. Aya's paws made the words.

"No one can reach that far unaided."

I can reach any Spirit alive or dead anywhere in the world or the Spiritlands given the time to concentrate.

It wasn't a boast and Ayria knew it. She had seen Aya demonstrate the skill. The exercise would either teach Ayria how her Spirit was connected to her body, and therefore allow her to project her living energies through the Spiritlands without actually being a Spirit, or it wouldn't. If she could do it, then she could also be taught how to allow a Spirit to possess her body and remain in control.

You will also need to retain a Watcher. That, Aya knew, would be a much harder task for Ayria. Having a Watcher Spirit required complete trust between the ta'el and their Ancestor Spirit. That was not all there was to the bond between a Watcher Spirit and the ta'el. There were many emotional factors. The bond to a Watcher Spirit was permanent, so you couldn't bind yourself to a Spirit that was even slightly incompatible, especially when you considered that many ta'el lived over three hundred turns.

"You're insane," Ayria said.

Aya just shrugged. *Hey, if you want to have a delightful experience with screamy possession death, you go right ahead and try to do it without the proper training.* Aya twitched her whiskers showing her sarcasm.

Ayria rolled her eyes. "Ugh, fine. Just trying to get out of smelling the Deeps through your Watcher," she grumbled.

Believe whatever you like. However, I would like to remind you which of us is almost always less prone to self-interest. Thank you for your assistance, Ayria.

Ayria turned and walked away waving her paw over her shoulder. "Yeah, whatever. You're welcome," she grumbled as she disappeared into the crowd.

Aya turned to Leylia. *How fare you on the hunt, Honored Ancestor?*

Leylia's face was concerned – ears flat, but not pinned, whiskers pulled back. She began to form pawspeak, but Aya waved her paws to let her know it wasn't necessary. Roan quickly explained the situation, and Leylia looked at her with some interest.

"That is quite the rare skill."

Aya just shrugged. *I'm not the only one to possess it.*

Silease's soothing music continued over their conversation but didn't seem to interfere with it. Her talent as a musician was clearly supernatural.

"No, but only a few hundred ta'el in the world ever develop it despite it being immensely useful. It is not an easy skill to perfect. Clearly, you were pronounced an Adept for a reason."

Aya's ears folded down and back expressing embarrassment and she looked away. She forced her paws to form words.

The business at paw, Honored Ancestor? Aya asked

Leylia grinned at her, but spoke to Roan. "Where did you find this one, Roan? She's really something."

"I take all the credit. She doesn't have a confident bone in her body without me," Roan said.

Hey, low blow when I can't talk, you old fart. Aya gestured. Roan laughed.

"The business," Leylia said. "What I have found is not good, but I think not as bad as you feared. I believe the breach was intentional. As you know, the wardnet that protects this portion of the city is kept by a number of Forest Spirits. A few spells back, we had that small tornado touch down on the edge of the city. One of the trees that was home to one of the little Elementals that keeps the ring was uprooted and flung it into the leeward river basin chasm."

Aya looked suspicious. *That's impossible. The wardnet trees are protected by their Spirits. They are well kept and are checked regularly. Why didn't the Spirit provide us with warning that its tree had been damaged?*

"I have no answer for that question. It's not as bad as you feared in the sense that I do not believe anyone in the city was responsible for the destruction. However, the tree's destruction had been camouflaged with a powerful illusion. It took almost all of the living energy you had provided me in combination with my own power to pierce the illusion. This is why I had to be Channeled across the veil again."

So opportunism, not sabotage. That still isn't good. I will be happy to provide more as soon as Sileas has finished her performance.

"There is no need. I have performed my task, though I would not object to a few more rounds in the Wild. I would very much like to visit my remaining family, and none are Channelers. I would consider it ample payment for my services. That being said, I tracked whatever did this for an entire round before I lost the trail to age. At first I suspected a Corrupted One, but the scent did not match any Corrupted One I ever encountered. It also doesn't explain why the Forest Spirit did not notify us. It was fretting over its tree when I arrived."

I will be sure to let someone at the Hearth know that a new tree will be needed for the Spirit, Aya gestured.

"Never once did the thing's tracks turn back to the city. They were not from here. However, the most disturbing thing is that once I took the time to consider the scent I believe that whatever casted the Illusion carried a Corrupted One within their body. They Channeled a Corrupted Spirit."

Aya shivered at the pronouncement. *Why would any Ta'el do that?*

"Who can say, Hearth Stone? Even ta'el are not perfect."

Aya turned to Roan. *So, now we have to find the Below Places and someone among the ta'el who has done the unspeakable at the same time. Could this get any worse?*

"That sounds suspiciously like asking for trouble, Little Aya."

They listened to the impromptu concert until the end. Thankfully, Sileas played a set of only ten or so songs before she finally took Aya's fingers from the strings. There was a short round of quiet cheers and applause. Sileas hopped down carefully from the rock, holding the guitar with care. She caressed the dark wood one last time and then turned to Irasai.

"Please do try to find it a home with a proper Player, but as long as you have it here and the Hearth Stone can make the time, I will happily come back and play for you all from time to time."

Irasai took the guitar reverently. He nodded to Sileas and then retreated into the dispersing crowd. Sileas brought Aya's body back to where she and Greatfather Roan were watching.

"I have never met someone with this talent, Ayasha the Speaker. I would be overjoyed if you would allow me to perform using your body from time to time."

Aya grinned and nodded. She held out her transparent paw and Sileas took it. Roan took the other paw of her body and tugged. Sileas slipped free from Aya's body as Aya used her living energy to pull her Spirit back into her body.

It took her a moment to reorient to being solid once again. She waited until the tingles that came from reconnecting her body to her spirit faded away before she opened her eyes. Sileas, now returned to her spirit form, smiled at Aya. She formed words with her paws much more fluently than Aya had.

"There are others who have the ability. I will endeavor to make a list for you if you agree not to share it with every Spirit you meet."

Truly? Silease gestured.

"It would be my pleasure. I ask that you not share the list only because it is a rare skill, and we all need to sleep sometime."

Aya grinned and Sileas covered her muzzle with a paw as she giggled. Aya was a little startled that the sound came through just fine. She tilted her head and dropped an ear in confusion. Before she could say another word, Roan interjected.

"Laughter is a pure expression of her feelings. She can't speak or make any sound with intent. There are a few sounds that come about without any intent of your own. She can still make those sounds."

If you will stay, I will fetch Ayrece for you, Hearth Stone, Sileas' paws said.

"Thank you, Honored Ancestor."

It is the least service I can provide for what you have done for me this round. She faded back into the Spiritlands.

Aya turned her attention to Roan.

"What do you think of the idea that someone from outside of the city breaking the wardnet? The penalties for doing such a thing would be stiff."

"That's putting it mildly."

"I just never thought I would see it, Greatfather. They told us there were ta'el who had become Corrupted, but..." Aya trailed off.

"You never thought that they actually existed."

"That obvious?"

Roan shook his head.

"We almost all feel like that the first time we encounter them first paw. It's not easy to realize that even though the gods made us with purpose, there are still those of us who seek power, greed, and chaos."

"No, it definitely is not," a new voice said.

Looking up, Aya found Ayrece the Record coming across the clearing. Aya had only met him once. Ayrece was a very special ta'el. He, much like Aya, was the only ta'el to hold his name. The Record was a title given only to one ta'el at a time. He was the sum total of the lives of all ta'el.

Even Aya had not known that he was all that he was advertised to be until the White revealed that the Heartstone Chronicle was real. He was the channel that all of the knowledge of every life of every ta'el flowed through. He almost certainly knew what her name meant, but she could not ask him. That was not how his magic worked.

"Hello, Ayrece the Record. I would like to ask you some questions, if you can answer?"

"You know the rules, young emta?"

"I do. I will accept whatever answers you may be able to provide."

That was part of the problem. Ayrece had access to all of the knowledge of all of the ta'el who had ever lived. He could instantly access the answer to almost any question he could be asked, but that did not mean he could always answer. Magic was a balance. If Ayrece could just use all of that knowledge at will, it would give him godlike power. It would have created a massive imbalance in the world.

His magic had been made as a preventative measure to make sure that what had happened with the humans could never happen again. Sometimes, though, if you were careful with the questions you asked, Ayrece could answer. Aya asked the first question that everyone always asked Ayrece when they met him.

"Can you tell me what species you chose?" Aya said with a little grin.

Ayrece was an odd looking ta'el. His face was somewhere between at cat and a bear. He was not much larger than Aya, making his species somewhat on the small side since ehta'el were almost universally larger than emta'el. He had midnight fur with almost grainy grey markings. His muzzle was bristling with an enormous amount of whiskers. As far as anyone was aware, no one knew what species Ayrece was, and he was known for giving out hints. It was a game he played with everyone, and ta'el all over the world kept track of the hints trying to figure it out. He didn't always give new hints, and she knew a lot of the hints already.

"I can tell you that figs are absolutely delicious."

Aya nodded. "Can you tell me what the Below Places are?"

Ayrece shook his head. "I cannot. That question is too direct. I know what you are seeking, Ayasha the Speaker. I cannot simply give it to you."

"Can you tell me where to look for more information?"

This time, Ayrece paused for a long moment, and then he grinned.

"I can tell you that you should investigate those ta'el known for **exploring**." His emphasis was clear.

Aya waved her tail in a feline gesture of thanks. Ayrece favored her with a toothy smile, showing that he understood.

"I appreciate your assistance," Aya said.

She turned away to where Roan awaited her. A weary sigh escaped her muzzle. She felt Ayrece's paw gently on her shoulder and she turned back.

"Remain determined, Ayasha the Speaker. We need someone like you."

"Have there been others like me?"

"Yes. Like me, there is only ever one like you at a time. Unlike me, a Speaker is something… more."

"I think you may be giving me too much credit and yourself to little."

"I am not." Ayrece's voice was so certain that it gave Aya pause. "Good luck to you, Ayasha the Speaker." Ayrece turned on his heel and padded away without another word.

Aya turned back to Roan. She made a wordless gesture of extreme confusion at the back of the retreating ehta.

Roan grinned at her.

"He is always like that. At least we have a direction to go?"

"About as general a direction as possible," Aya grumbled.

"So where too now?"

"Leeward. We have to close the hole in the wardnet before anything else."

Chapter 8

"FIND"

Aya combed the archives, her ire clear as she tore through tome after tome. She had been here for three rounds solid, and the ancient library shelves had long since become sickening to look at. She had read every book she could find about those who had held the name Explorer. None of them held anything about the Below Places.

"Hearthstone, can I…" the apprentice, one born of some sort of canine that Aya did recognize, began.

"No, you cannot," Aya snapped grumpily.

Roan's voice inside her head chided, *{Little Aya, you are being most unkind to the apprentice. Need I remind you of your manners?}* His words burned with his disappointment.

Aya had channeled Greatfather Roan because he blessed her with several magics that helped to improve her mental acuity. Aya paused and looked up to the black and white face of the canine. "I'm sorry, Arctah. I appreciate your help. If you find any further tomes that tell of Explorers, I would love to see them."

Aya only had two apprentices under her. Teaching apprentices was the last step in any Stone's training. She had never asked what species Arctah was, and he had never shared. It wasn't generally considered a polite question. She had only been so forward with the Record because it was well known that he would find it amiss if she didn't ask the question.

Arctah nodded. "I will keep looking, but I think we have dredged up everything up from the archives we are going to find, Hearth Stone. Perhaps if you could tell me about what you are attempting to…"

"Ayasha!" A high-pitched wail of anger drowned out the rest of Arctah's response.

The speaker was born of a species of ungulate that Aya had not seen before. She was a pudu, a tiny deer that gave her a size similar to most ta'el born of domestic felines. This made her quite tiny, several inches shorter than Aya. She was huffing indignantly through her nose, ad her normally small black eyes were wide with anger.

Usually, she had a blue-grey pelt with some brown on her legs. Her paws each had three fingers, usually tipped with small black hooves. Now, though, her pelt blazed neon red, spotted with perfect white dots. Her hooves, both on paws and feet, were bright neon green. She stood, fists at her sides, shaking with rage. She opened her mouth, and Aya held up a finger to quiet her.

"I do **not** want to hear it, Marisa. I warned you repeatedly that he would do this if you were not attentive to his habits. What did you forget… besides my title?" Marisa's anger was extinguished in the face of an angry Hearth Stone. "Elder Sangill is one of the easiest Spirits to please, and yet you cannot remember a simple routine in exchange for his daily assistance. No, you will just have to endure this or find some other emta to take your place."

Aya had become frustrated with the emta's complaints in only a single spell. Elder Sangill had done the very same thing to her when she had continued to forget to set up the stairs at the podiums where he read each night. Aya did her best to hold a stern face despite the absurdity of Marisa's situation. "It will only last for a round or two, especially if you simply do your duty to the Spirit. Do you want to be a Hearth Stone one round or not?"

"But Hearth Stone, I have to perform…"

Aya's cold stare was the exact same one that Elder Samasu used to give her when she complained that one of the Spirits was being unfair.

"You are granted his magic and time every round. He has only one small request, like any other Spirit. If you cannot remember to do it before you move on to your next duty, then perhaps you should attempt for another position within the Hearth. Is there anything of actual importance?"

Marisa sighed. "I'm sorry, Hearth Stone, but he is so abrasive if I don't have new books for him to read."

Aya smiled and reached into one of the pouches on her belt. She took out a folded piece of paper she had been holding onto for just this moment. The emta had to learn that the Spirits were always fair with their requests and punishments. If she had learned the more important lesson, how to ask for help sooner, it wouldn't have gotten to this stage.

Marisa sighed, "It's difficult to keep up and I really like him. He's got a great sense of humor but this..." She gestured to herself.

"Is a lesson in asking for help that you should have already learned," Aya finished for her.

Marisa deflated, and then nodded. "Yes, Hearth Stone."

Aya held out the folded piece of paper and Marisa took it into her neon paws. She carefully unfolded it, revealing a full sheet of paper with tiny, perfect handwriting on it. Marisa stared in awe at the hundreds of titles written on the front of the sheet. She turned it over and found hundreds more.

"Good. Now, those are all of Elder Sangill's favorites. When you do not have something new to read for him, substitute these in. You can add to the list as I have for the next ta'el who needs it."

The emta held up the paper as if it were stone tablets stolen straight from the Spiritlands themselves.

Aya continued, "They don't ask for much in exchange for what they give, Marisa. If you go back up to the Library and ask him very politely, he may undo this. However, if you simply endure it in good humor, he will respect you more."

Marisa looked down at the neon red polka-dot fur covering her body. After a moment, she sighed. "Alright."

The emta rummaged about in a satchel on her hip, pulling out a small book with a red leather cover. "Here's the tome you asked for, Hearth Stone."

The gold leaf letters on the spine read: *Undersides*. It was a book about Explorers who found some of the most expansive cave systems that humans could never access. Like those given the name Wanderer, those with the name Explorer generally had excellent relationships with Spirits related to travel. Unlike Wanderers, though, they did not tend to give traveling magics. They tended to give magics related to finding hidden places. She didn't have a single relationship with an Ancestor Spirit who had held the name Explorer. They were rare souls. It took a very specific kind of ta'el to shun the idea of ever having a home.

"Oh you're a treasure, Marisa. I've been looking for this for three rounds."

"Can I perhaps convince you to help me get my fur and hooves back to normal?" she asked brightly.

Aya laughed. "Not a chance. Go on, I know you are one of the best students in the latest martial arts class. If you want to have a chance at training with Wanderer Lane, you can't miss a demonstration."

"I'm not going to get any respect looking like this."

"You'll get more respect looking like that. They'll all know that this is a punishment for some mistake or affront given to a Spirit. That you continued the demonstration will show your resolve. At least you're not blue with pink stripes. I had to recite all twenty-one points of the feline dialects of Ta'eltesh to demonstrate my mastery looking like I was made out of cotton candy. Now go on, before you're late." Aya dismissed the emta and Marisa trotted away, her hooves clicking on the stone floor.

Aya turned back towards the restricted sections of the archives, where most human research was done. Aya made it back to the table piled with books, Arctah in tow behind her. She began to comb through *Undersides*. This particular volume was not a biography of a single Explorer as the books Aya had been reading previously. This was more a collection of discoveries labeled with Explorers' names. It was there, near the center of the tome, that she found an entry titled *The Below Places*. She began to read the entry, but what she found there did not please her.

The Below Places were a system of caverns that were inaccessible through any method but a Pathway. It was discovered by Huan the Explorer, deep beneath the surface of the Australian Outback. It was apparently almost a mile below the surface. She turned the page and found that halfway down, it was torn away. Several pages after that page had also been torn out of the book.

"Arctah?" Aya looked up from her reading but the black and white canine was nowhere to be seen.

"Yes, Hearth Stone?" Arctah's voice came from somewhere in the shelves of the restricted stacks.

"This book has pages torn from it. We need to know if there is a complete version of this book somewhere. Please fetch me the Archivist?"

A Spirit formed of blue mist floated through the nearest shelf, wearing a polite smile. An Avian of some small owl variant, she waved a wing in greeting. "No need. I am here, Hearth Stone. This book is one of only four known copies. The copy in the London archives is also missing these pages. The copy from Hong Kong has been missing for one hundred and thirteen turns. It's suspected by the Archivist that it was lost in the Elemental Shift that destroyed almost one third of that city."

The Elemental Shift had been a result of the mismanagement of the elementals in that area. It was a mistake that had haunted all of the ta'el who had lived there at the time. A typhoon the likes of which the world had rarely seen had obliterated Hong Kong Island and washed up almost two full miles into the city.

"And the fourth copy?"

"It was part of the Denver archive until three turns ago. It was taken from the stacks by Dedran the Explorer. He was expanding the maps of the Rocky Mountain Range. A moment, I am in contact with the Archivist in Denver."

A pregnant pause later, the Archivist began to speak again. "According to much of the military knowledge left behind by the humans of this land, there are hidden military installations there that contained a great deal of knowledge of human science. Some of the rear chapters of this book describe the hidden installations that were uncovered in the Adirondacks. Dedran though that perhaps they used many of the same methods to hide the installations in Colorado."

"So, if I want the full version of the book, I need to find it with the Explorer," Aya muttered as she flipped the pages back and forth. It was the only evidence of the Below Places that she had.

"Seems that way, Ayasha the Speaker."

The Archivist floated away, her light blue body sliding through one of the shelves and disappearing. The Archivists were some of the oddest Spirits. They could interact with the physical world almost as if they were still a part of it, unaided by any Channeler. They rotated out from time to time, which is why few ta'el referred to them by name. They were somewhat ubiquitous.

No one took them for granted, though, and Aya often shared memories of reading favorite books with them. They were all Spirits who were somehow related to books, but surprisingly, never libraries. They were never librarians or ta'el who simply made or cared for books. Their connection needed to be deeper to become an Archivist Spirit, always some ta'el who loved books so much that they did not want to leave them in the afterlife. These ones became Archivists. They knew everything there was to know about books.

"To Denver, then?" Greatfather Roan asked from over her shoulder.

"We can't right now. We have too many responsibilities here to go running off after my name," answered Aya.

"I disagree. Your students have their lessons. Besides, you have been told by The White that finding out what your name means is of extreme importance. If you trade on her name just a tiny bit, you can get some assistance with your students until you get back."

Aya shook her head. "Yeah, lets tick off a goddess. Great plan, right there. How could it possibly go wrong?" Aya snarked.

Roan rolled his transparent eyes. "Ayasha the Speaker, The White has charged you with a task. Is that not enough to motivate you to take some small risks?" Roan had changed to a formal tone that he only used when she was being particularly stupid or stubborn.

Aya cringed, narrowing her eyes at him. "Keep your teacher voice to yourself." After a moment, she let out an exasperated sound. "Fine, you cranky old mutt! I'll talk to Etria and see if there are any other Stones who can look after Arctah and Marisa."

Roan grinned at Aya, who she folded her ears back in annoyance.

"Might it be better to simply go to the Below Places themselves? You have learned enough to find them," he suggested.

"I've also learned that there are several pages to this entry that someone thinks no one else should know about. I think it would be prudent to know what is to be found therein."

Roan nodded his ghostly head. "I suppose that is a fair point. The Below Places could hold some dangers we would be unprepared for."

"Would you be so kind as to fetch Etria, Greatfather?"

"Of course, Hearth Stone." It wasn't very often that Roan used her title. He only did it when he was feeling particularly proud of her.

"Thank you, Greatfather. We are going to need some help."

"I think that would be a good idea." Greatfather Roan nodded, and then faded from sight.

Chapter 9

"VISCERAL"

The library at Denver was filled with silence when Aya came through the Tunnel. It was odd for a permanent traveling Pathway to empty out into a library, but apparently the library building was at the center of the city. The courtyard that the Tunnel lead into was enclosed, but had a wide gate on the south side that lead outside. She was surprised that the courtyard was so entirely empty of life. Tunnels should be bustling places. She turned, and headed for the Western entry into the library. Roan materialized next to her just as she reached the door.

"Where have you been, Greatfather?"

"Etria asked me to stay and give her a good idea of where your students were in their lessons. She has asked that you request a potion from your father." Roan paused.

"One of the meal potions?"

"It's all anyone asks for anymore. My son is the most talented potion maker on this side of the world, and the only thing anyone can think to challenge him with is food." Roan grinned.

"It's Dad's own fault. He won't give anyone the recipes for those potions. No one has any idea what Spirits he is charming to help him make those concoctions." Aya pulled open the doors and had started inside when she heard a small hissing sound coming from Roan's direction. She turned to see Roan's teeth bared.

"Be on your guard, Aya. There is something here that does not belong."

Aya's eyes narrowed on him. "This is a Ta'el city."

"Not anymore. We should retreat through the Tunnel and close it behind us Aya. Quickly."

"I will not. I need that book, and what if there are Ta'el here that need help? There haven't been any reports of problems here."

"Ayasha, I can sense no living Ta'el in this place. Not as far as my senses go. There should be a hundred thousand ta'el here. There should be at least some hundreds in the range of my senses. At least call for assistance. This feeling is so wrong. Can't you feel it?"

Aya closed her eyes and focused on the magical senses given to her as a Channeler. It didn't take her long to shiver.

"Yes, I do. But I also sense the living."

Roan shrugged. "You always had better senses than I ever did."

"Greatfather, there are strong Channelers here. They are hiding. Terrified. Siris the Lightmend leads here. That old Lemur has been fighting Corrupted Spirits for two hundred turns. I only met him for a few spells during my training, but I didn't get the impression he was afraid of much."

"He fears me."

The voice was oddly monotone. Not high, but not low, either. It was so lacking in any special qualities that she couldn't imagine a ta'el was speaking. The thing that appeared from the shelves of the library was alien in a way that made it impossible to recognize. It shifted smoothly from walking on two legs to four like any ta'el had a tendency to do. It was roughly canine in shape, but had no fur. Instead, it had shining skin the deep red of coagulating blood. It appeared as if it were made of gelatinous liquid, shimmering and rippling as the creature moved.

"What am I looking at?" Aya whispered to Roan.

"I have no idea," Roan replied.

She switched to purely telepathic communication. *{Is it Spirit or Flesh?}*

{It is neither.}

Roan's reply seemed cryptic to her so she just sent confusion in reply to his words.

{I do not know what this thing is, Ayasha, except that it is dangerous.}

Aya backed slowly away from the creature. Only a lifetime of training saved her as she moved on instinct alone when the creature blurred towards her. The speed made reflex her only option. She immediately began to call for Wanderer Lane.

Aya split her focus for only a moment to send the pulse of spiritual communication through the Spiritlands, and that moment nearly cost her life.

The thing flashed towards her again, leaping too fast for her eyes to track. Gripping the hilt of her Heartblade, she yanked it out and interposed the blade between her throat and the creature's claws. Sparks flew from the blade as it bit into the steel-hard material of its claws. She shoved it back and pitched herself into a smooth, backward tumble. She came to her feet in a defensive crouch, brandishing the Heartblade. Smoke rose from the surface of the blade where some viscous dark red liquid had spilled onto the shining surface and was burning away.

{I advise you not to let it touch you, Aya.}

Aya was amazed that the creature's claws had resisted the edge of her Heartblade. There were few things besides another Heartblade that would. *{You think, Greatfather?!}*

The creature circled to her left and she circled to the right to keep it in her sight. She was preparing to turn and run for the Tunnel. That was when she felt the presence of Wanderer Lane appear from the portal. She held out her free paw back towards him, and willed him into her body. It was rude to draw him into a Channel, but she would apologize later if she were not facing the Bardo. To his credit, he did not speak or do anything to distract her once he was inside of her head. She Channeled his magic through her body, and the world slowed down around her until she felt slightly safer.

{Wanderer Lane, do you recognize this monster?}

{I have an inkling. It matches something described to me once, but I never fought one. They called it a Visceral. It was described as a creature of the Nether. Your Heartblade is your best weapon against it. Since it is neither Spirit nor Flesh, the dual nature of your blade being both will do harm to the creature almost as if it were a Spirit. And as always, Fire destroys almost anything not born of Fire.}

Aya kept her eyes fixed on the creature as it circled opposite her. She hissed her orders. "Roan, make assessments as to how many injured and dead there are. Then fetch Siris and his Watcher."

The creature darted toward Aya, and she backpedaled, pivoting to the left. She brought her Heartblade across her body, knocking aside the claws slashing toward her chest.

"You tell him that if he doesn't get his tail out here right this instant, when I am done with him, he will dream fondly of death for the rest of his days!"

"As you wish, Hearth Stone." Roan didn't argue once she had made her decision.

{Lane, I wish to summon the The Heart, do you object to sharing my body with the Elemental?} There was a short pause.

{How did you… no forget it, of course you have befriended the most volatile Elemental in all the world. Why not? I do not object.} Lane said, exasperated.

"I call to the Heart of Fire for aid, and offer a piece of my own heart's fire to sustain your flame." Aya whispered the words to help her separate the sending from her sendings to Lane. The Heart of Fire would take some time to arrive.

{Are you sure about this, Aya? Giving up a piece of your own soul?} Lane asked.

Aya slid back away as the creature charged, claws slashing at her throat.

{I have done it before, Honored Ancestor. Can't befriend the Heart any other way. It's not fun, but I can do it safely. No more distractions please!} Aya sent desperately.

The creature had continued attacking during her brief exchange with Wanderer Lane. As it approached, it began to speed up in her sight. It was somehow increasing its speed by leaps and bounds, but still wasn't a match for Lane's magic. She took a step to the right, out of the path of the charging creature's arm.

Her Heartblade came down in a smooth arc through the creature's outstretched wrist. The blade severed the wrist with no resistance, and the hand fell away. The creature showed no sign that it felt any pain, and immediately turned and swung its arm at her. It had gotten faster still, and she leapt back out of the way. She avoided the blow, but drops of steaming ichor splattered across her chest.

Three droplets seared away her fur and attempted to soak into her skin. It was a poison unlike anything she had encountered. Not merely physical, it was somehow spiritual. Her connection with Wanderer Lane wavered. Aya knew if she allowed it to continue, their connection would be severed.

She danced back away from the creature and shoved her paw into her piece pouch. It contained not only the gold pieces of its namesake, but a number of small glass vials. Each one contained a tiny glowing simulacrum of a Spirit. She pulled out one that was glowing with pure white light. She downed the contents and tried not to flinch at the awful taste. The liquid, suffused with magic, would clear the poison from her system. She threw the empty glass vial into the creature's face. The remaining drops of the potion splashed across the creature's face when the vial smashed across its eyes. That got the reaction she expected.

The glowing white liquid sizzled like frying bacon into the creature's eyes. It clearly could feel pain because it let out a piercing shriek as the potion reacted with its flesh. She noticed something interesting then. The paw she had cut away had turned light grey, and was shriveling to dust as she watched. Then, blinded, the creature came screeching at her in a blur of motion that almost overwhelmed even Lane's magical enhancements.

She stepped back, spinning her Heartblade in her fist so it would lie along her forearm, supporting it with the full strength of her arm. The blade sparked as it clashed with the claws of the creature's remaining paw. Ducking a swing, Aya rolled smoothly back out from beneath the creature when it attempted to fall atop her. Coming to her feet, she skipped backwards as far as she could get before the creature could recover. Pulling a small cloth out of her piece pouch, she swiped the sizzling gunk off of her Heartblade. Dropping the smoking cloth the blade went back into the sheath at the small of her back.

{What are you doing, Aya?}

{I need to buy time for the Heart to arrive. It almost killed me just by surprising me with its blood. This is too dangerous.} Aya felt his mental affirmative.

{So, we are running? What if it doesn't follow.}

{I took its paw. It will follow me into the maw of the White herself, but in case it needs a little incentive,}

Aya scooped up a rock twice the size of her balled fist. She cocked back and threw it with all of her empowered strength. It smashed into the creature's face with enough force that it blasted the creature off of its feet. Its head snapped back hard enough to break any living thing's neck and the rock kept right on going. It embedded itself into the stone wall of the library, fifty feet behind the creature.

Aya cringed for a moment. She hadn't meant to throw it quite that hard. Then, she turned and bolted down the street in the direction she could feel the living energy of Siris. The creature's screeching roar of anger chased her down the street. She risked a glance back.

"Shit!"

She yelped in panic and then increased her pace as she saw the dark thing streaking down the street towards her. She bolted down the street, dropping to all fours for greater speed.

{Finally, you are in range. Keep going straight, Aya. The Lightmend is not hiding. He is tending to a rather large amount of injured ta'el. He has not even seen the creature you are fighting.} Roan's sending was concerned.

{Good news, but I am not sure he can actually do anything about this thing. Wanderer Lane informs me that it is a creature of the Nether, whatever that is supposed to mean.}

{Scales! I have heard stories, but I didn't think they were actually real. They are just stories.}

{The thing chasing me would suggest they're not.} Aya shot back peevishly.

{If it is a Nether creature, then Siris will only be able to destroy it. That will not tell us why it is attacking.} Roan seemed certain of his words.

{I highly doubt it is going to talk to us, Greatfather. I took its paw and, I am fairly sure, though it is not dead, that I caved in its skull quite thoroughly.}

{So diplomatic of you, Little Aya.}

{Pretty sure it was going to try to eat me, Greatfather, and I recall telling you that I have been chewed on by the cubs enough to last several lifetimes.}

{Not far now, Aya. They have a secondary building set up for healing and care near the residential section of the city. Aya, if you can destroy it some other way, we should not risk Siris. Lightmends are rare.}

{I have called the Heart of Fire. I do not know how long it will take to arrive, but if I can delay long enough, I can destroy it without his help.}

Ayasha kept up her pace, but Lane warned her that Channeling his magic for so long was going to cost her physically.

{Not a lot of choice, Honored Ancestor. Risking a painful recovery really doesn't stand up to letting that thing kill half the ta'el here.}

{Turn right, Aya. The city gardens are just a few blocks in that direction.} Roan sent.

Aya responded with a negative. *{If I Channel the Heart of Fire there, the gardens will burn.}*

{I realize this. There is a dead area of the city on the other side of the gardens. Siris warns that the area may sheer from the cliff face, though, so you should be ready to call on a Spirit that can provide you with flight.}

Aya turned right and ran as fast as she could. Even on all fours, the Visceral was keeping pace with her. It couldn't gain with Lane's magic running through her body, but that it could even keep up was absurd. She pushed herself to go faster, blasting through the gardens at top speed. She didn't want to risk any of the forest Spirits drawing this thing's attention when she still knew so little about what it could do. She saw the area where the restoration of the city had stopped and the dead zone began.

{Greatfather, are there any open areas where I can be sure this thing will not find a way to take me from behind?} The Visceral roared in frustration as it tried to run her down.

{Two blocks in, take a left then a right and go straight. Siris says the old city maps show an open square in that area.}

It took her only a short few moments to reach the square he described. There was a large broken-down stone… something in the middle of the square. She leapt into the air and spun herself, skidding to a stop with her claws scoring the pavement. The creature, though, did not stop. It bolted into the square and shot towards her, fully intending to take advantage of her recovering from ceasing her motion so abruptly.

Aya did not need to recover. She was not off balance. She had purposely dug her claws in, and wobbled when she stopped to make it appear as if she were shaken by the sudden stop. She whipped her Heartblade from the sheath at the small of her back and took one perfect step forward. She twisted her body, putting her free paw on the ground to assist with her forward roll. As she passed beneath the creature's flying body, she raised her arm.

Her blade slammed home, slicing through the creature's body from shoulder to crotch. Aya dug her claws into the pavement to cause her body to flip violently as she rolled. This spun her so that when she landed in a crouch she was still facing the creature, which had smashed into the broken pile of stone at the center of the courtyard and laid still.

She was under no delusions that she had killed the thing. She had noticed as it launched itself at her that its paw had been restored. She didn't even know if it was possible to kill it with purely physical attacks. The magic of her Heartblade did seem to do harm to it, but not permanent harm. She suspected if she were to deliver enough damage, the creature would be destroyed. She watched as the dead-blood flesh of the creature writhed back together.

She cringed in horror as the thing reformed its body. It was utterly disgusting to watch. She noticed, though, that the flesh that had touched her Heartblade had turned to grey dust and flaked away before it healed. It soon came to its feet. There was a blur of motion, and the creature faded from sight.

Aya blinked in confusion for a short moment, but then she closed her eyes. She drew in a deep breath, and perked her ears for any sound. Lane's words from her training played in her mind.

{Listen well, Little Aya. Observe your world not with your eyes, your ears, your nose, but with your entire body.}

She tried to do what Lane had been trying to teach her all those turns ago. She took deep breaths, and the creature's distinct scent came to her. It made her want to throw up, but the way the scent came to her told her that the creature was not moving so quickly that she could not see it. It was creeping towards her from the left. The sounds reaching her ears were the tiniest scuffs of paw over pavement, but they confirmed what her nose was telling her.

The creature had employed some sort of ability that made it invisible to her eyes. It crept closer as she stayed crouched with three paws on the ground. It was approaching from the side opposite her Heartblade. It would attempt to grapple with her so that it could poison her with its touch again. Aya held out hope the potion surging through her bloodstream would keep the toxins at bay.

A breath of wind through her fur warned her when the Visceral leapt at her. She turned and fell backward as the creature came down on top of her. She had made the assumption that like most predators, it would go for her throat, but the creature was attempting a tackle. It landed on her with its arms wrapped around her midsection. Claws dug at her back, and she screamed. Hot blood spilled from her back onto the street.

She slammed the pommel of her Heartblade into what she assumed was the top of the creature's skull, considering the crunching sound it made, but the creature didn't seem to mind, only continuing to sink its claws deeper into her. She still couldn't see the creature very well, even now, which made it impossible to cut away at the arms holding her. It was unbelievably strong, and if she didn't do something soon, it would rupture something vital inside of her. Sasu's healing magic would take care of injuries like that to a cein extent before the energy of the potion was used up, but she had to dislodge the thing, or it would rip her apart.

Aya switched tactics. She slammed her Heartblade home into the invisible thing smothering her to the ground. It yowled in agony as the Heartblade's magic poured into the creature, destroying everything it touched. Still, the creature did not let go. Suddenly she was having trouble getting a deep breath. One of the creature's claws had clearly punched through one of her lungs.

She gasped in breath after breath, but it was not enough as blood poured into her lung. She growled in frustration, considering her last resort. The last potion in her pouch might turn the tide, but it could be dangerous to use and was hard to replace. Her vision swam, and Aya made her decision.

Her paw released her Heartblade and plunged into her piece pouch, drawing out the second vial. This one glowed with deep viridian light. The tiny glowing simulacrum in the vial also appeared like a teddy bear but this one had deep brown fur, and was outlined with a green aura. She didn't pop the cork, though. This time, she had guessed right.

The creature immediately ripped its grip free of her body and strong paws gripped her wrist, trying to force the vial away from her maw. When the creature released her, the wounds in her back began to close. She grabbed the hilt of her Heartblade with her free paw and ripped the blade free of its writhing flesh. She brought it down in a slashing arc that passed through the empty air just shy of slashing her own arm. The Heartblade sheared through both of its wrists.

The creature became visible and reeled back away from her. She used what was left of her flagging strength to roll backwards away from the creature. She shook her arm to dislodge the severed paws, and then with all of her will, she suppressed the coughs that would bring the blood up out of her lungs. As much as it was harming her, she did not have time to keel over and wretch up blood at that moment. Her thumb touched the cork of the vial.

{Apologies for my tardiness, Adept.}

The voice in her head was like the roar of an enormous flame. Beside her, almost as solid as any living thing in the Wild, appeared the Heart of Fire. It was slightly taller than her and roughly the same shape. Its entire body was made up of a coruscation of flame. Its shape suggested feline, but it clearly was not. Two eyes burning like the heart of a star focused on her. Then, its head slowly turned, and those burning eyes locked onto the creature. She slid the potion back into her piece pouch. She would not need it after all.

{That... is a bad thing.}

{Indeed. Will you assist me, Honored Elemental?}

{You misunderstand Adept. Though not all remember, all Spirits are bound by our very existence to destroy this creature.}

The Heart's voice in her head became an angry roar that terrified her more than any single thing in her life ever had.

{I command thee, use my power to rend this horror from the Wild.}

There was no question of the Elemental's authority to command her to act. While no Spirit had ever directed her so forcefully, her sole duty was to the Spirits. If a Spirit that had bound itself to her commanded her to do something, she would do it or die trying.

{As you command, Honored Elemental.}

Aya held out her paw, and the Heart grabbed her paw in a powerful grip. She Channeled the Elemental into her body, and her body burst into flames. The broken pavement beneath her paws immediately began to soften from the intensity of the fire pouring forth from her body. Then, much to her staggering embarrassment, she broke out into a paroxysm of coughing. Bright red blood poured out of her muzzle as she vomited up the fluid that had filled her right lung.

The creature took the opportunity to attempt to attack her despite the fire pouring from her body. She could do nothing to respond, but she did not need to. It threw a large chunk of stone at her, and while the impact threw her onto her back as she attempted to cough up her very guts, the fire coming from her body was of such intensity that the stone softened into molten liquid before it even contacted her body.

The stone dribbled to the ground around her as she pulled herself to one knee and coughed up another spat of blood. The molten stone ran off of her like water off a duck's back. While the Elemental shared her body, she was utterly immune to heat. When she finally had her breath back, she found the creature was lifting a much larger stone.

The creature hefted the stone, and then pitched it at her. Its strength was immense. Aya lifted a paw, and a sphere of fire burning with heat just this side of the heart of a star burst into existence. The center of the stone vaporized on contact, and the hole was large enough that she passed through the center entirely untouched, the sight causing the creature to turn tail and try to flee.

"Too late for that now, beast."

On instinct born of knowledge passing straight to her mind, she simply leaned forward. Propelling flames burst from her hind paws, and she lifted off of the ground a few scant ticks. Then she shot forward in a blur that beggared belief with its speed. A jet of fire propelled her forward, skating along on the smaller jets of fire keeping her aloft. She caught the creature before it could even reach the edge of the square. As she shot forward, she slid her Heartblade back into the sheath and then lifted her arm. Just as she reached the creature, she willed the power of the Heart into her arm.

She Channeled the magic and swept her arm from left to right. A half-moon arc of blinding white fire slashed out from her arm just as she passed the creature. The burning arc of fire passed cleanly through the Visceral's center mass, nearly bisecting the creature. Aya leaned to one side, and the Heart responded, jetting flames from her body to flip her around. She slid to a stop, hovering a few feet away from the creature.

It fell into two halves on its next step. The top half tumbled away, and Aya raised her paw. She made a fist and two spheres of fire warped the air as they engulfed the two halves of the creature. When they vanished, nothing but black dust and blackened bones remained of the creature.

Aya stood there panting, the coppery taste of her own blood still filling her mouth. She coughed, and then spit blood onto the ground. It immediately sizzled and evaporated as soon as it was out of contact with her body. She dropped to one knee, and Lane finally spoke into her mind again.

{Are you all right, Aya?}

"I will be." Then she put her paws on the ground in front of her and was nosily sick onto the ground. She coughed up a few more small flecks of blood, and then turned over onto her back.

{Honored Elemental, would you be so kind as to take all of the heat of the melted things with you when you take your leave?}

{I will, but I do not wish to depart until we have confirmed that no further Netherspawn are present.}

Aya sat up in alarm. "There could be more of those things?!"

"No, not here." The voice was that of Siris.

"How do you know?" Aya asked.

"I could smell them. I smelled it the second it clawed its way up from the depths. That smell vanished as soon as you burned it. I couldn't corner it, though. It seemed to know when I was approaching. Whenever I did, it would injure more Ta'el and flee. It kept coming back to the Library."

"Of course it did."

Aya grumbled in annoyance. She did not rise as her wounds burned from the reaction of the healing potion. When it finally burned away, she was far from recovered, but her wounds were at least no longer life threatening.

"I don't think it found what it was looking for. Greatfather Roan informs me that you are looking for one of the Explorers. Estia the Archive sent to me that Dedran the Explorer has the book you are searching for, and while she does not know the location or condition of the book currently, she does recall that it was intact when it left our library."

"Of course it was." Aya's mood was not improved. "He lives here, though? Do you know if any of the local Spirits work with him?"

"I will introduce you," Siris said, "but first..."

Siris padded across the square to where she had burned the Visceral. His long, ringed tail lashed back and forth, indicating his unease. His species clearly used the feline dialect of Ta'eltesh, because she could understand his unspoken whisker twitches quite well.

"You don't think it's gone?"

He nodded. "Not yet. You could burn it until it was gone if the Honored Elemental so wishes, but I would ask you allow myself and my Watcher to take care of it from here?"

The still glowing stones around the courtyard quickly cooled as the Heart of Fire drew the energy from the fire back into itself.

{I shall respect the Lightmend's wishes, Hearth Stone. I will remain in the Spiritlands for a time so that I may be recalled quickly

if any other Netherspawn are discovered. They are anathema to life, and the Life Spirit commands their expulsion from our reality.}

She released The Heart of Fire back to the Spiritlands with feelings of gratitude.

{No, Ayasha the Speaker. Thank you for heeding my command. I chose correctly when I allowed you to call upon me.} The Elemental faded into the Spiritlands.

Siris walked a slow circle around the burned remains of the Visceral. Left behind on the ground were glowing white paw prints as he walked. He continued to walk until the glowing paw prints overlapped into a solid glowing circle. Then, Siris held out a paw to his left. White mist gathered and began to glow before forming into the shape of Siris' Watcher Spirit. Hestilam the Lightmend had been some sort of canine that Aya did not recognize, even though she knew his name.

The magic of a Lightmend was about healing and purification. Aya had never been terribly good at it. It was about fixing things in the Wild, and that had never been something that Aya was particularly concerned with. Maybe she should take up Kika the Lightmend on her offer to teach her about their particular magic.

"Hey space case, don't you think you should allow Wanderer Lane to go, and Channel my power instead?" Greatfather Roan's voice broke her out of the trance she had fallen into watching Siris work his magic.

{I apologize, Lane.} She released him from her body with a mental effort.

He formed in bluish white mist next to her. "No trouble at all, Little Aya. Would it be possible to join you in the Wild when you next practice your forms?"

"Of course," Aya said tiredly.

Allowing Lane to leave drained all of his strength from her body, and she immediately sagged. Ringing blotted out all of the sounds as she felt like she might collapse, but then she felt the touch of Roan's paw on hers, and she accepted his Spirit into her body. It didn't erase her fatigue, but it made her feel much better. She let out a sigh of relief.

"I have got to stop almost dying. I've been a full Stone for less than a turn, and I've already almost died twice."

{Adepts tend to live interesting lives, and if you keep doing things like this, you'll get good at not dying,} Roan assured.

"Doesn't matter how many times I get it right, only takes one time getting it wrong," Aya complained.

{I'm sorry, do I hear whining?}

"Shut up, ass."

{Or maybe clucking. I might have heard clucking.}

"Alright, shut up already. I'm going," Aya grumbled.

She put her hands on her knees and pushed herself up. The circle that Siris had been walking filled with white light that appeared as if it were liquid. It burned brightly for a long moment before the whole thing faded away. The remains of the Visceral had vanished with it. Siris turned to her, and she was astonished when he folded himself into a tight bow of respect.

"My thanks to you, Ayasha the Speaker. I am ashamed that I could not do more."

Aya waved her paws in embarrassment. "Please, Siris, I didn't do much of anything. I couldn't have healed all those Ta'el. I just did my duty. Any Stone would have done the same."

Siris stood up, and his whiskers folded back in contentment. Then they twitched up and down, adding a bit of mischief to his words. "Well, it might have been better if you could have done it without being poisoned and almost burning down half the city."

Aya rolled her eyes. "I'll keep that in mind the next time an insane beast is attempting fervently to feast on my liver."

{Little Aya, I must inform you that your body has reached its limits. You have a pawful of minutes before you will pass out.}

"Ayasha?" Siris called her name.

"Yes? You must be quick, Siris. My Watcher informs me that I have overextended myself and will be shortly unconscious." She swished her tail back and forth to add overtones of urgency to her words.

"May I assist?" Siris asked.

Aya shook her head. "No. My wounds are not very severe. I have simply exhausted myself with Channeling. Only sleep will help me now."

Siris nodded and continued, "Something was left behind."

He moved over to her and held out a small sphere of metal. Inscribed into the surface were two lines, and along those lines were strings of numbers in human language. Where the lines crossed, there was a dot drilled into the surface.

"Why didn't the fire destroy it?"

"The fire I Channeled from the Heart to destroy the creature wasn't nearly the hottest I could have used. It burned the body to ash, but it wasn't hot enough to destroy that. It's something made by the humans, a heat resistant metal. But I don't know what these numbers are. I have no idea where the creature got it." Aya's eyelids started to feel heavy.

{You'll barely have time to get home if you go through the tunnel now, Little Aya. Please.}

{Yes, Greatfather.}

"May I take it?"

"You defeated the creature. It is yours by right, though I am interested to know it's purpose if you discover it."

Siris handed over the small sphere. Aya dropped it quickly into her piece pouch.

"I apologize for leaving you with this mess, Siris, but my Watcher informs me that if I don't make it to my bed right this second, I will fall unconscious. Between my small injuries and Channeling the Heart of Fire, I have overdone it." Siris grasped her arm as she turned away.

Aya looked at him dumbfounded, and then a glowing white nimbus surrounded him. She felt instantly better. It wasn't going to keep her from passing out, but her small wounds had vanished.

"Not at all, please go. I can introduce you to the Spirits you wish to speak to after you have rested and returned."

Aya turned to Lane, who had waited for her knowing she would still need him.

"Honored Ancestor, can I request that you redirect the Tunnel for me for a moment so that I don't wind up with my muzzle buried in the dirt in front of all of the other Hearth Stones?"

Lane smiled, and made a gesture with his long-fingered paw. The opening to the Tunnel that would let her travel back to New York yawned in the air behind her. She turned to find that he had redirected the Tunnel directly into her bedroom.

"Bless you, Lane the Wanderer."

Aya had just barely made it through the Tunnel when whatever dregs of wakefulness she had left fled. She collapsed onto her sleeping pad gratefully and was unconscious before anything else could intrude.

Chapter 10

"DISPELLED"

Aya started awake. She had no idea how long she had been asleep after taking on the Visceral, but what had awakened her was clear. The world felt dead around her. Not like the round of her Confirmation. No, this felt like everything was dead. She could feel her connection to Greatfather Roan but nothing else. It was like the Spiritlands were gone entirely.

"I apologize for waking you, Little Aya."

"How long was I asleep, Greatfather?"

"A round, three shifts, and some change."

Aya made a petite groan. "This is the last good sleep I'm likely to get for some time, isn't it."

"Yes, but I also woke you because you have visitors."

"What is happening, Greatfather? Why are we so dispelled? Where are the Spiritlands?"

"I have information from the White concerning all of that, but you should see who awaits you first."

Aya let one ear fall and twitched her whiskers in counterpoint, expressing confusion.

"Just go see who is at the door, Little Aya." Roan was growing a little exasperated.

She ran her claws through her hair, pulling out a few tangles as well as any comb would. Then she pulled her long hair over her shoulder and began to braid it, letting out a tongue-curling yawn. Finally, she tied a blue ribbon around the end of the long seafoam colored braid and walked to the door.

When she pulled open the thick oak, standing behind it were two ta'el that she had not seen in two long turns. One, who had been standing with her paw raised to knock, was very nearly a mirror image of Aya, except where Aya had bright blue eyes, this emta's were a summery green, almost the same color as her hair. The mottled yellow, white, and black fur was almost exactly the same as Aya's own. Even the pattern of large cloudy black markings was identical to hers in nearly every way.

There were some small differences. Aya's tail, for instance, had three black rings – one near the base, one in the middle, and one at the end that covered the whole tip in black. Each ring had a long black stripe lengthwise down her tail on the top and bottom between them. The feline in the door, however, had at least a dozen rings running down the whole length of her tail. Still, it would not have been surprising to mistake one of them for the other without close scrutiny.

"What happened to the lavender? It went nicely with your eyes. Like a beautiful winter morning," Ayasha, her mother, asked as she moved her upraised paw to gently touch the seafoam lock framing Aya's face. Aya touched her braid a little self-consciously.

"I missed you, Mom." They stood there like that for a long moment, and then Aya backed up, swinging the door completely open. "Come in, come in." They had never seen her home, and so they looked around curiously.

She turned to her father. Sahone was born of the Fox. His pelt gleamed in bright, shining silver. Deep charcoal fur covered his paws from fingertips to biceps. Similarly, ebony socks of ebony fur traveled from his toes to just past his knee. His tail was a bar of deepest midnight with a bright silver tip like a shimmering star. Bright orange eyes peered out from his onyx-furred face, above a trim vulpine muzzle.

"Hello, Little Aya."

"Hi, Dad."

Aya threw her paws around his neck and hugged him so hard that he almost dropped what he was holding. He quickly set the box down on the small table beside the door and put his arms around her. He held her like he always had when she was a cub, her paws swinging off the ground even though she was slightly taller than him now. Sahone had always been physically powerful. He had a little paunch around his stomach, but that was only his diet. Even with the paunch, his body rippled with muscle beneath his fur. He didn't seem to have aged a round. He set her gently back on her paws.

"You're different, Little Aya."

"It's been a long two turns," she replied with a sigh, still exhausted.

"No, it is a compliment. You are stronger, surer of yourself than I've ever seen you."

Aya tucked some flyaway hair behind her ear a little, self-consciously. Her father had never been stingy with praise, but he had never ever given her false praise either. When she botched something, he'd told her so with all of the subtlety of a battering ram. When he was proud, though, it overflowed through his smile, just like it was doing right then.

"I don't feel sure right now," Aya confessed.

"Well, that's okay. I brought some surety with me."

He patted a paw on the box he had been carrying. She looked at it. The box was beautifully carved wood with twisted, fluted rods of gold at the corners. Its latch was magical, though she could not discern its purpose. There was so much magic invested into the box that it glowed in her sight. Magical items like this box were not uncommon, but to see one that was so new was amazing.

She heard cupboards opening and closing in her kitchen.

"Mom, I can make anything you would like."

"Nonsense, I'm just getting some tea, and your father is going to cook us dinner, if he finds your kitchen sufficient."

Aya looked hopefully at her father.

"Do you have everything I'll need?" he asked quietly.

"We might have to get some ingredients, but I have some little helper Spirits that will make sure whatever you need shows up at the door. At least, if they're still here," Aya replied.

"Never expected anything less."

Aya looked at the box, and her ears pricked in curiosity, causing her father to chuckle a little.

"It's your Confirmation present."

"About that. A lot has happened."

It was Sahone's turn to drop an ear in confusion.

Aya turned around and headed for the living area. Sahone picked the box up and followed, looking around.

"Quite the space you have. Roan caught us up on the walk over here from the Pathway exit." It wasn't a long walk from The Paths, but long enough for Roan to give her parents a play by play.

"You'll be a lot happier once you see the garden."

Aya's father looked at her in delighted anticipation. She showed them around her home while the water came to a boil. He wrote down a list of ingredients he'd need, and she showed it to one of the little messenger Air Spirits that drifted over an upturned fan near the door. They couldn't carry messages much further than the boundaries of the city, but they were apt to help get things delivered to her home. It read the list for a long moment, and then with a little wave, the faintly glowing white outline that looked roughly like ghosts drawn in human children's books faded away.

It was odd that the elementals were still around with their connection to the Spiritlands so interrupted. She chalked it up to the fact that many elementals were tied quite tightly to the Wild. She left her father picking a few things in the garden and came back into the living area through the sliding doors. Her mother was pouring tea, a jasmine blend that they both really liked, and her father enjoyed the flavor as well.

Sahone carried in a number of vegetables from her garden and put them down on the cutting board in the kitchen and returned with the wooden box. He held it out to her with a small quiet smile, barely baring his sharp teeth.

She took it from him and held it in her lap. Aya popped the latch, a small flame rendered in metal. It unfolded so that the two halves of the box laid flat on the table. The top of the box had a leather pouch that had something held within. Aya pulled it out, and and found that it was a beautifully tooled leather quick pouch. The square leather pouch was small, with a magnetic closure that could easily be flipped open. It was meant to allow one to quickly pull potions out and use them. Hence the moniker. Inside were six vials glowing with spiritual essence. It was made so that she could sling it across her body. If she were wearing a belt, the sling strap could be removed and the bag attached to it instead.

The bottom of the box held a dozen large potion ampules in velvet-lined cavities surrounding a smaller cavity holding just one single tiny vial. Six of the ampules were empty, and six of them glowed with active potions. The single vial in the center, though, glowed almost too brightly to look at. It seemed to be filled with bright white light, and she could see the simulacrum of the Spirit moving inside.

"Listen well, Little Aya. This box was carved and prepared by my own paws from the heartwood of a dying oak tree that wished to be of use one last time. It was blessed with magic by six Wanderer Spirits, once for each of the six cubbies that have full potions. Each of the six is linked together with one of the vial slots in your quick pouch. Put an empty vial into one of the slots of the pouch, and it will refill with the potion from the corresponding cubby in the Phoenix box until the ampule is empty. Each ampule can hold enough potion ingredients to refill your vials six times, but this one I suggest you wear around your neck."

He lifted the gleaming white crystal vial out of the tiny center cavity. Aya stared at it in wonder. She guessed at what it was, but she couldn't believe he had created something so precious.

"Is it...?" she asked.

Sahone nodded. "This is a single drop of Phoenix Blood. It may very well be the only drop in this entire reality. The vial has been enchanted to break only if you will it to do so. If you are dealt a mortal blow, you can crush this vial and it will restore you to perfect health. But, have a care. If it touches your skin and you are not harmed unto death, it will likely kill you. It will burn like the heat of a star. It is the most powerful potion I have ever made, and I would not relish making it again."

"Do I even want to know?"

He grinned his vulpine grin at her.

"Maybe one round, when I am gone to the Spiritlands and one of your little cubs inherits my talents, I will reveal to you where to find my Recipe Tomes."

It didn't sting her. Aya had many talents, but she knew that she was not a match for her Father's skills in making potions. It took a special ta'el to make potions. Unlike Channeling or direct favors of magic, for which the Spirits would readily tell you what the required price was, potions were more of a mystery. They would never tell you what they desired to give a portion of their spiritual essence to a potion. Her father was a small legend for having the talent for knowing those things. If anyone had known he had somehow gotten the essence of a Phoenix, his legend would not be so small.

"I can't accept this, Dad. This is…"

He held up a finger to stall her. "I know, priceless, and that is exactly why you will take it and wear it. Because to me, you are priceless." He lifted the crystal on a fine silver chain and hung it around her neck.

"But what would make you make this? It must have taken…"

Aya tried to calculate how long it would take to make such a powerful potion. Erasing wounds so far as to reattach a Spirit to the body was nearly impossible. A Lightmend could do it, but the cost was almost incalculable. Lightmends who had succeeded in such an attempt were on a very short list of quite legendary ta'el. Not only that, some of them had had to recover for multiple turns to recover their ability to Channel.

"I can make it very slightly faster now, but it took me six turns to make. It is difficult to use because very few ta'el have the senses of Spirit necessary to know precisely when their body has reached a point where you will not recover on your own. Channelers like you and your mother are the only ones who can safely use that potion." Aya watched her father, and he sighed. "I made it because of this." He gestured around to the world. "I know you never meant to be the kind of Stone who gets involved in the fight, but our world is changing."

Aya dropped an ear in confusion. "Speaking of that, how did you get here?"

"We were already here when the disruption began. We had just come through a Pathway when it snapped closed behind us, and we lost contact with Lewak the Wanderer. We are, unfortunately, stuck here until this ends," her mother answered.

Her father bustled into the kitchen and Roan materialized next to her.

"Time?" Aya asked tremulously.

Roan shook his head. "The White is making repairs for now. You have time for this."

Smells began to emerge from her kitchen as her father started cooking dinner.

"What's the matter, Little Aya?" her mother asked.

"I have been given a task, a name, and a title that I am not ready for. I am not strong enough. The Spirits prop me up and I am scraping by, but it's not gonna last." Tears ran down either side of her muzzle and suddenly, her mother was at her side.

"Oh, my Little Aya."

Her mother held her and made a comforting purring sound that Aya had not heard since she was very young. Her mother held her like that for a long time as the delicious smells of cooking filled her house. After a time, her mother used a thumb to wipe away the tears.

"I knew this round would come. You never faced the fact that you are more than my shadow. Long have other ta'el attempted to stand your mere twenty-three turns up against a lifetime of my work. They judged you lacking before you ever had the chance to prove otherwise, and you, to our dismay, believed them.

Your father hoped that if we let you develop without pushing you to understand how unfair the comparison was that you would understand it on your own, one round. He convinced me that if we gave you our support and love, that one round you would see it on your own. In this wisdom, he was not entirely wrong, but also not entirely right, I think."

"There was no perfect solution, my love. You and I both knew from the moment we saw how much she had chosen to look like you that ta'el would stupidly make the comparison," her father chimed in from the kitchen. There as a knock at the door and Aya looked up, but Sahone waved her off and answered the door to take delivery on the groceries.

"I did not say you were wrong, dear, just not entirely right," her mother said, a little sarcasm coloring her voice. She turned back to Aya. "All that being said, make no mistake, my daughter, you earned the title of Adept all on your own. And I'll tell you a little secret. You are never ready for the responsibility of adulthood, much less the kind of responsibility you have taken on as a Stone of the Hearth. We are, all of us…" She paused. "What was that human phrase you liked so much?" she asked over her shoulder to Sahone.

"Flying by the seat of our pants," her father shot back with a grin. Her mother nodded. Aya knew very well what it meant.

"It will be long turns before you have any true idea of what you are doing. Even then, it's just going to be an idea. There is no real planning for life, Little Aya. No matter how it goes, at least two ta'el will always be proud of you." Her mother hugged her again.

"And now that you have passed your Confirmation, I feel much more comfortable in telling you with no ego that I am absolutely green with jealousy about how easily you befriend all Spirits. I may be able to Channel more power than any ta'el on Earth, but I am an absolute amateur when it comes to the ability you have to make any Spirit welcome alongside you in the Wild. You are not weaker than me, Aya, and never have you been. Your abilities as a Channeler are simply different, and in many ways, you are stronger than I will ever be.

Do you know how many turns it took me to be able to call on the Heart of Fire? Ninety seven turns of auspices to even attract its attention. Then it snubbed me for another eight turns when I had no idea what to offer it to make it trust me. Imagine just how inadequate I felt when you called it up at the age of eighteen turns, and not only did it respond, but you carried with you an obsidian shard filled with a piece of your own Heart's Fire to facilitate your bond with the Spirit. You were not yet even close to the end of your training, and if I was not your own mother, I think I might have hated you." Her mother grinned at her. "Instead, I was just proud."

Her father came around the bar that separated her kitchen from the living room. A wave of good smells followed in his wake as he planted himself in her favorite chair. He looked down at the chair a little surprised. Clearly, he didn't think it would be as comfortable as it was. Then he smiled at Aya.

"Your mother is right. Life doesn't fit into neat boxes, Little Aya, so it's ok to feel like you aren't ready. For the most part, we never are. I certainly wasn't ready to be named Wildheart. I was certain that because of my potions and cooking, I would be named Brewsmith. I almost gave up on finding out why they named me Wildheart when I met your mother. She encouraged me to keep going. Together, we tracked down the meaning of my name. This is not me urging you to find a mate." Her father grinned wickedly. "Just making sure you know that you shouldn't give up. We only expect what we have ever expected from you, your best. No one can ever do more than that."

Aya cleared the tears from her fur, and sighed. "The Hound teased me with your name. Will you tell me one more story, Daddy?"

Her father grinned. "It's not as," he paused, searching for the word, "glamorous as my life might have been if I had received the name Brewsmith, but it is better, I think, than trapsing about the globe chasing rare potion ingredients."

"What does your name mean?" Aya asked.

"The name of Wildheart is not particularly rare so much as the ta'el that are able and desire to wear it are few. Like any other name, it requires a journey to discover its meaning. We do not tell the story to anyone who is given the name. So, know that you must keep it to yourself."

It was a custom that no ta'el would ever break. Interfering with the journey of another ta'el would cause lifelong backlash from the Spirits.

"Come on, spill, you old fox," Aya said, and her father's quiet grin sprouted teeth.

"Wildheart means a ta'el who is born with the ability to join the Spiritlands with the Wild. Unlike a Caretaker like your mother, who is tasked with purifying spiritual corruption and bringing Spirits back to their purpose, it is the task of a Wildheart to purify and heal the Wild itself. We seem less necessary to most, even if they know what we do.

However, there are times that balance cannot be restored by any Caretaker without the assistance of a Wildheart. Without us, there are places in our world that would remain blighted and unbalanced forever. Our magic also allows Channelers to perform cooperative magics with the Spirits that they could not otherwise do. The words are generally not sufficient to make most ta'el understand our place. Only Channelers like you or your mother can truly understand how important we are."

"But I'm not sure I understand." Her father's smile faded.

"Most do not, because they think that if a Wildheart can do all of that, then why do we need Caretakers?"

Aya did not like that it was exactly what she had been thinking.

"I am not a Channeler, Little Aya. I cannot use the great magics like you and your mother can. It is the place of a Wildheart, my place, to support others."

Aya understood then what her father had meant when he said his life would have been more glamorous as a Brewsmith. Her thoughts about him being far more famous if everyone knew what he could do came back to her. He had chosen a different path. She understood then why so few Wildhearts existed. Very few ta'el would be satisfied with living a quiet life where praise would be small and come infrequently, except from Channelers, who were also rare among the ta'el.

"I've been waiting your entire life to show you this."

Aya's eyes were forcefully pulled up to see her father's silver and black pelt pulsing with soft golden light. The light of the Spiritlands. The light spread out from her father's quiet form, through her house, and she gasped when it passed over her. Her entire home, the whole floor of her building was plunged into the Spiritlands. Every surface in her home took on a softly glowing sheen. Even her fur and sash began to glow with light corresponding to their colors in the real world.

It was possible for powerful Channelers to pull small areas of the Wild into the Spiritlands for short periods of time. This was only done occasionally because it was an enormous strain on the Channeler, for special occasions to bring large groups of ta'el closer to their Ancestors. It required massive amounts of Spirits working in conjunction with Channelers to perform the feat. Yet somehow, her father was doing it with no visible effort whatsoever. Aya realized her mouth was hanging open and she snapped her maw shut with an audible click.

"How, that's…" Aya stammered.

He pulled himself out of the chair, and ruffled her hair and ears like he had done when she was just a cub.

"You are meant to be the Speaker, whatever that is, Little Aya. This is what I am meant to be."

Then she realized that what he was doing was far more amazing. He couldn't fight like they did, though she knew he was physically extremely strong. He had been her sparring partner for years before she went to Lane the Wanderer's tutelage, but she could feel the power of the home of the Ancestors coursing through her body. It revitalized her in ways that she had not even known she needed.

It went even further than that, though. Even Channelers as powerful as her mother had limits. Pulling Spirits through the Veil between the Spiritlands and the real world, the Wild, was taxing on the Channeler, but what her father had done had completely removed that step. If you had the right Spirits available, even a single Channeler would only be limited by the sphere of her Father's influence. She eyed her mother suspiciously. Before she could say anything, though, her father cut her off.

"No, this is not how your mother achieved such amazing power. She truly is as powerful as she advertises. We have never been able to show you what she can do when we combine our abilities. "

Aya understood then. "That's why they didn't start calling you both together until just a few turns ago," Aya said.

Her mother nodded. "Yes. Your father's abilities are amazing, but they are also very difficult to work with, even for someone like me. By the time you started your training as a Hearth Stone, I had been training myself for many turns to work with his magic. It is true that I can do it now, but the first time I tried to Channel magic without first Channeling a Spirit through the Veil, I thought I was going to burn myself to death with the power. Channeling magic directly without the Spirit to act as a buffer required finer control as a Channeler than I had ever needed in the past."

Aya nodded in understanding. When you Channeled a Spirit and used their power, they assisted you in controlling the magic, but without that assistance, you were the conduit for the pure power itself. It was all up to you.

"I've missed this," Roan said as he came in from the garden. He was completely solid, as if he had returned to the Wild. Aya blinked.

"Can he..." She reached out and touched his russet red fur. He was solid. "How do you not draw crowds of Spirits with this? They can experience the Wild again?"

"I can't keep it up forever. A few shifts for a meal is no trouble, but generally, I do attract them when purifying an area like this. Why do you think I wrote down so much food?"

Her parents' Watcher Spirits came in from other rooms. Clearly, they had been exploring her home. Greatmother Sasu and Greatfather Strom were both much larger than all of them, one with deep brown fur, the other pure white. Bears were some of the largest of the ta'el. Aya bounded up from her sofa and leapt over the back. She dove into Sasu's embrace and wrapped her arms around the large bear.

"I missed you, Greatmother!" Aya shouted.

"And I you, Little Aya." She held Aya off the ground with no trouble.

Aya looked over to Strom. She had never met him in life like she had with Sasu. He passed a few turns before she had been born. She still missed him, though. He had taught her everything she knew about Spirits of the earth.

"You too, Greatfather. I don't have enough room in the dining room for everyone. We'll have to have a picnic in the garden."

"Oh, I think we will need even more than that." Her father pointed to the sliding doors to the garden.

Standing there were various creatures that Aya recognized only by how they felt. One was a somewhat frightening figure that was roughly the shape of a ta'el, but had no real features. It was just made of solid grey mist. This was her Witness. Despite her appearance, she stood shyly, holding one arm behind her back with the other. One looked like a small figure made up of various stacks of rock roughly in the shape of a four-legged animal. It wasn't much bigger than a small dog, but this was the Elemental that guarded her home when she was away.

The last of the three figures was oddly bird-like in its mannerisms. It kept twisting this way and that, as if things were startling it. That really wasn't the case at all, it was just the nature of a Hearth Spirit. It was attentive to everything in its domain. It stood on two legs, and had two arms. It had no head. Its body appeared to be made up of twisted bars of gleaming brown hardwood, as if a sculpture made by a master. The hardwood figure was the Spirit of her home. Of all the homes in the building. It made certain that the building stayed sound, and that everyone within felt safe within. Aya often left offerings for these Spirits to make sure they always felt welcome in her home.

Aya slid down from Sasu's embrace. "But I don't have anything for…"

Her father closed her oven and came across the room carrying a basket that she had not seen before. "Where did you get that?"

"Oh, your old dad gets to keep a few secrets." He grinned as he pulled a small metal box out of the basket. "Go ahead and fix yourselves plates to take into the garden while I tend to the appetites of those who do not enjoy my more regular fare. The food is all laid out."

He carried the box and the basket out into the garden and waved the basket to invite the Spirits to follow him. He knelt in front of the little figure made of stones and flipped open the box. Earth Spirits were tied to the land where they were born, and Aya knew that they adored sampling stones from other parts of the world. Her father obviously knew it too, because inside of the box were a collection of six perfect spheres of stone that he had brought from Alaska.

For the Spirit made of twisted tree roots, he pulled out a stone bowl covered with a heavy lid. Inside, there was a glowing green liquid that smelled heavily of herbs that Aya didn't immediately recognize. Glowing inside of the liquid was a simulacrum of a Spirit. Aya blinked and stared wide eyed.

"Where did you get that?" Aya pointed, her eyes agog.

The simulacrum was a tiny plush-looking version of a deer made of plants. Its antlers were soft, round tree branches, and its body was made of soft green moss. Her father grinned at her. The Spirit who had embodied that green potion was one that she knew of, but had never met before. It was without a doubt the most powerful nature Elemental on the planet, the Spirit of the Amazon Forest. Aya felt like her brains were going to dribble out of her ears.

The Spirit of the Amazon was one of the most elusive and skittish Spirits in all of nature. It was like finding a single specific grain of sand on a beach, and then somehow turning that single grain of sand into the most beautiful glass sculpture in all the world.

"You are cheating somehow. That's so unfair!" Aya spluttered.

Her mother patted her on the head. "He wouldn't even let me meet the Spirit of the Forest. He said there was no way it would come out of hiding if he brought anyone with him. What's worse is I know he was right," her mother complained.

Her father squinted at her in annoyance. "Oh yes, so unfair. So when was the last time you whistled up The Grey himself?" her father sniped, and she blushed underneath her fur, remembering what had been said to her about having the guts to speak to the Grey so casually.

"How did you know about that?"

Her mother rolled her eyes, and then chuckled. "There are precisely eleven Channelers on the planet who have been granted permission by the Grey to call upon him. You are number twelve. We tend to notice when he befriends someone new, especially when they are our junior by a century or more." Her mother narrowed her eyes a little.

"I don't do it on purpose!" Aya complained and went to fix her plate.

"Anyway, the potion will protect your Hearth Spirit's physical manifestation from all sorts of pests, fungus, and infections for at least a century. And don't you dare tell anyone where you got it. Ta'el would track me across the earth to get their paws on this, and as far as I know, there are only two or three Brewsmiths who can coax out a Spirit of the Forest strong enough to make this. And last but not least..."

He took a bottle out of the basket as the rest of them started to settle themselves in the green grass of the garden clearing. The bottle was blue crystal, and appeared to have liquid made up of a rainbow of colors inside. Each color was its own distinct collection of liquid in the bottle, and none of them mixed.

Aya blinked. "Is that a rainbow catcher?"

"Yes, and yes, there is more than enough here for everyone to have some."

From the bottle, he poured some of the swirling multi-colored liquid into a small dish. He held it out to the shape made of mist. The bottle was something that only someone with the skills of a Brewsmith could make. You could set it out in a rainstorm, and if there was a rainbow after the storm it would magically convert the light of the rainbow into a light delicious liquid that could be enjoyed by both Spirits and the living. The flavor was different for anyone who drank it. It was one of the small things that Brewsmiths made that were purely for the joy of it.

It smelled like fresh wind blowing through a forest on a warm summer round. It was more or less the best thing you could taste, and the rainbow catcher was so hard to make that her Father could trade or sell it for almost anything she could think of. Making the bottle required the assistance of nine Spirits, but she had no idea what nine Spirits were the right ones. She didn't know anyone who did, except apparently her father. Her father had, in the usual marvelous way, made a different dish for everyone who he had to feed. She watched everyone enjoying the things her father had made.

"Almost time now," Roan said around a mouthful of spiced rice.

"Pig," Aya chided, and Roan swallowed.

"I am a Coyote, thank you very much," he said with as much dignity as he could muster, but what he said had brought Aya back to the reality that not everyone was able to feel what she could feel right now. Her father had used his personal magic to make their conspicuously missing connection to the Spiritlands immaterial while they had enjoyed their meal. That was not so for the rest of the Ta'el.

Right now, they were all terrified that they would never see their Ancestors again. Maybe some of them were even speculating what many of the Channelers had first thought. Their world was under attack, and maybe even dying. Many of the Spirits thought that she could do something about it. This meal with her family though was precisely what she had needed to give her certainty.

"I'm ready, Greatfather. I am going to find out what it means to be the Speaker."

Chapter 11

"EXPLORER"

Aya's parents spent two rounds sleeping in her spare bedroom before the White was able to make repairs to the connection to the Spiritlands. On the third round, her Hearth Spirit informed her that a visitor had appeared outside her door. Aya tugged the thick oak door open to find an unfamiliar Avian occupying her hallway.

She had enormous golden eyes like all ta'el born of the Snowy Owl. Curiously, unlike most of her species, she had no black markings in her feathers at all. They both stood there for a long moment not saying anything, and then the Owl tilted her head and looked down at herself. She lifted her wings.

"Does something stain my feathers?" she pipped, her voice high and musical in the way of Avians.

She turned her body slightly, her head spinning eerily past the point of pain in most species to spy her tail feathers in search of defects. Aya blinked and then noticed a very slight transparency to the Owl's body. Realization assaulted her like a punch in the whiskers. She immediately bent into a bow.

"I apologize, White! Be welcome in my home. You need not wait at the door."

"It is only polite. This is not my home," The White said, her head pivoting back to fix Aya with her golden gaze.

"Please come inside." Aya swung the door wide and The White stepped inside with the odd, bobbing gait of many Avians. She shook her feathers and settled her wings.

"Are your parents still here?" she asked.

"Out in the garden. You may be more comfortable out there. My heart tree has limbs low enough for comfortable conversation," Aya offered, and the White nodded.

"Very thoughtful, but it is raining."

Aya shook her head. "It's no trouble. My Hearth Spirit keeps a thick canopy on most of the gardens."

She pulled aside the sliding glass door and, though it was dark in the clearing, aetherglow from a dozen small Spirits gave gentle illumination to the tiny grotto formed of thick, vibrant vegetation. Brilliant blue and purple bell flowers almost seemed to glow, blooming despite the tree canopy blocking most of the direct sunlight.

Aya's parents knelt in the carpet of lush grasses in meditation, calling to the Spirit of Lewak the Wanderer to assist them with their travels. She had offered to call the Wanderer for them, but they had insisted they would manage themselves.

The White spread her wings and flapped them in a powerful downbeat that lifted her to the first limbs of the trees a few scant feet overhead. She gripped a branch with her talons, but took care not to damage the tree with the sharp edges of her claws.

"Your hearth is very strong, Ayasha the Speaker, and made stronger still by a blessing from a Forest Spirit."

"My father brought a potion that he crafted from the Spirit of the Amazon's freely given essence."

The White nodded. "Who is your father?"

Her father spoke slowly, a hallmark of someone who was deep in meditation. "I am Sahone the Wildheart, Creator."

"Ah, I have heard some stories of you. Not many Wildhearts left, these rounds. A shame that more of my children do not seek such quiet fulfillment as you have. Conceit is not a problem among your kind, but still, many seek admiration."

Her father chuckled. "You will not find conceit a problem with my Little Aya." Her father still spoke with the slow-paced cadence of his meditation.

"Would you and your Watcher grace us with your power, Sahone the Wildheart?"

"Would you be so kind as to allow me a moment to finish assisting my mate, Creator?" Sahone asked.

"If you will call me White instead of Creator, I would be far more inclined."

A slow smile spread across her father's muzzle. "As you wish, White."

"Aya, might you prepare us some of that delightful tea?" The White asked. Aya nodded, and slid the doors closed behind her.

"She will not be long," Sahone said, finally opening his firelight eyes. His voice returned to its normal cadence.

Ayasha the elder continued in her meditation.

The White tilted her head in an Avian gesture of confusion.

"I am not a fool. You could have asked her for tea before ever coming into the garden."

The White looked to the sliding doors as if to gauge how long it might take Aya to make the tea. She did not look back before she started to speak.

"Sahone the Wildheart, you know what her name means for her. You are one whose tangible connection to the Spiritlands makes you aware of many things that even the Spirits themselves are not, and you are old enough to remember the last, even if he has been erased from everyone else's memories."

Sahone grimaced and nodded. "I remember the last Speaker. I remember why he was so named by the Spirits. I remember, my father being certain my mate would not be the one to carry that mantle. He was certain it would be our little Aya." The corners of Sahone's muzzle turned down into an angry frown.

"I also remember when he and everyone else lost their memories of the last Speaker. He passed shortly after, and Aya was only a few rounds old. He could never tell me what he saw in our little girl that made him think it would be her. It was decades before I understood. Why did you make them forget, White?" There was no hesitation in his accusation. He knew exactly what had happened.

She finally turned back to him. "Because like your path, they must journey to find the meaning of their name, but unlike you, the knowledge of what the Speaker can do is quite dangerous. To lose a Wildheart to another name because of accidental foreknowledge is not so grievous a wound." The White turned her head back to watch Aya moving about in the kitchen. "To lose a Speaker, though,"

"Is something more," Sahone finished in a whisper, letting out a breath he did not know he had been holding. He ran his paw through his chest fur looking down in contemplation.

She nodded, not taking her eyes off Aya.

"I don't know if she can do what is required of the Speaker. She has the intelligence, and there is no question she will make the hard decisions if she has to, but Ayasha the younger, my daughter, has been ever unsure about when it was time to make those hard decisions. Almost too patient, she always looks for a better way, especially when it is violence that is required of her."

"She obliterated a Visceral."

Sahone nodded. "Because she knew there was no other way to keep everyone safe. But when it is less clear, she will spend tremendous time thinking things through. Sometimes too much time. I do not suggest you attempt to use that as a motivator. I have yet to see anyone successfully manipulate my daughter into doing something she does not think is right." He grinned mischievously at her. "I do not doubt your abilities, my Creator, but all abilities have limits."

She let out a little hooting laughter at that.

"I promise you I would never knowingly attempt to manipulate someone with the talent to be named Speaker. Even with all of my power, I am not so arrogant as that. I simply wanted your assessment. You daughter does not reveal herself easily. It is the way of someone like the Speaker."

"How do you know I'm not overestimating her?"

"Your consultation is not the only one I have sought."

Sahone's brows drew together in concern. "My daughter will pass your tests, White. When she does, will you watch over her?" he asked with the morose uncertainty of a parent whose child has chosen a very dangerous path to walk.

"I will do what is within my power, Sahone the Wildheart, but if what all of my children have told me holds true, I think you have prepared her very well to watch over herself."

Aya came back carrying a tray with four cups and a teapot on it. One of the cups was shaped differently from the others.

It was larger, almost the size of a dish, and instead of a D-shaped handle, it had a horizontal wooden dowel as a handle. It was a cup designed specifically for Avians who, by necessity, would pick it up with their talons. The White was more impressed with this young emta every time she met her. She had prepared herself to accommodate and make everyone feel welcome.

The respect she was prepared to show to all ta'el, no matter who they were, was admirable. The White noted that the handle even had the traditional hook on the end so that she could hang it from her perch when she had finished the beverage. Aya came to the trunk of the tree just as Ayasha the elder opened her eyes. Aya held the tray up above her head for the White to reach down with one talon to take her cup, and then let her parents take two white mugs with different colored paw prints on the side to make it easy to tell whose mug was whose. Aya took her own and cupped it in her paws.

"Lewak will be indisposed for some time. We will likely not be able to return to Tongass for another round," Ayasha the elder said with some small frustration.

"I can call Lane if you like?" Aya folded her legs beneath her, kneeling comfortably in the grass.

Her mother opened her mouth to protest, and Aya narrowed her eyes, her whiskers turning down to say she was not making a suggestion.

The White put her beak into the cup, and after a long moment, she lowered it. She adjusted herself to make herself comfortable standing on a single leg. "Siris informed me that something was left behind when the Visceral was dispatched."

"There was."

Aya pushed a paw into the opening of her piece pouch. She took out the gleaming silver sphere. The two lines crossed over a dot on the surface. Numbers were written along the lines in both directions as they ran around the surface. She held her paw flat with the marble in the center of her palm paw pad. While an Avian ta'el's vision was not precisely like their animal counterparts, it was still the sharpest of all Ta'el.

She would have no trouble making out the large metal marble from her perch in the tree.

"I do not recognize this thing. It must have been made in the time we were away creating other worlds. However, the numbers must mean something."

"I recognize it, or at least I have heard of a thing like it," Greatfather Strom spoke as he emerged from the Spiritlands to join them. He was quickly followed by Greatmother Sasu, who materialized floating just behind Aya's mother. "You need to speak to an Explorer about that marble."

Aya groaned.

"I need to speak to an Explorer to get the book. I need to speak to an Explorer about the marble. Where in the seven sides am I supposed to find,"

Greatfather Roan made a throat clearing noise and held up a paw, palm towards Aya, in a pausing gesture. He then pointed at Greatmother Sasu. She was holding up a single finger with her mouth partially open as she waited for Aya to finish her rant.

"Apologies, Honored Ancestor," Aya said and then waited.

"I think, if you would use your gifts, Little Aya, you can call to Lishi the Explorer. She may assist you," Greatmother Sasu explained.

"I don't think so. I've tried to call to several Spirits of previous Explorers from the Tome of All Names, including Lishi. None have responded."

Sasu's semi-transparent muzzle pulled a frown. "I just spoke to Lishi not two spells ago. How many did you attempt to call?"

"I don't recall, at least two dozen before I gave up and decided to go looking for Dedran in the flesh," Aya replied.

Sasu's frown deepened. "White?"

The White spread her wings in a shrugging motion that said she didn't know, but she would try to find out more.

"So, what do I do?"

"I suggest continuing your quest to find Dedran wherever he might be," The White said.

"Right. Siris said that his Watcher Spirit was about, but that's another odd mystery in itself. Why would he go anywhere without his Watcher?"

"It's not entirely uncommon to leave your Watcher behind to relay messages, as you well know," Roan proposed.

"If I know where I am going, what I will be doing, and that I will be away too long to make running back and forth practical. I would never go into an unknown situation like trying to hunt down a hidden human installation without you with me, Greatfather."

"She is not wrong," The White sang agreement.

"Then we should get going to meet this Watcher and see if we can get some answers," Aya said, tipping herself backwards into a crouch before standing up. She closed her eyes and concentrated on reaching into the Spiritlands with her voice. "Lane the Wanderer, might I ask your assistance?"

The blue-white mist of the Wanderer Spirit appeared next to her. He yawned meaningfully at her and stretched his lithe body. She explained her request.

"I think I will ask something in return this time."

Aya rolled her eyes.

Lane put his fists on his hips. "Not very good manners, Ayasha the Speaker." Lane could only hold the straight face for a few seconds before his cheeks puffed out as if he were holding water in his mouth. Then he blew out a raspberry, and laughed.

"Whatever you would like, Honored Ancestor."

"I think just a kiss will do."

Aya's mouth almost fell open in astonishment, but she controlled herself with an effort of iron will. She blushed, and was thankful for her fur that her cheeks would not turn red. Aya had had a small crush on Wanderer Lane since he had become her martial arts instructor at the age of fourteen turns. It was nothing serious, but she admired him. He was strong, wise, and gorgeous to look at, especially when she had seen him in his living colors. She coughed spasmodically and pounded her chest as if she had breathed in a bit of her tea. She finally got control of herself.

"If you would be so kind as to redirect the local Tunnel for my parents to return to Tongass?"

"It would be more energy efficient to create a Pathway for them," Lane suggested. "We are a little far away to keep shifting the Tunnel's endpoints."

Aya dropped an ear in confusion. Pathways, basic teleportation portals, were energy inefficient in the extreme compared to Tunnels. Lane shook his head sensing her thoughts.

"Tunnels work with the Spiritlands, but because they occur naturally, the farther we move their end points, the more energy it costs. I moved the Tunnel to get you home the other round because you were in no shape to create a Pathway." His ghostly eyes roved over her in languorous interest. "Your shape is just fine now."

Ayasha the elder rolled her eyes this time. "You old lecher." She grinned.

Lane shrugged. "She is an adult, Ayasha the Caretaker, and the love given in sharing a kiss is a wonderful thing."

Aya's mother held up her paws in surrender. "He's right, Daughter." Then she eyed Lane mischievously. "Though your father is quite a good kisser. I'm sure he wouldn't mind paying the cost."

Aya's mouth fell open when her father waggled his eyebrows at Wanderer Lane. Not in surprise, but amusement. Then she burst out laughing because the look of apprehension on Lane's phantasmal face was priceless.

Same gender pairings among the Ta'el were just as common as opposite gender pairings. Dispositions of femininity and masculinity were a determination of personality as Ta'el reproduced magically and had no physical gender. It was quite normal to have many partners with whom they exchanged intimate Spiritual encounters. As her father had made her understand, variety is the spice of life. No pairing that involved genuine love and mutual admiration was looked down upon. However, Ta'el did have preferences, and Lane's definitely did not that way. Her father, on the other paw, had no such preferences. Aya gasped in air as she tried to get her laughter under control. Her father grinned at her.

"No, it's fine. Lane's request is very fair," Aya said, overtones of laughter still in her voice, and Lane looked relieved.

She reached out her paw, and Lane took it. She drew his Spirit inside of her. She concentrated, and created a small mental landscape where they could share a few moments as if it were the real world. At least she didn't have to worry about her parents having to watch her make out with Lane. The memory was of a small cabin in the Adirondack Forest that she had visited every summer when she was a cub, a place where she had stayed during much of her training for the Hearth. It was no coincidence that her mind had gone to this place, it was where she had her first kiss. Wanderer Lane was there with her, looking out the window of the cabin at the pristine forest outside.

"This is a special place," he said.

"It is. Let's get this over with."

"Is it really such a dismal prospect?"

The smile on his short muzzle was roguish. He held out his paw, and she took it. He pulled her close, and it was clear that he knew what he was about. He cradled the back of her head and pulled her into a kiss like only a couple she'd had in her life. When he finally pulled back, releasing her from the kiss, she was a little breathless.

"I guess that wasn't so bad," Aya said, far more relaxed than she had been.

"No it was not. More to the point, you have made me feel alive again. Thank you, Aya. Come, let's build your Pathway."

Aya let the mental landscape collapse, and she was back in her garden. Clearly, the relaxed smile was still on her muzzle because her father winked at her. She went and hugged her father and then her mother.

"Please don't wait so long to visit again?" Aya asked.

"We won't. We didn't visit because we didn't want to interrupt your training. We would have been a distraction," her mother said. She wasn't wrong. Training to become a

Stone was intense. Her mother should know. She had gone through the same training.

{Are you ready, Lane?}

{Of course, Little Aya. Walk the circle.}

Aya began to walk in a perfect little circle, placing her paws carefully, one in front of the other, so that the toes of one paw touched the back of the other. Each step left a glowing blue paw print in the grass. She was extremely careful to make that sure each print touched the last. When she took the last step, and the paw prints formed a solid circle, there was a flare of soft white light. The paw prints melted together into smooth line of luminescence. Then the area inside of the circle faded away, leaving a window into another place.

Lush green forest populated with conifers stretched away in the view. Her parents stepped over the odd window into another place. They tipped forward and fell through the hole, and then they were standing in the forest through the window. They waved in farewell, and the window slowly faded away as the glowing line dimmed. The ground reasserted itself and she began to walk a new circle. She was rolling the marble in her paw, staring at it. The little round shape looked so familiar to her. She wasn't sure why, but she knew she had seen something like it before. Something about the numbers seemed so familiar, but she could not place it.

"Where are you going next?" The White hooted musically.

"Back to Denver. I've got way too many questions, and not enough answers." Aya narrowed her eyes at the White. "Is all this really necessary? I don't feel like I am learning anything about my name," Aya criticized, and then realized who she was complaining to.

Before she could say anything further, the White spread her wings and curled her primary flight feathers in an odd waving motion that asked Aya to calm herself in Avian Ta'eltesh.

"I understand your frustration, young emta'el. It is necessary. Much like your father's name, there are some parts of yours that cannot be explained. They must be experienced to be understood."

"And how long am I expected to neglect my duty to discover the meaning of my name?"

Aya did not show the frustration simmering deep inside of her. Her parents had told her to dedicate herself to whatever felt right in her life. She had done that very thing. Walking through the city the last two rounds, seeing the fear and disquiet on the faces of all of the Ta'el without their magic, and not being able to do anything about it but research her stupid name had been profoundly upsetting.

The White flapped her wings and landed in front of Aya. In her owl form, she was smaller than Aya by several inches. She lifted a wing and curled her primary feathers around Aya's shoulder. A gentle, comforting touch.

"As long as you feel that you are still doing the right thing, Ayasha the Speaker. I will never force any Ta'el to fail in what they see as their purpose. No matter how important it is, that is more important."

Aya sighed. "I apologize again."

"Ayasha the Speaker, never apologize for being who you are. I may be the Creator of the Ta'el, but you are you, and even I would not attempt to make you someone else," the White sang.

She walked across the covered clearing and into the rain, where it ran down through the opening of the smaller exercise clearing. Water ran off of her feathers in small rivulets not penetrating her feathers. She tipped her face up to the sky, and she drew in a deep breath. Then she flapped her wings once and disappeared over the side of the building, the same way she had gone at her last departure.

Aya turned and finished walking the circle of her own Pathway. Light flared, and the library courtyard in Denver appeared through the new circle. Aya fell forward into the circle, and vanished.

Chapter 12

"LOST"

Siris had been carried off to his rooms to sleep off the soul sickness caused by healing the over two thousand ta'el that had been injured by the Visceral. Aya couldn't believe the scale. The cursed thing had hurt so many. Lightmends and other healers were not the rarest of Channelers, but they certainly were not common. There were only a pawful in any city, and in Denver, Siris was the only one.

Many ta'el were still injured when Aya arrived, but given the welcoming committee, one could hardly notice. It seemed that someone had let slip that it was she that had saved them from the Visceral. In fact, they told her as much when help had finally been summoned. She had been half carried to the city's massive denlodge for what she had been told would be a small celebration in her honor.

Passing between the two massive trunks of the building's twin heart trees, she entered a cavernous room filled with at least two hundred ta'el. Four massive limbs, two from each of the heart trees, snaked away from the corners of the room to support the ceiling. Trefoil leaves covered the branches racing away from the central limbs to paint a fresco of mother nature across the trappings of lost mankind. She eyed Kian the Denmaster and flattened her ears in annoyance.

"Small?"

"It's smallish."

Kian trundled his black and white bulk behind the long bar that had been grown from the wood of the heart tree. Twenty feat of gleaming maple had been painstakingly carved in such a way that the bas relief did no harm to the living wood. Fanciful creatures trotted across the frontage and waving spiral designs adorned the top surface, over which Aya spent a long time talking, laughing, and telling the very recent story of what she had done to dispatch the Visceral.

"Alright, Kian, I must get to see Siris. He has to be awake by now. It's been shifts." There was a round of jeers from the Ta'el in the denlodge common room.

The Panda held up his massive paws, "Alright, alright, everyone. Calm down. Let us show the Stone the respect she deserves."

The motion lifted his spotless white apron that was akin to a badge of office. Aya was convinced that they all had some magical talent for keeping those aprons so bright and clean. Kian the Denmaster moved around the bar and over to Aya. He lowered his booming voice to converse with her.

"Siris stays up on the tenth floor of one of the buildings nearby. There are several buildings here that are part of the denlodge. Go two buildings to the west. The Hearth Spirit there will be waiting for you. Just touch the heart tree and they will help you find him."

"Thank you, Denmaster," Aya said, and Kian waved her along.

"Not at all, Hearth Stone. Please do come back and enjoy our hospitality whenever you are here. I will always have a free room for you to refresh yourself in, even if it is in my own home."

Kian grinned at her and stuck a shoot of bamboo in the side of his muzzle before turning back to the rest of his patrons. Aya had to stop several times as various ta'el thanked her one last time for what she had done.

"You look embarrassed, Ayasha the Speaker."

The voice that broke through the surface of her thoughts was deep and a little playful. She realized that she had almost missed the building where Siris was supposed to be staying. Siris leaned against the building, waiting for her. Aya had walked completely past, dwelling on her embarrassment over all of the bowing and scraping that everyone had been doing around her. She realized that all of her emotions were showing in her whiskers and ears. It was quite literally written all over her face.

"Very." She crossed back to where he was waiting.

He pushed himself away from the smooth grey wall of builtstone, bending himself into a deep bow, his long, ringed tail curling into a perfect circle behind him.

"Perhaps you should accept that despite how you feel, your actions speak much more loudly of your character than do your words."

Aya shook her head in stubborn denial. "I just did what any Stone would do."

"But not, I think, what any Stone *could* do. I might have defeated the creature, but I could not catch it. You, though, the creature mistakenly thought you weak, and you used that to your advantage. Even uncertainty about one's own abilities can be a strength if one does not allow themself to be crippled by it." Siris straightened, and then went back inside, waving a paw over his shoulder to indicate that Aya should follow.

She touched her paw to the trunk of the tree clinging to and running through the face of the building. She conveyed a hello to the Hearth Spirit through the tree, and it responded in kind, and that it would recognize her in the future.

"Dedran the Explorer has an apartment in this building as well. Unlike New York, most of the ta'el in the city live here, either in the denlodge buildings or near to them. The geological instability of many parts of the city prevents them from rebuilding there. We have been attempting to raise the Spirit of the Mountain for hundreds of turns in an effort to stabilize these areas, but it does not respond. Many fear that it was somehow killed when the humans destroyed the Balance. We believe the city was originally much closer to the edge of the mountains then than it is now. The old maps show the topography has changed drastically in some areas of the Rocky Mountains."

"I learned that in training. A few ta'el actually urged me to come here instead of staying in New York, but I don't have my mother's talents with teasing out Spirits that do not want to be found."

Siris nodded. "We have been hoping she would be available soon, but the Spirit of the Forest in Tongass is far more critical. That forest is by far the largest remaining natural wildland outside of the Amazon. If that Spirit is not recovered soon, the forest will shrink even further. That could be problematic for the entire world, especially with how difficult a time they are having expanding the Amazon, even though the Spirit of the Forest there is so active."

Siris dropped to all fours as he started up stairs that were made of an odd rock that was apparently created by the humans. They had determined how it was made with the help of earth Elementals, but the human name for the concoction was lost to time. Ta'el called it builtstone. Aya followed suit. Stairs were so much more comfortable on all fours. She followed him up to the third floor and stayed on all fours when Siris did not rise. He turned right, and turned down the hallway, stopping at the second door.

"This is Dedran's apartment. His Watcher Spirit awaits you within. She is somewhat distraught, so please be gentle." He pointed to a solid looking door whose wood had been stained with a vibrant green dye of some sort, then padded away down the hall.

"Thank you, Siris, for everything."

In reply, he waved his long tail languidly in a gesture that said he hoped to see her soon.

Aya smoothly got up onto two feet again and knocked softly on the door before turning the handle. It popped open, and she slipped inside, closing the door behind her. The apartment within was what Aya would have generously described as unlivable. She found herself in a kitchen joined with a small dining area, with a much larger living area beyond, free of any walls separating the rooms.

Every available flat surface beyond the single stretch of cut marble countertop that contained the stove and sink was covered in scrolls and books. The walls were plastered with maps, and various bundles of red string outlined paths that joined maps to other maps. The only distinguishable features of the living area were a large half-moon of a couch and two very comfortable looking leather chairs surrounding a large table. This was situated exactly far enough away from each of the seating arrangements to be used as a writing surface.

There curled up on one of the chairs was the Spirit of a very small emta'el. She was made of soft orange mist, and as she lifted her head, two large circular ears popped up over the arm of the chair. A thin triangular face followed. She had been one of the smallest ta'el species in life. She had been born of the Mouse.

"Hello, Honored Ancestor. I apologize for intruding into your space."

The Spirit appeared bleary-eyed, and her thin tail laid limply over the side of the chair. She shook her head. "No, not at all, Ayasha the Speaker. I am Eleena the Wildheart. Siris informed me that you would like to speak to me about Dedran?"

She swung her paws over the edge of the chair. They did not even come close to reaching the polished hardwood floor. Aya was surprised that this tiny ta'el had once held the same power as her father.

"I'm attempting to find a book that your partner has taken from the Archives."

The little spirit nodded. Much like Roan, Eleena seemed to interact with the world just as if she were still alive. It was an oddity even among Watcher Spirits to retain such trappings of life. "The book you seek is here," she said, sliding herself off the chair and floating lightly to the ground. She was just slightly taller than half of Aya's height, and she was utterly adorable in her mannerisms.

Eleena brushed her whiskers back in a quick grooming gesture and brushed back the orange bob cut hair framing her face. She walked around the entire living area, weaving around the battered furniture, stopping at each table for a moment before moving on. She checked the books in the kitchen, and then went down the hallway that disappeared from one side of the living area.

Aya heard a door open, which must have been taxing for the little spirit, considering how much trouble Roan had with moving physical objects. She came back a moment later, carrying the tiny hard bound book. She held it up to Aya, who took it with all haste, to take the burden off of the Spirit. The way the Spirit moved, so aimlessly, was disturbing to Aya. She set the book aside and touched the tiny Spirit's face.

"Honored Ancestor, I apologize if I cause you any distress, but I must ask. What troubles you?"

Aya knew that something had happened to Dedran. If it had not, his Watcher would not be here in this state. No ta'el would ever leave his Watcher behind to linger like this. In that moment, the little Spirit broke down. She threw her arms around Aya's waist and buried her muzzle in the fur of Aya's stomach. She was a very light but tangible presence in a way that the average untethered Ancestor could not be.

"Please, Honored Ancestor. Tell me how I can assist you?" Aya asked.

"I have lost him, Ayasha the Speaker. My ties to my charge have been somehow blocked, and I cannot find him."

Aya was shocked. She did not know of anything that could shut off a Watcher's bonds to their charge. Outside of her experience during her Confirmation, she would have said it was impossible.

"Greatfather Roan, would you be so kind?" Aya asked, and Roan appeared next to them. Eleena's eyes went a little wide, and then she stepped back from Aya. Roan caught her by the shoulder.

"Hello, Eleena, it has been a long time."

"I'm sorry, Roan the Trickster. I'm not myself."

"Do not apologize, Eleena. It is we who should apologize to you for allowing you to linger in this state without assistance. Why is there no Hearth Stone helping you?"

"It's not their fault. Dedran went missing a few rounds past, just before the Visceral appeared and began to kill ta'el around the city. Everyone has been so occupied attempting to set that right that I didn't want to trouble them with my issue. Dedran has often left me behind to relay messages. When my sense of him vanished, I assumed that something bad had happened, but that is the life of an Explorer. Many meet their fate suddenly, and he had told me he was going into a very dangerous area of the mountains in search of a human military installation." The Spirit could not shed tears, but she swiped a paw across her eyes as if she were.

"But my connection to Dedran is not broken like it would be if he had been killed. This is much worse. He's alive, and he's in great pain, but I cannot tell where he is." It was no wonder Siris had described her as distraught. This kind of emotional stress would be abysmal for a being made up of only memories and life energy. Aya touched the book as Roan held Eleena.

"She's a former student of yours, Greatfather?"

Roan chuckled. "No, Little Aya, quite the opposite. I am a former student of hers. Eleena taught me everything I know about being a Stone of the Hearth, and by extension, she did the same for you. She even taught me a thing or two about what it is to be a Trickster, and how important we are to the world."

"So, this is the Mouse that turned you into an insufferable wiseass?" Aya asked, the corners of her muzzle turned up in a gentle smile.

Eleena let out a little sobbing laugh. "I think I like this one, Roan. How did you end up with her?"

Roan grinned. "She's my Greatdaughter. When my son asked me to watch over her, how could I refuse?"

Eleena seemed taken aback. "This is Sahone's little one? She's got so big! I remember when she was just a tiny ball of fur!"

"I don't recall ever meeting you," Aya said, her ear drooping in confusion.

"You would not. I passed into the Spiritlands when you were only a few spells old. I only got to see you the one time, because this one would not stop pestering an elderly Mouse on her deathbed."

"That's not how I remember it. I seem to recall being thumped on the head with a stout stick and some shouting about you not being dead yet," Roan replied.

Eleena looked down at the floor and stepped back from both of them. "I apologize for troubling you, Ayasha the Speaker. You have your own tasks to fulfill."

Aya shook her head. "Honored Ancestor, my first duty is to you, the Spirits and ta'el I joined the Hearth to help. I will find out what happened to Dedran, and I will return him to you if I can."

Eleena shook her head. "You don't know it yet, but your name fits you very well, Ayasha the Speaker."

Both Aya and Roan stared.

"You know what my name means?" Aya blurted out.

"Any Wildheart old enough to have been alive when the last Speaker was still in the Wild would know what your name means," Eleena explained.

Aya's eyes narrowed. "And how long ago was that?"

"He passed from this world about two hundred and eighty turns ago. There are likely only a handful of Wildhearts in the world who knew of him now."

"One of them being my own father." Aya said, somewhat indignantly.

Eleena's squeaky laughter filled the room. "Do not be upset with him, Ayasha the Speaker. None of us could tell you what your name means. That is a journey you must take yourself." Eleena's tiny smile was unexpectedly comforting to Aya. "May I accompany you, Ayasha the Speaker, on your search for the meaning of your name? At least until you find Dedran?"

"I would be delighted to have you. Do you offer the same sorts of powers as a Wildheart like my father?"

Eleena shook her head. "Unfortunately, the innate magics of the Wildheart require one to have a living body in the Wild. However, I can provide you with magics for what I was most well-known for in my time: stealth and guile."

Ayasha blinked, realizing that her father had not Channeled a single Spirit when bringing them into the Spiritlands. Her father's power was far more amazing than she had realized. "Really?"

Magics that involved improving one's cunning were exceedingly rare. Various versions of Stealth were very common magics offered by many Spirits, though many had to be applied judiciously, as they were more successful in some situations than others. Guile, though, was a rare power indeed. It revealed traps and discovered lies.

Eleena nodded and twitched her whiskers. Many gestures of the rodent dialect of Ta'eltesh were shared with the feline dialect. This particular twitch, back, then up and down, indicated confidence.

"Not that I would ask you to share those magics with me. You are not my Watcher."

"Some of Roan's magics are similar as well. While it would be improper for you to ask, it would not be improper for me to offer. You have freely offered me what aid you can render; it would be terrible manners if I refused to reciprocate such kindness." Eleena's Spirit dimmed as she turned back to the room. "But where do we start?"

Aya hopped up onto the couch. "That's a good question. There has to be a clue in here as to where Dedran was planning to hunt next." Aya followed the red strings going from map to map with her eyes and realized that some of the strings terminated further up. She turned her head and followed the lines.

More maps had been plastered across the ceiling. It was like he had turned the room into a giant globe to map his travels. That, though, triggered something in the back of her mind. Some long ago remembered thing.

"Perhaps if we," Roan began.

"Ssh."

Aya held up two fingers pressed together like one in response to the annoyed look she knew he'd be making. It was a gesture that she and Roan shared for when they were thinking. Roan quieted and Aya focused, trying to tease out what her brain was trying to tell her. A globe, but not like this makeshift thing Dedran had used this room to create. She had seen it a long time ago, when she was just barely old enough to start learning about the purpose of the Ta'el. Not long after she had been told the story she had told to the cubs the round of her Confirmation. She wracked her brain trying to make it puke up the information.

"Globes."

She took out the mirror-polished marble, and held it up. Then the image appeared in her mind, a large hollow wooden ball mounted with an axle through the middle. The axis had been mounted on a large, wooden stand so that you could easily spin the ball with your paws to see different parts of the planet. Her mother had told her to be careful with it because it was so old that the only thing holding it together was magic.

"Some of the ones the humans left behind had lines on them, a grid that covered the entire surface of the globe. That's what this is, a tiny globe." Aya shook the marble in her fist, feeling the lines cut into the smooth surface as it rubbed across her paw pads. "It's directions. The dot is a specific location."

Eleena was looking on with some interest now. "The humans had names for the lines, but I could never make the sounds." Most, if not all, Ta'el were taught to read many human languages. Mostly English, Mandarin, Hindi, and Spanish, but very few ta'el had voice boxes capable of making the all of the same kinds of sounds that humans made when actually speaking them.

"The book that I read explained that there were numbers that worked with the lines to give precise locations in the world," Aya mumbled.

"Right!" Eleena's ghostly paw latched onto Aya's. Unlike most physical objects, Aya's status as a Channeler meant that most Spirits could touch her as if they were still alive, as long as she didn't stop them. Eleena tugged on her paw. "Dedran had a book like that, and he made it part of the Cartograph."

The tiny Spirit pulled Aya down the hallway towards the other side of the building.

{Why didn't you tell me you knew Dedran's Watcher?} Aya sent to Roan.

{I had no idea. I have not seen Eleena since just after you were born. I knew that she had passed the Bardo, but I hadn't had the opportunity to see her again,} Roan explained.

Eleena pulled Aya excitedly towards the last door on the right.

{Is she always like this?} Aya sent, and Roan's answering chuckle warmed her.

{Seeing Eleena sad or upset would be stressful for anyone because for her, it is an utterly alien state. She was always excitable, always joyful, and always ready for an adventure, whether she was five or five hundred turns old. She smiled even through death itself. I know, I was there for that part. I can't imagine her staying in the Spiritlands for longer than her required period of rest before choosing to be born again.}

Eleena tugged Aya through a door and into a massive room that was at least as large as the rest of the rooms in the apartment put together. If the rest of the apartment was a disaster, this room was immaculate. It was like the rest of the apartment was a testing floor for what was finished in this massive room. As soon as Aya stepped into the room, everything lit with aetherglow.

Where the other room had been an attempt at creating a globe, this room was the culmination of that attempt. It was like he had somehow peeled the paint off of a globe whole and pasted it onto every surface of the room until you were surrounded by the entire world. Everything was outlined in the ghostly light of the Spirits. The entire room was a magic unto itself. The water in the oceans moved and flowed as if she were looking through a window onto the real thing. Forests waved in an unfelt breeze wherever they were, and even the land itself seemed to breath as the light moved to outline every surface.

A single vibrant line of blue shot from place to place. It was differentiated from any other part of the representation by its brightness and color. It was like the red string in the other room, but somehow, she knew just from looking at it that it was more permanent.

The other room was a plan for the future, but this room was a record of the past. Tears gathered in her eyes as she beheld the life's work of Dedran the Explorer. Like healing or magically invigorating the Heart Tree of a home, it was a magic so beautiful that it was almost impossible to look upon it, for in each of those things, there were so many emotions, so much given into it that it could not be simply taken in or observed in a single glance. Blood, sweat, tears, pain, and joy: all of these things were represented in this room. Aya noticed that the incandescent blue lines joined equally bright points of blue light.

She reached up, and as soon as she touched the point of blue over a place on the map near her home in New York, an image appeared in the air next to her. It was like a golden representation of a hand written scroll. It was transparent, and when Aya reached out to touch it, it felt solid, as if it were real paper. It was a detailed account of what Dedran had found at a place a few hundred miles to the northwest of New York, called Cornell. He had accessed human computer systems there, and with the help of several other ta'el, had deciphered the text held within.

They believed that what they had found was a small but important part of what the humans had done to cause their own extinction. Dedran had summed up the discovery in his notes. It had been part of a technology that could be used to open doorways to other dimensions, like Pathways that reached beyond the boundaries of this reality. Aya knew that other realities existed, and even that with the right magics, it was possible to travel between them, but the Dragons had warned them that those were magics that should only be used if there was some dire need. The records of how to perform the magics and what Spirits were needed to do so were closely guarded secrets.

"This room is wonder made manifest," Aya whispered.

Eleena made a small noise of agreement. "Dedran spent many turns of his youth working on this magic. Spirits of light and water, earth and air, spirits of guile and wit like myself as well, we have all lent our power to this tool," Eleena explained. She pointed to the center of the room.

There, floating in the exact center of the room, was a sphere of what she first thought was glass, but as she approached it, she realized that it was made of various shades of quartz somehow forged into a single brilliant crystal. It was an opaque rainbow of colors, and each layer contained a different spirit. The quartz acted as a physical channel for the power of each small Spirit within, so that they could all work together to act upon the Wild without assistance from a Channeler.

"Scales," Aya swore in awe. "This is a masterful creation. He must have had more help than just Spirits."

"Indeed. Several Channelers participated in the creation of this sphere. It should show me where Dedran is right now, through the magic I have added to its function, but as you can see, there is no green dot anywhere." She gestured around the room.

Aya took her paw away from the blue dot and the transparent scroll she had been reading faded away. "We will find him, Eleena, but how does this help with the marble?"

Eleena stepped away and moved to the sphere. She put her paw on its side. Instantly, a transparent grid of lines emerged from the images projected around the room. Each line was no thicker than a hair, but easily seen due to its soft violet radiance.

"How do we use the numbers on this?" Aya asked.

Eleena grinned and wiggled her whiskers in a way that said 'like this,' or 'watch this.' Then, numbers appeared on all of the lines. Ta'eltesh characters emerged, marking off each line. Aya looked at the human numbers and made the conversion to Ta'eltesh. She walked around the room, following the lines, still not quite sure how they worked.

"How come the numbers up here are the same as the ones down there?" Aya pointed to the northern hemisphere of the room and then the southern hemisphere.

"Numbers like these always include a cardinal direction. There are two main lines that are like the center of the system, and the numbers radiate out from them."

Aya looked at the silver marble in her paw. She didn't see any directions. She rubbed her paw pads over the lines and numbers. At the end of each string of numbers, she felt an almost imperceptible bump. She held up the marble and turned it slowly. The two lines of six numbers were broken down into groups of two with symbols between them. At the end, though, there was another symbol that Aya had not recognized at first. It was a simple triangle, but at the end of each string, the triangle was clearly pointed in a different direction.

"But which direction is which?" Aya mused. "It's something the humans made."

The ta'el used a great deal of the human information structure for the sake of simplicity. Trying to decipher things about the humans while stacking on the extra layer of complexity of translating concepts and ideas into their own language was simply too frustrating. However, not everything could be translated well. Sometimes, they had to do things the hard way.

One of the strict differences between ta'el maps and human ones were the cardinal directions. Humans had used precision instruments to know which direction was which. Ta'el needed no such instrumentation. They had several inborn senses that humans lacked. In some ways, their animal natures also gave them some handicaps that humans did not have. This was not one of them. Ta'el always knew what direction they were facing.

Because there was no need for instruments to make precise judgements of a direction, ta'el had no generalizations for directions. They all used a simple numbering system to indicate the direction being faced. Ta'el knew the cardinal directions that humans had used, but they barely used it at all because it was so imprecise by comparison.

"Does Dedran have any actual human paper maps?"

Eleena didn't respond right away. She just stood looking around the room. Her ghostly orange form turned slowly in a circle before she stopped facing the side of the room that covered Asia and Australia. She glided across the room and pointed to the blue dot that covered the city of Sydney.

"Here. Most of the maps Dedran uses don't have human markings. He has a habit of copying and converting the scales to Ta'el measure, but here he found a map that was an estimation of what the world looked like when all the land was one continent that fascinated him. It had human markings. I can't touch the magic without disrupting it. It's meant for living paws."

Aya followed her across the room and touched the dot. This time, dozens of printed pages appeared in the air. "How does this work?"

"If you grab them by the vertical edge, you can view that particular document in greater detail. If you push the horizontal edges up or down, it will move through the different documents stored here."

Aya pulled up on one in the middle and the documents moved, some disappearing at what was the apparent top of the viewing area. Eventually, one of the documents that floated into the view was larger than the others. It was clearly a drawing of the world, but all of the continents had been forced together into one massive land mass. She pulled it forward and looked it over until she found the compass rose in the upper right-hand corner. She had not studied human mapping methods in any depth. It just wasn't her area of expertise.

The fact that she had known about the grid lines had just been a random memory. She had realized what the gridlines were for, but didn't really know much more about them. She had left that to the Explorers. Unfortunately, there were no Explorers here. The compass rose had the four cardinal directions, but more importantly the map also had a number of lines of text printed on it. This helped her orient the page.

North, as the humans had called it, was pointed towards the top of the page. She turned the marble so the first set of numbers was right side up. The arrow at the end of this set pointed up, just like the arrow on the compass rose that pointed North. She turned the marble for the other set of numbers. This one pointed to the left which matched up with West. Aya touched the blue dot on the wall again and the images vanished.

"So, the first one is North, and the second West. What do we do with the rest of the numbers though?"

Eleena shrugged and one of her ears fell in confusion. "I've learned a lot, but I am no Explorer. I'm not sure how to apply those numbers to the map."

Roan interjected. "I don't think Dedran would have wanted to fight with human calculations on every map or document he unearthed, not with the magic of other Explorers to aid him. Did he have any Explorer Spirits help him with the construction of this?" Greatfather Roan gestured towards the quartz sphere.

Eleena nodded. "Several assisted."

"Touch the sphere and send it the coordinates mentally. It might not work, but I have worked with Explorers before. They work hard to gain all of the necessary knowledge to understand these things themselves, but they are not book learning folk. They're adventurers, which is why they generally meet sudden ends. They're a folk without regrets and without time for anything that might slow them. They are ever looking for ways to get back out on the trail," Roan pointed out.

Aya went to the sphere and did as Roan asked. There was an immediate reaction. A bright white line streaked across the floor to the northwest. It did not go very far from the Sphere before it burst into a bright orange x over a spot not terribly far from their location in Denver.

"Is something that dangerous really that close?" Aya asked.

Eleena nodded. "Yes, there is. It isn't as close as the map makes it seem, but there is an open lava flow in that area. The entire area is unstable, and there's also some sort of Spiritual upheaval there. Dedran must think the installation is there somewhere, but how could it have survived all the destruction in that area?"

"I don't know, Eleena, but I know this much. This marble was left behind after we destroyed the Visceral. It must have had it for a reason."

Chapter 13

"AID"

"We need help. If there are more creatures of the Nether, we will not be enough to destroy them," Roan said as they emerged onto a street where twilight had overcome the day. The evening was oddly empty of other ta'el, unlike the buzz of constant activity that New York gave off.

Aya chalked it up to everyone licking their wounds after the Visceral attack. "I can't ask anyone to go into something like that, Greatfather."

"Can you not?" Roan asked knowingly.

Aya sighed. "I will not involve my friends. This is my path, not theirs."

"I have not said this sooner because up until this point, you were enough, but, going further without help is foolish. Still, if you are bent on this course, then ask help from those in the city."

Aya shook her head again, and her voice came out in a low growl. "I didn't ask for whatever this is, Greatfather. I knew that I might have to fight Corrupted Spirits and maybe even other ta'el if the need arose to protect others, but that is not this. You are not aiming me at the life I envisioned. I refuse to drag anyone else into whatever this is."

Roan looked a little taken aback as burning blue eyes pinned him where he stood. Not by the ferocity of what she said. Aya had never been petit. It was more in how angry she was at him and how bad it made him feel. Because she was right. He was trusting that the Spirits and the White knew what was best for her. He knew exactly how he would have reacted if anyone had tried to steer him like that. He had heard Sahone warn the White about trying to steer Aya. **How could I have been so stupid to try to do the same thing?** It didn't matter that he had done it unwittingly. He had still done it.

"Aya..."

She held up a paw index finger extended to stop him. "I'm no fool, Greatfather. I can also see that the White took advantage of her position to try to shove me along in a direction and she used you to do it. Creator or not, there will be a reckoning for that. I would never insult the Spirits unprovoked, and I will demand the same courtesy in return. If I walk down this path, it will be because it's what I want." Aya shook her finger under his transparent snout and snarled. "Not because it is what someone else wants me to be. Do you understand me, Greatfather?"

Roan nodded somberly. "Yes, Ayasha the Speaker. I understand."

"Good." Aya closed the subject with a sharp smile.

"I still think that you should enlist help for this. There are ta'el in Denver that owe you their lives. Powerful ta'el. At this point, some of them would trade away a body part to help you, I think." He flashed her a small, mischievous smile.

She sighed. "Alright, I will ask, but I didn't do that much." She turned to Eleena, who had been watching their exchange with an expression of awkward amusement painted on her face. "Can you help me find the ta'el who would be best suited for this task, Honored Ancestor?"

"I will," Eleena said.

Aya opened the door and went out into the hallway, leaving the two Spirits to exchange a glance.

"Well, she is certainly your Greatdaughter," Eleena quipped.

"You have _no_ idea, my teacher," Roan replied as he watched Aya turn into the stairwell.

"We'd better catch up. I get the feeling that if we let her out of our sight, we might not get the chance." Eleena faded into the Spiritlands. They caught up to Aya at the exit to the building, on the way down the street towards the main building of the denlodge.

"My first suggestion would be to see if you can enlist Siris."

Aya shook her head. "He isn't a fighter, and I won't take anyone who has cubs."

"Do you know a Lightmend under four hundred turns that doesn't have cubs?" Eleena asked.

It was a fair point. Lightmends almost never had cubs of their own, but because of the relative safety of their calling, they generally took in orphans. There were not an overwhelming amount of orphans among the ta'el, but there were always a few in every city. Ta'el were killed. Even her own position on the Hearth was not safe in any way at all. Corrupted Spirits could often be deadly. That was not even counting the purely mundane ways ta'el got killed while trying to repair the disaster the humans had left behind.

"He's still not a fighter," Aya said.

"Few Lightmends are."

"I'm not winning this argument, am I?" Aya asked.

Eleena shook her head. "They might not be fighters, but I bet he can dodge like you wouldn't believe."

Roan chuckled at Aya's rolled eyes and then turned to head down the street.

Eleena went on, "Besides, just because they don't fight doesn't mean they can't. True, they will never be your equal in combat, but have you ever thought of what it would be like to fight a Lightmend? How would you win?"

Aya paused. Every Lightmend had a Watcher Spirit that had also been a Lightmend. They were universally healers, and while Aya could call on Spirits to heal her body if there was dire need, Lightmends' bodies healed instantly, as long as they were Channeling their Watcher Spirit. They weren't invulnerable by any stretch of the imagination, but they would be damn hard to kill.

"Alright, fine!" Aya growled, "but only as a last resort. If we don't have enough help, I'll ask for Siris."

Eleena pointed down the street, slightly off from center. "He's that way-ish. He's not my charge, but he is Channeling his Watcher right now and I can feel their magic. But if you are going to collect other aid, there are places you should stop along the way." Eleena glided across the street toward a part of towering brick buildings and Roan shrugged, following.

"He'll be in the courtyard this time of round."

Eleena crossed the street, pulling them towards the buildings on the other side. She floated between them, past one's Heart Tree. Aya couldn't fit through the space, so she touched the Heart Tree to send a hello to the Hearth Spirit of the building. It took only a moment to gain permission to climb the tree. Aya sunk her claws into the bark and pulled herself up into it. Eleena was waiting when she dropped from the branches on the other side. She watched Aya for a long moment, expression inscrutable.

"What?" Aya asked.

Eleena didn't respond. Instead, she turned and drifted away once more. Aya followed her out of the alleyway into an open space between several buildings. Green verdigris raced up every building surface of the enclosed courtyard. The buildings began to fade from her senses until the breath of nature filled her with the sense of an ancient forest.

There was a clearing in the middle, about fifty feet across, a small expanse of flat grass. In the center was a medium sized poplar tree. There, not far from the tree, was a ta'el practicing fighting forms. He was about her size, and his movements were smooth and economical. Aya didn't recognize him right away. There was no wasted movement, and she watched him with a critical eye. He was not as liquid as Wanderer Lane, or even Aya herself. She was about to speak when, with the flick of a foot, an odd-looking staff with a short blade at one end leapt into his paws.

While he had been excellent unarmed, with the polearm in his paws, his movements became entrancing fluidity. The weapon became an extension of his body, and he flowed through the forms with a liquid grace he had not been able to obtain with his paws alone. He finished his forms, and then leaned the polearm against the branches of the Heart Tree. He picked up a towel, and then seemed to notice he had had an audience. Aya knew better than to think that he hadn't seen them before. Now that she could get a good look at him, she realized he was also a feline.

She thought a Puma from his tawny coloration, but couldn't be sure. He mopped some sweat out of his fur, and then she saw recognition in his eyes,

"You're the Speaker. You killed the Visceral," he said, a little astonishment in his bass voice.

Aya just nodded.

He turned to the Spirits and bowed. "Honored Ancestors. Eleena the Wildheart, I apologize for not being able to spare time to look for Dedran. Thanks to Siris I am now fully recovered. I will organize an effort to search for him soon."

"May I suggest now? Ancestors, will you introduce me, please?" Aya asked.

"Ayasha the Speaker, this is Arno the Wanderer."

Aya lifted her paw, palm forward in greeting. Arno mirrored her, and they touched paws. Aya had thought at one point that she would become a Wanderer herself. Much like her, they tended to help where they were needed, but Wanderers had no home. There were places they tended to travel through regularly, but the road was their home. Not only that, but Wanderers also enjoyed combat almost as much as they did seeing new places. Aya didn't like fighting. It didn't matter that she was good at it. Hurting things made her feel bad. Wanderers had a completely different outlook on it.

"I'm ready. I'm not crazy about facing another of those blood creatures, especially without my weapon, but I will not shirk my duties out of fear."

Aya allowed an ear and her whiskers to fall, asking what had happened.

"I was helping to outline the edges of a collapse on the eastern edge of the city when it attacked us. I didn't have my Heartblade with me. I didn't think there was any need."

Aya eyed the long staff. The blade affixed to the end was much too long to call a spear, but wasn't any longer than her own Heartblade. It made sense. Wanderers traveled the Wild, and one of the talents that she didn't have that was bred into every Wanderer was a supernatural sense of when danger was near. There was no way to sneak up on a Wanderer if you meant them harm. They could use that sense to feel out how dangerous an area or situation was. He would be perfect for a task like that.

"I fully endorse bringing your Heartblade with you. Do you know of others who might come with us? I need to find Dedran to help Eleena before I can continue with my own journey," Aya explained.

"Will there be more of those things?" Arno asked.

Aya shrugged uncertainly. "I hope not, but if there are, they must be destroyed." Arno looked a little unsure. Aya went on. "When I called the Heart of Fire to help me deal with that thing, it told me that it was bound by its very existence to destroy it. It commanded me to use its power to destroy the Visceral. You ever have a Spirit command you to use its power?"

Arno's eyes went a little wide and his whiskers and ears folded back in astonishment. "It gave you an order?"

"I have never heard of a Spirit commanding anyone to do anything, either. Even when dealing with Corrupted Spirits, they would request our assistance but never give orders. What are we dealing with that a Spirit felt the need to <u>command</u> me to act?"

"You think these things took Dedran, don't you."

Aya nodded. "I do, and I also think that he has uncovered a secret. I think that's why he was taken."

"I know a few ta'el with the right abilities for this kind of hunt. Come, Ayasha the Speaker." Arno quickly attached a strap to the staff of his Heartblade. He slung it across his back and then fell to all fours. His tail waved, indicating that she should follow. Aya dropped to all fours and they began to run. He led her in a straight line across town, towards the main building of the denlodge. Aya caught up and ran beside him.

"Where are we going?" Aya asked.

"To the denlodge. The first ta'el that you should bring into this fight is Kian the Denmaster."

"Truly?" Aya seemed skeptical.

"Kian has a deep bond with one of the stronger earth elementals nearby and is an excellent fighter. Besides, he would be furious if we left him out. That thing almost killed his Greatson and his son is more than ready to be Denmaster in his place if anything happens to him. He will want to be a part of this."

"I can only trust your assessment, Arno. Collect whoever else you think we need to form a search party. I'm going to go and try to recruit a friend to help us," Aya finished and split off from him, heading towards the library.

"Do you know where Ireana is, Greatfather Roan?"

"I have a fair idea."

"Is she ready?"

Aya had not seen her best friend in almost two turns. She had gone into the heart of the Amazon Forest to finish her own training, fully expecting to emerge with the name Stalker.

"I know that she passed her Confirmation several stints before you did. I don't know why she hasn't returned," he replied as he floated along next to her, unperturbed by how fast they were moving.

"And you didn't tell me?"

"You didn't ask, and your last few stints have not exactly been a docile experience. I assure you that training as a Stalker was no less intense for Ireana than it was for you. I had every intention of telling you when there was a lull."

Stalkers were important parts of searching for missing or Corrupted Spirits, among other things. They were always as scarce as true Channelers like herself. Not only were they trained in all methods of tracking things down, both mundane and spiritual, but they also had a knack for finding their way into places they needed to be without being noticed.

Aya needed a quiet place where she could sink into the proper mental space to reach out to her friend with her Spirit.

"Turn right here," Roan said.

Aya turned and loped down the alleyway between the Library and the buildings next to it. When she got to the next block over, the alleyway opened out onto a large somewhat clear space. Pathways paved with beautiful cut granite hexagons in a riot of colors stretched away in various directions. The area she entered was a collection of perfect square spaces. Each space was centered by an ancient tree, each of a different species.

She slowed and pushed herself back onto two paws. She padded onto the grass, and the gentle quiet of the space enveloped her. She slowed as she concentrated. She could not sense anyone else nearby. She approached the small tree supporting a canopy of deep burgundy leaves. The leaves brushed the tips of her ears as she placed a paw against it. She took a deep breath, but there were no scents of any other ta'el. The tree gave her a joyful greeting and she sighed in contentment. She dropped to her knees in the grass and made herself comfortable. She cupped her paws in her lap and let out her anxiety about seeing Ireana again with her breath.

"Please warn away anyone while I concentrate, Greatfather?"

Roan nodded.

Aya closed her eyes and focused. She took a deep breath and relaxed her body. Then she emptied out all of her thoughts. She pushed them away until her mind was a clear space. Once she had, she could see, as if it were projected onto the back of her eyelids, the thick rope of energy that tethered her to the Spiritlands. She reached out with her mind and touched the rope, sending it into the Spiritlands searching for Ireana's Watcher Spirit. Nobian the Stalker had agreed to be Ireana's Watcher when she had first begun her training.

{Ireana the Stalker, I seek your attention,} Aya sent down the rope. A moment later, the response came.

{Who calls for my Charge's attention?} Nobian's response was a little clipped, as if he were distracted.

Ayasha was about to answer when his sending came again, *{Ayasha? No, not just Ayasha anymore.}*

{You are far enough away that you would not have heard yet. The Spirits confirmed me as Ayasha the Speaker.}

{Congratulations, but I must ask. It has been over two turns. Ireana was certain that you had forgotten about us.}

Aya sent a feeling that was the equivalent of a snort of derision. *{I simply thought that if Ireana's training was anything like my own, she could do without the distraction.}*

{You were not far off the mark. She has been waiting to hear from you, but we have not returned to New York because Ireana's tutor asked her to stay and assist with various duties until her other apprentice was ready to take over for her. We were planning on coming home in a couple of spells.}

{Are you both ready, Nobian?} Aya tried to keep her feelings out of the question, but when Nobian responded, she knew she had failed.

{She has changed as much as you have, if I am any judge. Ireana is perfectly capable of taking care of herself. We all have our doubts when we start down a path, but Ireana has earned the name Stalker.}

{Then, Honored Ancestor, I need your help,} Aya finally admitted.

{You have changed. Ireana is about to wake. Since it is she that you reached out to in the first place, I will pass the connection now,} Nobian said.

{Mmm, Is it morning already?} Ireana's voice was as silky as it always had been.

{Not yet. I am sorry to wake you, my Charge, but there has been a request for our attention,} Nobian informed.

{Hi, Ireana,} Aya sent hesitantly.

{Ayasha! I've been waiting for spells for you to find out why I hadn't come home yet,} Ireana said excitedly.

{Things have been moving fast since my Confirmation, Ireana. I'm so sorry I didn't contact you sooner. It's been...}

{Too dangerous for me?} Ireana's voice was not angry like it used to be when Aya had tried to protect her best friend.

{You know how I feel. I'm not going to try to hide the fact that I don't want you in danger, not anymore. But I need your help. I need a Stalker and her Watcher Spirit. Will you come back and help me find my way?}

Chapter 14

"GATHER"

Aya reached the denlodge about a shift after she had left Arno. It had taken some time to arrange things with Ireana so that she could free herself from her duties in the Amazon. She wouldn't be able to arrive for some shifts but would be there in plenty of time to join them.

Passing between the massive heart trees to find an empty Denlodge unsettled Aya. Denmasters had large, extended families or an abundance of apprentices to ensure that the denlodge was always open. Crouching in readiness, Aya crept into the room on silent paws. Roan appeared next to her, forming from crimson mist. Aya inhaled deeply. There were many scents in the room, but they were shifts old, but for a handful, which lead towards the bar. At one end of the massive bar was a set of swinging double doors that her nose told her lead into the kitchen. At the other end of the bar was a door that looked much stouter. A carved sign over the door proclaimed "Denmaster" in flowing Ta'eltesh script.

Carved with hypnotic whorls, the door stood silent. Aya turned her ears forward to listen, but still heard nothing. She reached for the handle. The door popped open and swung inward. Aya's Heartblade was in her paw in an instant as she slid back away from the door. Kian's black and white bulk paused, a slow smile creeping onto his muzzle.

Aya narrowed her eyes and slammed her Heartblade back into its scabbard. "Why is the den empty?" Aya just managed to keep the hiss out of her voice.

"There are four main den rooms since almost everyone in the city takes their meals in our lodge. I have closed this one so we are not disturbed." He stood aside. "Thank you for organizing this, Ayasha the Speaker." Kian bowed to her.

"Please, Kian. I don't..."

The Panda straightened and waved a paw.

"Speaker, if you think that I will ever hold you in anything but reverence, you should observe my Greatson playing Pahn with his friends in the central courtyard and attempt to protest again."

"I'm far too young to be held in reverence."

Kian just shook his head in the face of her weak protest.

"Age has little to do with it, Ayasha the Speaker. As you well know, actions matter. Whether you are five turns old, or five hundred." Kian grinned and turned back to the room.

Inside, there were several ta'el. The room wasn't packed tight, but it was definitely crowded. Everyone watched where they put their paws and tails to make sure that noone's sensitive bits got stepped on. Aya squeezed in at the table. A large map had been rolled out onto it and weighted at the corners with smooth stone discs. Kian made introductions of the eight ta'el in the room.

"These are those who are willing to join us in our search for Dedran. Ayasha the Speaker will be leading this expedition, and if you are to join us, we will be following her orders."

Everyone exchanged a look. Aya rolled her eyes.

"Despite Kian's overzealousness, I will take all advice in areas where I am not well versed, but he is not wrong in one thing. I will find Dedran because I require his help to find out what my name means."

"Good to see that you have a fair head upon your shoulders, Ayasha the Speaker." One of the figures was born of some animal that she did not recognize. He was solidly built with a mottled yellow and brown coat. He was definitely canine-adjacent, but she knew not what to name his species.

"Ayasha the Speaker, this is Iral the Loreseer. He will not be going with us, but I asked him here to give us an advanced look at what is happening at the Downpour right now. That was the last place Eleena had a sense of Dedran. Further, the position that you say that human marble leads to is also dangerously adjacent to the Downpour."

Aya had only heard of Loreseers. They were thought to be some of the most important ta'el when trying to determine what the humans had done. They could see the memories of items and how those items connected to the world.

"You already met Arno." There were several other ta'el crammed into the room, two emta'el and three ehta'el that Kian hadn't introduced yet.

"There will be one more, my best friend, Ireana the Stalker," Ayasha said.

"How long will she be in arriving?" Kian asked.

"Not long. I told her how to make her way here when she arrives. I expect her to arrive within the shift."

"We should be nearly ready by then." Kian continued the introductions, pointing to an emta'el with flowing red hair and a long, ringed tail. She was not born of the Raccoon or the Lemur, as her fur was a festive decoration of red, white, and black. "This is Iryeka the Firecaller." He then pointed to a muscular canine that was almost as large as Kian himself. He had dark grey fur with a collection of white markings. "Karoon the Provisioner." Kian pointed to the next ehta. He was a species she recognized right away because he shared it with Lane the Wanderer. Born of the Banded Mongoose, he waved a nervous paw at her. "Ipsal the Shadeweaver."

Next in line was a squat powerfully built ehta with deep brown fur. He had powerful looking paws with long claws. "Baan the Iceheart." The last ta'el seemed almost delicately built, but when she got up, Aya could see whipcord muscle rippling beneath her pelt. She was a little shorter than Aya, and had a grey and yellow coat covered in large black spots. Her long tail was also ringed, but Aya couldn't identify her species. She spoke before Kian could introduce her.

"I am Kyara the Shimmer." Unexpectedly, she threw her arms around Aya, and clutched her in a hug. "You saved my life. When you came out of the Tunnel and drew the Visceral away, it had been stalking me." Tears dripped from her large, citrine eyes when she pulled back. "Thank you."

Aya smoothed the emta's hair with a paw. "You're welcome, but I didn't do much."

Kyara looked a little incredulous, and then Baan spoke. His voice was deep, and a little raspy.

"Humility is a fine quality, Ayasha the Speaker, but not false modesty." He stared her down when she met his eyes.

Aya just shrugged. She wasn't about to argue the point. It was something she had struggled with all her life. She wasn't going to overcome it just because she had done her duty.

Ipsal was the next to speak up. "What can you tell us about how you killed the thing?"

"Did all of you have an encounter with the Visceral?" Aya asked.

Everyone nodded. Shadeweavers were extremely dangerous in a fight. Their Ancestor Spirits allowed them to shape and solidify shadows. It meant they could attack from any darkness as if it were an extension of their own body. If he had had trouble with the Visceral, it meant that only her connection to the Heart of Fire and her willingness to quench a Heartblade had saved her.

"Does everyone here have a Heartblade?" Aya knew the likely answer was no. The making of a Heartblade had a serious cost both emotionally and physically. The final step of making a Heartblade meant quenching it in your own heart's blood. You had to impale yourself through the heart upon the blade. It wouldn't kill you, of course, but it was not a fun experience.

Aya remembered it very well. The blade had saved her life twice, and she didn't regret going through the process of making it. Only Baan reached behind his back and drew out an enormous knife that was almost a shortsword. It had a wide blade with an oddly flat point that would not allow it to be used for stabbing. However, the thick, cleaver style blade would be very advantageous when blocking. She had already seen Arno's bladed staff. Everyone else shook their heads.

"Does everyone at least have the training to use one properly?"

Nods went around the room, and a variety of blades came out of sheaths and scabbards. Aya frowned. She didn't want to push them to do this, but a Heartblade was the only sure weapon that she had seen work against the Visceral besides fire.

"Is there a Spiritforge in the city?" Aya asked, and everyone who did not already have a Heartblade blanched.

"There are three," Kian said.

"We can't leave for three rounds. I must ask that anyone who is going with us have a Heartblade by then."

"What about fire spirits?" Kyara asked.

Aya shook her head. "That won't do."

Kian nodded in agreement. "There are ways to keep away all but the strongest of Fire Elementals. Not only that, but fire is dangerous for most of us in close quarters."

Ipsal looked at his two blades and swallowed, regret in his eyes.

"You can do them both at once, Ipsal. There is no need to go through it twice. Talk to the Spiritforge. They will help you create a pair of blades that are comfortable for you and act as one blade as well," Aya assured.

Kyara, though, looked absolutely terrified. "I want to go, but I'm not sure I can. The blade scares me."

"Nothing to be ashamed of, Kyara. Quenching a Heartblade is not something everyone has to do. I just know with certainty that a Heartblade hurt the creature."

Kyara looked down at her reflection in the gleaming edge of her straight, thin-bladed sword. She clenched her jaw.

"I will not be afraid like that. Not ever again."

Aya touched the hilt of her own Heartblade in the sheath. Despite the unpleasantness of the making, her blade had always been a comfortable presence.

"I can't do this for you, Kyara, but I will be happy to go with you. We have three rounds. I will even take you to New York with me, and you can meet the Spiritforge who made my Heartblade. She's very gentle, and has a lot of experience getting ta'el through quenching a Heartblade."

Kyara nodded. "I'd like that."

"If we could proceed?" Iral said in a deep bass voice completely out of place on someone his size.

Aya nodded. "I killed the Visceral with fire, but my Heartblade hurt it. I sheered away its hands, and while it grew new ones almost immediately, it was unable to reuse what I sheered away. It turned grey and withered almost immediately."

Iral held his hand out in a gesture familiar to almost any Ta'el. He was Channeling a Spirit that none of them could see. "This is the Downpour." He put his index paw pad down on the map on a spot in the nearby mountains colored in orange. When he pulled his paw away, an image appeared in the air. A flat plane of light that showed an Avian's eye view of an area littered with spears of jagged volcanic rock. There were many black paths surrounded by glowing orange rock flows. In the center was a deep pit, much like the peak of a volcano. It churned with glowing orange lava. The light of the illusion made shadows dance on the carved teak wall panels.

"Currently, there is only one marginally safe path to get to the coordinates you provided, Speaker." The floating image pulled back to show a larger section of the area. Iral pointed a finger at a flat plane of volcanic rock that lead around the rim of the pit. "This area has been examined by Earthwards many times, and they all agree that it is stable."

A knock came at the door, and a very small emta'el cracked the door. She had white fur, tiny pointed ears, and a very long torso. Her face was conical, with a respectable amount of whiskers about her muzzle.

"Sorry I am late," she said shyly. She slipped inside in a sinuous motion, her body almost curling around the edge of the door before she pushed it closed.

"We were not sure if you could make it. Thank you for joining us," Kian welcomed. "This is Lilandra the Earthward."

"Thanks, Kian."

Earthwards were an important part of helping to stabilize, balance, and understand areas of the world where the earth behaved unusually. The Downpour apparently was one of these areas.

"Well now that our expert is here, she can explain the situation," Iral said.

"Please call me Lily. Can I control the image, Iral?"

Iral nodded. "Just gotta stick your paws in it to change the position or shape."

Lily looked around. "Um, I'm going to need a stool."

Kian chuckled, "Sorry, Lily, I wasn't sure if you would make it." He trundled out the door, and was back a moment later, carrying a heavy wooden bar stool. He put it down in front of the image. Lily scrambled up onto the stool and sat behind the semi-transparent image. She stuck a finger through the path that Iral was explaining earlier.

"We are not exactly sure why the Downpour is where it is. We have been attempting to speak directly with the Earth Spirits that inhabit this area for almost two hundred turns at this point. The problem is that there are none. We have to go almost a hundred miles in any direction to speak with Earth Spirits. All they will say is that this is a bad place."

"Why do you call it the Downpour?" Aya interrupted.

"Give it a few minutes and I'll explain that," Lily went on. "The instability of this area is extremely localized. The pit in the center is only about two hundred feet across. We have been able to traverse the magma venting down past the crust, and it is an almost perfectly straight shot, as if someone drilled straight down past the crust until they broke a magma vein, but I don't see the point of that. Regardless, this means that geologically, the area is much more stable than it seems."

Lily trailed off as the magma in the image began to bubble violently. "Here it comes."

A massive jet of molten rock at least twenty feet across burst up from the surface of the lava. It shot into the sky at least two hundred feet before blossoming into a liquid orange flower. From this safe vantage, it was quite beautiful to watch. However, a moment later, glowing stars of liquid rock began to fall from the sky like rain. Most of it managed to fall back into the pool of lava, but tiny raging dots shot out around the pool, landing on the ledges and pathways in all directions. There was no question exactly why they called it the Downpour.

"The way the plate floats above the mantle in this area creates regular eruptions from the pool. However, there is no danger of a mass eruption like in regular volcanic areas. The pressure release is too regular for the kind of massive buildup that is required for a larger eruption, at least at this time.

There is always at least one Earthward monitoring the situation."

"Is this image actually what is happening there right now?" Baan asked.

Iral nodded. "My magic works in very useful ways with items like maps. I can get a real-time image of any area the map depicts."

"Can't we just use your power to search?" Iryeka asked.

Iral shook his head. "No, the map is tied to the land, so I can only see that much."

"And the coordinates?" Aya asked.

Iral put his paw into the image. He swished it to the right, and the image moved in a blur until he spun a finger in the image and it zoomed down. "We are not sure what is special about this area. Lily, were you able to approach and search the area while submerged?"

Lily shook her head. "We could get close to it, and there is definitely something there below the surface, but the underground area felt very dangerous to my Watcher Spirit. Ireyane said we would be in great danger if we entered. She thinks that it may be a nest of Corrupted Spirits."

Everyone looked towards her at that, and the petit emta'el shrank under their eyes.

Nests were extremely uncommon. For a nest of Corrupted Ones to happen, there had to be something metaphysically broken about the area. There had only been a few hundred nests discovered in over seven thousand turns of their history. Most notable of the horrors they had discovered in the world had been a massive area of the northeastern United States. It was said that the abomination they found roaming the land there was what had finally killed The Grey, who gave his life to cleanse the immense amalgamation of thousands of Corrupted Nature Spirits and what the Grey believed was one old god of the native human peoples.

Aya swallowed. "So, do we think that something abducted Dedran and pulled him into the nest? It would explain why you are unable to locate him, Eleena." The Spirits had up to this point remained invisible to make the room feel less crowded, but now Eleena faded into view.

"It is a possibility. He may have also gone into the place on his own, unaware of what he was getting into. Dedran's sense of self-preservation in the face of completing his work has never been what I would describe as exemplary," Eleena posited.

"Regardless of how he got there, I think Aya's instincts are right. I can't imagine where else he would have gone. We will either find him there, or we will find his body," Arno said. "We will bring him back either way, Eleena."

"I appreciate that, but why are we waiting three rounds if your Stalker is coming in so soon?" Iryeka asked.

The door clicked open.

"Here so soon," a feminine voice said from the door. Ireana entered the room. She was the largest ta'el present except for Kian. She should not have been, considering her species, but Ireana was the statistical outlier. Born of the wolf, she had a mottled grey and brown pelt with black socks on her paws and feet that ran to the wrist and ankle. Long silver hair was tied into a tight bun on the back of her head.

"Welcome. Everyone, this is Ireana the Stalker, my best friend."

"Welcome, Stalker. It will be great to have a Stalker along with us. I'm not a fan of ambushes."

"I warn you that I have all of the necessary training, but I do not have an abundance of experience. However, with some help from my Watcher, I should be able to perform up to your expectations," Ireana said before moving to Aya and putting her arms around the smaller emta. The hug lasted a little longer than was strictly comfortable for everyone in the room, but Aya didn't let go until Ireana stepped back.

"Sorry, everyone, it's been a long time," Aya said.

"Do you have suggestions for approaching this, Stalker?" Baan asked.

"Fill me in."

It didn't take long to bring her up to speed. At first, she let everyone else go on while she sat staring at the image Iral was projecting. Her tail swayed back and forth slowly, telling everyone who understood the canine dialects of Ta'eltesh that she was concerned, but still thinking. Finally she spoke, and somehow, it cut through all the other conversation in the room.

"I don't like this single approach. The lava in the area has made even this simple approach suicide. If someone is ready to defend this position, especially if they are creatures that are tough enough to give Aya trouble, we are going to be in far more danger than I find acceptable. I know we have to look for Dedran, but I think maybe our group is too small for this sort of thing."

"I have to go with or without help," Aya said plainly.

Ireana looked at her and dropped an ear quizzically. Aya pulled her whiskers back, and tilted her ears to the left, saying she would explain later.

"If we have to go, then I would like to suggest that we employ some assistance from the Earthwards to make us an alternate path, if they would be willing?" Lily twitched her whiskers backwards and shook her head.

"The land is dead there. We can't coax any Spirit to go near the place."

"Might I speak to your Watcher?" Aya asked.

Lily shrugged. She held out her tiny paw to the left, and a moment later, a Watcher spirit formed from viridian mist. Aya nodded to Lily. Interestingly, the spirit was almost a twin to Lily.

"Honored Ancestor, please explain what makes you so reluctant to enter this area."

"Nisane the Earthward. There is a darkness in that place. I do not wish to go near it, and you will not find a Spirit that will willingly venture anywhere near that place."

"Honored Ancestor, I have a task from the White. As it would be immeasurably rude of me, I would never try to force you to do this, but I need your assistance to keep everyone safe. I do not believe what Ireana is suggesting will take you inside where you do not want to go. I believe she simply wishes for you to shape the land around the area to provide us with a different approach.

If you can use the Earth to pierce into whatever facility the humans have left behind, I will not ask you to enter. Simply make a door and hold it open for us. If you are offered any resistance after we pass inside, I would wish for you to flee. I know you are not all fighters."

"All ta'el are fighters, Ayasha the Speaker. We just do not all do our fighting with our fists." Nisane paused seemingly to consider, but a moment later, she sighed. "I will speak with the other Earthwards. However, your request is more than reasonable, Hearth Stone. It must be a request, but the others will agree."

Lily looked a little green, and her whiskers wilted along with her tail, which said she felt sick.

Aya put a paw on her shoulder.

"Do not worry, Lily. You will not need to fight, and if your Watcher Spirit agrees to allow me to be her Channel, I would be just as happy to have you stay in the city."

Lily nodded, but a moment later, her whiskers stood out and her face hardened. "No, I will go. I am used to moving earth and moving through it. You're not. You need me."

Aya nodded. "We'll keep you safe Lily, and I give you the same advice that I gave to your Watcher. If you are offered any resistance, you should leave us and flee. We are fully capable of taking care of ourselves. I would ask that some of the Watcher Spirits stay nearby in the Spiritlands so that I might call on them if I need them to assist in our escape."

Lily nodded.

"Back to your earlier question, Ireyka. We need a few rounds for proper preparation. Ireana will need time to actually investigate the area. I'm sure she has some ideas as to how to improve our approach, but we will need to investigate first paw to make a truly effective plan. Not only that, I believe that each of us having a Heartblade will be crucial to survival going into this situation.

It will take a round to forge each Heartblade and a round to recover from the quenching. It's taxing for the Spiritforge doing the work. We cannot even simply use the ones in the city because they will need to rest between forging the blades. I do not know all of you, and it may take you a little time to work up the nerve to quench a Heartblade. That is perfectly understandable."

"Also to make us as prepared as possible, there are some other ta'el that we should visit. Your father should be able to provide us with some simple potions to keep us alive," Ireana suggested.

Aya nodded. "I don't know what his supply looks like these rounds, though. They haven't been home in two turns just like you, Ireana."

"Knowing your father, I fail to believe that his supply has dwindled even knowing that." Ireana's tail wagged a little more quickly which said encouragement.

"I thought about contacting him, and asked Greatfather Roan if he would make the trip this evening to get permission from him to raid his stores."

"We will get to work on our Heartblades," Ireyka said.

"I want you all to come with us, but make no mistake I am far more interested in your survival. There is no shame in not being able to perform an act like quenching a Heartblade, but you should not come if you cannot," Aya said.

Everyone nodded.

"It's a fair requirement for what we are about to do," Baan said, and there were agreements around the room. "We should get to it."

Chapter 15

"ENOUGH"

Kyara followed Aya and Ireana out of the denlodge.

"I don't mean to be presumptuous, but do we have enough ta'el for this?" she asked.

Aya seemed distracted by the nearby unrestored remnants of human civilization partially reclaimed by overgrown nature. Finally her ears came up and she turned back to Kyara

"If you were worried about that, why didn't you bring it up in the meeting?"

Kyara looked away shyly when Aya eyed her.

"Kyara, despite the confidence I'm showing, I promise you that I am no more experienced than you are. I have some experiences that others do not. Still, I have only been Confirmed for two short spans. Ireana, not much more than that. If you have opinions, you have to speak up."

Kyara's ears folded back shyly and she put her paws behind her back, grabbing one arm with the opposite paw. It was such a bashful posture for someone Aya knew had been trained in combat. Kyara wouldn't have been in that room if she wasn't excellent. There had never been a Wanderer born that was not a great fighter. Arno would not take anyone who he didn't respect in that regard.

"Ireana, do you have a Heartblade?"

The wolf shivered and shook her head. "I don't know how you did it, but I will find out," Ireana said determinedly.

"Then we will need to see Leona."

Kyara looked at her with some interest.

"She's a gentle soul," Ireana reassured. "She has been the Spiritforge in New York for two hundred turns."

"She is also Ireana's Greatmother."

Kyara's interested look intensified. "But..." Kyara began.

"Nope," Ireana said immediately.

Kyara opened her muzzle and Ireana glared at her.

"Look. See this?" She held up her balled fist. "This is what you are about to ask." She held up her other paw. "And this is the nope bag." She smashed her fist into her other paw. "And that over there," she pointed into the distance. "That's the nope ocean." She drew back her paw and threw the nothing in the direction she pointed. She narrowed her eyes at Kyara. "Get the picture?"

"She's a little sensitive about the fact that no one can understand how a Spiritforge produces a Stalker."

It was not incredibly common for children to take on the callings of their parents among the Ta'el, but some callings almost always passed from parents to children. Spiritforge was one of those. Creating Heartblades was not the only thing a Spiritforge could do, but it was what they were most well known for. Their trade, imbuing metal with magical energies, was a trade that took a lifetime to learn. Most Spiritforges held their first hammer before they learned how to walk upright.

Ireana had never been a Spiritforge, even though almost all of her ancestors had been among their ranks. There were never ever enough Spiritforges. It made Ireana's choice one that most other ta'el didn't grasp. The idea that a Spiritforge would not produce another Spiritforge was somewhat alien. Ireana squinted at Aya and held up a balled fist, but Aya just shrugged.

"Anytime you think you've got what it takes, skyscraper, I'll take care of that problem for you."

Kyara burst out laughing. Ireana had at least thirty pounds on Aya and a good four inches of height. She looked at Kyara.

"Oh no, she's not joking. She would have me wearing my ass as a hat in a minute or less," Ireana said, without the slightest bit of ego. "I may be bigger and scarier **looking**, but you don't ever want to get into a scrap with this one. Never seen anyone fight a Wanderer to a standstill before."

Kyara looked a little stunned.

"I've fought Arno dozens of times and I've never beat him. He's so strong and fast. It's like he never gets tired," Kyara said, looking at Aya with a little awe.

"Stop it. You're embarrassing me, and you know I don't like fighting. I'd be happier being known for what I really like doing, helping other ta'el." Aya's annoyance was clear.

"Alright, I'm sorry, Ayasha," Ireana apologized, "but honestly, I'm the embarrassed one. I've always been bigger than Aya, and she thrashes me like I'm an amateur whenever we spar. She always has."

"Cats are just better," Aya said with a smirk.

Ireana swatted at her, and Aya stepped out of the way without any trouble at all. Kyara was watching them both with a quiet smile. Foot traffic picked up as they got closer to the library, and the conversation trailed off as they dodged around other ta'el.

"You two are…" She trailed off when they both looked at her with interest, "mated?" Ireana looked to Aya, who looked away.

"Nothing like that. Just best friends," Aya said.

Kyara shook her head. "Just friends don't look like this."

Ireana laughed. "We aren't there yet, Kyara, but I'm hoping this ball of fluff will come around to the idea eventually."

Ireana was so candid about the fact that she had been chasing Aya since they both understood what it was to be mated. Aya was so busy praying to anyone who might listen that neither of them scented her embarrassment that she didn't even notice she had reached the portal square. It was a sad little hope, considering how good Ireana's sense of smell was. She suspected Kyara was no slouch in the nose department either.

"I've never been through the Tunnel before," Kyara said.

"Just don't stumble when you take the last step. It can be jarring the first time," Aya instructed. "Let us go through first, and we'll catch you on the other side if you fall down."

The metaphysical Tunnel had been attached to a large stone archway in a courtyard just outside of the library building. It filled the arch with a whirlpool of glowing light. Most of the whirling glow was a deep purple color with lines of bright white light swirling through it. Aya walked through it and vanished. Ireana walked through behind her. She appeared in New York, and Aya was standing there waiting for her. Then, both stood to one side of the Tunnel. A moment later, Kyara's head popped through, and then she jerked forward, stumbling. Ireana and Aya each caught an arm before she could fall down and stood her backup.

"You have to just walk through. Everyone falls down the first time they go through the Tunnel. It won't tolerate you being in both places at once, so if you don't just walk through, it will sort of puke you out the other side. Everyone hesitates, though, because it's so weird," Ireana explained.

"That's why Pathways are always walked out on the ground and you fall through them. They aren't as stable as the Tunnel, but they work the same way. Because of their instability, if you lingered at all, there is a chance you could get…" Aya paused, trying to find a gentle way to say it.

"Ripped in half," Ireana finished.

Kyara paled and her face went a little slack.

"I've been though a Pathway at least a dozen times," Kyara said slowly.

"Well, as long as no one figures out how to walk one out on a wall, you'll be fine," Aya replied.

Ireana led the way towards Shop Row. She had not been home in two turns, and her mother had no idea she was coming. She had not had time to send any messages ahead.

"Then how do you know what would happen?" Kyara asked.

"Because some damn fool figured out how to walk one out on a wall," Ireana grumbled.

Aya snorted sardonically. "A long time ago, a very foolish young Wanderer thought that he could find a way to make permanent Pathways without working with the geography of the Spiritlands. Unfortunately for him, he discovered the problem of lingering for even a moment between two ends of a Pathway," Aya explained as they moved about the dozens of ta'el still flooding the streets of New York despite the late hour.

"We should take the roofways," Aya said.

"Not all of us can easily climb massive heart trees," Ireana complained.

"Some Stalker you are. A little tree climbing slows you down?" Aya teased.

Ireana made a sound of annoyance. "Not without my climbing grips. I usually have them on me, but I was carrying a lot of stuff when I came through the Pathway. I left it all at the Hearth when Lane brought me through because **someone** told me I needed to drop what I was doing and get my tail to Denver preround."

Aya sighed and reached into the pouch at her side, taking out a small potion ampule. Inside of the bottle was a tiny simulacrum that looked like a plush version of Aya herself. Anyone who drank it would get her normal talents through a minor shapeshifting magic. It didn't provide anything truly magical, but rather only things she possessed as a clouded leopard. One of those was the ability to climb. The potion also made someone look like an interesting hybrid of their species an Aya's own. She held out the phial to Ireana.

"Thanks, Spots." Ireana looked to Kyara.

"I can climb extremely well." Kyara suited her own words and leapt onto the side of the nearest Heart Tree. It was holding up a three-story building with a large staircase leading up the front of the building. At each floor was a large balcony connected to the staircase.

Ireana downed the potion and her body shivered. Amazingly, her fur lightened from mottled brown and grey all the way to an almost blonde yellow. Her claws changed, lengthening slightly and sharpening to bright razor points. Her tail thinned until it was much more feline, though it still had a rough of fur that made it shapelier than a feline tail. She jumped onto the side of the tree as easily as any feline and followed them to the roof.

"That's amazing," Kyara commented.

"It's a fairly simple potion. You can make it too. Almost anyone can, but it means dulling your..." Aya paused, looking for the words, "Felineness? It's the only way I know to say it. The potion takes in some of your essence, so you will feel odd for a shift or two after making it. I can show you how, if you like."

They hopped down from a branch of the tree that extended over the flat roof of the building and headed for the other side.

"How do you know how to make it? Don't you need magical talents to even know what to put into a potion?"

"Sort of. Some simpler potions, once you know the ingredients, you can make even without a Brewsmith, especially when the potion is so personal to you."

Aya paused at the gap that had been cut into the short brick wall surrounding the roof. A wide bridge with short wrought iron railings extended across to the next building over.

"How long am I going to look like this?" Ireana asked.

"Couple shifts tops. I think you look amazing."

"Thanks?" Ireana said. She ran her paw through her shoulder length hair, which was an odd shade of steely blue as opposed to its typical silver. She held it up in front of her eyes.

"Your natural color comes through in the potion?" Ireana asked.

"A little of everything comes through. You're basically getting a little dose of my essence. It gives you most of my physical abilities, but you also get a mix of some of my looks. I thought you liked my hair."

"The blue looks great on you," Ireana grumbled. "How… feline do I look?"

She reached up and touched her ears, feeling around the edge. They had gone from two sharp triangles to shorter, more rounded shapes. "Scales! I have round ears!" Ireana griped.

Aya waved a paw. "You look fine. Come on, we don't have time to mess around."

"I can't go home looking like this!"

Aya rolled her eyes. "Yeah, because your mom has never drank a potion that had some side effects in her entire life."

Ireana sighed. "Fair point. She lost all her hair to that strength enhancing potion for an entire spell, even though the potion wore off after a shift. Looked like an ehta for spells."

"She wanted to forge an Essence Siphon entirely by paw without any help from the Spirits."

"She did it, too."

"That emta has too much pride for ten ta'el."

Ireana shook her head. "She doesn't like anyone thinking she is foolish, so she proves ta'el wrong when they tell her she can't do a thing. What's prideful about that?"

Aya shrugged it off. She was not fond of Ireana's mother's attitude toward her daughter. They followed the roofways across the city. Shop Row was a twenty bout walk from the exit to the Tunnel, but none of them was moving slow, so they made it in ten.

"So, about the earlier question of having enough ta'el," Kyara asked.

"It's a good point, but the fact that we really don't know what we are getting into means that taking a huge force of ta'el into the place could be an even bigger disaster than not taking enough. With a small force, we can be mobile. Get in and out. Considering this area is underground, it is unlikely that superior numbers will be good for much. If there was a massive cave where they could surround us, it might be a problem, but I think that Aya is planning a little insurance to make sure we all get out just fine," Ireana said, and Aya nodded in response.

"If you would be so kind, Honored Ancestor?"

Aya didn't want to bring him fully through into the Wild, but she held out her hand, and Lane the Wanderer took it. He appeared next to them, walking in lock step across the rooftops. He didn't say anything, but waved to Kyara. Aya had not brought him through fully enough to speak. Kyara paused, and then bowed to Lane. They all stopped and watched Kyara with interest.

"I've never actually met a Wanderer Ancestor before. I've been through plenty of Pathways but never actually met the Spirit making the Pathway." Lane paused, and returned the bow.

{She's respectful. I like her,} Lane spoke into Aya's thoughts.

{She doesn't know you that well,} Aya replied with a grin.

{That's a fair point.} Lane shook a little with silent laughter.

{We will need more than one of you, Lane. If we must split up, we will need multiple Pathways to get us out of there.}

{Will it be a huge inconvenience to gain assistance from that many Wanderers?} Roan broke into the conversation, though he didn't appear visibly. It was a fair question. Get too many Wanderers into the same place and there was bound to be a fight.

{I don't think it will be a problem,} Lane responded. *{As Spirits, we are able to get along a little better than in life. Aya, I would like to investigate the Below Places. If you intend to go there, you should let me find out more about it.}*

{I get the sense that maybe The Below Places are more than just the place in that book. We might need to go there to finish whatever this is, but I feel like we are on the right path.}

{I don't feel like you are wrong, but I also feel like there is a lot we are missing. These creatures are powerful, but I don't think they have the kind of power necessary to Dispell the connection between the Ta'el and the Life Spirit even for short periods of time. Even the mystery of how Corrupted Spirits passed our barriers into New York is currently beyond our reach. There is so much to do,} Roan said.

{Thankfully, one of those two mysteries have been passed along to someone else. I cannot do it all, Greatfather,} Aya said.

{That is wise of you, Little Aya, wiser than I had expected you to be.} That came from Lane. There was no accusation or criticism in his words. He actually sounded proud.

{Thank you, Lane.}

{And one other thing I would like to clarify as I have been told by many that I was not clear. The round I pronounced you competent, I meant that you had learned everything I could teach you. I knew that you had no love for fighting so I thought that competent was what you needed to hear.}

When she didn't respond, he went on.

{Ayasha the Speaker, you might not ever surpass me as a martial artist, but you are my equal, and have long since surpassed me as a ta'el. You never hesitate for even a moment to do what is right. That is more than I can say for my choices in life.} He could feel that Aya was stunned to hear that confession from him. A wan smile crossed his face. *{We all fail, Ayasha the Speaker, but not every failure is honest. Many of mine certainly were not. We are almost to Shop Row, and they are starting to notice you are not with them right now.}*

Aya pulled herself from the flow of the mental conversation.

"...doesn't actually hurt you physically. It's just that when you watch hundreds of ta'el willing to stab themselves in the heart with glowing hot steel it gets a little..." Ireana shivered.

"Then how do you know?"

"Well, before I decided that I wanted to be a Stalker I was training to be a Spiritforge myself, so I've been cut with Spirit imbued steel before. It's part of the training. You have to know it's not going to hurt for yourself before you can convince anyone else, but watching other ta'el do it over and over again as I got a little older didn't have a positive effect on me."

Ireana made a face. "When I threw up the last time I was in the forge, my mother decided that my insistence that I wanted to be a Stalker was something more than a childish phase," Ireana explained.

"If it was that disconcerting for you, how are you going to do it now?" Kyara asked.

"I don't know, but it's been turns since I was that cub. I've trained long and hard to become a Stalker. I can only hope that training has hardened me enough to be prepared for this."

"It's not easy. I know I was worried sick for rounds about it before I did it, but Leona knew just what to say to help me. Most Spiritforges have a talent for it, and Leona is no exception."

They crossed the mid-town bridge which stretched a long way across a massive street that was just over a hundred feet wide. Then they followed the roofway south until they made it to Shop Row. They slipped down the Heart Tree to the second floor of the building that held Leona's shop.

"Why are we stopping here?" Aya asked.

"She's not in the shop. Leona is only in the shop in the early morning these rounds. With my brother and sister as apprentices they, she says, have too many smiths in the forge. She only goes down when there is something special that needs forging that Mom can't handle alone. She'll help them start a new forge soon."

"Isn't she a little old for that?"

"She's four hundred forty turns old, but if our family is an indicator, that's about middle aged," Ireana chuckled as they stepped onto the balcony.

"Besides, if you call me old again, child, I will have to thump you." A voice that was much like Ireana's, but a little deeper in pitch came from the porch wrapped around the second floor. "Welcome home, Ireana."

The emta'el standing on the porch was almost a mirror image of Ireana, if quite a bit shorter. Her coat was a deep gray that was almost black, and she had bright green eyes. As soon as Ireana's paws hit the porch, Leona wrapped her arms around her shoulders and pulled her into a hug.

"Congratulations on your confirmation. Your brother and sister will be overjoyed that you made it out of the Amazon with your..." She paused and held Ireana out at arm's length. "What in the Wild have you done to yourself?"

"It'll wear off in a little while. She drank an essence potion so she could climb with us. She was in a hurry to get to me at my request, so she left behind some of her things that would have aided her. I felt it only proper that I provide assistance since she was answering my call," Aya filled in.

"Oh ho." Leona laughed. "Imposing upon our new Hearth Stone already are we?" she teased.

"More like she is imposing upon me," Ireana said, gesturing to her features. "Wait, our Hearth Stone?" Ireana gave Aya the side eye. Aya just shrugged.

"Well if I am being honest, it's certainly a different look for you. Not bad at all. I like the color." Leona gently touched one of the bright blue highlights threaded through Ireana's silver hair.

"Yeah, well, I can get a less invasive potion if I want some colors in my hair," Ireana complained, "but my natural color is much better for blending in."

"Suppose that is a valid concern for you, these rounds," Leona said. "Who is this one?" Lenoa gestured to Kyara.

"This is Kyara the Shimmer. We both will require Heartblades, and we only have three rounds to acquire them. Can you help us, Greatmother?"

Lenoa looked a little startled. "I didn't think you'd ever be asking for that."

"Me either, but our new Hearth Stone requires us to have them for an important task."

"It is doable, but we'll need your mother's help." Ireana's expression soured a little.

"Is that a problem?" Kyara asked. Aya pointed off to the side where Ireana couldn't see. She lowered her voice to a whisper while Ireana talked with her Greatmother.

"Ireana's mother Tiana is a lot like Leona. She's an excellent Spiritforge. The problem is she has never approved of Ireana not becoming one herself. They are always in such short supply that Tiana has always felt it is the duty of anyone in her family to take on the job of providing the magical items that all Ta'el need. She is not precisely spiteful to Ireana, but she is not exactly pleasant. Every conversation becomes about that."

Aya had always felt a little ire when it came to the way Tiana treated Ireana, but she never felt it was her place to say anything about it. Stalkers were just as rare as Spiritforges.

Leona gave her a meaningful look when Ireana turned away. The look said, "You're the Hearth Stone, do something about this." Aya realized that at this point, she could do just that. Harmony among the ta'el was part of her business. Still, she wasn't sure she could be impartial in this. She tried to think of the situation objectively.

Ireana had been sad because when she was younger she had had an excellent relationship with her mother. It was only when she chose not to be a Spiritforge that their relationship degraded. She didn't feel right doing it, though. While she wasn't certain that she was ready to have a mate, Aya was certain that if she ever was, it would be Ireana. Aya drew herself up and stifled a sigh.

"Leona the Spiritforge, may I speak with you in private?" she said formally. Everyone turned to her, and when they did, their expressions changed. She must have used the correct bearing, because from the way they bowed their heads, all three of them saw not Aya, but a Stone of the Hearth.

"Of course, Hearth Stone." Leona held out a paw towards the sliding door to the small rooftop garden that was part of almost every ta'el home in the city. Aya went out and Leona slid the door closed behind them.

"I'm so tired of this. I have tried to set Tiana straight so many times. Will you please help me?" Lenoa began.

Aya shook her head. "I don't think I can. I don't think that Tiana will listen to me either. She knows just as well as anyone else that if I ever do take a mate, it will be Ireana."

Leona grinned knowingly.

"That being said, she will not believe I am being objective. She will think that I am just defending her daughter because of the way I feel. Instead, allow me to offer this. Allow me to speak to someone else in the Hearth, someone that I think Tiana will listen to."

"Scales," Leona swore. "Please, Hearth Stone. I will take whatever advice you have to offer to mend this stupid divide between them."

"It will take a little time to speak with the right ta'el, but I will help you, Leona. I just don't feel like my own personal intervention is what is needed here."

Leona sighed. "Well I suppose I should have expected that. I accept, Heart Stone. Thank you."

Aya sighed in relief. "Now that that's done, why don't we simplify this? I assume that if we get you a place that you can work, we can keep Ireana away from Tiana until her issues are resolved?" Leona nodded. "We'll have Kyara stay here, and Tiana can make her Heartblade. I'll talk to Hurun and get him to open his forge to you so that you can work on Ireana's blade."

"Hurun will not let me work in his forge."

"He will if I tell him to clear out or I'll make sure that every wind spirit will vacate his forge for the next hundred turns. I haven't the time for stupid matters of pride." Aya shook her head.

"Hurun is every bit as talented as I am. Ireana could simply ask him to forge her blade."

Aya shrugged. "Is that what you really want?"

Leona shook her head. "I could just punch Hurun out if it would be more convenient?" Leona offered, flexing impressive muscles in her right arm. Aya rolled her eyes, and Leona laughed. "I gratefully accept your offer, Hearth Stone." Leona bowed to her.

"I'd do a lot more than clubbing sense into Hurun to make sure this goes easy for Ireana. She's not ready for this. I certainly wasn't."

"You were eleven turns old when you marched into the forge with Wanderer Lane. Barely halfway through your training. I hadn't often seen many ta'el so determined to get a Heartblade, especially after counting only a decade of turns."

"I was terrified! Lane gifted me that blade as part of my training, but when he told me how it was made, I almost couldn't work up the courage."

"Oh, I know, but you have never been one to let fear stop you from doing anything."

"She's going to need your help, not Hurun's. He's a talented Spiritforge, but his approach to getting ta'el through quenching a blade is not the right one for Ireana."

Leona straightened from her bow.

"I hope you find what I can offer sufficient," Aya said.

"It is indeed enough."

"Thanks for not treating me like the cub whose nappies you used to change on occasion."

Leona shrugged. "You're not that cub anymore, Ayasha, and considering the way you are handling this, everyone would do well to remember that. And frankly, everyone would do well to remember that about Ireana as well. I just hope whoever you have in mind will be able to drive that point home through my daughter's thick skull."

"When you see who I have in mind, I think you will have few doubts of that."

Chapter 16

"THE BLADE ITSELF"

Ireana watched as her Greatmother fed a small log of seasoned oak into the kiln beneath the open face of the forge.

"Normally, I would speak with Spirits to determine the best blade for you. However, while you are not a Spiritforge, you've had enough of the training that it is unnecessary?" Leona asked.

Ireana nodded and drew two feet of pattern-welded steel from a scabbard slung at an angle across the small of her back. She flipped it from her reversed grip to something more standard. The blade's thick blunt spine opposed a straight edge that curved upwards at the tip. The edge gleamed bright and was well cared for.

"This blade shape fits me well, but the blade is slightly unbalanced. Not a fault of the smith, just what I asked for. I have since learned that it doesn't quite suit the style that Aya and Lane the Wanderer have drilled me on. I need something with a lighter spine."

"Worried that you'd break the spine using it for blocking like that?" Leona guessed.

Ireana nodded. "And for powerful blocks, it's better to have one blunt edge so I can twist the blade to catch strikes on the flat and brace with my arm."

"Alright, now for the most important question," Leona began.

"I am a Stalker. My blade must be simple and strong. Not just an instrument for killing, but a tool to fulfill my duties."

Ireana sat down on a stone bench with a leather pad. The interior of Hurun's forge was surprisingly different from their own. As much as it was a place where dangerous work was performed with hot metal and spiritual power, her mother and Greatmother had attempted to give the forge a welcoming feel for those times when Heartblades had to be forged and quenched. It comforted the nerves to be in Tiana's forge.

Hurun's forge by comparison was almost clinical. Stark white stone walls enclosed the workspace of an obsessive. Tools in racks next to the forge were polished as if they had never been touched. Tiana and her brothers and sisters never let their forge lapse, but there was a certain amount of lived-in-ness about it. Hurun scrubbed his as if it were an operating theater.

A bench of white marble topped with black leather pads stood nearby for visitors to use. They were comfortable and stable, just what was needed for quenching a Heartblade. The forge was a perfectly scrubbed amalgamation of hardened clay and solid stone tucked neatly into the corner of the large room. A single, solid piece of carved crystal served as the anvil. It seemed as if it would shatter the moment a hammer touched it. Still, Leona did not hesitate a moment to tap one of Hurun's forging hammers upon it. The note that rebounded from the strike of the hammer was pure and musical. Leona smiled at the sound.

"Can't say Hurun doesn't do good work, even if he *is* wound tighter than a launch spring."

"Place is creepy," Ireana responded.

Lenoa chuckled and reached into a leather satchel. "I though you might think it was, so I brought something from home to improve the ambiance."

Leona pulled out a stuffed toy shaped like an eastern dragon. It was crafted with amazing detail, with hundreds of shimmering emerald scales made of buttery soft leather somehow polished to a lustrous sheen. She set the toy on the bench next to Ireana.

"I know you're not a cub anymore, but I though that he might help make this place feel a little more like home."

Ireana's muzzle curved into a gentle smile. "Thank you, Greatmother. Juji is a comfort."

Soft footsteps came from behind her, and she turned to see Aya entering through the door to the forge. Leona got up and went to the wall of neatly stacked bar stock, leaving them to speak.

"Sorry, it took me a moment to finish chasing Hurun out of here. How does anyone get a Heartblade from that flat-brained blowhard?" she wondered. Leona chuckled, accompanied by the clinking of metal bars.

"Some Ta'el are partial to that gruff sort of straight forward support. No one can accuse him of being a slacker. Would you be so kind as to infuse some of his stock so that we do not use any of his, Hearth Stone?" Leona addressed Ayasha professionally.

"I've never done it before, but I know the principle. I'll try." Ayasha moved to the shelving and stood next to Leona.

Leona took several bars of steel out of the rack and held them out to Aya. Aya touched the metal with one paw and then reached up to the neat shelving that was, nonetheless, made of the living Heart Tree of the building.

{Honored Elemental, if you would be so kind as to provide me with some of your magic?} Aya sent to the Hearth Spirit.

The Hearth Spirit sent back warm greetings and an affirmative response. Warmth flowed up Aya's arm as the Hearth Spirit provided a neutral energy.

"Ok, so I have to be careful not to touch this with any of my own Spirit, correct?"

Leona nodded. "Pure neutral energy accepts the Spirit of the blade's user more readily. There is usually some sort of personal investment attached. From what I understand, it's extremely difficult to keep it completely free of personal investment."

Aya nodded. "I can't keep it completely pure. There are only two ta'el I know of that are skilled enough to do that, The Matron Keystone and my Mother." She shook her head and sighed. "I need to concentrate for a minute to do this right."

Aya took the small collection of steel bars out of Leona's paws and then climbed onto the bench beside Ireana. She folded her legs into the lotus position, and laid the bars across her lap. With some effort, she held the energy in her body away from her own Spirit. To infuse the metal, she would need to use her body to complete a circuit to pass the Spiritual energy from the Hearth Spirit through the bars.

With an effort of will, she moved the energy through the bars, back into her body, and through the bars again in a loop. She repeated the process, mentally forcing the energy to remain separated from her own Spiritual essence as much as possible. Finally, the energy filled the bars and they glowed with a soft white light. Ayasha opened her eyes.

"Best I can do." Aya held out the bars to Leona.

Leona held them for a moment. "Good enough."

"I'm more than a few decades from that kind of delicate control with Channeling," Aya apologized, and Leona shook her head.

"It's good work, Ayasha the Speaker, as good as most of the stock we get unless we have to request something with a high purity for things like Essence Siphons. Your Spirit is compatible with Ireana's, so her energy will replace yours just fine." Leona turned, moved to the forge, and arranged the bars neatly within it to be heated.

Aya noticed that Ireana was staring intently at the metal being heated. There was a slight tremor in her right paw where she was gripping her leg. Aya put her paw over Ireana's. "You can do this."

Ireana sighed. "I'm not okay right now. I might throw up before we even get to the stabbing myself to death."

Aya giggled. "You know better than almost anyone that it won't hurt."

"It's morbid work. I don't know how my whole family does this day in and day out. Do you know they made a Heartblade almost every other day last year? Do you know how dangerous this is, how easily you can kill the Ta'el you are working with?"

Aya shook her head. The knowledge of the work of Spiritforges was limited to the small amount she knew about Heartblades and the infusing of metal, which is a task that every young Channeler at the Hearth must do.

"Watch what she does as she forges the blade. I can't see the flow of the magic very well any more since I stopped training for this years ago, but I know the process in my sleep. You imbued the metal, which she can't do, but she will move the energy you put in the bars into a specific configuration. The pattern of the energy must be in perfect negative synergy with the Spiritual signature of the blade's owner." Ireana fidgeted with one of her small throwing knives, twirling it in the fingers of her free paw.

"So, she is making a pattern perfectly opposite to your own so that when your energy enters the blade, it will mesh perfectly, like puzzle pieces fitting together." Aya concluded.

Ireana nodded. "If it is off, by even the slightest margin, the effect can run anywhere from extreme pain to deadly. I can't deal with the stress of that, the idea that I might have shoved a blade into someone one day and injured or killed them." Ireana shivered with fear. "Look at her, Aya."

Ireana gestured to Leona as she worked diligently at the forge. She shuffled the bars using only her hands. The heat of the forge did not touch her as she adjusted the glowing steel bars to her liking. She stood watching them with a critical eye.

"She's about to forge a blade that she is going to shove through her own greatdaughter's chest. Does she look concerned she is going to screw it up to you? Looks like she's about to fall asleep to me." Ireana sighed. "I never had that in me. I can face down a charging gorilla and steal into the most terrifying stronghold of Corrupted Ones without a twinge of fear." Ireana pointed towards Leona where she was now removing the glowing bars of metal from the forge. "But I can't do that."

Leona stacked up the bars neatly atop the crystal anvil and took the hammer up. She tapped it rhythmically on the anvil, and then pounded the bars of metal forcefully. The bars deformed, pressing into one another and fusing together. Sparks flew as she pounded the metal relentlessly, forge welding the bars into one. Aya watched as the energy she had pushed into the metal changed shape with each swing of the hammer. Over and again, Leona returned to the forge, heating the metal then pounding it into shape. Slowly, the blade began to form, and it became clear that the hammer was more than just a tool.

It became an extension of Leona's body. Aya watched as magic from the building's Hearth Spirit flowed up from the floor, through Leona's body, and then down into the metal through her hammer. Each blow shaped both the metal and the magical essence within into a recognizable pattern. Finally, Leona set aside the larger hammer for a much more delicate set of tools. She began to shape the hilt, and used chisels and other tools to carve whorls as well as some abstract designs that came together to give the impression of flowing water across the blade. Leona kept glancing up and squinting at Ireana, just as she had done when she was making Aya's Heartblade.

"Why does she keep eyeing you like that?" Aya whispered.

"She can see the shape of my Spiritual Essence. It changes slightly, even as observation continues. Watch the pattern she already laid down near the hilt. When she strikes new designs into the blade, it will ripple throughout the entire pattern right up until the last few seconds before we…" Ireana swallowed, "quench the blade."

"You can do it." Aya squeezed Ireana's paw. "As your Greatmother advised me, you are not the same cub who ran away from this place any more."

Shifts passed as Leona carefully embellished the blade while they watched in growing agitation. By the time Leona lifted her tools from the beautiful glowing blade, night had fallen, and the glow from aetherlamps lit the inside of the forge.

"Are you prepared, Greatdaughter?" Leona asked.

"Scales, no, I am not prepared. Are you sure," Ireana paused, and her ears fell in shame. "I apologize, Greatmother. I'm terrified, but not foolish enough to call your skills into question." She caught the flew on the right side of her muzzle between her canine teeth as she always did when frightened.

Leona just chuckled. "I have known you all of your turns, Ireana, and you should know by now that you need not apologize to me for nothing. To answer your question, I assure you that the alignment of the essence within this blade is a perfect negative of your own personal signature." Leona turned the short blade so that the hilt was towards Ireana. She swallowed and released Aya's hand.

"Do I need to advise you on what taking this blade means?" Leona's voice was gentle.

Ireana shook her head. "I know that once I take the hilt, I must finish or suffer the pain of being separated from the blade." And the pain would be immense, like losing a limb. Ireana gripped the hilt of the blade with purpose.

"Good emta. Remember, this won't hurt a bit. It will just be as scary as looking down the maw of a Dragon," Leona comforted.

Ireana nodded and turned the glowing blade in her fist. It was, like all Heartblades, a work of astounding beauty. Aya's blade was the plainest looking Heartblade Ireana had ever seen, but like Aya, if you looked closer, it revealed itself to be complex. The swirling pattern inscribed across the flat of Ireana's own reminded her of ocean waves, and the spine of the blade held a stylized solar eclipse. It was without a doubt the blade of a Stalker. The blade of Ireana the Stalker.

"Take your time. We have all the time you need."

Ireana laughed nervously. "We have until Hurun wants his forge back."

"We have as long as you need. I was quite clear what would happen if Hurun interrupted us," Aya reassured her.

Tears gathered at the corners of Ireana's eyes as she stared into the glowing surface of her Heartblade. "I can do this." She took a deep breath and spun the blade in her fist so the point was toward her.

Leona set a stool down to Ireana's left. "Ireana, you are one of the strongest Ta'el I have ever known. You stood up to your mother when she tried to force what she wanted for you down your throat. Compared to that, what challenge is this?" She gestured to the blade.

Ireana's eyes hardened.

Leona put her paw over Ireana's on the hilt and grinned toothily. "Ready, kid?"

"I'm ready."

Ireana lifted the blade and rested the point of the blade just over her heart.

"Remember, smooth pull and just hold still while I do the work," Leona reminded.

Ireana took one last deep breath and then pulled the sword toward her. The blade passed cleanly through her chest with no resistance whatsoever. Her heart fluttered once more and then stopped. She was about to open her mouth when Aya patted her free hand.

"Only temporary. You're going to get terribly cold in a moment, as you know," Leona mumbled. She was so focused on the blade that Ireana wondered if she was even with them. Her grip slacked on the hilt of the blade for a moment and Leona's paw tightened around hers.

"Don't you dare let go of this hilt, young emta'el. I will have your hide if you screw up all this hard work," Leona growled, but Ireana could hear the grin in her voice. She shivered as her body started to cool.

"Just, the, final, alignment, right?" Ireana's teeth chattered as she waited for her Greatmother to finish bonding the blade to her Spirit.

"A few more seconds and it will synchronize." Leona took her paw away from the blade and warmth flooded through Ireana's body.

"Now pull it free carefully."

Leona stood up, grabbing the stool away to set it back down directly next to the bench. Ireana drew the blade from her chest, and held it across both hands.

"Forge and fire, that feels just as weird as you always described it. I can feel the hole, but there isn't really a hole. It just feels like it. Can I," Ireana made to poke a finger into the glowing hole in her chest, but her Greatmother slapped her paw away.

"Don't touch it, you'll go blind," she joked.

Ireana and Aya both giggled together.

"Ok, I'm going to go keel over from stress now," Ireana groaned.

"Wait, we've got something new since you left your training. An enterprising young emta'el from Japan came up with something far more comfortable to cover that hole in your chest. Found an old process for creating elastic fabric in an old human book."

Leona fished in her bag and came out with an odd scrap of black fabric that shimmered slightly in the light of the aetherlamps. She demonstrated its elasticity by stretching it over her head, poking her head through a hole in the top of the garment, and then pushed her arms through two holes on either side. The garment stretched across her chest just over her heart.

"It's much better than the leather vests we used to strap on to keep wind from blowing annoyingly through the hole."

She slipped the garment off and handed it over to Ireana. Leona took the blade from her paws and the metal's glow faded. Ireana donned the garment immediately, sighing in relief as soon as it settled into place.

"Well, if this doesn't confirm that you made the right choice to your mother, I can't see much else doing the job."

Leona held up her Heartblade. The metal had turned, and the color was striking – a black darker than midnight that seemed as if it should gleam like a mirror under the high sun. Still, it did not, it drank in the light. The breathtaking illustration etched into the blade was outlined in lines of matte black. The whorled design carved into the hilt had brightened to silver, but they would never betray their wielder with reflected light, for they too were brushed and matte.

"This is undoubtedly the blade of a Stalker." Leona held the hilt of the finished blade out to Ireana once again. "I assume that you can grow her a scabbard for the blade, Hearth Stone?"

Aya nodded. "Of course. Leona, can I invite you to share a meal with Ireana and I in exchange for your services?"

Leona dusted off her paws and began to clean up the tools and mess left behind from her work. While she would never scrub her own forge clean of all signs of her work, she would absolutely not leave Hurun to say she had failed to do so in his workspace.

"Grow the scabbard while I clean up and I would be delighted," Leona said.

Aya turned away to head towards the Heart tree growing through the corner of the otherwise pristine room. Ireana began to follow, but Leona caught her by the arm. She turned back.

Leona spoke in a low whisper. "If you want that emta, you are going to have to do it yourself. She will never ask you."

Ireana grinned, "I know, Greatmother."

"You take that Heartblade and watch her back. The places she is going, she will need you, no matter how strong she is."

Ireana's smile fell away, replaced by grim determination. "I will."

Chapter 17

"THE WAY IN"

"The only way I can see to easily approach without exposing ourselves to the danger of the Downpour is to approach by widening this tiny path from the north." Ireana plotted, tracing her finger over the map unfurled on the thick oak table.

Ayasha listened nervously as Ireana explained what she had found on her scouting run to the Downpour. The large, neat office of Kian served as their meeting room once more. The aetherglow from the lamps at the corners of the office allowed shadows to dance along the teak wall panels. The fanciful creatures carved into the wood seemed to be jostling to watch them as they planned their approach to the task at paw.

"It's not really large enough for any of us to fit through as it is, but I was able to follow it all the way to here." Ireana pointed to a spot on the map at the north western edge. "The entrance is little more than a hole in the stone wall above the lava pit. There is an extremely thick steel door blocking the entrance. I got close enough to prod it with my Heartblade, and I didn't have much trouble cutting it, but it was so thick that my Heartblade didn't reach all the way through the door." Ireana finished, and everyone's eyes turned to Ayasha.

"I can clear the door, but I do not think that it is where we will be making entry. I'm going to ask the Heart of Fire to act as a distraction so we can make our entry more easily. With a little help," Aya paused when the door cracked open and Lily poked her head inside, "from our resident Earthwards. Perfect timing, Lily." A transparent near duplicate formed of glowing green mist followed Lily through the door.

"Honored Ancestor, how did your talks with the others go?" Nisane nodded to Ayasha.

"The Earthwards are agreed. We will provide you entrance into the human facility," Nisane said. "Some have even agreed to go with you into the facility. If this is a nest, then it cannot be allowed to stay near our home."

Aya nodded. "I agree, but I will not take anyone with us that does not have proper protection. I can take two more, but only if they are good fighters in possession of Heartblades."

Nisane and Lily exchanged a look.

"There is only one that fits those requirements, Hearth Stone, but we understand. Gris will go with you without a doubt," Lily said.

"It would be greatly appreciated," Ayasha accepted. She looked to Ireana.

"I know how to get us in. Strategy about how many ta'el that will be useful inside is your department," Ireana responded.

Ayasha shrugged, and leaned into the padded back of the carved stool. "Doesn't mean I don't want your opinion."

Ireana flicked her tail out of the way and planted herself on one of the carved wooden barstools. She drummed her fingers on the map for a moment.

"We don't know enough about what the inside of this place looks like to give an informed opinion."

"Then we set goals. Once inside, we should have three. As I see it, if this is a nest of Corrupted Spirits, then that news must escape with some of us. To that end, I will task two of you to leave immediately once we confirm this. Second, find Dedran and get him out. Third, find out exactly what took Dedran into the place."

Ayasha held out her right paw and Channeled Lane the Wanderer through the Veil. Almost everyone recognized Lane, but Arno, Baan, and Ipsal all stared with mouths agape. Arno clearly wanted to fight him, but Baan and Ipsal were just as clearly in awe.

"Everyone, this is Lane the Wanderer. He is going to provide transport out of this dung heap. I realize that some of you may want to stay and fight for your own reasons, but I will need two volunteers," Ayasha said.

Everyone exchanged a look. Kian lifted his large paw. Ipsal followed him quickly.

"I'm the best choice. I can use the shadows to hide us no matter where we are while the Honored Ancestor uses Kian's body to walk our Pathway out."

Aya Channeled again, pulling through three more Wanderer Spirits through the veil. "These are Andra," she pointed to a lone emta'el formed of white mist, a feline of the variety that humans had domesticated. "Lidal," she pointed to the stout fluffy looking ehta'el who had a large shock of fur down the back of his neck and spine formed of amber mist. "and finally, Miras." She pointed to a wiry looking ehta with short fur formed of light yellow mist. Faded but distinct dark spots covered most of his body.

"I have compensated them for their assistance and their willingness to allow themselves to be Channeled by anyone involved in this effort. Keep in mind that if you are not traditionally a Channeler, there could be some uncomfortable consequences for performing this act," Aya warned.

Everyone nodded in response. All ta'el could Channel Spirits, but not all ta'el were compatible with all Spirits. Only Channelers like Aya could Channel any Spirit freely.

"What sort of consequences?" asked Kyara.

Aya looked to Wanderer Lane. It was a valid question. Someone who was not compatible with an Elemental could easily kill themselves attempting to Channel one.

"Wanderlust. For those of you who are not Channelers and are not compatible with channeling a Wanderer Spirit, you will likely feel anywhere from a few rounds to a few spells of Wanderlust. You won't feel comfortable staying in any one place for more than a few shifts. Best thing to do for it is to simply get moving. Our magic will filter out of your body faster if you just do some wandering about," Lane explained.

"Thank you, Honored Ancestor," Ayasha said. "Can you tell us who would be best to use to avoid that?"

Lane shrugged. "Only Arno and you will be immune in this group."

"That being said, I think Arno should go with Ireana and be the primary team for gathering information about the facility to carry out as soon as they have confirmed it is a nest. Ipsal and Kian will be our contingency."

Ireana opened her muzzle to protest, but Aya spoke over her. "Ireana, much like Ipsal, you have the ability to hide yourself and others for short periods of time. That would give Arno more than enough time to walk a Pathway for the two of you."

Ireana snapped her muzzle shut with an audible clack and gave Ayasha a hard look. She knew for certain that Ayasha would not leave the facility until they had searched the entire place to find Dedran and anything else she was after. Even if it killed her.

"Other than that, this is a simple search. Once we find what is hidden within, we will track our paths to make sure there is no back tracking with these." Ayasha pulled a small blue marble out of her piece pouch.

"These were made after I allowed a Spiritforge to examine one of the devices in Dedran's room. Keep it in your piece pouch or on you somewhere and it will record a perfect recollection of everywhere you go. Hold it in your fist and it will be able to lead you through any place that you have carried it through." They all stared at the marbles as she handed them out.

"Are these...?" Baan the Iceheart started.

"Yours to keep as a reward for your assistance to the Hearth. I hope that they serve you well. These are the least I can offer for your help," Aya interjected.

"You must have offered quite something in trade or one heck of a pile of pieces for these," Ipsal said.

Aya shrugged. "I don't spend many pieces. This is worth the cost. Anyone who doesn't have a Wanderer Spirit with them will regroup with me and I will take us out."

In truth, it had cost a lot of pieces, but Aya had plenty to spend. Money did not have the same importance in the ta'el world as it did in the human world. One couldn't just buy anything one wanted. For the most part, ta'el used a barter system to trade for what they needed. Still, there were times when coin was used, usually when there was no time to work out a proper trade. Aya was not wealthy in coin, but her parents had gifted her quite a sum when she had entered training as a Hearth Stone. Even what she had spent had left her with a considerable sum of pieces, and she had not hesitated to spend them on something like this.

"Questions?" Ireana finally asked when she noticed that Aya was finished. Many heads around the table shook a negative reply.

"Then, Lily, if you would collect the rest of the Earthwards, we will meet you at the entrance to the Downpour."

Chapter 18

"THE DOWNPOUR"

Ayasha stood at the rim of the Downpour. A few scant
moments had passed since the bubbling magma had blasted
up from the boiling pit into the sky. The blossoming flower of
molten shards had been a breathtaking cascade of falling stars.
Standing next to her, Lily cringed as she stared at the molten
rock.

"Nothing to fear, Lily. We'll be gone soon." Ayasha held
out her right paw and Channeled the Heart of Fire.

{Honored Elemental, may I offer you a piece of my inner fire as
payment for your services?}

{In this case, no payment will be necessary. Do what you must,
Ayasha the Speaker.}

Aya nodded and then held out her paws. The gestures
were not really necessary, but rather something that helped
her focus the Elemental Spirit's power. The lava in the pit
below her began to bubble more violently. It lurched up out of
the pit in a torrent ten feet wide, streaming into the air. Aya
drew back her paws, willing the boiling rock to follow their
motion. She took a step back, holding her fists at her sides,
then a step forward before turning her body, letting fly with a
single perfect punch.

The flow of lava surged forward as if blasted from a
massive fire hose. It smashed into the door like a volley from
the cannons of a battleship. Aya dropped her fist and stepped
back. She wavered on her feet as the massive expenditure of
energy hit her. The flow of lava fell off, splashing back into
the pool and throwing off molten shrapnel. Aya steadied
quickly and jumped into the hole that Lily had left next to
them.

Lily landed next to her a moment later and the rock closed
up behind them, protecting them from any backsplash.
Ayasha nearly stumbled from the massive amount of magic
she had just channeled, and Lily put a steadying paw her

Aya's side. She took a few deep breaths, allowing her racing heart to slow.

"Thanks," Ayasha said.

Lily nodded.

Ayasha watched for a moment as the black rock began to flow like water under Lily's magic. The tunnel began to fill in behind her as she backed down the tunnel. Ayasha dashed off down the tunnel. She quickly outpaced the much smaller emta'el, but that wasn't a problem. Lily would finish closing up the tunnel behind them.

Aya skidded to a halt at the junction between two tunnels and turned left, still not waiting for Lily. She bolted down the tunnel at top speed, dropping to all fours, digging her claws in to help her turn a second corner. She slowed down as she came into the small cave that the Earthwards had created directly adjacent to the steel wall of the human facility.

"It's done. I blew a hole the size of a heart tree in the side of the mountain. Anything inside that can be distracted is. Let's go," Aya said.

She panted for a moment, waiting for Lily to catch up. There were two other Earthwards in the area, but they were working on their own part of the plan. They were creating other breaches to try and draw more enemies out into the maze of tunnels they had spent shifts creating over the last two rounds. It was dangerous work, but their particular skills would keep them safer than everyone else.

Lily finally came scurrying down the tunnel on all fours. She was panting hard, but stood up and took a few deep breaths. She put her tiny paw against the steel wall that abutted the open area. The steel seemed to iris open as if it were a circular doorway. As the metals were pieces of the earth, they could be manipulated by Earthwards as well. The wall opened further, leaving behind a hole more than large enough for any Ta'el to fit through. On the inside of the steel was a thick layer of concrete. Everyone rushed inside. Aya put a paw on Lily's shoulder.

"Remember, don't reopen this door unless your Watcher Spirit tells you it is safe. We all know the stakes here, Lily. I'm

not asking you to put your hide on the line for us." Aya
waited until everyone else was inside. "If we don't return by
sunrise tomorrow, you can assume we are all dead. If that
happens, the Wanderer Spirits have orders to visit you, and if
they cannot find you, they will go to the Lightmend.

I'm counting on you to get out of here alive to warn
everyone that this place needs to be destroyed even if it does
hold the secret to what the humans did. If there is something
here that can destroy Spirits, then it must be stopped. Word
has to get back to The Record," Aya emphasized.

"Why the Record?" Lily looked confused.

Aya blinked. "Because," Aya drew out the word. "The
Record is the most powerful ta'el in all the world. While he is
usually unable to act directly, in some cases, he can step in.
Knowledge is power, Lily, and there is no one more
knowledgeable than Ayrece. This is a task equal to his power.
He will destroy this place for the good of all ta'el."

Aya turned and headed through the opening, pausing
when Lily spoke again. "Dragon's Break."

"Talon's Touch to you, Lily," Aya called on the luck of the
Dragons.

It was dark within, and Aya slipped a paw into her piece
pouch. She pulled out a small, round glass ampule. This one
was much smaller than one for a potion. Inside, a tiny figure
sat in a quiet, cross-legged posture. The entire figure seemed
to be made of golden light. Yet somehow, the burning
incandescence failed to blind. It opened large white circles
that served as its eyes and looked up at her.

"If you would be so kind, Honored Elemental?"

There was a hook tied to the neck of the ampule, and she
slid this onto a ring on the belt of her small pack. Light spread
from the ampule in a flash. It was unlike any other simple
light source. Once the flash passed, the light did not seem to
emit from the ampule, but from all around her as if she were
standing in full sunlight, the source so far away that it seemed
to be everywhere around her.

"What is *that*?" Kian looked at the ampule wide-eyed as she came along to illuminate the entire area around her waiting party. Clearly, he already suspected the answer.

"This is a Source Elemental. I found her by accident when I was just a cub. Her name is, obviously, Light."

Kian's face fell slack, and he stared in speechless awe. He shook his head. "That's," Kian just spluttered. "Just who are you?"

"What's so special about it?" Baan asked.

Kian stared at him, his rounded ears drooping with incredulity. "It's a source," Kian started to explain.

"If we make it out of this alive, I'll explain it to everyone. For now, my little friend will help keep us all safe," Aya interrupted. She gestured for everyone to gather closer to her and then grasped the ampule of the little elemental. "Light, will you gift my friends?"

The tiny Elemental stood up from her meditative pose and looked at each of the ta'el gathered around her as if judging them in some fashion. She turned back to Aya and nodded. Aya held out her free paw.

"Everyone grab my paw."

They did as bade, and suddenly the light in the tunnel grew and spread out. It illuminated bare concrete walls that someone, or something, had been maintaining for the thousands of turns since the humans had constructed it. The ceiling was constructed of interlocking metal panels.

"The light has been attached to each of you, and will last until the Honored Elemental takes it back or until you dispell it. She has changed the nature of the light so that only we can see it. You can dispell the light by touching a finger to your forehead and concentrating on releasing it. Everyone knows what they are supposed to do. Let's go."

Everyone stared at her as if they all wanted to ask what she had done until Iryeka stepped up next to her. Everyone snapped into motion, darting away down the hallway. There were several branching hallways, and their lights veered off down them, disappearing into the darkness.

Chapter 19

"CLEAR"

Kian crept through the door, checking the corners of the massive laboratory for threats. His round ears one black, one white twitched as he listened to the sounds of the facility around him. He spoke to the Earth Elemental he shared his body with.

{Do your senses reveal anything, Honored Elemental?}

Kian kept his paws spread, arms up and ready to defend himself.

{Something hides, in this place,} the grating stone voice of the elemental filled his mind.

Kian crept further into the room his green eyes roving around the room. Broken beakers, and odd glass constructions of swirling tubes connected to rubber corks covered the steel countertops. None of that was what grabbed Kian's attention. To his left in the back corner was a darkness deeper than shadow. Limbed in a line of purple light that bled motes of sickly violet energy. He gripped the tiny ampule containing the Lightning Elemental.

{I have found a portion of the nest. I don't see any Corrupted Spirits, but a Shadowgap limbed in purple just like Sirius described.}

Kian reached into his quick pouch, and pulled a small potion bottle glowing with white energy. Inside was a simulacrum with a long black and white ringed tail, and a somewhat apish appearance.

The warning came a moment late to save Kian's right ear. The Elemental sharing his body saw the creature emerge from one of the air ducts in perfect silence. It lunged at Kian's back. At the elemental's warning Kian dropped rolling to his right. Pain lanced through his ear as a claw sliced his left in twain. He came to his paws facing a creature that appeared to be formed from deep red blood. A grin formed on its muzzle as it held up its bloody claws.

Kian grinned back baring teeth at the creature, and he Channeled the power of the Earth Elemental within. His fur stiffened increasing in density and weight until he was near impervious to damage. He popped the cork on the potion bottle, and drank a small sip from the potion. Light glowed from his split ear, and the two halves drew back together healing as if the wound had never occurred. His paw snapped forward whipping the potion bottle into the black void of the Shadowgap.

"Come, creature. One of you caught us unawares before. Let us see how well you do without an ambush."

Kian leapt forward driving a fist empowered by the power of the Earth Elemental within into the creature's chest. The Visceral crossed its arms before Kian's fist, but the power of the strike blasted the creature off the ground. It smashed into a steel table. Glasswork shattered as the table was ripped from its moorings, and folded around the creature like wet clay. White light burst from the pool of darkness as the magic of the potion intermingled with the Shadowgap. It began to fizz, and pop as bubbles of white light consumed the patch of deepest blackness.

Kian was distracted only for a moment, but the creature took that time to lunge at him. It's claws bit into the hardened fur but it was unable to penetrate to Kian's flesh. Kian stumbled back from the force of the blow, but his paw came around claws biting into the wrist of the creature.

The Panda turned his body into a roll dragging the creature over his shoulder in a throw. He tumbled to the ground as he flung the creature into the bubbling white puddle.

Kian reeled back from the screech that resulted from the creature coming in contact with the Lightmend Draught. It was pitched agony of such volume that Kian knew only the power of the Elemental he held kept his ear drums from bursting.

The creature flailed its way free its right arm dissolving as the potion attacked the creature. Smoke boiled off of the side of the creature where its body attempted to cope with the damage.

Kian jumped back as the creature flailed towards him in an astonishing blur of motion. He was not quite quick enough, and while his fur, hard as stone, was excellent protection the creature managed to hit one of the vulnerable points of his defense. Kian had a number of scars on his forearms from his younger days before he found his calling as Den Master. No fur grew in these places, and while they were thin gaps in his protection a flailing claw struck one laying open his left forearm to the bone.

Blood reddened the downy fur of his stomach. It splashed across his face, and stained one eye. A second jump back put a little distance between Kian, and the Visceral. Then he drew his Heartblade from the horizontal sheath across his spine. The firm grip of his right paw stilled the weapon with unwavering resolve. The blade was eighteen inches of rectangular steel. Sharp only on one edge it appeared to be a massive butcher's cleaver.

The Visceral shook its head, triangular ears flapping, and then it focused on Kian again. It surged forward, and Kian held his blade in a low guard his poise perfect. He did not move as the creature roared towards him. The creature would attempt to throw him off balance using superior speed. Den Master he may be, but he had not left behind the cub who thought he might one day become a Wanderer.

He could feel the motion of the fight in his bones. In a smooth motion he snapped his arm up turning the blade edge up. He slid forward swinging toward the ceiling. At the last moment the Visceral jerked back, and then leapt to Kian's right attempting to bypass his blade. Claws sought his throat, but Kian was not fooled. Balance perfect he pivoted with smooth grace that belied his bulk. His Heartblade passed cleanly through the creature's arm. He slammed his free palm into the creature's chest smashing it back with the force of a charging bull.

Ipsal's silhouette appeared in the doorway one Heartblade in each paw. Shadows lifted from the floors and walls resolving into sharply pointed tentacles that twitched and swayed around Ipsal.

The Visceral looked to Ipsal, and then back to Kian. Kian stood blade back in the low guard position ready to continue their conflict. The creature fled. Leaping onto one of the tables to smash more of the glassware it scrambled into the ductwork vanishing before either of them could make another move.

"Hmpfh." Kian snorted. "The Lightmend Daught works to clear the Shadowgaps." Kian said. Ipsal nodded.

"I found two gaps in another room down the hall, they have been cleansed. The rest of the floor seems clear."

"Let's get back to," Ipsal's round grey ears twitched as he trailed off. A dull roaring sound permeated the room almost more a feeling of vibration than a sound.

"I hear it too. Let's go."

Kian pulled a cloth from one of the pouches on his belt, wiped his Heartblade clean, and threw the cloth to the concrete floor where it began to smolder. He slid the blade back into its sheath, and headed for the door.

"You're hurt."

"A flesh wound." Kian replied. He fished in his quick pouch for another Lightmend Draught. A quick drink and the wound began to seal. The roar got louder as they both dropped to all fours and ran flat out.

Ireana slipped into the grip of a shadow as she trailed the rotten stench of one of the Viscerals. Aya had given her the scent by sharing her memory of it, and while she did not relish the scent, she was thankful for the warning. Arno slipped along just ahead of her.

Ireana watched Arno move, and sent her hopes to her ancestors that she could move like Arno one day. Every movement was smooth, graceful, perfect. Even the way he touched the staff strapped across his back to keep it from even touching any obstacle to give away their position.

He gestured her forward, and she gripped the sheath of the Heartblade at her waist. She slipped forward padding on silent paws to reach Arno's side. He pointed to his eyes, and then to two of the glass cells filling the enormous room just a few yards ahead. He made a circling gestured around his head to tell her to keep her eyes open for the rest of the room that they could not see around the corners.

Ireana nodded, then she lifted her cloak, and swung it around her shoulders enfolding her in a curtain as dark as the shadow around her. The cloak was a magic unto itself, and as long as she had some shadow to stand in it would keep her invisible from even the sharpest senses.

She made a fist and held it up to Arno, and then she pointed over her shoulder with her thumb. He gave her a nod that he would be watching her back. Crouching slightly to shift her balance, she slipped forward into the room. Even after so many thousands of turns one of the odd lights the humans had left behind still gave off an amber glow that lit part of the room.

While the light that Aya had gifted them with was invisible to everything else it saturated the room to her eyes. Whatever that Elemental had been was beyond any magic that Ireana had ever seen because she could still see the room as it was without the light. Shadows somehow remained visible even though the light illuminated what was hidden within. The way the magic manipulated her sight was powerful beyond her ken. She cleared the doorway, and froze still as any statue.

The room was four hundred feet square divided by into four sections by to halls that crossed in the middle. Each section had ten glass walled cells each one twenty by twenty. Several of the walls were shattered across the floor. Amber reflections from the one remaining light veiled the contents of several of the cells, and even the magic of the Elemental that saturated the room with light did not reveal them.

One of the senses any Stalker honed was a sense of when they were being watched. It was a sense she had learned to trust turns ago, and it had never failed her. She always knew when something had focused on her with intent. Those senses whispered to her that she had been seen despite the protections of her cloak. It was a rare thing for anything to see through the magic of an Interlopers cloak. Even more interesting to her was the fact that she couldn't pick out the creatures watching her.

She realized that meant that there was something between them and her, physically, and they were not concerned that it would slow them down. She held a paw down by her waist just outside of the cloak. She held up three fingers. Arno's eyes locked onto her paw, and he gave the barest nod to let her know he understood.

She made a fist, then pointed with her index claw. One directly to the right, then she held up two fingers, and pointed slightly further to the left, then three fingers, and to the left but not completely to the left.

Arno nodded. She reached into the quick pouch at her waist, and lifted a Lightmend Draught from one of the compartments. Arno nodded again. He pulled a bottle of the draught from his quick pouch, nodded and then bolted past her into the room. She was right behind him, and he turned right towards the end of the room where there were two Viscerals. He was the better fighter there was no question if one of them should be taking on two of those things it should be him.

Ireana slid her Heartblade from its sheath with her off hand. She knew she wasn't ready to take this thing on in a fair fight. Maybe after a turn with training with Aya she would be, but for now she was going to cheat. She whipped her Heartblade towards the far corner of the room snapping her wrist with supernatural speed causing the blade to spin like a blurring airplane prop. It smashed through the glass panel without slowing at all. It sliced through the desktop on the way toward the steel grate seated in the wall behind the desk. Before it could reach the grate burst open knocking the whirring blade aside. It slammed into the concrete all the way up to the hilt.

Emerging from the grate in a blur, one of the Viscerals roared and surged towards Ireana. She skidded to a halt, claws scrawling across the concrete, and the paw holding the Lightmend Draught hurtled forward. Almost on top of her there was no time for the creature to dodge, and the potion bottle shattered against its skull.

The scream that emerged from the creature as the potion completely covered its head and upper body threatened to shatter Ireana's ears. She did not slow. Blown ear drums would heal. She straight kicked the creature in the chest blasting it back through the shattered opening in the glass. It slammed into the remnants of the desk, and flipped backwards to slam into the concrete wall. A second bottle of Lightmend Draught came out of quick pouch, and was shattering across the creature's thrashing body before there was any other chance to recover.

The screams grew in intensity as the creature thrashed through the bubbling white liquid. It began to lose shape, and Ireana watched in horror as it dissolved into liquid. The potions never lost their color as the purified the matter that made up the Visceral. The screams trailed off as the creature finally fell completely apart.

The sounds of furious combat behind her snapped her out of her revulsion, and she snatched her Heartblade out of the wall, and turned on her heal to bolt towards Arno. When she got into the hall, and saw the fight in one of the cells on the far wall she realized she needn't have hurried.

Arno controlled the fight. One of the two Viscerals had clearly been splashed with Lightmend Draught. Aya had told Ireana of her fight with the Viscerals, and they had both realized that most of the danger had been in not knowing what the thing could do. That was how the first one had injured, and killed so many people. The things were not pushovers to be certain. Arno had a few scrapes, and was bleeding from a ragged tear that had clipped off the top of one of his tawny ears.

The grin on his face showed the real truth of it. Like all Wanderers, combat gave him true life. Each time the injured Visceral rose to attack, Arno would smash the staff of his Heartblade polearm into the creature's head in an almost off handed movement keeping it on the ground while he concentrated on its sibling.

He wasn't completely toying with them, but it wasn't far off. Ireana watched in stunned silence for a few moments as Arno flowed from one movement to the next with all the grace of his feline heritage. Then she shook herself and began forward the night black Heartblade held in a high guard.

She knew he saw her when she crept into the hall a few cells away from the one where he was fighting. She just paused, and waited not wanting to interfere if he did not need her assistance.

In a single smooth attack, Arno's foot smashed into the head of the uninjured Visceral. It crashed to the floor in a roll and smashed into the concrete wall with bone shattering force. Arno spun his staff the blade at the end slicing off the injured Visceral's leg which darkened to grey almost before it tumbled to the ground. Arno planted a hind paw into its chest, and it smashed through the glass right towards Ireana.

Ireana hopped back as the creature tumbled through one of the glass walls, and splayed at her paws. It pushed itself up to three paws, but Ireana didn't hesitate. She swept her Heartblade down in a vicious arc toward the creature's neck.

It rolled away, and her blade sliced a line across the concrete floor. It came to three paws again its leg already in the process of reforming. Turning her wrist, she brought the blade back up towards its chest, but the creature's hardened claws came up to strike the sword with a musical chime. Her sword bound against the creature's claws, but Ireana focused her intent and pushed with all of the potion enhanced strength of her body.

The blade bit deeper into the claws like they were made of soft cheese. They sliced through the claws, but Ireana was forced to jump back when the creature sacrificed its balance to swipe claws at her face. She snarled in pain when they cut through her cheek, and slice across her nose just missing her eye.

"Scales!" She swore, and swiped her blade wildly in an arc in front of her driving back the creature. Blood filled her left eye where the claws had clearly caught her brows just above her eye blinding her on that side. When she regained her balance she turned her body so that her unblinded eye was facing the creature just as Aya had drilled into her.

She tried to recall all the times that she had fought with Aya, who had never fought with a weapon to make their sparring more of a challenge for Aya.

You're going to lose your sight at some point in a fight. Split brows, gouged out eye, it is one of the vulnerabilities that enemies aim for. When you do, turn and present only your working eye. Deny your blind spot to the enemy, or better, use the blind spot against them.

Aya's words saved her life, because it the creature tried to circle to her blind side. Instead of following the first bit of advice, she moved to the second. She let the creature circle to her blind spot. With all care, she did not twitch her ears in the direction of the creature. She did not need to hear its every move, only one move. The creature was not fooled into thinking it had the drop on her. She had failed to show the proper vulnerability. She was to collected, and the creature could sense that.

Still, she waited because it would not give up the opportunity to attack her blind side. The sound came, the slap of a bare paw against concrete. A whiff of the creature's stink was the last warning.

Ireana spun away from the creature, falling to one knee, she spun into a roll extending her arm her Heartblade whistling through the air with supernatural speed. As with everything she had cut with the blade there was almost no resistance when the blade past through the Visceral's midsection as it flew over her head.

The two pieces of the creature flopped to the floor a moment later. To her amazement, it was not dead. The top half scrabbled at the ground trying to attack her. The deep red color bled out of the bottom half until nothing but grey sludge remained.

Ireana took one of the ampules of Lightmend Draught from her quick pouch. Drank a small swig of it, and poured the rest on the struggling creature. The reaction was immediate, and violent. The creature began to disintegrate under the cleansing magic of the potion. She turned to see if Arno was all right.

The remaining Visceral smashed through one of the glass panels, or at least the pieces of the Visceral did.

"Are you all right Stalker?" Arno asked.

"Yes, just a scratch. Lightmend Draught did its job." Ireana said. Her ears twitched as a dull rumble filled the room.

"Do you hear that?" Arno asked. His ear continued to drip blood into his fur.

"Would you use a Lightmend Draught on that?" She complained. Arno rolled his eyes.

"Would rather not waste what someone else can use. This is nothing." Arno replied. Ireana rolled her eyes, and held out one of the potions from her quick pouch.

"Look, if Denver is short on potions someone might have to be uncomfortable. If you lose an ear, you might get dead with what you do. I'll just have Aya's father make enough Lightmend Draught to last the city a year."

Arno lifted a brow, and dropped an ear in question.

"Her father is more or less a Brewsmith." Ireana said, and her ears twitched as the dull rumble ramped up to a louder roar. "We should probably go find out what that," Ireana trailed off as something caught her attention. One of the glass cells that was still in tact was completely empty, but on the floor of the cell were black marks.

"Stalker?" Arno asked. Ireana waved him forward, and she slunk towards the cell. The door opened with a creak of hinges that had lacked oil for centuries.

There on the floor were footprints, but no ta'el had made these. Ireana knelt next to them, and put her paw down on one. It was not just a mark, the footprint had been imprinted into the stone of the floor. Ireana trailed her paw pads against the edges of the prints which were mushroomed up from the service.

"What made these?" Arno asked.

"A human." Ireana whispered.

"What does it mean?" Arno asked.

Ireana shook her head. "I'm not sure it means anything, these are old." Ireana wished that her Watcher Spirit was there to help her, but she could feel it. They were not just old, they were ancient beyond imagining. Yet, there was something about the feeling. The floor began to vibrate, and Ireana pulled her paw away.

"We have to go. Something is happening, both my own sense, and Lane the Wanderer's senses are warning us it is time to move."

Ireana nodded, and pushed herself away. Arno clipped the strap to his polearm and swung it onto his back. Then he dropped to all fours, and darted out of the glass cells. They found no Shadowgaps, and left the laboratories with haste. They galloped down the long hall past the rest of the floor they had already cleared. They burst into the stairwell, and the roar was almost overwhelming.

Ireana snatched the ampule from her belt realizing that it had caught on the sheath of her Heartblade and she hadn't been able to hear the communications.

{...the sixth floor is filled with Corrupted Ones. The entire floor is has dozens of Shadowgaps. We have to decide what to do. The Speaker is not answering.} The voice was Ireyka's, and Ireana cut in.

"Baan, Gris take the Honored Ancestor, and get out of here. The rest of us will retrieve Aya." Ireana said.

All of them drew weapons when the sound of paws slapping on the stairs reached their ears. A moment later a Ta'el emerged from the darkness. Dedran panted in exhaustion.

"Take Dedran with you." Ireana began.

"I'm not going with them. She saved my life, and I may even get my tail back because of her. I'm not leaving without her." Dedran denied.

Ireana rubbed the bridge of her muzzle. "Fine, your butt is attached to Ireyka. If I see you more than five feet from her I promise there will be literally zero lag between that moment and my paw hitting your ass. You are what we came in here for, and Aya will beat me like a rug if we lose you. Got it?"

"Yes, Stalker." Dedran replied without hesitation. Ireana's eyes went from Dedran, to Ireyka standing one floor up, and then back to Dedran. He scurried away up the stairs.

"Which floor is the problem?" Ireana asked.

"Eighth." Ireyka replied.

"Did the rest of the floors get cleared?" Ireana asked. Nods went all around.

"We didn't want to break whatever seal is on the Eighth floor before it degraded." Baan said.

"Baan, Gris, go now." Ireana said. Baan nodded, and Gris began to walk a circle right there on the landing. Glowing paw prints trailed behind him as he completed the circle. A moment later they jumped through the Path, and it vanished behind them.

"The rest of you, hopscotch rotation one team per floor." Ireana asked. Ireana and Arno darted down the stairs, and the rest of them followed.

Chapter 20

"IN THE DARK"

Iryeka waited. "Why did you take me as your partner?" the large emta asked. She had been quiet most of the time, putting in only a few words. She had a deep, barely feminine voice.

"Because I am carrying the Heart of Fire with me, and you are the only other ta'el available who has any acquaintance with the Honored Elemental. While you have not formed a bond with them, they have agreed that you are the only option for Channeling their power if something happens to me."

Iryeka's deep amber eyes went a little wide.

"You're also the only other ta'el who can Channel a Spirit that will make you immune to fire. We are going straight down, Iryeka. No one else is following us. Do not hesitate to burn anything that gets in your way. If you feel it is too dangerous, I will open a Pathway for you to leave."

"Are we certain that these things are related to that creature that killed my brother?"

"Can't you smell it?" Aya asked. "There is no question."

Iryeka lifted her nose and took a deep breath. "There are more of them here. I will empty this place of Corruption, even if it kills me." Her resolve was like a mountain, and Aya nodded.

"Good. Now listen to me, Iryeka. I need you to watch my back, but please do not interfere unless I ask you for assistance."

Over the three days they had spent acquiring Heartblades, she had sparred with each one of the group. She would not take anyone without first paw knowledge of their fighting skills. Only Arno had truly given her a challenge. Lane's relentless training had allowed her to prove victorious in that match. As much as she had hated him when he was her teacher, she would kiss him again when all of this was over for pressing her so hard.

"That doesn't really explain why you picked me."

Aya sighed. "Because you're not prideful like the others. You won't let your pride force you to get in the way."

"I'm not sure if I should be insulted or flattered." Iryeka dropped an ear in confusion.

"Flattered."

Aya she turned and padded away down the corridor. As they traversed the concrete halls, Aya began to detect an odor. It was faint at first, even to her extremely acute nose. They found a stairwell leading down. They knew at least that the facility was nine floors. Each group of two ta'el would investigate two floors. Aya and Iryeka would investigate the last three. The Earthwards had explained that the last floor was almost entirely a metal box. It was some sort of extremely durable alloy that they had not seen before.

"How good are you at climbing?" Aya asked as she leaned out over the railing.

Iryeka shook her head. "Not my best skill."

"Follow me as quickly as you can. I'm going down the fast way," Aya said.

Iryeka nodded.

Aya leapt over the side of the railing and shot down the center of the stairwell. She let three floors pass before she judged that her speed was near to being faster than she could handle, and then reached out and caught the railing. She flexed her arms, and her descent slowed, but she did not hold on. She opened her fingers and fell again, repeating the process until she saw the final landing rising up to meet her.

She turned her body in the air so that she could land with all four paws and flexed both her arms and legs. She bent all four limbs the second her paws touched the concrete, absorbing the impact without issue. She landed in almost complete silence. She did not wait. She had split up from Iryeka on purpose, to give Iryeka a chance to work in the stairwell. The other teams of ta'el would have cleared the first four floors of the facility, but with the aid of her Elemental, Iryeka could bathe the rest of the stairwell in flame.

She would temporarily clear the stairwell so that when the rest of the teams finished searching their floors, they could secure it. It was not a perfect plan because it would split the teams, one ta'el to search a floor while the other held the stairwell to prevent reinforcements from other floors. But they knew how large the floors were, and had come prepared.

Aya pulled a small white crystal out of her piece pouch. Inside the perfectly clear sphere was a tiny figure made of light and jagged blue edges, a Spirit of Lighting. The little ta'el shaped figure of electricity shook itself at her, and she gripped her fist around the sphere. The tiny Lightning Elemental had the uncommon ability to split itself into two identical Spirits. They could reside in two crystals and transmit electromagnetic waves to each other. Combined with the ability of most ta'el to work with Spirits to communicate telepathically, the crystals could be used to transmit thoughts between two ta'el over long distances.

{What does it look like in the stairwell?} Aya sent.

{Clear for now, Hearth Stone. I had to burn out two of the creatures and some of the stairwell melted, but it is cooling. The others are joining with me now to secure the stairwell.}

{Keep me updated. I'm starting on the seventh floor. Has anyone seen any Shadowgaps yet?} Aya felt an affirmative before the reply came.

{Several. Kian is injured, but not terribly. There are a large number of Corrupted Spirits on the other levels, and Kian also ran into a Visceral. This one though was not as persistent as the one that came to Denver. It fled as soon it discovered Kian was carrying a blade that could damage it. We suspect it is going for help,} Iryeka explained.

{They will come through the stairwell. Prepare yourselves, and tell everyone to call upon any Spirits that you have for aid. They will come to kill creatures of the void.}

{What about you?}

{I'm going to find Dedran. He's down here. I can both sense and scent him, though the scent is faint and overpowered, it is here.}

Aya paused at the seventh-floor landing, inhaling deeply to try to catch a better scent of Dedran. A moment later, it was clear that his scent continued down the concrete stairwell. "Of course it does," she thought as she descended to the eighth floor.

Here, too, the scent descended. As she reached the last landing on the ninth floor, a spirit formed from mist beside her. The Spirit was dim and almost grey, with just the barest hint of orange, lacking the personal glow of a Spirit visible to anyone else.

{He is alive,} Eleena said with relief.

{What are you doing here, Eleena?} Aya asked.

Eleena shrugged. *{I had a theory after you left. I was right. I can sense him. He is on this floor. That way.}* Eleena pointed toward the stairwell door. *{But something is disrupting my connection to him.}*

{Great. Love it.}

Aya was starting to get an uneasy feeling in the pit of her stomach. This was going far too easy. If this place was the source of the Netherspawn, then where were they? Aya slowly pushed the door at the end of the stairwell open. Fur bristled along her back as dread crept into the pit of her stomach. This place was enormous by Ta'el standards, including the doors. Humans had been huge by comparison to the ta'el. Only the largest ta'el were the size of humans.

She crept into the room, and the smell of Dedran grew pungent. There was a distinct overtone of decay in the scent. The room she entered was about fifty feet long and thirty feet wide. On the left, a door opened into an adjacent room that was much larger. Next to the door was an opening as large as the wall itself. She suspected it had once contained a window. On the right, there was a stairwell leading up to three levels. Each level had many desks with sleek looking slates of glass propped up on them. Some of the slates were broken. On the third level, she found Dedran the Explorer. She swallowed in dread and approached him.

Dedran's unconscious body was tied down to one of the large steel desks, which had been cleaned off of everything else. His legs and arms were each lashed down to the sides of the desk. It was clear that the restraints had been drawn so tight that his limbs had been hyperextended. Each joint was pulled completely out of its socket. He was breathing, at least, but there were dozens of tiny cuts all over his body. Drizzles of drying blood streaked his grey pelt. His long, ringed tail looked to have been amputated one small piece a time, and the pieces were lying on the desk in a gruesome facsimile of his tail as it had been when it was still attached. Aya watched the entire room and mentally asked Light to expand the illumination to fill every corner of both rooms. The light expanded like water, filling the room.

The expanded light revealed nothing. The previously shadowed corners held nothing at all, but Aya did not relax. She crept forward with all the paranoia of a hunted thing and expressed her claws to remove the binds holding Dedran down. She wanted to move him to the floor so she could tend to his wounds. As she reached towards the ropes, one of his deep green eyes cracked open. It rolled to lock onto her.

"They found The First Word," he whispered hoarsely.

"Quiet now."

Aya fell into a space in her mind where she could reach out to Spirits far away. There would be a cost for doing this. The energy to do what she did was pulled from her life force. She would lose some small portion of her life, but Dedran would lose his life this moment if she didn't do something.

{Kika the Lightmend, I request your aid.}

Aya felt the affirmative response immediately. She reached out not with her paws, but with her life force. Energy that she would never get back streaked out across the Spiritlands, stretched, attenuated, and then snapped back towards her. Tethered uncomfortably to the light of her own Spirit was Kika. She joined the two other Spirits sharing space inside of Aya's head. Roan and Lane seemed amicable to the arrangement, but Kika was a little startled.

{How many Spirits can you hold?} she asked, a little incredulously.

{Five, but any more than three will give me Soul Sickness for sure. The output from that much magic isn't meant to pass through a living body. At least not my living body.}

Two was a stretch for most channelers, and she couldn't approach her Mother's power to hold over a dozen. Still, she felt Kika's surprise.

{But you can do more than five, can't you,} she asked.

The space she felt between her, Roan, and Lane inside of Aya's head was considerable.

Aya sent a mental shrug. *{I've never tried. I am wary of trying to hold more than five. The task at paw, if we could?}*

Kika sent a mental nod. *{You need not ask leave to use my power. I have offered, you have accepted. I trust you, Ayasha the Speaker.}*

Aya looked back to Dedran. She slashed her claws through the bindings holding his disjointed arms and legs.

"Dedran, I'm not going to be able to do anything about your tail. I am not skilled enough. I can leave it untouched, and a more skilled healer can repair it," she whispered, trying to look everywhere. She didn't think any of the Nether creatures would be stupid enough to come near her while she was holding the full power of a Lightmend, but she also didn't know if they could sense that power in her.

"Stupid thing was always in the way anyways," he rasped, and then grinned at her with bloody teeth.

Despite herself, she let out a little chuckle. "I defer to your wisdom. I know nothing of healing." She reached into the satchel hanging at her hip and took out a small roll of bandage.

"I'm going to roll you over so I can bandage the stump properly. It will hurt, and I don't trust this place, so please try to keep the noise to a minimum."

Dedran nodded and gritted his teeth. Aya took the time to carefully lift each of his limbs and arrange them on the table around him before she got on with it. He let out nothing more than grunt and a slowly hissing breath as she rolled him onto his side. She did it slowly so that his broken limbs were not jostled too violently. Once he was on his side, she carefully lifted the stump of his tail and wrapped the bandage around it. Once the bandage was tightly wrapped and covering the barely bleeding stump, she rolled him back.

{How much is this going to take?} Aya silently asked Kika.

{He is very broken, Ayasha the Speaker. If we arrived much later, we would have found a corpse. Several of his internal organs are bruised, and he has a ruptured kidney that has allowed poison to leak

into his body cavity. I fear that if we heal him completely, I will be of no further use to you for many shifts.}

{I do not wish to be greedy, but do you know of another Lightmend that might aide me in that time? I fear this is not the first healing we will need,} Aya hedged.

{You are here on the business of all ta'el are you not?} Kika asked as her power began to suffuse Aya.

{I believe it to be so. I believe Dedran may have found a very important clue here to fulfilling the purpose handed us by the Dragons.}

Aya felt the mental nod from Kika as she Channeled the healing energies from the Lightmend into Dedran. She was careful to heal all of the damage besides his tail. She did not have the skill necessary to regenerate the missing limb. She was not practiced enough with healing magics granted by a Lightmend to do a healing requiring that much anatomical knowledge.

Still a moment later, Kika's power faded and Dedran laid on the desk, looking up at the ceiling. All of his wounds, bruises, and even fatigue seemed to have been wiped away. The magic had inhibited his pain while his joints had been reconnected, so the loudest sound was the popping of his joints repairing themselves.

He didn't get up right away, though, having apparently received such healing before. Aya unclipped a steel canteen from the side of her satchel. She held it out to him, and he took it carefully in one paw. She held out her free paw, and he took it. She pulled him to a sitting position. Aya nervously checked her surroundings while he sipped from the canteen. he held it back out to her, then lifted a paw, and pointed into the other room.

"The humans discovered the First Word. That is what was done to destroy this world," Dedran said, a note of triumph in his voice. "They tried to use it to open a Pathway to the other side of the world. When they did, though, they failed to fully understand how the magic functions. One of the doorways used incorrect Runes. I can't see the Runes of the First Word, but I was able to access their computer systems to find what had happened."

Aya turned and looked through the hole that she assumed had once been a window. Inside were several large square frames. They had been constructed by joining large beams of metal together. The frames had no doors within, and stood in the middle of the room. The inside of the second door from the left shimmered with what appeared to be a transparent white curtain through which only blackness could be seen. Aya could tell there were symbols carved into the steel of the frames, but when she squinted to try to get a better look, it only seemed to make the symbols look more blurry.

She had heard of the First Word. It was in several texts she had studied at the Hearth. It was supposedly the first written language ever created in the history of all universes. She didn't know much more about it, but she was inexplicably drawn to look at the symbols.

"Where does that go?"

"That Pathway opened into the Nether. Netherspawn poured into this world and killed every sentient creature, but the materials used to create these Pathways were not designed to deal with the prolonged output of so much energy. It began to degrade, and thank Scales the humans put some protections into the Runes they used. I think that the Pathway was designed to draw everything that comes through back into it in some fashion. The Pathway only opens at random now, and once it opens, it only stays open for a few rounds before closing again. That is the only reason we are not swimming in Netherspawn. We have to leave."

Dedran began to rummage about in a pile of detritus in one corner of the third level. After a long moment, he pulled free a leather satchel. Aya, though, was drawn to look at the Pathways. She walked towards the door that would lead her into the other room. Before she got two steps away, a paw closed around her arm.

"I don't know who you are, but we have to go. The Pathway will be used again soon." Dedran's face held surprisingly little fear considering his treatment.

"I thought you said it was random."

"It is random, but if you watch it open as I have, you can tell when it starts to get that diaphanous sheen to it, like a curtain made of light. It will disgorge more netherspawn soon."

Aya pulled her arm loose from his grip. "How many have come through?" Aya asked.

Dedran shrugged. "A few rounds ago about a dozen, but one of them was not like the others. I didn't see it get pulled back through the Pathway. I think it may have defeated the protections somehow, but I am only making guesses. I don't understand everything I have seen at all. There is so much information I took from their computers left to process. Not only that, a thousand of them could have marched through that door and not gone back while I was unconscious."

"Ayasha the Speaker," she supplied.

"We have to go, Ayasha. We have to find a way to contact the Dragons. They are the only ones who can use the First Word."

Aya shook her head. In a lifetime of training her senses, both physical and aethereal, she had never sensed anything like what was tugging at her to get a closer look at the symbols on the door frames.

"I have to stay. I have to try and stop this. You can make it back out through the Downpour. We have set up a path for everyone. Go find Iryeka at the stairwell. She, Arno, Kian, and Ireana should come to join me. You should take the others and leave. What you have found must reach the Hearth."

Dedran reached for her again, but stopped. "You'll die. You can't fight that many. If they find someone here that can fight, they will send more through to fight you."

Aya shrugged. "Then I'll die doing what I have decided I was put here to do. Go on, Dedran. Tell the others to come and support me only if they are prepared for what may come of it. I have to stay and undo this."

Aya made her way to the opening. She didn't bother with the door. It was likely jammed shut, considering the twisted look of the door. She leapt down the five feet to the floor.

Dedran watched her approach the door frames for a long moment, and then took a long look at the bits and pieces of his shorn tail. He shivered, turned, and fled.

Chapter 21

"DOORS"

As Aya approached, it became more and more difficult to look at the symbols on the standing door frames, but Aya did not look away. Something inside of her drew her closer. The transparent curtain of dim illumination fluttered more quickly, but Aya paid it no heed. She could feel the magic coursing through the door frame. She reached up, and the pads of her left paw brushed the symbols.

Magic rose up and lanced into her like a striking snake. It tried to push the Spirits from her body, but a lifetime of training at Channeling magical energies had left Aya well prepared. She focused, and the energy passed through her feet, grounding itself into the floor, where it dissipated into the concrete. She yanked her paw away, but it was too late.

The Runes of the First Word were now completely clear. She could see the symbols, though she had no idea what they meant. She staggered back from the door frame and fell to her knees.

{Aya, you must center yourself,} the voice of Lane the Wanderer reminded. *{I feel we have little time.}*

Aya took one deep breath and then another as she tried to put the magical energies coursing madly through her body into order. Slowly, she succeeded, but it had taken far too long. She hurriedly stood up and turned towards the door frames with a snarl. She mentally called to the Heart of Fire.

{Aya, do not do anything rash,} said Greatfather Roan.

{This is not rash. I have considered the danger, and I am going to burn these things to slag.}

The burning elemental appeared next to her, and Aya reached out immediately.

{I am not attempting to dissuade you from doing this thing. I am saying that we do not understand the magics bound up in these artifacts. I know very little about the First Word, but I know that it is orders of magnitude more powerful than our Channeling. Those

Runes are the material of the universe. I cannot imagine how much energy might be released if you melt that steel with them still active.}

{I don't know how to deactivate them first.}

{I think you simply have to mar them. Fire will destroy them, but Fire is pure energy. It might synergize with the Runes and cause an enormous release.}

Aya dashed forward and drew her Heartblade. Seven symbols stood before her. She aimed for the easiest to slash through, the symbol about halfway up the left-paw side of the frame. The Heartblade cleaved through the steel with no resistance, and the glowing symbol winked out immediately. It vanished from the doorway, but the fluttering curtain of energy did not dissipate. Aya tapped Lane's power and her body sped up. Faster than reflex, she slashed through all seven Runes in a blurring instant. The steel door frame scraped softly, and then clattered to the ground in over a dozen pieces. The eerie black square of emptiness with its fluttering curtain stayed precisely where it was.

{Why is that still there?} Aya asked. She could feel that the magic energy feeding the thing had faded away. The fluttering of the curtain of energy had ceased, at least, which seemed a good sign.

{Remember what Dedran said. He said something came through that had somehow beaten the protections. It could be because of the way the First Word was used to bend reality here. It might stay like this until the creature is forced back through or destroyed.}

{We are out of our depth here,} Aya responded, and felt a mental nod from Lane the Wanderer.

{I am not completely,} Roan responded. *{Each symbol of the First Word is the thing itself in all of its forms.}*

Aya moved to the next door frame. This one did not have as many Runes carved into it. Still, some of the Runes were the same. Roan sent a request to control her body.

{I am fairly confident that nothing else will be coming through this Pathway. This symbol here is the only one that I know, and oddly, I have no idea how I know what it is for.}

Under Roan's control, her paw pointed to the symbol he was trying to indicate, three circles overlapping each other. *{It is Time.}*

The way he said it was somewhat odd to Aya, like the symbol was the actual thing itself rather than the name of the Rune. Her thoughts drew an affirmative from Roan.

{That is exactly what I am saying. It is Time itself. You have to understand, I am guessing from a discussion I once had with a few of the more magically gifted Spirits from our history about the nature of our magic. Most of it went flying over my head, but what I do know is this. The First Word is the language used to describe the mechanics of our reality. It is unusual for anyone to even be able to see the runes themselves, but to be able to invest them with intent and power is almost impossible. Because it is the fabric of our reality, using it as they've done here could change the very nature of reality in this space. If there were protections like Dedran said, then perhaps because the First Word changed the nature of this little piece of reality, it will not return to normal until the conditions of those protections are fulfilled.}

Aya felt his control of her body slough away and breathed a sigh of relief.

"I get the feeling that the First Word has something to do with my name. I was just," Aya tried to quantify the sensation from moments before, "enchanted by those runes, somehow. I couldn't read them before." Aya looked down, feeling uncertain. "I can now." The words came out as a whisper.

A shuffling noise range out behind her, and Aya spun. Her nose had told her that four ta'el she knew had entered the outer room. A moment later, Dedran trailed into the room behind the others. She narrowed her eyes at him.

"I told you to get out of here. I've broken the Pathway, but Netherspawn are not the only danger in here, and you need to take this news to the Hearth."

"They convinced me that it would not be very courageous of me to turn tail and run."

Aya growled softly. "I'm sure they did."

"I'd like," Dedran began.

"I don't care what you would like. You are so out of sorts that you have not even noticed your Watcher attempting to draw your attention," Aya said heatedly. *{Lane the Wanderer, a Pathway to New York, if you please?}*

She felt an affirmative, and began to walk a circle right there in the middle of the floor. It was a tight circle, and it would create a Pathway just large enough for a single ta'el. Just as she completed the careful circle and the Pathway opened, a screeching roar came from the entrance to the room. Everyone clapped paws over their ears and spun to face the doorway. Aya called their attention back.

"This will take you to New York, Dedran. The rest of you can follow him if you like, but I suspect that the denizens of the Nether were attempting to get the rest of these Pathways working so that they could spread the contents of this Nest anywhere they wanted. I, for one, am not going to allow that sort of corruption to spread from here."

"We saw at least two dozen Shadowgaps, but I am sure there were a lot more. We saw dozens of Corrupted Ones, but there could be hundreds more nearby. I will stay and fight," Kian said. He was missing part of one of his small rounded ears, and it looked ragged as if it had been bitten off.

Dedran jumped into the Pathway, and Aya watched him disappear. She had to make a decision. Shadowgaps were a product of Corrupted Spirits. If enough Corrupted Spirits gathered in a place, the run off of spiritual energy from them would create pools of discordant energy. In the natural course of things, Corrupted Spirits happened over time when something damaging happened to a Spirit.

They should be rare, but the world was a big place, and bad things happened in it. In a nest, where Shadowgaps could form, Corrupted Spirits could capture other Spirits and forcibly corrupt them by submerging them in the aethereal pools of energy. With that many Shadowgaps available, there was no telling how many Corrupted Spirits were about to flood the room, but she couldn't leave the Nest here to fester. She was going to have to do something drastic, something stupid if she wanted to be sure this place would not spew darkness forth into the world.

"Are you all willing to buy me some time? I need a few moments to concentrate," Aya asked.

She knew she was asking them to risk their lives, but this many Corrupted Spirits, if unleashed, could easily overrun the city of Denver and kill every living soul within. She suspected that without the Netherspawn here to control them, they would not long stay within the nest. Normal fire would be of little use against them, though enough of it could disperse their energies. Only the Heartblades they carried would save them from what was about to burst into the space.

{Lane, we must widen the Pathway. Do I need to walk a new circle?} she asked, and felt a negative reply. The opening of the Pathway expanded to at least ten feet across. Kian, Iryeka, Ireana, and Arno all seemed to reach their decision at the same time.

"Iryeka, fire won't destroy them very quickly, but it will keep them back for a moment," Kian said.

The large grey and white canine stepped forward. Her body wreathed itself in flame. She lifted her paws, and a huge torrent of flame spewed forth. It spread in a jagged wall between them and the control room. Then, she walked a large circle around everyone, spreading a massive wall of fire. The heat in the room became nearly unbearable, but Aya didn't feel it like the rest of them. She had called the Heart of Fire into herself once more. She released Kika with a sending of deep gratitude.

{This plan is not advisable, Hearth Stone. Your body may not survive Channeling such power,} the Heart of Fire advised.

{If I die, it is what I must do to keep ta'el safe. This is not the largest nest we have seen, but it isn't far from it.}

{I will grant you the power you ask, Hearth Stone.}

The screeching roar of Corrupted Spirits sounded again. They attempted to batter their way through the wall of fire. Shouts sounded from the other ta'el in the room as they fought and destroyed Corrupted Ones. Still, Aya blocked it out. She Channeled the power of the Heart of Fire and mentally reached out to the Downpour. Aya fought down the shivers of terror at what she was doing.

Through the magic of the Heart of Fire, she could feel the boiling lava. What she had done earlier was a mere fraction of what she was about to do. It was without a doubt the most idiotic thing she had ever attempted. To destroy this place, she would need to move thousands of tons of molten rock. Even her mother would find such a feat difficult, with or without the Heart of Fire.

There was no other way. She rolled herself up to her feet and spread them apart, before crouching and holding her paws out in front of her. She made a grasping gesture with both paws. She could feel the flow of the lava as if it were a writhing serpent squirming in her paws. She took a step back and Channeled the power of the Heart. She felt as if her blood might boil in her veins. Forcing the feeling down, she concentrated and squeezed her paws into fists. She felt it when the flow of the lava began to change. At the same time, she felt herself beginning to burn up on the inside.

Just when she thought she would literally burst into flames, she felt the lava rise from the pool. She yanked her fists back to her sides, and there was a sudden release as an enormous mass of molten rock was yanked out of the pool outside. She tumbled backwards to the edge of the Pathway.

"Go!" She managed to rasp out before she began the downward spiral. She saw Kian turn, and then there was an enormous rumbling. It wasn't a sound, it was a feeling. A vibration. Something that permeated her entire body. Everyone froze for a long moment. Spirits, Corrupted Ones, and Ta'el all stood, locked in terror. The rumbling brought with it an undeniable feeling of dread.

"Go!" Aya shouted one last time, but in her weakened state, it came out it came out more like a wheeze. It was all her body could handle before she fell into the black depths of unconsciousness.

Chapter 22

"BURN"

Aya did not come back to full consciousness. She could just barely hear voices around her, as if they were extremely far away.

{What did she do? Her internal organs are boiled!}

The voice was somewhat unfamiliar. The sounds faded out for a long moment. It came back with Greatfather Roan's voice, mid-sentence. There was fear in his voice, and also a touch of awe.

{… lava flows out of the Downpour and into the…}

The sound faded again as she lost her grip on consciousness. It came back an indeterminant time later. She attempted to pull her eyes open, but her eyelids didn't respond to her request.

{… can't fix this, Roan. She has somehow damaged the connection between…}

She recognized the voice as Siris, but it faded away again. Again, some length of time passed, and when she could hear again, it was her mother's voice that was speaking.

{… will add my power to yours, but so help me, you will attempt to fix her, Siris!}

Aya finally pulled her eyes open, and though her vision was blurry, she could make out the glowing red shape of Greatfather Roan next to her bed. The room was a simple one, about ten feet square, with calming bluish grey walls. There were no windows, and only a single door. The cot she was lying on told her that she was in a clinic somewhere - just comfortable enough to sleep, but not so comfortable that one wanted to hang around.

"Roan? What is going on?" she rasped in a whisper. None of the shouting ta'el seemed to hear her, and Roan sent to her inside of her mind.

{When you pulled the flow of the Downpour out of whack and down into that Scale-cursed hole to destroy everything, the energy you pulled from the Heart of Fire burned your body and your Spirit. Before we could all get out of there, the room flooded with Corrupted Spirits, and while we destroyed many of them, before the lava burst into the room to take care of the rest, some of them managed to attack you.

With your Spirit so damaged already, they were able to rip your Spirit to ribbons. You're currently clinging to your body by a thread. My thread, actually. The only thing holding you together right now is your will binding me to you, but I'm getting tired. I can only clutch your Spirit to your broken body for so long. Try to stay conscious and hold on, Aya.

Siris is unwilling to risk the corruption bleeding back into him when he attempts to heal your Spirit. He is not confident that he can do the job without being poisoned himself. He's hiding cowardice behind the idea that he cannot risk himself for the good of his city. However, considering the look on your mother's face right now, I believe that if he doesn't acquiesce to your mother's demands, she will make good on her promise to eat his still-beating heart. I have rarely seen a look quite that furious on your mother's face. She does not well abide cowards...}

He continued on, but Aya wasn't listening. There was something happening inside of her head. The symbols of the First Word that she had seen on the doorways were appearing on the ceiling of her mind, as if they were being etched across the vaults of her consciousness. They seemed so simple for something that granted so much power. One of the symbols began to glow. This one also looked like three circles overlapping each other, but they were in a completely different configuration than the symbol that Roan had identified as Time. It glowed intensely with blue light, and then another lit up, this one with white light.

Aya floated inside of her own mental thoughtscape. Since she was so near to death, she assumed she had come here to avoid the pain of her body. She had been wrong. She had come here to see these Runes of the First Word. She reached out with ephemeral fingers and touched the first Rune that had lit up. She had never seen anything quite like its shimmering glow. The moment she touched it, the symbol flared with light. In this place of thought, it could not blind her, but it was startling and she pulled back. Still, warmth suffused her body, and she felt much better. Distantly, she could hear her mother.

"What is happening to my daughter?" her mother growled.

Aya felt a gentle paw on her forehead, but then she saw the second Rune begin to glow. She wondered how many Runes composed the First Word. Here, she saw only two. The second one was an odd, twisted looking symbol that looked almost like a stylized version of the humans' letter S, made of ribbon. This one glowed in a shimmering white. She wasn't sure what the ramifications of what she was doing might be. Still, she was certainly going to die if something wasn't done, and her mother would do something unpleasant to force Siris to do his duty if she didn't find some way to help herself. She just hoped that was what she was doing.

She touched the second symbol, and it flared to incandescent brightness. It felt like her entire body was about to burst into flames again. She tried to scream, but she knew she didn't make any sound. She was not properly part of her body in that moment. Getting it to respond was impossible. It was her very spiritual essence that was burning.

Suddenly, her pain faded away and she sucked in a startled breath. Her eyes sprang open, and she threw herself to her paws. Several ta'el gathered around her cot jumped back. Every muscle in her entire body creaked with strain. She was taut, teeth bared, and ready to attack. Her claws had slashed the coverings on the cot to ribbons before her brain truly reconnected to her body. She collapsed face-first, back to the cot in the tatters of her coverings.

"Little Aya?" her mother's voice came from somewhere above.

"M'fin," Aya mumbled into the cot, but she was better than fine, not that she actually felt good. She felt like she did after her first training session with Lane, and she had bruises in places she didn't know she had places. It was a good kind of pain, though, the kind that told you that you had done good work and it was time to rest. Aya would not rest in the face of this, though. In agony, she lifted her paws and slid them off the side of the bed. She pushed herself up with excruciating slowness until her feet hit the floor.

"Aya?" Greatfather Roan asked.

She walked across the room straight to Siris. Then, in a blur of motion that hurt more than anything she had ever felt in her life, she drew back her fist and slugged Siris in the jaw. Despite the physical pain, few things had ever felt so good. There was a loud crack, and Siris smashed into the wall behind him. He slid to the ground, and Aya limped over him to loom.

"You Scale-Cursed coward! I put my ass on the line to save your city and you repay that sacrifice with letting me die?"

Siris reached up to attempt to fix his broken jaw, and Aya hissed in a way only a feline could manage.

"If you use one measure of healing magic on that jaw, I swear by the White herself, I will separate every part of you from every other part of you. You don't need to talk. Be thankful that a busted jaw is all you have to deal with, because if you had stood by like the worthless pile of shit you are and let me die, no amount of healing would have saved you from her." Aya gestured to her mother who was actually glowing with latent power.

Aya did not have much of a problem with fear in the face of things that you were not equipped to deal with. Sometimes, fear was the correct response. She hadn't expected Siris to fight. He was, after all, a Lightmend, but cowardice in facing up to the very task for which you were given your chosen abilities to do was unacceptable.

Just then, Siris' Watcher Spirit manifested next to him. This Spirit was, unexpectedly, an Avian of an owl species that she had not seen before. Avians did not often go down paths that involved being so tied to the ground as becoming a Lightmend. She looked from Aya to Siris disapprovingly. For the first time in her life, it was not her immediate instinct to attempt to smooth things over. She had come very close to giving her life to protect the ta'el that Siris was responsible for. The least he could have done was try to help her survive it. She certainly wouldn't have given up without trying a lot harder than he had.

"Apologies, Honored Ancestor, but at this moment, I care little for your charge, and I would hope that you would both endeavor to improve your fortitude for the work in the future."

Aya turned and limped away very slowly towards the door. Before she was halfway there, her father Sahone had bent to slide a shoulder under her arm to help her walk. Her mother was on her other side, and between the two of them, they made the walk much lighter.

"Where are we?" Aya whispered.

"New York. Siris came after you dropped everyone into the Hearth's garden here. Usually, Adronis would be on duty here, but both he and the next closest Lightmend, Syna, were called away to help with a small disaster on the Florida coastline. Sirus reconstructed Dedran's tail, healed some lacerations, and fixed Kian's ear. When you wouldn't wake, though, Roan came to fetch us," her mother explained.

"What did you do?" her father asked.

"How should I know? I saw symbols of the First Word inside my mind. When I touched them, I got better."

Her father drew in a breath. She eyed him, and he shook his head. "I can't," he said, and she smiled at him.

"I know, Daddy. What happened to me? I only heard part of the argument."

"You Channeled an astonishingly stupid amount of power through your body from the Heart of Fire to pull half a mountain's worth of molten stone out of the Downpour and into the place where you found Dedran. The magic generated enough heat runoff that even with the Heart of Fire inhabiting your body, you simmered your internal organs like you were using your insides as a pressure cooker."

"Joy," Aya groaned.

"Why? We haven't had a chance to get the story from anyone else. Dedran left the book you were looking for and ran off to find the Record the moment his tail was healed. He grabbed your things when the straps holding them to your body burned."

"We found what the humans had done down there."

Her parents both stopped, forcing her to stop as well.

"Dedran figured it out, but I would have as well, once I saw the Doors. Someone among the humans summoned the will to make use of the First Word, but something tells me that it wasn't properly utilized. I don't know how I know that, I just do," Aya explained. Her Father nodded. "Further, the entire place had become a nest for hundreds of Corrupted Ones. With the Netherspawn driven out, they had been unleashed. I had to destroy everything and cleanse those Spirits in fire."

"We don't know a lot about the First Word," her mother said as they started to walk again.

It turned out, as they got outside, that they were not far from her home. Clearly, they had moved her to one of the Hearth's clinics that were only a few streets over from home. Even at her reduced pace, it did not take them long to walk the three blocks to her building. Her parents settled her on her sleeping pad, and her father went off to cook a meal. Aya watched her Mother as she roved around her bedroom.

Aya's mother stopped to inspect the various weapons hanging on the wall above her bed. A pair of curved swords hung horizontally on a stand, one above the other. The lower sword was shorter than the upper one, but they were otherwise identical. Vertically next to them was a long spear, twice the height of any Ta'el. These were clearly human weapons. To Aya's left, where her mother wandered next, a set of two dozen cubbies were built into the wall. Some of the cubbies held plants while others contained carved figurines in stone, wood, and ivory. Ayasha the elder recognized several figures from the history of the ta'el. A pristine likeness of Lane the Wanderer stood in jade above a cubby containing a bonsai tree.

She continued to the next wall, a solid plane of pure white unlike the others, which had been floor to ceiling wood panels. Ayasha knocked a knuckle against it, and it clicked like stone. Written across it in black charcoal were hundreds of sentences and phrases in Ta'eltesh. Some were lines of poetry, and others were humorous quips. Still more were thoughtful lines of text that seemed taken out of context.

Aya watched as her mother stopped in front of the wall of glass that looked out onto her rooftop garden. When Ayasha the elder turned back, there were unshed tears in her eyes.

"Mom?" Aya asked.

Her mother wiped away the tears. "It's nothing, Little Aya. I'm just terrified for you and proud of you. You are who you want to be, and that is more than I could have ever hoped for."

Aya felt herself blushing. Before she could say anything, her mother went on.

"You used the First Word to heal yourself."

It was not a question, but Aya shook her head anyway. "It was the First Word that fixed me, to be sure, but to say I used it would be a stretch. I had no idea what I was doing, only that if I didn't do something soon, they would be sweeping Siris into a dust pan. You don't need that kind of discord with the Spirits."

"To be fair, Greatmother Sasu was moments away from ripping away control of Siris' body to do the work herself." The shimmering white bear appeared next to her Mother and grinned toothily at Aya.

{I think you handled that lickspittle quite nicely,} Sasu sent, and Aya grinned.

"Lickspittle, good word." Then she sighed. "Not my best moment, I think."

Her mother shook her head. "I think it was good that you saved me from frothing and strangling Siris to death."

"He didn't strike me as the cowardly type when he disposed of the Visceral."

Sasu shook her head. *{I don't think he is. I think he saw something when he looked upon your Spirit that frightened him. I haven't had a chance to examine your Spirit free of your body to see what that might be.}*

"Would you like to?" Aya asked.

Sasu shrugged. *{After such a trial, I don't think it would be a good idea to separate your Spirit from your vessel at this point, Little Aya. I suspect with the magic I saw suffuse your body, there is little chance whatever he saw remains, in any case.}*

"As you wish, Honored Ancestor. I do feel fine, though, despite my body feeling as if I have been beaten soundly with a stout stick."

Roan formed of blood red mist next to her. *{I'm not finding anything amiss at this point. Our connection is as strong as ever.}* Roan's pronouncement made her mother groan.

"You're going to run out of here next round and try to get yourself killed again," her mother stated as she folded herself into a cross-legged position next to Aya's sleeping pad.

"I don't think I have a choice. This isn't over. Dedran said that something worse than the Viscerals came through just while he was down there. He said he didn't think that the Pathway was just open all the time. I need to learn more from him."

"He is waiting for you in our house."

Her parents' home was outside the city limits. It was much larger than her apartment, but it had to be. When her mother wasn't off doing her duties as a Caretaker, she generally taught other Channelers. Her home also sometimes hosted classes that her father taught for Brewsmiths. Once Aya had been released from Lane the Wanderer's tutelage, she had taught a few students of her own at Lane's request.

"I will come as soon as my body doesn't feel like Greatmother Sasu trampled me with Greatfather Strom riding on her back."

Sasu's mental chuckle rang inside of her mind.

{Will you accept healing, Little Aya?} Greatmother Sasu offered.

"Gladly, Greatmother, but not tonight. Next round," Aya said, and Sasu nodded, "if you are going to be here that long."

"Not even the White herself could pry me away until you are well again."

Aya inhaled, and smelled perfectly prepared fish.

"If Daddy is going to make meals that smell that good, it won't be long," she said with a grin.

Chapter 23

"UNDERSIDES"

After a night of rest, Aya felt like she had only been beaten with a rubber hose instead a stout staff. She wished she had time to spend a few rounds just lying in bed. Greatfather Roan had reminded her that she had solved the mystery assigned to her entire species by their Creator. Her parents had shown up at her door to make sure she was no longer dying, and breakfast made by her father had destroyed any hope of sleeping in.

The first rays of the sun spilled between the overgrown buildings as they made their way onto the street. Blossoms on heart trees spiraled open the moment they were kissed by the light. Aya took a deep breath as her city woke around her. She dropped to all fours to walk more comfortably, and her parents paced her easily.

"We could have had him come here," her mother offered, but Aya shook her head.

"I could use the walk. Besides, I want to stop by the Hearth and check on my apprentices, and I need to speak to the Matron."

"How is old Luxia?" Sahone grinned knowingly.

"She's fine, same twelve-hundred-turn-old bird monster thing she will always be," Aya said with a fond smile.

"Gryphon, dear," her mother supplied.

Aya rolled her eyes and twitched her whiskers, saying 'whatever.' She turned down the street towards the outskirts. "You don't mind waiting?" she asked when they made it to the Hearth's large compound.

Her father shook his head and switched smoothly to walking on two paws. Her mother also stood up, and they exchanged a look. They both dusted off their paws, and her Mother twitched her whiskers and raised her brows, asking how long.

"It shouldn't be long, and it's just going to be a boring conversation where I ask her to go speak with Ireana's mother about an attitude adjustment," Aya explained.

"Well, it's about time someone did," her mother said.

Much like her daughter, it had never sat well with her how Tiana treated Ireana. Her father shrugged, held out his arm in a gentlemanly way to her mother, and they padded off down the street, arm in arm. Aya knew she would find them at their favorite little café down the street when she was finished.

Aya rarely went in through the large institutional-looking façade of the Hearth. The massive columns of carved stone that had once supported and adorned the building were long gone. Each one had been replaced by the trunk of one of the building's many heart trees. The ta'el had restored the carved statues above the entrance, though they were now outlined in the branches and vines that have been woven into the construction of the building. Pure white blocks of stone that had replaced missing pieces shone between their worn and grey relatives from the original construction. Much of the construction had already been quite old when the human civilization had ended, so the magic that had been used to preserve what was already there could not make it new again.

Checking on Arctah and Marisa only took five bouts. Most of their apprenticeship was book study at this point. It wouldn't be too long before Aya would need to start teaching them to Channel in earnest or hand them off to another Hearth Stone. When she was finished, she turned to head to the Matron's office and almost ran muzzle-first into Ayrece. The Record tilted his head curiously, and Aya took a step back. Caught on the spot, she had no question for him. He grinned toothily at her and twitched his whiskers, conveying amusement. She had never been sure if he could actually hear other ta'el's thoughts, but she though that perhaps this was a small confirmation.

"Hello, Ayrece," Aya gave a quick bow.

"Just the emta I've been looking for. You found it."

Aya shook her head. "Dedran gets the credit for that."

"I rather think not," he said, and Aya dropped an ear in confusion. He continued. "Dedran rushed into a situation without even telling his Watcher what he intended or suspected concerning that place. Had it not been for you, this would have gone much differently, I think."

Aya had not thought about it that way. She paused, thinking it through. "How close was Dedran to dying?"

Ayrece gently tapped one of his claws on her nose. "That, Little Aya, is the right question. Be careful with what you learn from Undersides. What you will find in those pages is important for you to know. Be mindful, Ayasha the Speaker, if you continue on your path from here, there is no turning back." He stepped around her and walked off towards the exit.

She stared after him for a long moment, knowing that he had said everything he would. He would not talk to her any more, even if she tried to stop him and ask more questions. He was always like that. It was part of his magic. He had to be very careful what he revealed to others. Then she scowled.

"As if there was ever any turning back from this mess."

She made her visit to the Matron, who was happy to intervene on her behalf to set Tiana straight. When she finally made it to Starlight, the café her mother liked so much, she was surprised to find Ayrece once again. Seeing him twice in a round was extremely odd. As soon as she came through the door, he excused himself and quite literally disappeared. Aya scowled at the chair where he had been sitting, and then sat down with her parents.

"What was that about?"

"Just inquiring on our progress in the Tongass forest. We told him it was going as well as could be expected until our daughter went on a rash of suicide attempts."

Her father grinned at her sour expression. He burst out laughing when she made a rude gesture at him. A young feline with mottled black, white, and tan fur appeared at the side of the table and carefully put down a glass and a small square pastry with a drizzle of transparent red syrup atop it. A white powder had been dusted over the whole thing.

"It's been years," Aya said, a little amazed that her father had remembered.

"It's food, dear. I never forget."

Aya carefully picked up the pastry and bit into it. Delicious sweet and just very slightly sour flavors burst across her tongue. The drink, though, was something really special. It was made with blended strawberries. These berries, which had been widely described in a lot of human cooking recipes, grew only in wild places and were quite difficult to find. Aya looked up at him. Her whiskers and ears did a complicated little dance that expressed more than curiosity. She wanted to know where he had found the strawberries. Her father shrugged.

"I didn't. Nevian did."

That midround went so quickly. They discussed small things. Aya enjoyed the short few shifts because that one cryptic sentence spoken by Aryece had somehow burrowed deep into her subconscious, giving her the certainty that she was about to live through interesting times. Considering her last few spells, if things got any more interesting than they had been, she would certainly be facing the Bardo quite soon.

When they finally arrived, Dedran was sleeping off the left-over fatigue from being healed. They entered into a large room with bookshelves on all the walls, filled with entertaining books. Like most ta'el common rooms, the furniture surrounded a pit in the center where ta'el could relax or sleep. However, Aya found Dedran draped over the arm of one of the large blue cloth couches. His head was hanging upside down and a little drool leaked out of the corner of his muzzle. Aya shook her head and examined his tail while he snored contentedly.

Despite the fact that she'd like to club Siris, he did good work. After his ordeal, she didn't want to touch him. She watched him for a moment longer, and decided that a gentle mental sending would be best. She had never tried it unaided by the Spirits, but it should be possible over this tiny distance, as long as she kept it simple. Aya concentrated and sent

Dedran's sleeping mind a gentle jostling. His eyes popped open, but he didn't startle. He just sighed.

"This is the most comfortable piece of furniture I have ever plied my carcass to," he said with a grin.

A moment later, orange mist formed into the small shape of Eleena, swinging her tiny feet off the edge of the couch. She bowed her head to Aya in deference, and Aya returned the gesture.

"How are you feeling, Honored Ancestor?"

{Much better now that this idiot is no longer about to be eaten by Corrupted Ones.}

Dedran sprang up to his feet and reached over the end of the couch. He scrubbed the drool from his muzzle with the back of a paw and came up with a weather-beaten leather backpack in the other. He flipped open the top and began to rummage through it. A moment later, he produced a small book bound in black leather with gilt lettering on the cover.

"You dropped this, Hearth Stone." The cover read Undersides in gold leaf. "I checked it this morning. It is complete, but before I could read any more of it, The Record told me I would not like what would happen if I read the rest of the entries. Since I am driven, not suicidal, I decided it would be best to heed his advice." He proffered the book to her, and she took it.

"Thank you, Dedran, and Eleena, for everything you have done."

Dedran bowed very deeply to Aya.

"No, Ayasha the Speaker, thank you. I would not have survived to tell this tale without you. I was stupid, reckless, and I should have called for help the second I realized what I might find down that hole. You have allowed me to culminate the work of my life. I have achieved the task our race was given by the Dragons all those millennia ago. Or more accurately, I should say *we* have. I think I need to go find something else to do with myself now. Perhaps explore some things just because I want to know what is there."

Dedran bowed to her parents, respectful but less deep than he had to Aya. "Thank you for the rest. I truly needed it." Aya's mother nodded.

"My Watcher, what say you?" Dedran asked Eleena.

"I think that sounds like a nice way to spend a few turns."

Dedran turned to Aya's parents. "I do not wish to be rude to such gracious hosts, but I believe that I should converse with the Speaker alone."

Sahone shrugged, took Ayasha the elder by her paw, and lead her off deeper into the house.

"I have come to some questions to which I do not like the answers I have drawn. I think that you need to know," Dedran began.

Aya gestured for him to go ahead.

"From what I extracted from the computer systems in that place before I was attacked, I have now calculated some figures concerning how often the creatures of the Nether were given access to the Pathway. It seems that the Pathway would open at random over the course of several spells every thousand or so turns. It isn't at any set time, so I suspect that not many of the Netherspawn could get through, but considering what I have seen them do..." Dedran trailed off when Aya's eyes lit with comprehension.

"Seven thousand and twenty-one turns. That is how long it's been since the first ta'el were made by the Dragons. So, what happened to the Netherspawn the other six times the Pathway opened?"

"What indeed, Ayasha the Speaker. Clearly, if they were allowed to run rampant, we would have more stories about them. Someone stopped them, and the thing that came through while I was bound to that desk was nothing like one of those filthy Viscerals. I am no Channeler, and even I could feel the power coming off of that thing. I suspect there are no more than ten ta'el on the planet who would stand a match for that. The Record, perhaps your mother, some of the Mythics." Dedran shrugged.

Aya lifted a paw causing Dedran to pause. "Will you show me?"

Dedran frowned. "Are you sure? You know if I let you peak into my memories, you will feel everything I felt. I feel no shame in telling you I lost all control of my faculties when that thing came too close to me."

Aya did not particularly want to, but she had to see what he had seen. She nodded.

"As you wish, Hearth Stone." Dedran held out his paw.

Seeing into the memories of another ta'el was not always an option. It required that both ta'el have a Watcher Spirit looking out for them to help transfer the thoughts from mind to mind. She took his paw in hers and concentrated on opening her mind to his memories. She blinked, and she was back in that room. This time, though, she was bound to the desk, her wrists and ankles lashed down to the legs of the cold metal desk beneath her.

The pain crashed into her like a charging elephant. She could see the severed pieces of her tail on the desk one level down from hers. She twitched her tail, and could tell that around half of it remained. The movement made her cringe in pain. Everything hurt, and she knew without any doubt that she would not last much longer. The last round of beatings had broken something vital inside of her, and it was only a matter of time, now. She was about to close her eyes and pray for unconsciousness when she felt it. A current of chill air blew through the fur of her face. She slowly turned her head enough to see the Pathway fluttering. The current of air came through the doorway, but it did not move the curtains of energy.

Her eyes widened as misty tendrils of seeping black, something, started to flail its way out of the door way. Worse, as more of the tendrils emerged from the Pathway, she began to feel a sensation, a sinking, twisting of her guts as the foul creature emerged. The tendrils were drawn back towards the door as a black figure stepped slowly through. They twisted and wrapped around the roughly ta'el-shaped figure, but there was no doubt that this was not any ta'el.

Aya released Dedran's paw and collapsed onto red couch opposite the one where he had been sleeping. Dedran took a step forward, but Aya waved him off.

"I'm fine. Go on."

Dedran nodded. "Killing something like that should be part of our records, but I have asked Eleena, and she has asked everyone else she can contact. They know what these things are, but nothing more than that. I think my dear Watcher may be keeping back some details." He paused, and Eleena shrugged.

"I promise I have left out nothing of true importance. I have only not told you what I know about who fought the Netherspawn." Dedran sighed and turned back to Aya. "I feel that you especially will find out precisely what they are."

Ayasha shivered a little. She remembered what Ayrece had said to her about there being no turning back just that morning. "No turning back," she whispered.

Dedran hummed in question.

"Nothing. Thanks for letting me see that memory."

Dedran shook his head. "It was nothing. Thank you again, Ayasha the Speaker. I offer you any help that I can give, now or in the future. My life, such as it is, is yours. Call to my Watcher if you ever have need of me. I will come. I will come even if it means my death, for you have given me every moment I have left to enjoy in this world." He bowed, and then turned to go, his ringed tail swaying gently behind him.

"I may hold you to that, Dedran."

He paused for a moment, and then nodded. He said no more, and headed for the door. Aya was moved by some impulse she did not understand. She reached out and caught him by the bicep. Something happened, something she did not understand at all. Tingling warmth flowed down her arm. Dedran's eyes went a little wide. She finally released him, having no idea what she had done.

"Be safe, Dedran the Explorer."

He nodded again, and disappeared through the door. Aya put the book on one of the couch cushions, and then pulled herself up onto the couch. She pulled the book open and riffled through the pages until she found the entry labeled The Below Places. There, she began to read. She skipped past the first two pages and sighed in relief when the next several pages were intact. What she found, though, made her certain that what Aryece had told Dedran was true. It was an absolute fact that he did not want to know what she found in those pages.

Chapter 24

"CHOSEN"

Aya sat staring at the book for long minutes before she felt the presence of Roan materializing next to her. He could tell she was distraught, and so he said nothing. Clearly, though, he didn't think that doing nothing was enough, as a moment later, her Father came into the room. She knew Roan had summoned the Fox.

"Tell me the truth, Daddy. I know you know, and after reading what is in this book, I think I know too. What happened when the Netherspawn came to this world before?"

Her Father tilted his head and his eyes roved over her slowly, judging her.

"You do, don't you," he said slowly, as if he'd seen something that told him she had figured it out.

"Aryece was right, there is no turning back."

Her father nodded. "Then make yourself comfortable, my cub, and I will tell you a small story."

What she had found in those pages was what Huan had found in The Below Places. That there in those caves, never meant to be seen by living eyes, was a tributary of the World Well. She did not know much about how things functioned in the background, but every Channeler knew that reality was created by a great magic. That was what the First Word was. It enforced all of existence. Each living world had a well of power that was created using the First Word, and there were tributaries of that well that carried the energy throughout the world. But that knowledge was just a vague idea, more legend than any sort of manual for how it functioned.

The Runes of the First Word were a mystery to her. Even now, having touched them inside of her mind and in the real world, she couldn't fully remember them. She wasn't sure how she had accessed them, or that she had accessed that kind of power at all. It was possible that someone else had assisted her, somehow.

However, the last part of the entry in Undersides made it very clear exactly what her name meant, even if it didn't tell the whole story. The entry had been written by Huan after he had been taken into The Below Places on a mission with another ta'el. They were to seek out one of the tributaries of the World Well to help Anaran, the last Speaker, fulfill his quest to realize the meaning of his name. To learn to speak the First Word. to learn to shape the magic that was reality itself directly, without the assistance of Spirits.

"You know that when the ta'el were first born unto this world, The White and the other Dragons charged us with discovering what the humans had done that had so thoroughly scoured this world of intelligent life. What most do not know is that they knew it had to be something to do with the creatures of the Nether, because this is not the first time such creatures have attacked a world in our reality. They only ever try to kill intelligent life, because animals do not try to oppose their destruction of any given world. The Dragons could not find what had been done to allow the Netherspawn into our world.

They believe that in a last ditch effort to stop their destruction, the humans had done something drastic to keep the Netherspawn from pouring into our world. This is what had finally destroyed them. They couldn't be sure, though, and they had obligations to the other worlds in our realm, so they created the ta'el to search for answers and defend this world in their stead. They made certain that all of the lingering Netherspawn had been destroyed. They taught us to Channel and use the magic of the Elementals. They informed us that as we died, we would also be bound to the Spiritlands, and we could choose to aid our descendants, or not, as we saw fit.

When they finally felt we were ready, they told us one last thing. Be mindful, they said, for the spawn of the Nether could return at any time. If they do, if whatever the humans did to stop their rampage is ever broken, a ta'el will need to be chosen to stop them. This ta'el will be chosen not for their magical might or their ways with the Spirits, but for their mind, a mind that can think with the fluidity of one who does not believe in the impossible. One who would not stop at a solution simply because it seemed unreasonable. Only a mind this flexible can learn to speak the First Word, and only the First Word can send the Netherspawn back into the darkness with certainty that they will not return. It was a thousand turns before the first Speaker was forced to choose to fight the Netherspawn, and the White returned to our world to train them. I am sure you have guessed that you are the seventh Speaker. The Netherspawn have come again into our world and now, my daughter," Sahone let out an unhappy breath, "you have chosen to stop them."

"Did they attack the Life Spirit last time as well? Do you know how I can stop them?"

Her father shook his head. "I was alive only for the last forty turns of the previous Speaker's life, and only met him once, but I can tell you that they did not. The last time, they attempted to use the Tributaries to poison all of the intelligent life on the planet. We intelligent folk tend to be tasked to disrupt their plots, but the previous Speaker was somehow able to wring from the Netherspawn that those who sent them would reabsorb all of the living energy still available on the world when it was destroyed. That is why they do not just attempt to kill everything before destroying a world. It was a process."

Aya looked like she wanted to ask more questions, but her father held up a finger. "I, sadly, don't know anything more, Little Aya, or I promise I would tell you. You know now what you are getting into, and there is no prohibition against me telling you everything I know at this point. It is clear that knowing has not deterred you."

Aya shook her head in response. "There truly isn't anyone else, is there?"

Her father shook his head. "Not likely. Speakers are one of a kind, and while there are likely many with minds flexible enough to perform the task few have gained the rest of the skills necessary."

"So, I did actually do this to myself?" Aya grinned.

"Undoubtedly. The reward for work well done is more work, as the humans used to say." Her father chuckled.

"You don't seem as worried about me putting myself in danger as I thought you'd be."

Her father's smile gentled down to something more earnest. "I do not relish the idea that because of your chosen path, I may outlive my daughter, but I am not nearly fool enough to think that I could stop you from doing what you feel is right. I've known since long before you started counting your turns that trying to stop you from doing what you think is right is like standing in front of a tidal wave and expecting it to go around me. For you, it would. The rest of us mere mortals have to get out of the way."

"I'll do my best to make sure you keel over before I do, old fart." Aya joked, and her father grinned. "Do you know if the Netherspawn can use the First Word?"

Her father shook his head immediately. "They are entirely alien to any living reality. The only way they can enter our reality is with assistance from those who already live within."

"Why would the Dragons hide this from everyone?"

"There are several reasons, I am certain, but the one that I can see is that such knowledge is dangerous. There are only a few like myself and the Record that, by our nature, are unable to be confounded by magic, even the First Word. Not only that, the First Word itself is extremely dangerous.

It is nearly impossible for anyone to learn the First Word without permission from the Dragons, but not completely impossible. There are ways it can happen, as we now know it did with the humans. Leaving knowledge of the Nether would also mean leaving knowledge of the First Word. It would not precisely make it less difficult to learn the use of the First Word, but it would give more ta'el access to it.

There are some with a mind like yours that could learn, if they were given access to the materials. The issue is that not all of those minds are prepared to deal with power on that level responsibly. It takes proper training and, more importantly, an inborn sense of right to handle absolute power with any sense of safety, Little Aya."

Aya nodded. That at least made some sense. She couldn't help but feel like they had made the job harder, though. She said so, and her father shrugged.

"In what way? The Dragons only knew that creatures of the Nether were the likely culprits for the damage. Had they told us, don't you think that it might have biased us to look only for sources of Nether creatures, and not necessarily what the humans had done to allow them into the world?"

"Maybe you are right. I guess that we will never know. Clearly, though, they had reasons."

Her father nodded. "Come on, Little Aya, it would be my honor to serve a fine meal to the new Speaker."

Her mother was waiting for them in their ample dining room, where her father had laid out a fine feast indeed. Ireana was waiting there as well. Aya had known that this was coming at some point. Fighting unknown supernatural monsters that wanted to eat her alive was practically boring compared to how hard this was going to be. Ireana stood up and came around the table. She threw her arms around Aya and pulled her into a hug.

"Thank you, Aya. My mother apologized to me this morning and said she would do her best to make sure she respects my decision in the future." Aya's ribs creaked as Ireana squeezed her.

"I didn't do anything," Aya wheezed.

Ireana released her and stepped back. She pointedly rolled her eyes. "Yes, because the Matron Keystone just found time out of her schedule to appear in our forge and unleash a tirade that humbled _my_ mother." Ireana scoffed. "Yes, you had nothing to do with it."

Aya thought she had dodged the proverbial relationship bullet and she let out a sigh of relief. Then Ireana's face went still. She smiled Aya's favorite quiet smile, her fangs showing just a tiny bit. She reached into her pouch, and produced a small object which appeared to be carved from blue crystal. Aya's breath caught when she saw it. She knew that it was actually made of sapphire, and Ireana would have had to bargain with a Spirit to have it made, since no naturally occurring sapphire was ever large enough to carve two bracelets. It appeared as one bracelet, with two bands interwoven around each other, impossible to separate. They were often worn by mated pairs, and their magic tied together mate to mate, right down to their very Spirit.

This was a powerful magic, and one had to be very certain of their feelings indeed to seek such an object, because their bonding magic would not function unless both ta'el were compatible and willing to be bound together. It was an extremely personal magic, one that worked a little differently for everyone. Ireana held out the bracelet in both of her paws, offering it to Aya.

"Ayasha the Speaker, would you be my mate?" Ireana sounded more tentative than Aya had ever heard her. She was always so confident, even when proclaiming her own inexperience, but right at that moment, she was terrified that Aya would say no.

Aya took a deep breath. She wanted to tell Ireana no. What she was getting herself into was not going to be any sort of life she would want to put a mate through. That, though, was the lie her protective instincts would use to try to wrap Ireana in soft blankets like she was fragile. Aya knew that would be the stupidest thing she could do. Ireana was not a fragile flower that needed Aya's protection. Noone fragile could take the name Stalker. Even in the few rounds that they had been back together, Aya had admitted to herself that if she were to have a mate, it would be Ireana.

It was amazing, but having not seen Ireana in two turns, she only loved her more. Ireana was her heart. She realized that she had been thinking for much longer than she had intended when her father cleared his throat in the most minute of ways. She mentally berated herself for not being ready for this. She had known it was coming at some point. She opened her mouth, but nothing came out and Irena maintained her smile. If anything, it deepened. She was enjoying Aya's consternation immensely.

"I think you broke her," her father said. Her mother snorted a laugh but then covered her muzzle, shaking silently with laughter.

Wordlessly, Aya reached out and took the free side of the bracelet. As soon as her fingers curled around it, the vibrant blue crystal began to give off a soft green light. This really wasn't a choice for Aya. Much as she had tried to keep her feelings for Ireana entirely platonic, she knew the second she had come into Kian's meeting room that those feelings were anything but.

"Yes, Ireana, I will be your mate."

The twisted bracelet came apart into two beautifully carved bracelets woven like sapphire rope. The one that Aya held stayed crystal blue, but then tiny rivulets of light began to run through the bracelet. It gave off a very soft light. The circle of crystal had an opening on one side, and Aya bent to slip it around her ankle. She knew it would leave a mark when it closed, and she would much rather have it on her ankle than a wrist. Ireana slipped her paw through hers, fastening it around her wrist. Her crystal had turned dark, like the midnight sky. What looked like dark smoke blew in a wind within the crystal. As soon as she fastened it, both bracelets faded to transparency and then tightened, sinking into their fur, and then into the very skin.

Aya felt a warmth as the magic ran through her, bonding her Spirit together with Ireana's. The bracelets were a very permanent bond. It would last even through death and rebirth. While they might not be mated again if they were both reborn, they would be drawn to each other. Even if they didn't know why.

When the warm magic faded, she could feel Ireana, but not in the way she had always had it explained to her. The Heartbond was not a widely used thing. As much as no one wanted to admit it, the depths of love, like any other feeling, were not a shallow pool. They had varying depths. Using the magic of a Heartbond showed you precisely how deep those feelings ran. Not many were ready for that kind of knowledge. Most found that they could feel the ta'el on the other end of the bond. Knowing they were alive and there strengthened their relationship. Aya, though, was a Channeler. She knew precisely how the Heartbond's magic worked. The deeper your feelings when you made the bond, the more you could feel about the ta'el on the other end.

At that moment, Aya was almost distracted by how clearly she could feel Ireana's love. Aya was not exactly the best at exploring her own feelings, but to have precisely how much she loved Ireana so starkly laid out was startling. The Heartbond had formed so strong that it took her breath away, and both of them quickly reached for the new patterns marked into their fur by the bond. A quick touch, and the feelings coming from their new bond were tamped down to something almost unnoticeable. Aya was relieved to see that the bond had been just as overwhelming to Ireana as it was to her, but then she was putting her arms around Ireana as the wolf clutched her.

"I love you, my heart," Aya said, and Ireana had similar regards. She noticed her parents out of the corner of her eye. They were watching with happy grins. She turned her head just slightly towards them. "Not a comment from either of you two peanut gallery residents." Her parents had been subtly hinting for turns that she and Ireana should be mated.

"I'll comment all I like, and my comment is, let's eat," Sahone chuckled.

Long after they had finished eating, Aya and Ireana sat together on the rooftop viewing platform, watching the sun set.

"We'll need to go down to Shop Row tomorrow for a bigger sleeping mat."

"We'll need to discuss when we are going to take our expedition to the Below Places," Ireana replied.

Aya opened her mouth to protest and then closed it.

"That's a wise decision, my heart," Ireana said, knowing that Aya had been about to try to keep her safe. "I do not need you to keep me safe. I need you to love me and be by my side, just like you need the same from me."

"I don't know what I am going to find there. I might not come back, Ireana."

"Why do you even have to go? Sahone told me that you know what your name means."

"Because I don't think knowing what it means is enough. I feel like there is still more to the journey. The White said I need to start in the Below Places. I think she actually meant that is where I will start to be the Speaker."

Ireana nodded. "Alright, then whatever you find there, we will face it together."

Aya sighed. "Alright, but not right this second. I'm still worried about that bigger sleeping mat. I can be a little sharp and pointy in my sleep so you might not want to snuggle up right next to me until I get used to you being there."

Ireana chuckled. "Don't you threaten me with a good time, Ayasha the Speaker." Ireana put her arm around Ayasha's shoulders. "I missed you."

"Missed you too. It was a long two turns. I just hope it lasts."

Ireana glanced at her sideways. "You made a Heartbond with me, Aya, what makes you think it won't?"

Aya shrugged. "Because I haven't the slightest idea what I'm doing." She giggled nervously.

"You keep saying that like any of us ever really do." Greatfather Roan materialized from crimson mist. He smiled at Ireana and gave her a polite bow. "All the training and teaching in the world can prepare you. Preparation, though, is never the same as doing. No plan survives the battle, Little Aya. When it all goes wrong, it is always better to face it together instead of alone."

Chapter 25

"INTO THE DARK"

Aya slung the pack over her shoulder. She couldn't imagine them staying in the Below Places for one moment longer than it was necessary to find the Tributary. Ireana came back from her bath, her fur fluffed until she looked like a stuffed animal. Aya stifled a laugh. Irena tilted her head and narrowed her eyes.

"Give me a brush, you grinning fool," Ireana growled.

"It's a good look for you." Aya tossed a brush to her mate.

Ireana started to smooth down her fur, and put her hair into order. "I love your bathroom. Where did you get the idea for that, what did you call it?"

"Our bathroom, and it's called a shower. The idea came from human books. Did you have any luck?"

"With finding a Shadeholder?" Ireana shook her head. "I put the word out with the local Spirits. If anyone has seen one, it will appear."

"I have been meaning to ask you, Where is Nobian? I haven't seen your Watcher since you got back."

"He will arrive soon. Our training partner was not quite ready to take over our duties. Since they did not have a Watcher of their own yet, Nobian and I felt that he would be doing better service by helping to finish Arask's training. We think that he'll reach a skill level high enough to attract the attention of his own Watcher any round now."

Aya sighed. "Alright, but you've been slacking on your sword drills during your training." Ireana opened her muzzle, but Aya put a finger on her nose. "I am not being rude, my heart. I know that you had a lot to learn, but I kicked your ass the other round, and you were better than that when you left. You don't use a sword to wrestle gorillas in the Amazon."

"But I will need all the skill I can get for the kinds of things you will be getting into. I still have some training to do. I will happily accept your instruction, my heart."

Aya nodded. "For now." She took her quick pouch down from the hook next to the door. She held it out to Ireana and explained what her father had told her.

Ireana took it very tentatively. "Aya, I can't take this. It is," Ireana paused, "priceless."

"If I have to accept you will be in dangerous situations, you will accept that I will do what I can to protect you. I'll have seven powerful Spirits helping me to stay alive. My father meant it for me, but I can't think of a better use for those potions than to give them to you, at least for this trip." Aya pushed the quick pouch gently into Ireana's paws. "The six potions in here are some of the most useful potions my father has ever made, according to him. The thing that makes them so useful is that you can drink all six at once without any side effects."

Ireana's eyes turned to saucers as she stared at the pouch. "What do they do?"

Aya flirted her tail, the equivalent of a shrug. "It's my Dad. Nothing would surprise me at this point, but I haven't had a chance to inspect them all. I've been a little busy. I only know the white one in the first slot of the pouch on the outside is Lightmend Draught, and the green one in the slot next to it on the inside is Blood of the Mountain. Those are the only two I recognize without holding them." Ireana seemed speechless, and Aya giggled at the look on her face.

"Yes, I know those two potions usually work against each other. You tell Dad he can't make them work together."

Ireana lifted the next vial in the case and handed it to Aya. This one had a soft turquoise glow, and the simulacrum within appeared to be the stuffed toy version of an otter, one Aya didn't recognize. Aya held it for a moment, then let out a low whistle.

"This is Spirit Tears. It will make you incorporeal until you dispel the effect." Ireana exchanged it for the next one, which was glowing a glacial blue that was almost white.

"Elixir of Icy Veins. Makes you immune to heat, for the most part. You could take a swim in a volcano with this potion and come out feeling refreshed." The second to last vial was crystal clear like water and gave off a muted white glow. Aya took it, and after a moment, her mouth dropped open. She goggled at the vial.

"This is Featherbound Brew," Aya stammered.

"No it isn't. No one has been able to make Featherbound Brew for three thousand turns," Ireana responded instantly.

Everyone knew about the potion. It was a potion that allowed a ta'el to fly without regard for wind currents or gravity. It required a blessing from a Spirit known as The Silent One. The Spirit in question, much like The Hound, was the progenitor of all avian species. When the ta'el were unable to save the owls native to the planet, the Silent One had become extremely distressed. It had rarely been seen since the species had gone extinct, and no ta'el had spoken to the Spirit at all. They suspected it was why so many ta'el born of Avians chose to be born of owls. It was speculated that newborn Spirits could feel the sorrow of the Silent One and were attempting to soothe the ancient Spirit by choosing to be born of one of the lost species of birds. It was impossible to be sure since none among the ta'el could remember what made them choose their species when they were born.

Aya shrugged to Ireana's response. "Ask it yourself if you don't believe me. This is the simulacrum of the Silent One or I am the daughter of a goat."

"We can't ever tell anyone about this. Brewsmiths the world over would delightedly scoop out their eyeballs to be able to make Featherbound Brew," Ireana said, and Aya nodded in agreement. Then her expression turned sour.

"I had to eat <u>worms</u> to experience flight," Aya grumbled. "He <u>knew,</u> and he <u>let</u> me eat worms!" Aya's scowl was full of teeth and Ireana chuckled. She was going to have words with her Father when this was done.

Ireana carefully replaced the vial in the quick pouch. She took out the last vial and handed it to Aya. This one contained a liquid so dark that it was difficult to make out the simulacrum within. It glowed with a gentle purple light.

"This is just what we need. It's a Draft of Stolen Breath. Scales, this is supposedly the potion that The Grey used to protect himself from the vacuum of space. This is like a life support potion."

Ireana lifted her own pack to her shoulder as Aya received a sending from Greatfather Roan.

{There is a Shadeholder waiting outside of your protections, Aya. The Spirit tells me that it is answering a call for one of its kind.}

{Yes, Greatfather, please allow them past the protections.}

{These things are so creepy.} Roan's sending had a little shiver to it.

Shadeholders were especially useful in places without much light. A moment later, Aya felt the mental pressure of the Spirit announcing its presence. She reached through the veil and Channeled the Shadeholder through. Creepy was an accurate description. The Shadeholder was entirely alien to their world. Its body appeared like a thick sheet of paper so black that it would drink in all the light around it.

The body was shaped like a triangle with the tip cut off, making it into an odd rhombus-like shape. Long, spindly, insect-like legs adorned the corners. Its head was on a thin stalk that seemed to wave irrationally about, giving no indication of where the creature's attention was focused. The head itself was some combination of a sphere and a cube, with two thin, multi-joined antennae. The head split in half, showing dozens of sharklike teeth with a small hole in the middle. A long tendril snaked out from it and reached toward Aya. Aya held out a paw until the tendril touched her index paw pad.

"Greetings, Honored Elemental. We wish to enlist your aid in helping us remain safe on a dive into a deep place."

Ireana made a small, unsettled noise. Being a Stalker, she would have been taught about Shadeholders, but Aya didn't think she had ever seen one in person. There were many ways to do what the Shadeholder would help them with, but in a place were the only source of light would be what they carried with them, the Shadeholder was the best choice. It would use the darkness and shadows of the place to create illusions around them, confusing anything that attempted to attack them.

Shadeholders did not care for light, so when you were using their power, only a minimal amount of light could be used. Usually just enough to create shadows. Aya, though, planned to ask the Source Elemental she had befriended to do much more than that. She could use Light to provide them with illumination that did not touch the Shadeholder, giving them the best of both worlds.

Aya belted on her Heartblade and looked to Ireana, who was doing the same.

{For the protection you seek, I request that you make a dark place for me to rest in the Wild for one full stint at a future time of my choosing, Ayasha the Speaker.}

{Agreed, Honored Elemental. Are there space concerns or is something as small as a closet agreeable?} Aya had never worked with a Shadeholder before.

{Size is of no concern. Even a small place such as a chest or even a tiny box kept from the light of the sun is acceptable.}

Aya went out into the garden where Lane the Wanderer awaited them. He lacked the personal glow letting Aya know that only she would be able to see him.

{I don't suppose it is appropriate to ask for a kiss this time.} Lane's sending bubbled with amusement.

Aya just shrugged. *{If that is what you wish for payment, I do not think my mate will object.}*

Lane shook his head. *{Not this time Little Aya. You are going to the Below Places?}*

Aya nodded.

{I will take you, but I will require something far more valuable and powerful than a simple kiss.}

Aya was about to speak about the oddity when Lane went on.

{Something is attempting to keep this place from being accessed, Little Aya. To break through that barrier, I will need a piece of powerful magic. I will need an Aethershard.}

Aya sucked in breath through her teeth and narrowed her eyes.

{You <u>knew</u>. You knew all about the Below Places and you made me go through all of that to find the information,} she accused.

Lane shook his head quickly. *{Not until you told me you needed me to take you to the Below Places and how to find it. I investigated just this past round.}*

Aya looked to Ireana. Aethershards were powerful magic indeed, and there was a cost to making one. Only two ta'el who were extremely close both emotionally and metaphysically could work together to make an Aethershard. They had various uses, but the most important one was the birthing of newborn ta'el. The cost was that two ta'el could only make an Aethershard extremely infrequently. While it varied depending on how large the population of ta'el on the planet was, generally, a pair of ta'el could only make an Aethershard once every fifty to seventy turns.

It wasn't the same as giving up the life of a cub. The Aethershard was simply used to start the process of birthing a new cub. They were living energy solidified into a jewel. Aya wasn't even sure that she an Ireana could make one yet. It wasn't exclusively mates that could make an Aethershard, though.

"Could you be any more distracted? Just ask me whatever it is your brain is trying to churn through, already," Ireana said.

"Lane tells me that someone or something has constructed a barrier around the Below Places. He will require something of equal power to break through. We would need to make a Aethershard."

Ireana paused for a long moment. It was one of the reasons that Aya had been uncertain about becoming her mate. Ireana had always been the kind of emta that wanted a cub, possibly more than one, which was often made possible by requesting Aethershards from the Hearth. There were many mates who had no interest in cubs. Often they would donate their Aethershards to the Hearth, who sometimes used them to create important magical items.

Aya held out her paw and Channeled Lane through the Veil into the Wild. "Would it be too much to ask that we are allowed to acquire a Aethershard from the Hearth?"

Lane shook his head. "The only way to pass the barrier is to overload it with energy tied to anyone going through it."

"Of course it is," Aya groused.

Ireana smiled. "This is important my heart. I will gladly donate to this cause. We can always request an Aethershard from the Hearth when we are ready for a cub, or just wait. We will still be more than young enough to handle a cub by the time we can make another shard."

"I don't want to take this from you."

Ireana just held up her paws palms out. "I didn't think it would go quite this fast, but that's life. It's what makes it fun. You're more important to me than any desire I have for motherhood. When we do finally have a cub of our own, I want us both to be ready, and I think it will be some time before that is true for you, my heart." Ireana wiggled her fingers invitingly and grinned.

Aya took a breath and then held up her own paws. The Heartbond had allowed them a glimpse into how they felt about each other, and would again whenever they wanted it to, but making an Aethershard was different. To mix your living essence with another was to briefly be the other ta'el within that mixture. It was a joining of Spirits that was prodigiously intimate, and Aya would have liked to save it for when this was over.

Aya looked back to Lane. "Are you sure we have to do this right now?"

Lane shrugged. "Only if you are hoping to finish this."

"Fine!" Aya groaned with annoyance and Ireana chuckled a little.

"Afraid I'm going to love you more?" she teased.

"No," Aya snapped right away. Then more softly she said, "Just didn't want to force this, and didn't want it to be all for me."

Ireana shook her head. "It's not. It's for us."

Ireana shook her paws again. Aya took a deep breath, and then put her paws up, pads facing Ireana's. She pushed her paws against Ireana's and then intertwined her fingers with the much larger wolf's. Ireana pulled her close, and Aya sighed happily as she was held. A long moment passed as they both tried to open their minds and Spirits to one another, and then the connection opened. The torrent of energy was overwhelming. It was too much to feel, too much to absorb all at once. Aya knew that was the point of the melding to create something that was a part of both her and Ireana. The feelings and memories seen through Ireana's eyes were so revealing.

Ireana had held feelings of love and devotion to Aya from almost the time they had met. She had never believed that love could happen so easily, and while her own feelings had taken many turns to develop, Ireana was not the same. Aya felt for a moment like she wasn't good enough. It had taken her so long to realize what Ireana meant to her. Ireana had known almost right away.

{Stop being silly. How you are different is what made me love you in the first place,} Ireana sent, but the comfort was as much for herself as it was for Aya.

She, too, felt somewhat inadequate in the face of the staggering presence that was Ayasha the Speaker. Her mate would never bend. She would never turn away from doing what was right no matter what it cost her. Ireana strove to be like that, but she was unsure of herself in so many ways that Aya had never been.

Nothing could change Aya, not interdimensional monsters nor gods. The universe itself would crack in two before anything would break the will of her mate, but it was clear she had not gained that will for free. It had been hard won over the turns of her childhood and even more so since she had begun counting her turns. She had wanted to live up to her Mother's legacy. It had forged an emta'el like Aya. It was amazing to Ireana that they could have been so close but were so different.

The magic flowing between them surged and the sense of absolute knowledge of the other faded. What was left behind, though, was almost as powerful. The crystalline shard of rainbow light settled between their four paws. With it came an absolute sense of who their mate was. They had instinctively brought their paws together to cup the pearlescent shard of pure magic. It glittered with a soft rainbow of light. The light died down in the shard until it was moved again. Then the glow brightened showing the potential of the shard. The Spirit of Lane the Wanderer let out a low whistle.

"That is powerful love to flow betwixt two ta'el," he complimented.

Aya felt herself blushing furiously and could tell by the look on her face that Ireana was doing the same. Lane held out his paw for the Aethershard. Aya exchanged a look with Ireana, who pushed the Aethershard gently into her paws encouragingly. Aya handed it to Lane, who held it reverently for a moment, one of the very few things outside living flora and fauna that were both living and Spirit at the same time.

He headed for the garden. When he got to the large patch of grass just outside of Aya's den, he walked in a tiny circle. Each step left behind a glowing paw print, tracing a perfect circle. In the center, he placed the Aethershard. Then he turned to Aya and held out his paw. She took it and Channeled his Spirit into her body.

{Walk your circle around the smaller circle. When we open the Pathway, it will use the magic of the Aethershard to punch a hole through whatever is keeping us from getting to the Below Places.}

Aya followed his instruction, creating a much larger circle. As soon as the last paw print completed the circle, there was a flare of blue magic. The Aethershard seemed to melt into a puddle of rainbow-colored light. It filled the smaller circle and began to break apart into tiny, shimmering flecks. The flecks floated up into the air like dandelion fluff until there was a shimmering stream of light connecting the ground to the sky.

{Oh shit, cover your ears!} Lane squeaked inside of Aya's head.

She clapped her paws over her ears, and Ireana followed her lead, even though she had not heard Lane's warning. There was a flash of pure white light that strangely did not hurt Aya's eyes at all. Then came the roar of sound, so loud that if Lane hadn't warned her, she knew her eardrums would have blown apart like wet tissue paper. When she pried her eyes open, the Pathway had resolved. It was a circle of pitch black.

"What in the seven sides was that?!" Aya yowled angrily.

{I apologize. That was utterly my fault. I clearly underestimated how powerful the Aethershard would be. It didn't just punch a hole in the barrier. It blew away the entire thing. It created a large energy imbalance and likely destroyed a small section of the nearby cavern.}

"Are you ready for this?" Aya asked.

Ireana checked her Heartblade in its scabbard to make sure it was clear, and then made sure the quick pouch was secure on her hip. She nodded.

"Scales, glad one of us is," Aya said.

"Remember, if there is too much for us to handle, we come back for help," Ireana admonished.

Each of them took a drink from the Draft of Stolen Breath. Aya nodded and then stepped forward over yawning black abyss, disappearing into the dark.

Chapter 26

"DIVERSION"

Aya instinctually reached out for Ireana and found the comforting touch of her mate a moment later. The Pathway had snapped shut the moment that they had come through, extinguishing all sources of light. Thankfully, the Draft of Stolen Breath had provided them with air and protected them from many of the harsh environment's other dangers.

{Was that supposed to happen?} Aya sent to Lane.

{Yes. Your Aethershard obliterated the barrier, but whatever is down here will know where we came through if I leave the Pathway open for too long.}

Aya nodded. This deep below the surface, the heat within the rough-hewn cavern walls was almost unbearable. Aya hadn't accounted for this.

"The Elixir of Icy Veins?" Aya asked and pointed at the quick pouch on Ireana's hip.

She nodded and flipped it open. Aya would survive the heat just fine carrying around the Heart of Fire with her, but Ireana was built for cold more than heat. Aya drank down half the potion because even having the Heart of Fire protecting her didn't make the heat comfortable. The cooling effects washed over her, and she held out the remainder of the vial to Ireana, who downed it. She slid the vial back into the pouch. Aya drew in a slow, deep breath, and then paused.

"Do you smell that?" Aya asked.

Ireana made a sound of acknowledgement – the acrid dead-blood-smell of Netherspawn. Aya reached down to her belt where Light rested in her tiny glass ampule. Aya touched the ampule.

{Light, we have purchased the protections of a Shadeholder. Would you be so kind as to provide us with Light that only touches us?}

The tiny elemental stood up inside of the tiny glass container. Her sleek body made up of the substance of Light stared around the darkness. The tiny amount of light that the

Elemental Spirit gave off did not go further than the borders of the glass. It did make it possible to see her, but magically, it did not light the area around them. The Elemental nodded, and suddenly the cave was awash with brilliant light. It revealed a bleak landscape of dark stone, nearly free of rock formations. The ceiling was high above, and Aya was certain it would have been hidden by distance if not for Light tampering with the nature of reality.

Ireana blinked. "This could be dangerous," she whispered.

"Only we can see this. To anyone else, there is no light."

Ireana gawked for a moment. "You never made good on your promise to explain about the Honored Elemental there."

"Light is a Source Elemental. Unlike most Elemental Spirits, she is not any sort of projection or representation of light. She _is_ light itself. She is the source. She can change the very nature of light as we know it. I don't know why Light decides to lend aid. Sometimes she doesn't. I can only ask, and if she sees fit, she will help."

Ireana shook her head. "How does that work? Is she the only one?"

"Yes and no. I don't know everything because these elementals are part of the..." Aya paused, unsure how to explain. "Part of the _background_. I believe there are more than one of them, but they are also all the same one? I'm only guessing, but I think she has a set of rules she has to be careful not to break. That's why she pauses to consider every request."

"Seems unreliable," Ireana whispered, and the tiny element narrowed its large burning white eyes at her. "I mean no disrespect, Honored Elemental. It is meant in a purely functional sense."

The tiny Elemental stamped her foot and shook a tiny finger up at Ireana.

"I think you insulted her." Aya giggled.

"I apologize, then. It was not meant as an insult." Ireana bowed to the tiny spirit.

Light shook her tiny head, turned her back on Ireana, and folded herself into the lotus position.

Ireana drew in another deep breath through her nose. "I smell what you smell, and something else. Cubs, blood, fear, pain, death. Netherspawn. A lot of Netherspawn. There were only two or three in Denver. I can detect at least a dozen scents here. This place is..." The fur of Ireana's neck bristled, indicating both fear and anger.

"How are there ta'el here without protection?" Aya wondered.

Ireana shook her head and her flirting tail said she had no idea.

Aya's paws clutched into fists. "How are there <u>cubs</u> here?" she hissed.

Aya was sharing her mindscape with more Spirits than she had ever Channeled at once before. Seven Spirits, she had discovered, was doable but after a short period of time, there would be a cost. There was a very real possibility of severe Soul sickness after this. She addressed one in particular.

{Kika, what are you sensing?}

{At least a dozen Netherspawn. Like Viscerals, but there is something worse, and something else entirely that I cannot identify. There are also at least a half dozen ta'el cubs down here. They are gathered somewhere to the north.}

{Can you be more specific?}

{At forty-two degrees by my estimation.}

Aya turned between what she could sense as north and northeast until she was facing the direction Kika indicated.

"Alright, cubs first," Aya said.

Ireana caught her by the arm and shook her head. "In this situation, we have much better odds of getting those cubs out alive if one of us makes a distraction while the other finds them and gets them out."

"Then I will be the distraction," Aya said. Ireana looked like she wanted to protest. "I'm the better distraction. You have Lewak the Wanderer with you, but you are not used to using his power, and I am the better fighter. We can't wait to go get reinforcements now."

Ireana grabbed Aya by the bicep. "If we die, they will still be stuck in here with whatever those things are doing to them."

Aya put her paw over Ireana's for a moment before gently pulling it away. "I will not leave them here while we scurry away for help."

"I'm not suggesting that we should. I'm suggesting that we should take the time to send a Spirit for help while we move forward."

Aya turned in a circle, gauging the direction of the Tributary from the information the Deep Dweller was projecting into her mind. As she was turning, white mist began to seep from Aya's body. A moment later, the tiny figure of Kika the Lightmend formed.

"Honored Ancestor, will you please go to the Sydney Hearth and explain the situation to the Matron Keystone. We request assistance. Explain to them how to reach this place?" Aya asked.

Kika nodded. *{But what if you need healing?}*

"We have the Lightmend Draught until you can return. If you would be so kind?"

"Of course, Ayasha the Speaker. I will return with all haste."

Kika floated up towards the ceiling far overhead. She would have to traverse the distance to be sure that she could stay in the Wild and speak to someone at the Hearth as quickly as possible. It would take a little time.

"Do you think you can find the cubs?" Aya asked.

Ireana lifted her nose and inhaled slowly. "Yes, I can."

"Good. I'm going to make a lot of noise on my way to finding the Tributary."

"Do you have any idea where it is?" Ireana worried.

Aya's whiskers twitched up and down, saying "sort of".

"The Deep Dweller knows. I don't think I can kill a dozen Viscerals and whatever else is down here, so I'm not going to try to fight them all. Just get all of their attention and get them to follow me to the Tributary. Then I will use the power of the Dweller to seal them up in a cave of their own for a while so that I can I do what I must," Aya explained.

Ireana nodded. "Alright, my heart. I trust you. I will meet you back home."

Aya lifted her nose and scented around her, finally picking up a single scent that went in a direction by itself. She would start with a single Visceral. She mentally focused on the presence of the Shadeholder in her mind.

{Honored Elemental, can we attach your illusions to my mate without being in her vicinity?}

The midnight whisper of the Shadeholder replied, *{For a time. Perhaps a few shifts at most. That long will have a cost in power for you.}*

{Acceptable.}

Aya Channeled the power of the Shadeholder. With the Elemental's help, she attached shadowy illusions to Ireana's Spirit. This caused her body to blur to the naked eye. Then, a secondary shadowy body appeared next to her, and then another. As she moved, each one moved with her, but they were all slightly out of sync with her own movements. Not only that, the Shadeholder's illusions were so real that they transcended all senses but touch. Even her magical senses told her that there were three ta'el standing before her. She felt energy trickling out of her.

It wasn't a considerable draw, considering her personal stores, but after a time, it would tire her. She couldn't cycle the power through her own body like she could for her own illusions, since the Shadeholder did not have a presence in Ireana's body.

"Find the cubs and get them out of here. I will do the rest. I love you," Aya said, then started off at a jog.

"Love you," came Ireana's reply, and then she dashed off in almost the opposite direction, following the scent of the cubs.

Aya Channeled her own illusions as she picked up speed. She thought she had come here just to find the Tributary and complete whatever it was that the White had in mind for her. This was so much more. Something down here was killing cubs. She would find it, and end it.

Aya fell to all fours, galloping down the tunnel at speed until she saw the shining blood skin of the Visceral. The rippling effect of its skin disgusted Aya as it whipped around to face her. It had known she was coming, but took one step forward and then stopped. It held the shape of some generic feline, though Aya could not tell more than that because it lacked any other identifying features. It tilted its head in a mockery of confusion. Aya, though, did not bother to stop. She took advantage of its confusion.

She leapt at the creature. Her Heartblade cleared its sheath in a draw so fast that she could not have made it without Lane's aid. She let out a roar as she soared towards the Visceral. The sound echoed off of the walls of the cave, and would inform everything within earshot of her position, just as she wanted it to. She swung the blade with all of the brutal might she could muster. It cleaved through the creature's neck with so little resistance that it almost made Aya stumble. She skidded to a halt a few steps past its tumbling body, her claws scraping across the stone floor. She turned and focused her mind on the Heart of Fire.

{If you would, Honored Elemental?}

Aya held out a paw and Channeled the power that welled up from the Heart of Fire. A burst of flame so intense that it seemed a solid thing seared the air. She dragged the fire across the entire body of the Visceral. When the fire faded and she could see again, the creature was crumbling into ash. The stone of the floor around it glowed with run-off heat, and she was thankful for the protections of her father's potion that kept her comfortable even with the added heat.

{We cannot produce much more heat of that intensity, Ayasha the Speaker. Your personal energy cannot support it,} the Elemental warned.

{Understood. It was not my plan to attempt that again.}

Aya switched her focus back to Lane. *{I fear most of this mission's burden will fall upon you, Lane.}*

Lane sent back a sensation of confidence that bolstered Aya. Her ears caught the sound of footsteps rushing towards her. She changed her focus once more to consult with the Deep Dweller. The Earth Spirit was one that the Earthwards in Denver had introduced her to. The Spirit had been able to make a complete map of the cave system within moments of the magical barrier being breeched. It'd had an immediate sense of where the Tributary was.

Even though they could not open a Pathway straight to it because of the magical distortion it generated, Aya knew where to find it. She wished she still had Kika with her. Without her, Aya had no idea if she had managed to gain the attention of all of the Neatherspawn roaming the caverns. She wracked her brain for ways she could make herself more attractive, but nothing came to mind.

One of the Spirits she had Channeled within her drew her attention. The Spirit had told her that she wasn't prepared to Channel his magic yet, but Aya had been relieved when he had agreed to join them.

{The only thing keeping Netherspawn like Viscerals contained here is the lack of sentient Spirits. You can be assured that now that you've used Lane the Wanderer's magic to enhance your body, every one of the lesser Netherspawn will be coming for you,} The Grey sent with some worry.

With the help of the Deep Dweller, she had planned a circuitous route through the massive cave system to reach the Tributary. She needed to be sure that at least all of the Viserals were not going to attempt to kill Ireana. She trusted Ireana to take care of herself, despite what she had told her mate about her swordplay.

A scuffle of paws on rock sounded behind her, and Aya turned and backpedaled. It was the only thing that saved her. Crimson claws streaked at what would have been her back a moment before she had spun.

Aya Channeled Lane's power into her body. She drew her Heartblade and struck in a single, perfect motion, slicing the creature's swiping paw off at the wrist. She spun to the left, away from the claw. Its body still tagged her, causing her to stumble. She let the movement flow into a roll, allowing her free paw to touch the ground for balance. She did not wait for the thing to recover.

Seeing several silent, blood red figures approaching from behind the one that had lost its paw, she turned away and bolted. She swiped her Heartblade in an arc to free it of as much of the liquid lingering on its surface as possible and slid it back into the scabbard at the small of her back.

Aya leapt from her dash onto all fours, allowing her to run much faster than she could on two. She would not be caught too slow again. She risked another glance, and now there were over a dozen creatures chasing her. Aya poured on the speed, using up another measure of her personal power. She carefully drew on Roan's connection to her as her Watcher Spirit to make herself even faster than Lane's magic could do alone.

{Have a care, Little Aya. You are stretching the limits of your body,} Roan warned.

{Thank you, Greatfather.}

She did not use both magics for very long, just long enough to pull away. She couldn't fight them all. They'd tear her to pieces. Instead, she turned as soon as she judged she had enough distance to focus. She skidded to a halt using her claws, spinning her body around to face the onrushing wave of bloodstained death. She switched her focus releasing, Lane's power.

The minor added boost that Roan's Spirit offered stayed. As her Watcher, he could Channel his magic through her without her involvement if she allowed it. Instead, she focused on the power of the Deep Dweller. She brought her paws up sharply, making fists, helping herself to focus the magic. The ground began to rumble as the Viscerals neared her.

Just as they were getting a little too close for comfort, two dozen massive sharpened spikes composed of the surrounding stone shot up like a tripped booby trap. The stalagmites blasted through some of the Viscerals and tripped up others. This gave Aya not only a few necessary seconds without having to worry about being torn apart, it also gave her a necessary view of the cavern behind the tripped Viscerals.

She raised her paws over her head and focused, Channeling a massive amount of the Deep Dweller's power through her body. She knew it was dangerous. Too much of any of the Elemental magics could have various detrimental effects to the living body, especially magics one was not especially attuned with. Aya had never had much affinity for Earth and Air. As a Channeler, she had been taught how to bypass her inborn limitations, but that didn't make it comfortable.

Her body felt heavy and sluggish as the magic passed through her body and into the Wild. The cavern began to shake more violently, rocks breaking from the ceiling and smashing to the floor all around Aya. The struggling Viscerals didn't have a chance to free themselves from the trap Aya had set for them before a massive wall of stone grew up from the floor behind them. Several clawed themselves past the trap, and they nearly reached Aya before a second wall of stone shot up from floor, neatly bisecting the tunnel. Aya nearly collapsed as she listened to the muted scrabbling of claws against the stone wall. They would burrow their way through the wall before long, but it would be too late.

Ireana stumbled when the ground began to shake beneath her feet. She turned wide-eyed to look back down the tunnel she'd come from. She couldn't imagine what Aya was doing that could cause so much destruction. Parts of the cave were falling to pieces, and she hoped that the cubs were all right.

"Thank Scales that someone smoothed out all the formations in here or I'd be dodging giant murder spikes," she mumbled to herself as she followed the growing scent of the cubs. She didn't bother trying to hide herself, knowing that only she could see the light surrounding her. To everything else down here, it would be pitch black.

Anything that could live down here would not use eyes to see her. Still, as she had been taught, she was careful not to make any sound that would give her away. Controlling both her breathing and focusing on keeping her claws from clicking on the floor, she crept along in total silence, growing ever closer to goal. She kept a grip on the hilt of the sword at her side.

Her Heartblade still sent a distracting buzz through her paw as Aya had warned her it would. She had come to a junction of three paths, taking the one to the far left. This took her further north than east, but the scent was strongest down this path. She wondered how she was able to smell anything in a place so devoid of air. She suspected it had something to do with the Draft of Stolen Breath. She hadn't thought any potion could contain such power. Leave it to Sahone to prove her wrong. The opening to this tunnel was much smaller than the others, and it didn't look like it widened out very much.

That was when she heard the howl. It was absolutely a canine sound, from a cub in dire pain. Ireana wasted no time. She took off her sword belt and the quick pouch and pushed them ahead of her into the tunnel. She wriggled through with a speed she had no idea she could muster. Frantically, she clawed at the walls of the cavern, pulling herself forward.

Short bouts later, she pulled herself through another small opening and into a cavern. She whipped her sword belt and the quick pouch around her body and crouched. The light did not spread far from her body in this place, defying all logic as it had easily penetrated every darkness the rest of the caves had to offer. Those thoughts fled her mind.

There was enough light to behold the horror. Scattered around her like broken, blood-spattered toys were bodies. The smell hit her nose a moment later, as if passing the tunnel had somehow released the putrid reek of decay. The cave was large, made of dark grey stone. Pillars of rock had formed

It took all of Ireana's considerable willpower to force down her bile and remain analytical. She searched for the cub who had made the awful puling noise that had drawn her through in such a hurry. One of the bodies near the edge of the light moved weakly. It was her instinct to rush over and help the child, but her training smashed those instincts down.

Ireana stood there in a low crouch, just as she had been taught. Something was in here killing these cubs, and anything that was intelligent enough to steal the cubs away from their parents was also intelligent enough to use them as a trap for any would-be rescuer. That was when she saw it.

At first, she had no idea what she was looking at, only that something had twigged those predator instincts that she had worked so hard to train as a Stalker. On the roof of the cave, she saw a pulsating blob of... something. It was definitely moving, though only in the slightest twitches, almost as if it were anticipating her rushing forward beneath it. She judged her best course of action for a long moment, and that was when the smell finally reached her nose.

Over the blood, vomit, and waste of however many cubs had been killed in this Scale-cursed hole, a stink far more powerful smashed into her like an ocean wave. She knew without a doubt that she did not want whatever that thing was to touch her. A thought tugged at the back of her mind. Aya had told her that when fighting the Visceral in Denver one of the only things that had caused it pain was her Lightmend Draught.

The creature was too far away to throw the contents of the vial across its rippling surface. She continued to scan the cave cautiously, making sure that there were no surprises. Unfortunately, there was no way to pierce the darkness beyond the light. It made it clear that this darkness was not a natural phenomenon of the cave lacking access to light. This was also a magical effect. She couldn't wait too long. Like the rest of the broken bodies, the whimpering cub's limbs had been shredded. If she did not get one of the vials of Lightmend Draught into him in the next few bouts, he was going to bleed out.

She remembered that Aya had told her that even touching a Visceral had poisoned her. She paused for a long moment considering her options. She didn't want to reveal the potions, but if she waited to down one until she needed it, it could be too late. She decided the tactical advantage the potions would offer was worth any advantage lost by the creature not knowing she had them. She flipped open the quick pouch and pulled out two vials.

It seemed as though the creature had not noticed her wariness as it did not move to stop her as she stalked forward toward the cub. Even though the light that surrounded her let her see the creature clear as round, it would have no idea of her advantage. Ireana was careful to keep the small vials clutched in her paw, not allowing even a tiny bit of their glow to escape. She lifted the vials to her mouth, and almost made a mistake.

These vials had been blown and cast with magic. There were no stoppers in them. The liquid would not flow out of them unless it was her express intent to drink it, or pour it out. Her fangs against the glass vials would have definitely given away that she was doing something. She downed both potions and slid the vials back into the quick pouch. The reaction was instantaneous.

She had never taken Blood of the Mountain before, but she knew what it did. It hardened her body so that it would have the weigh, and durability of stone without putting any strain on her muscles. It essentially gave her super strength and durability because her body was now dozens of times heavier, but still able to move with the same fluidity as if her weight had not changed at all. It didn't last for very long, but it was a potent potion.

She was almost beneath the gelatinous surface of the creature when it sprang. Using some unidentifiable form of locomotion, it flew directly at her as if had been shot out of a catapult. Ireana moved without thinking, diving into a roll to one side. One of the things that she had learned from Aya that many of her martial arts teachers had not taught her is that a dodge is always the better alternative to being hit. Even if you think you can block a strike dodge first.

She was glad she did when the creature struck the floor. In the blink of time it had taken it to strike the floor, hundreds of spines had sprung from it's body. It had taken on the appearance of a sea urchin the size of a small bear. What was more, she wasn't even sure the durability her potions had lent her would be enough. The spines had plunged directly through the stone, causing chips to fly off in all directions. Still, the Blood of the Mountain potion did not give her body the durability of any mere stone.

Whatever the thing was sat there quivering for a long moment, and then it flowed toward her. It didn't roll or move like anything else she had ever seen. It flowed like a blob of black oil. Spines and blades seemed to melt into its surface only to re-form moments later as it came towards her. Ireana didn't hesitate. She drew her Heartblade and spread her feet into a stable stance. Her tumble had put her between the creature and the dying cub. She would not relinquish that space, not even if it cost her life to hold it.

She would fight this thing until Aya came to help her get the cubs out or die in the attempt.

Chapter 27

"SOUL BOUND"

Aya dropped to all fours and ran with everything she had. She had no guarantees that she had trapped every creature of the Nether, and so she pushed her stressed body as hard as she dared. Once they had gotten past the barrier, the Deep Dweller had known almost instantly where to find the Tributary. The dark, uneven stone walls flashed past as Aya drew on Lane's power to make herself faster. She drew so much power that Lane decided he had to intercede.

{Aya, you are drawing too heavily.}

{I can't go slower, Lane. There is no time. Ireana is in danger. You're sharing my head. You can feel some of what I am feeling through the Heartbond.}

{You are of no help to her if you kill yourself with Soul Sickness.}

{I'll die tomorrow. There is no time right now.}

Aya ran. She streaked past dark corridors that hid unknown dangers. There was simply no time if she wanted to save everyone still alive down here and make sure she completed whatever it was that the White had sent her down here to do.

{To the left, Ayasha the Speaker,} the Deep Dweller directed, its gravel tone voice rattling inside of her skull.

She darted left and skidded to a halt when she almost crashed into a field of steel-colored stalagmites. The spears of sharp stone did not completely block the path, but they were packed tightly together. Aya snarled in frustration.

{Can we...} She directed her thoughts at the Deep Dweller.

{You may be reaching beyond your limits, Speaker,} the Deep Dweller warned.

{I am aware. I have no time to worry now, Honored Elemental.}

{As you wish.}

She felt the power of the Earth well up within her. She lifted a paw and made a fist, gesturing to one side. She Channeled the earthen magic and the spikes began to slide away from each other. They didn't need to be moved much to let her pass, and as soon as the passageway opened, she darted between the spires of rock. She stumbled a few steps in and tumbled to the ground as the shock hit her.

The Deep Dweller had been right. She fought for consciousness for a moment, and after a dizzying few seconds, her eyes snapped into focus again. She pushed herself back up to all fours and began to stumble down the path.

{It's close,} the Deep Dweller said, and Aya slowed.

She pushed herself upright, and then the light went out. She looked down to the Elemental in the ampule hanging from the strap of her pack. The tiny glowing form held up her facsimile of hands in a tiny shrug, and then pointed into the darkness. She slid free of the ampule, and Aya held out a paw to touch her.

{We Spirits cannot pass here, Ayasha the Speaker. This place is only for the living.}

Then she saw it, the dim glow in the darkness that was beginning to intensify. There, carved in light upon the side of the pillar, were four bright Runes. Red, Green, Blue, and White. Aya slowed as she neared the pillar. She turned, and walked around it. There were ten runes in total, carved in three groups upon the triangular spire of stone. It stood at about the same height as Aya. She tried to focus on speaking to the Spirits within her only to discover she was entirely alone in her own head. Light had apparently meant that no Spirits could come into this place. She was suddenly a tiny bit frantic. What if trying to coeme closer with those Spirits within her had done them harm.

{We are fine, Little Aya.} Roan's voice inside of her head helped her calm down. *{We cannot approach the Tributary. We are living energy, as are all souls, but we do not have physical bodies to anchor us to the Wild. The Tributary is pure power. We cannot approach because there simply is no room. To us there is a solid sphere of energy that we cannot share space with.}*

Aya's eyes were drawn to one of the symbols near the top of the pillar. It was glowing with a silvery grey light. It was a color that clearly could not exist, but somehow, it was being emitted from the Symbol like two intricately stylized squares overlapping each other. She reached up to touch it, and suddenly the world vanished. She stood on a flat expanse of nothingness, like a white sheet laid out across the surface of the entire world. Except there was no sky, no borders, no limits. Just a pure, blinding white expanse with no definition.

"So, you're number seven," a soft, very high-pitched voice came from seemingly everywhere around her. It was not a child's voice, but more like that of an Avian emta.

"I... guess?" Aya stammered. She started to say something else, but the effeminate voice interrupted her.

"No, no questions. Do not worry. Time isn't passing in your world while you are here. Still, there is no time for questions. You will learn all that you need to know without any help from this one. Now that you have touched the Tributary, you must be marked to do what you came here for. Know that you have earned what is given."

Aya started to open her muzzle again, then a searing pain in her upper right arm stole her breath away and the world disappeared again. Aya fell into unconsciousness. When she startled awake, she was standing with her paw against the pillar, all of her muscles locked and rigid. It felt as if she had been standing that way for shifts. The voice had said that time was not passing, but who knew what she had really just experienced.

That was when she realized that there was knowledge inside of her head which she had never learned. What was more, there was a vast amount of, something, that she knew was available but that she could not access. It was like she was standing in a library surrounded by the all of the knowledge in the world, but until she took out each book and read it, the knowledge was beyond her reach.

Still, what had been pushed forcibly into her brain told her precisely what it meant to be the Speaker. Speakers were called into the world to protect the ta'el in times when the Nether somehow gained access to their reality. It gave her the knowledge of how to use the First Word. Like her ability to Channel, the First Word gave her a means of manipulating reality to her will, but, it was impossible to compare the two.

It was like holding a candle up next to a star. The First Word would allow her to manipulate reality with few limits, and with no need for assistance from the Spirits. A power only necessary when higher creatures of the Nether somehow gained access to their reality. At that point, only the most potent Channelers would be their match. Even then, it would only make those Channelers targets. The Speaker, though, did not have that problem. Properly used, she could make herself literally poisonous for creatures of the Nether to even draw near to her. That wasn't quite in her reach yet. She would have to master the basics first. Still, the tiny bit of information she had been given was more than enough to do what she needed to do here. Just as the voice had said it would be.

Aya held up her paw and extended a single finger. She drew in the air, and a glowing violet line trailed behind. She drew the symbol for Space, and as she did, she formed her intentions inside her head, just as was required. The Rune both described and was all things related to open space. Using it, she could create a Pathway without help from a single Wanderer Spirit. She finished the rune, and then drew a circle around it.

It wasn't perfect, and she understood that if she could make the circle better, the process would be faster, but it was good enough, because it began to fill with violet light. This Pathway was personal. It would accept only her, and her alone. When the circle completely filled with light, the Rune in the middle seemed to fade until there was a perfect negative space in the shape of the Rune. Aya pressed her paw through the Rune and vanished.

Ireana backpedaled frantically and her Heartblade darted back and forth in her fist. Each swipe cleaved away tiny pieces of the creature's tentacles. The waving mass of limbs protruding from the enormous blob moved as savannah grass blowing in the wind - mesmerizing, and difficult to track each blade as it danced about. She had learned that even the Blood of the Mountain potion had not been enough to keep the creature's appendages from piercing her flesh, though it had helped to keep the wounds small while it lasted.

She sensed frustration in the creature, but she didn't understand why. It was clearly just toying with her, and she knew that soon she would have to make a terrible decision between saving one of the cubs and saving them all. The creature pulled back for one moment, and Ireana saw her opening.

Her free paw darted to the quick pouch. She flipped open the lid and yanked out the first potion. She swiped it towards the creature and the full vial splashed across its surface. The reaction was nothing like what Aya described. It was immediate and violent. The creature reared back, and the part of it that was smeared with the potion exploded.

Ireana dove into a roll, dodging half a dozen steel-hard spikes that had been blown off of its flailing extremities. She felt one piece shoot through her calf, and she let out a yelp that she quickly stifled. Part of a Stalker's training was how to keep silent, no matter the situation. Her Master would have applied a paw directly to her ass for that yelp. She didn't waste what little time she had. She slid the vial back into the quick pouch, and it refilled immediately.

She dashed across the cave, leaving the smoking body of the creature flailing in her wake. Ireana slid to her knees, scraping cuts into her legs and not caring one bit. She wasn't sure she was in in time, as the cub seemed unresponsive. She frantically opened the cub's muzzle and drizzled a little of the potion into the cub's bloodstained maw. The glow of the potion intensified for a moment, and the cub coughed.

"Drink this down, little one. It will make you better."

She left the potion vial in his tiny paws and took up her Heartblade again. When she turned, the creature was barreling towards her. She tensed, knowing she could not mount a defense in time. A flash of light blinded her for a moment, and then Aya was there between her and the Creature.

Flames roiled across her body as she held up her paw as the creature's tentacles streaked forward. They slammed into Aya's paw and raced up her arm, shredding her flesh. Blood flew and became steaming droplets as it burned through the fire. Aya screamed. The sound mutated quickly from agony to a roar of rage.

Ireana had never seen such a look on Aya's face as the one that resided there in that moment, a cold, blank fury. It was the face of someone that moved mountains and killed gods. Ireana almost shied away, but she knew how much that would hurt her mate. That fury was not aimed at Ireana, but still it terrified her.

White hot flames blasted from Aya's shredded arm, boiling away half of the quivering mass of ink black tentacles. The force slammed the creature back across the cave and into the opposite wall. It seemed to sag there as if it were a burst blister. The contents did not flow out, though, and it was clear that the creature was not dead when it began to twitch. Aya turned, lowering her destroyed arm.

Her teeth gritted in pain, she settled the shredded limb at her side. She knelt next to one of the bodies of the cubs that had been torn to pieces and then looked at the rest of them huddling in a corner of the cave.

"Mate, walk a Pathway circle, please. These cubs need to be made safe." Aya's voice was even. Emotionless.

Ireana jumped to obey. She picked up the shivering canine cub who had finished the Lightmend Draught. He was covered in filth and dried blood, but was mostly healing. It looked like one paw could not be recovered by the magic, though. That part of his arm had fallen away and the stump had healed over. He would survive, but Ireana thought that he would never be the same ehta he would have been.

"Who are you?" the cub whispered.

"I'm Ireana the Stalker, and that is Ayasha the Speaker. She's a Hearth Stone. We are going to get you back home."

Ireana carried him over to the motley collection of children: one canine, two felines, four whose species didn't immediately jump out at her, and one stout little ursine with pure white fur.

She set the healing canine down next to the others. When she went to step away, he caught her paw.

"Don't leave." Tears welled up in the cub's eyes.

Ireana smiled gently, touched his nose with her finger, then pointed to each cub in turn. "I'm not leaving without every one of you."

She released his paw and moved back to the circle. She looked to her mate. Aya was still crouching over the body of one of the dead cubs with concern, but she focused on the Wanderer Spirit waiting patiently within her. Channeling Lewak had taken a lot of coaching from Aya before they had left. Ireana was no Channeler, and sharing her mind with a foreign Spirit was not part of her normal skill set.

{Honored Ancestor, can you assist me in constructing a Pathway to get these cubs to safety?}

{Of course. Walk the circle, and be not concerned for your mate. She is a Speaker of the First Word, now. No mere Netherspawn alone is a match for her.}

{I am not worried that the Netherspawn will hurt her, Honored Ancestor. I am concerned what she will do to herself.}

Ireana began to walk in a circle, making sure each paw print she laid down touched the last. It was not the best circle, because walking while almost stepping on her own paws was not easy. It took her only a few seconds to walk out a circle big enough for everyone to get through, but it seemed like an eternity. When she was finally done and the Pathway flared to life, the view of Aya's garden appeared. She looked up to Aya who had stood up and turned to face the creature.

"The Pathway is ready!" Ireana shouted. She began to hustle the cubs through.

"Go," Aya said, and Ireana began to protest. Aya turned that glacier stare on Ireana. "Mate, I love you beyond all words, but the cubs are more important. Please."

As soon as the cubs hit the Pathway, they vanished. A moment later, they reappeared in the cave next to Ireana, where they had been before they jumped through the Pathway. Ireana blinked in astonishment. Aya narrowed her eyes. She peered at the cubs for a long moment and then Aya hurried over to them.

"They have been Soul Bound to this place. We can't take them away. They will just get pulled back to where ever the Darkheart is," Aya whispered, too low for the cubs to hear.

"Darkheart?" Ireana whispered back.

"That thing. It's what the Speakers called them. They feed off pain, fear, and torment. It's why it was killing these cubs. Nothing hurts or fears as purely as a cub. It'll be back up in a moment. We need to hurry."

"Why can't we go?" one of the cubs asked, voice quivering with fear.

Aya turned fully to the cubs. "You can. I just have to fix the Pathway," Aya said, but Ireana gave her a hard look. Aya turned away from the cubs and back to her mate.

"It's going to hurt. I can't make it not hurt. They won't understand," Aya hissed.

"Hurt is better than this." Ireana gestured to the killing floor between them and the Darkheart.

Aya knelt down next to the Pathway. She began to draw with the finger of her uninjured paw across the stone. Perfect black lines were left in the wake of her moving finger. Frantically, she drew a symbol that immediately blazed to life with light. She explained as she drew. Every few moments, she would pause to breathe, the pain of her destroyed arm clearly taking its toll.

"The Darkheart has forced, something, from the Nether into their bodies to tie them to it. We can't take them away from it because of the tether. This will break the tether as they go through the Pathway, and they won't pop back up here after they go through."

She drew a near perfect circle around the symbol. Aya wished that she were not so enraged at the White at that moment so she might call for the god's favor in this. She did not want to be responsible for killing these cubs. The circle began to fill with light the same color as the Rune. When it completely filled, the Rune seemed to fall away as if it were a window into the void of space.

"They are going to be hurting and upset on the other side. You go first. It won't hurt you." Aya looked her up and down. "Well, not more than you are now. Take another Lightmend Draught."

"Is that safe?"

Aya squinted at Ireana and nodded. "Yes, the power has run through healing up the wounds. Hurry," Aya said and turned back to the cubs. "Hurry, little ones. You can make it through, now. Just follow my mate."

The cubs lined up behind Ireana. Aya turned back to the broken body of the cub she had been looking over. She knelt over the body again. Ireana wondered what she was looking for, but there would be time to ask her later. She jumped through the Pathway.

Chapter 28

"FEAR"

Aya's eyes pierced the gloom of the cave, focusing on the black thing as she touched the cub's face. "I'm sorry I wasn't fast enough." She rose from the tiny, broken body of the cub it had savaged, a child that had not even had a chance to truly live. Roan's voice sounded in her mind.

{Aya, please, you cannot face this alone.}

{Please take your leave, Greatfather.} Aya's voice was a whisper fabricated of a pure rage that he had never seen in her before.

The First Word blazed across the canvas of Aya's mind. She was turns away from being able to use the First Word as well as her Channeling, but whatever had been done to her in that white expanse had taught her enough. She was the only ta'el that could speak the First Word. It was not a language of sound, but a language of her will, spoken to the universe itself, for the universe was created by the First Word.

She touched the blood running down her shredded left arm and willed a Rune into existence. Her finger moved, writing the Rune in azure fire upon her arm. She had no words to describe the vibrant illumination shimmering from her arm as it filled the circle around her Rune. It was a simple shape. One that she knew anyone else could draw and nothing would result. With the will of the Speaker to drive it, though, it was a magic that required no Channeling. She knew it was the basis for all living fauna, and had a very basic understanding of how to heal herself with it. There would be a cost, though, in pain.

Using her will, she Spoke the words to the universe. The Rune seared itself into her arm, and she clenched her teeth over the scream that tried to claw itself from her throat. When the fire faded, her arm was whole once again. Only the rivulets of blood through her cornflower fur were any indication the injury had even happened.

{Aya,} Roan began, but she sent over him.

{*Now, please, Greatfather. Please.*}

Roan's glowing red mist slid from her body and he spoke aloud. "I would rather stay."

"Now, Greatfather!" Aya roared.

He could see the tears spilling down either side of her muzzle, and he shrank back from the cold hatred coming from her. Her searing, cobalt eyes shifted slowly from him to the oily creature clinging to the corner of the cave. Her wrath was not aimed at him.

"Please go." Aya's voice broke a little.

Only then did he realize why she wanted him to leave. She was not concerned that the Nether creature would harm him. She was concerned he would see her, that he would see what she was planning to do. She didn't want him to think less of her for doing what she needed to satisfy her justified anger. **How could the creature not feel her fury?** The creature flowed down from its perch in the corner of the cave, rolling down the wall like a partially formed blob of oil.

"Please, Greatfather, into the Spiritlands. Find Kika the Lightmend. Those cubs will need her healing, and I will deal with <u>this</u>."

The way she said this, as if the creature were so much refuse to simply be thrown away, chilled Roan, and he shivered. Still, she knew the meaning of her name, and now, so did he. Whatever magical dam had held back the knowledge of the Speaker had broken. This was well within her abilities.

"As you wish, Ayasha the Speaker." He bowed, and then faded away into the Spiritlands.

Aya turned her full attention to the oily black creature that was creeping towards her. It barely had any solid form. Tentacles and blades sprouted from the gelatinous mass at its center. Aya gritted her teeth and put her finger in the air above her chest. She quickly moved her finger, leaving behind a glowing green trail as she willed a new Rune into existence. When the glowing Rune was complete, she drew a circle around it. The circle filled with green light, and the Rune became a negative space in the light. Aya put her paw over the Rune and it felt like a physical thing. Pulling her paw to her chest, she pressed the Rune into her fur.

The change washed over her, making her entire body as impenetrable as the hardest stone. She knew intrinsically what she was doing was extremely dangerous to her. If she applied the Runes directly to herself without any modifiers for too long, they would have permanent side effects. But this would not take long. The Darkheart paused when the Rune burst alight.

"From what I have read, your kind cannot feel. That you are not of this reality, and were made only to destroy."

Aya lifted her paw and drew a new Rune. This one was the fundamental embodiment of Fire. She drew a circle around it, and then duplicated the Rune. This second Rune burst apart, flinging spheres of Light throughout the cave. She didn't need them for what she had planned, but they would make her plan more effective. She took hold of the circle surrounding the other Fire Rune and twisted it like a dial until the Rune was upside-down. This, she pressed into her arm.

She felt it immediately. Light fled from her body. Even the illumination left behind by the magic of the Source Elemental dimmed until almost the entire cave was swallowed in shadow. Only small areas of light existed around the glowing magical spheres. Her body began to fade from view.

"You tortured cubs to gather your strength. Fed on their pain, and their fear." Tears streamed from her burning eyes as she considered what this thing had done to them. "For that, I will teach <u>you</u> to fear."

She stepped back into the deeper shadows nearby and was consumed by them. Her fiery sapphire eyes were the last thing to fade into the darkness. The Darkheart's body turned left and right as if it were searching for her, but no amount of sensory input would tell the creature where Aya was. She had become a literal part of the shadows. She walked through them as if they were tunnels and hallways, and then stepped out. The creature really didn't have a back or a front, though she thought that perhaps it had some sensory blind spots, but it didn't truly matter.

She was only interested in if it would react every time she appeared. She wanted it to see her emerge, and know that it could not stop her. It whirled as soon as her body began to appear from the shadows. She stepped back, and the shadows consumed her once again as black blades like razor wire spun through the space where she had been. She slid from the shadows again, this time beginning to draw a new Rune.

The Rune flared with impossible grey light. New instincts implanted with the new runes to emerge. She spun her wrist with a finger extended, and a near-perfect circle enclosed the Rune. She put her paw against the Rune and shoved it forward. Razorlike blades wrapped around her arm as she drove the Rune into body of the creature. The magic held, and the blades were ineffective in penetrating even her fur. Her glowing eyes filled with a fury that she had never felt in her life. The Rune burned into the body of the creature, and a mouth of needle fangs ripped open on the side of the Darkheart. A scream burst from it of such volume that rocks were shaken loose from the cave ceiling.

Only the reinforcement from the First Word saved her hearing. Aya stepped back, the shadows closing around her. The razor wire tentacles wrapped around her arms fell loosely to the floor. The creature spun wildly, looking for her. It lashed out with tentacles covered in spines, scrapping them along the walls of the cave in horrifying chalkboard screeches. Aya watched impassively.

"What have you done?!" the creature screeched in a voice that ripped at Aya's eardrums. The sheer volume was unbelievable. Its Ta'eltesh was awful, as if were trying to speak through a throat filled with gravel.

What she had done was burned feeling into the creature's very existence. The Rune she had used was the basis for all sentient thought. The creature's mind, though, was nothing like the minds of living things in her reality. Nothing, at least, until she'd used the Rune to instill all the feelings that the creature had been missing into its very existence.

She could not kill this creature, only send it back to the Nether. Instead, she had done something much worse. She had given the creature feelings that it was never meant to have. She stepped out of the shadows and expressed her claws, dropping into a crouch. The creature's tentacles whipped towards her, and she turned her body, letting them pass. Her claws shot up, slashing through the creature's tentacle, cutting it to ribbons. A new scream ripped from the horrid maw that had grown upon the side of the creature. This one was pure pain.

"What is this?!"

The creature grew spines and blades over its entire body, attempting to protect itself from something it had no experience in feeling. Aya said nothing and grimly turned to her work. Dozens of flailing, misshapen limbs grew from the creature's doughy flesh. These were thicker and heavier than the tentacles, multi-jointed and ending in heavy, rending talons. It spun wildly in a circle, trying to anticipate where Aya would appear next.

Aya cursed herself. She could not stop the furious tears from spilling down her face. She had to cry herself out at some point.

"This is justice," she sobbed furiously.

She stepped out of the shadows and drove her claws into one of the thickly jointed limbs. She slammed her foot into the creature, and the spines that covered its body shattered against her hardened fur. The creature began to scream again, and Aya forced her claws into the limb, beginning to pull. It flailed at with her with its other limbs, but its buffeting blows had almost no effect.

She continued to pull, applying more and more force until a sound like cracking bones emerged from the limb. The screams did not die off, and she wondered how the thing was maintaining the sound. She paid it no mind and yanked at the limb. The vile, rubbery flesh let out a catastrophic tearing sound and she ripped the limb away.

The creature extruded new blades, which slammed into her hardened fur with no effect. She threw the limb aside and wrapped her arm around the blades it was attempting to spear her with. With a sharp twist, they snapped off like brittle wood. It was not enough. Aya's rage over what this thing had done went on and on. She latched onto one of the other jointed limbs and began to pull. The creature's screams died off to whimpers.

"What is this?" it said again, but this time, it wasn't a scream. It was a pitiful, pleading whimper. Before, where it had felt only pure, cold emptiness, there was now a searing sensation so alien that the Darkheart was unable to process it. They flooded the creature's empty thoughtscape with unbearable noise and fury. Every time this hated otherworlder ripped away another piece of its substance, the noise got louder, shrieking off of the vaults of its mind.

Aya did not respond, she simply pulled. All she could see were the dozen tiny corpses she had found torn apart in this thing's skulking place. She methodically ripped away its next limb and threw it aside. She was certain it could heal itself just like the Visceral had, but unlike the Visceral, this thing could now feel all of the things she was doing to it. It couldn't cope with all of that and attempting to control whatever foul power kept it ambulatory.

"No more," it begged, but this only enraged Aya. She would make this thing suffer until it was destroyed. It would pay the same price it had extracted from everyone it had killed.

"Is that what they begged as you violated their bodies?"

She stepped back away from it into the shadows. She had to remove the First Word from her body soon, or it would cause her serious harm. She had promised to teach this thing fear, and there was time enough for that.

Its doughy body started to tremble as it undulated its tentacles, turning in a tight circle. It had not grown any new limbs, so Aya stepped from the shadows and raked her claws over its body, leaving oozing gashes in her wake. The creature yelped in pain and surprise. It spun to try to see her, but she moved back into the shadows once more. When it finally spotted her with whatever senses it possessed, she was already fading into the darkness.

"Where are you?!" The creature screeched its shattered gravel scream.

Aya stepped from the shadows and cleaved away another piece of the Darkheart with her claws. She slashed at it over and over again until it lay quivering and mewling on the floor of the cave.

"Please, stop. No more feeling."

Its disgusting body shook with tremors of fear. When she stepped from the shadows for the final time, it flinched away from her in pure terror. Aya dispassionately lifted her paw and drew a Rune of Fire, which burst alight in lurid red. She sketched a circle around it, and it, too, filled with blinding red light.

"Return to this place and I will be waiting."

She pressed her paw against the Rune and shoved it toward the creature. It screeched and tried to writhe away, but was far too slow. The Rune floated forward for only a bare second. Aya turned away as it flared to incandescent brightness, and a blast of brilliant blue flame thick as a tree trunk flashed across the cave. When it disappeared, there was no sign that the creature had ever existed. The stone of the floor glowed bright orange where it had melted to slag.

Aya's rage had not cooled at all. It would never be enough to pay for all of those tiny bodies. She would keep her promise to the creature, and maybe one round, she could at least say she had done her best to make it enough. As she neared the Pathway that Ireana had left standing open, movement caught her attention. The illuminating magic left behind had almost faded as the energetic connection to Ireana thinned through the Pathway.

Skulking in the blackness to her left, she saw a figure. It was perfectly clear to her what she was seeing, and yet it was completely impossible. The figure was a horrific facsimile of a human being, decrepit beyond what Aya would have considered to be death. It appeared as if it were made of rubber stretched thin over a collection of sticks that had been assembled into a macabre parody of humanity. Its grey skin, if it could be called skin, was splotched in spots of black so deep that they appeared as holes through its substance into the darkness of deepest space.

It turned its head towards her, and even though the eyes were empty pits into the darkest abyss, she knew it was looking at her. Aya's paw flew in a blur, scribbling the First Word onto the air itself. She scrawled the embodiment of Fire onto the air, but before she could release it, the figure turned.

As soon as its back was to her, it was swallowed by the darkness. She did not stop. She knew without a doubt that the creature she had seen was the literal source of what had happened to every human being on the planet. She thrust her fist forward, slamming it into the Rune.

Fire.

It was unlike anything she had ever unleashed, even with the full might of the Heart of Fire at her disposal. A bar of blue-white as thick as her arm flashed across the room. It burned away the darkness, blinding her completely, and if not for the inherent protections granted by the First Word, it would have killed her, without a doubt.

When her vision cleared, there was a glowing hole melted through the far wall of the cave. She had no idea how far it went, and for a trembling moment, she considered that it might not have stopped at all. It might have gone straight through the world and shot out of the other side. A moment later, however, that vast store of knowledge that had been shoved into her head answered her question.

There were ways to calculate just how much power you were using when initiating magic using the First Word. There was a lot to the explanation that filled her mind, but what it boiled down to is that she hadn't gone quite so far as to put a hole in the world. This would have burned a hole a few hundred feet through the cave system. The information streaming into her brain went on to caution that if she was not careful, she could very well burn a hole through the entire planet. Aya shuddered, just thinking about whatever that thing had been. She turned and jumped through the Pathway.

Chapter 29

"SPEAKER"

Aya stumbled out into the small glade that bordered her living room and the Pathway snapped shut behind her. The air was filled with the whines, shouts, and crying of the cubs that they'd pulled out of that slaughter pit. When Ireana had almost quieted them all, Aya came over to join her. Ireana's ears folded back when she saw Aya's haunted expression.

"What happened?" Ireana resumed shushing and petting the cubs.

{Little Aya, can we assist you with these little ones?} Roan's voice in her head was a relief, and then Aya saw Kika the Lightmend standing off to one side. She held out her paw and Channeled Kika into her body.

{I would be overjoyed to accept help at this point. I do not have any idea what I am doing when it comes to healing with the First Word. They just need something to keep them pain free until their Spirits are able to settle back into their bodies properly,} Aya explained to Kika.

{Of course, Speaker. Simply touch each one, and I will provide the magic you need.}

Aya carefully brushed fingers through each cub's fur, Channeling Kika's spells out into the Wild. The cries fully subsided into sniffles. Aya sighed and turned towards the apartment, startling back when she nearly ran into another ta'el. Once she focused, she noticed it was a Spirit, a figure in a dark cloak that she recognized from earlier that round.

"Honored Ancestor, can I assist you?" Aya asked, a little astonished that he looked so close to being in the flesh. She had not given him any energy to stay in the Wild.

The Grey pulled back his hood, revealing soft, round features that Aya did not recognize as any species she had ever seen, round cheeks with downy grey fur and a short, powerful muzzle. A huge ruff of fur that looked akin to a lion's mane encircled his neck, though his features were clearly more canine than feline. Hanging from a thick, golden chain that emerged from his mane was an ornately carved sphere. His bright blue eyes flashed with internal light, and unlike most Spirits even here in the Wild, he retained what she assumed was his natural coloring. Stormy grey fur covered his body, yielding only to black on his fingers and toes.

It took her only a moment to realize he was a Mythic of some stripe. Something in the human Asian mythos, if the markings carved into the sphere were any indicator.

"I am simply here in my capacity as the first Speaker to inform you that you have completed your journey. You bear the mark of the Speaker, and I will be at your disposal as your teacher in using the First Word. Call on me when you have need." The Grey bowed, and then vanished back into the Spiritlands.

"Unceremonious much?" Aya half shouted and half giggled. She continued her shambling walk towards the doors leading into her living room. Ireana caught up to her a moment later.

"What happened?" she demanded with a little more concern.

"I saw something," Aya shivered. "Shouldn't you be watching the cubs?"

Ireana took her by the shoulders and turned her. All of the cubs had curled up in a huge pile and passed out. The night was warm enough that they would not suffer any ill effects from a night outdoors, and Aya's garden was more than enough protection to keep them safe.

"I don't think they have slept in a long time. Even the ones who did not receive the attentions of that thing are not physically well. Don't change the subject. What did you see?"

"Something. You wouldn't believe me if I told you," Aya said, and Ireana shook her head.

"I will not think you are mad, my heart, and I have been treated to vistas of things that will live in my nightmares for turns to come. This will be only one more."

"It was a human," Aya said.

Ireana did not seem shocked. Infact her eyes narrowed in deep thought. "Aya, there was something I forgot to tell you.

It didn't seem important at the time, but a human. I think it came from that place in Denver that you turned into a volcano."

"Why?" Aya asked.

"When Arno and I were clearing that floor I found some footprints, human footprints. They had been, melted, into the concrete." Ireana said, but her eyes went back and forth as if she were trying to remember something more.

"What is it?" Aya asked.

"Well, there was something more, but I didn't trust it at the time because we were rushed, and I didn't have Nobian to help me feel it out better. Still I got a sense that," Ireana trailed off, but she shrugged a minute later. "well it's not any weirder than you seeing a human. I got the sense that whatever had left those foot prints was still alive."

Aya nodded, then looked up to the sky. She thought for a long moment, then narrowed her eyes.

{Grey, I have questions,} Aya sent into the Spiritlands with annoyance. The Spirit appeared immediately. He must not have been joking when he said he was at her disposal.

"It was the human, wasn't it. The one who opened the way for the Netherspawn."

Her mind had been tearing at what she had seen, and it was the only logical conclusion. Only by magic could anything be made to live for over seven thousand turns.

"I do not know. I have never seen that… **thing** before. None of the other Speakers have either, to my knowledge, but I would reach the same conclusion, yes."

"Then the only reason it would show itself to me is because it knows that we have figured out what was done. It wouldn't have remained hidden for this long only to show itself now if something hadn't changed. That has to be it," Aya reasoned, but the Grey shook his head.

"Or he or she believes that they have found a way to finish what they started."

Aya nodded uncertainly. "It doesn't feel like that, though. That room with the doorways, and what Dedran said. We'll have to read what he found there, but that felt like a mistake.

Like they were trying to work their way towards an understanding of the First Word and just went too far, too fast for safety," Aya reasoned.

The Grey's black whiskers went up and down saying maybe she was right.

"Why were you so abrupt earlier?"

The Grey shrugged. "You're going to be buried in ceremony once the Hearth finds out you have come into your ability to use the First Word. Besides, a little humor in a situation like this is never a bad thing."

He looked over the resting cubs and then his eyes roamed up and down Aya's bloodstained body. Aya sighed. He wasn't wrong, and she smiled weakly. Then what he had said registered.

"Why is that?"

The Grey's muzzle split in a grin that in no way made Aya happy. "Because you're the leader of the Hearth now."

Aya's muzzle fell open, and she lifted a paw with a finger extended, but no sound came out. Then she turned away from him.

"Nope. Not happening."

The Grey's grin turned into a frown. "It's not exactly optional. You accepted the name of Speaker. You bear the Speaker's mark now."

"There is literally not a single chance, at all, that I am ever going to take the place of First Stone."

"Oh no, you wouldn't be First Stone. The First Stone is, and always has been, the aide to the Speaker, even when there is no Speaker. They do our job for us as well as possible when there is no Speaker, and they will continue to run the Hearth. They are simply doing so at your direction now."

"What's going to happen if there are no more Speakers? If we manage to close down the way for the Netherspawn," Aya began, but The Grey shook his head.

"No, Ayasha the Speaker. There will always be the need for the Speaker. There is no permanent way to guarantee the Netherspawn will never return. Even if one of us manages to undo whatever the humans have done to this world, and I'm

not sure that we can, there are still ways for the Netherspawn
to attack us."

Aya thought for a long moment, and then sighed.

"So, by solving the mystery of what happened to the
humans we could have, in theory, made the problem more
likely to happen?"

"Absolutely. There are no certainties in life, Ayasha the
Speaker." The Grey nodded, his shaggy mane swaying almost
comically with the movement of his head.

"This isn't over. That… whatever is left of a human is still
out there," Aya mumbled.

"And it is undoubtedly your job to stop it. To perform feats
such as those, you must have help. You must have the entire
Hearth at your disposal."

Aya's ears folded back and her shoulders slumped. Then
she looked up again, her ears pricked forward with curiosity.

"What do you mean I bear the mark of the Speaker?"

In answer, the Spirit pointed a thick finger at her right arm.
She lifted her arm, and there, marked into her fur in blue, grey,
and white, was a small diagram. The diagram was three
circles. A larger central circle had a Rune she had seen on the
Tributary inside of it, two stylized squares with their corners
overlapping. It glowed with impossible grey light. The two
other circles were smaller and formed the points of a triangle
with the first circle. A single line was drawn between each
small circle and the large one. The lines and circles themselves
gave off a blue-white color. The second symbol was three
overlapping circles and glowed with a bright indigo color.
The last symbol was an odd, twisted looking symbol that
vaguely resembled the human letter 'S'. Its soft, golden glow
seemed to make her feel warm while she looked at it.

"Before you ask, no, you cannot give this mark to someone
else using the First Word. Applying Runes of the First Word
to a living being permanently is an extremely complex and
delicate process. You are dozens of turns away from being
able to do such magic, and even if you could, this mark is
given only to the Speaker. Even if you could decipher the

intent that was used to create that mark, by its very nature, it cannot exist more than once in this reality."

Aya sighed. Ireana came up behind her, and put her arms around her neck.

"You can do it," Ireana whispered into her ear.

Aya shrugged a little. Her mind was churning with the thoughts of everything that had happened to her on her way to dawning the mantle of the Speaker. They settled on one singular thought, and her anger sprang up white hot again.

"I know I can do it. I don't know if I want to do it. I didn't imagine such a thing would be part of taking this name. I don't want to be responsible for sending others off to do dangerous things. Isn't it enough that I have to endure seeing these horrors? Isn't it enough to fight things that no one else can? I'm not going to complain about having to risk my own life to keep others safe. Isn't that enough for any Ta'el?!" Aya shouted the last sentence.

She shouted it with all of her Spirit behind it, sending the shout into the Spiritlands. She could sense the White before she appeared. This time, she chose to appear in the form of a pure white feline. A lioness, near to the same height as Aya. The White saw the anger and frustration. Aya pointed a finger at her.

"There were things you could have told me. You kept everyone in the dark. You let those cubs die all for what?" Aya snarled.

The White remained quite calm. "I sent you on the journey that any Speaker must take to truly understand what is at stake. You are given the power to shape the universe to your will in a way that is usually reserved for gods. I understand that you were only seeking to protect Ta'el, and you could have done that very well as a Hearth Stone. The world, though, would not have done very well without the power of the Speaker with what is to come."

"You want to ask more of me than you let on. Did you think you could manipulate me without consequences? I know that my father warned you against that in the little talk you had in my garden," Ayasha said.

The White's eyes widened just slightly, and Aya caught it.

"Yes, I know you spoke to him about my suitability for my name. It is <u>my</u> garden. I birthed the Spirits of those plants myself. Every blade of grass and leaf speaks to me, White. You should have seen that. I will never be manipulated into doing a thing that I do not think is right. I waited for you to help all this time, and you chose not to. I understood the need for the journey, but you could have done more to help speed me along without ruining it. Still, I tried to understand. I made no protests because I trusted that as our goddess, you must have your reasons. Even now, I know that is true, but there are no reasons equal to the task of answering for what I discovered those things doing to cubs!"

Aya began to shout again. "You are a Dragon! If you had put forth even the tiniest effort to speed me along, maybe more of those cubs would have made it out of that stinking pit. You never did. Even if you didn't know what I would find down there besides the Tributary, that was your choice, and you made it." Angry tears were spilling down Aya's cheeks, creating tracks through the blood and dirt coating her fur.

Aya's voice became cold, and hard as an ancient glacier. "So, I don't need you. I will be the Speaker, but I will do it without you. I can't make you leave me alone, but I will treat with you as do two hostile families who must work together to achieve a goal. Other than that, I don't ever want to see you again. You will be the only Spirit I have ever thought of as unwelcome in my home. That is what your machinations have brought you. Please leave my home and do not return."

The White looked taken aback, and The Grey's muzzle fell open. He stared wide-eyed at the White. The position of his ears and whiskers showed uncertainty. He wasn't sure how the White was going to react. Aya wasn't certain herself, but she was so angry about what had happened with the cubs that at that point, she really didn't care. The White took two steps back. In seven thousand turns, The Grey had never seen the expression on her face. Her ears fell, tail sagged, and whiskers pulled back in shame.

"I didn't know. Despite what you may think about my power, I didn't know about the cubs. I knew that you would find the Tributary in the Below Places, that it would cement you as the Speaker and open you up to the knowledge of the First Word. I knew there might be Netherspawn guarding it from you. They do that sometimes, but part of the Speaker's journey is fighting the Netherspawn." The White sounded unsure, which was also something that was not at all in character for her.

"I am, sorry, Ayasha the Speaker." The White said formally, and then turned to The Grey. "You will need to teach her in my stead, since I have made a fine mess of this situation." The Grey bowed his head in acknowledgement. The White actually looked pained as she began to fade back into the Spiritlands. "Thank you, Amyran."

"Of course, White."

The White vanished into the Spiritlands, and The Grey scowled at Aya.

"That was unwise and unfair, young one."

"You can go too if that is the way you feel, Honored Ancestor. She was wrong to do what she did. She is a goddess. She could have done better."

"None of us are perfect, not even The White."

"She <u>could</u> have done better," Aya repeated stubbornly, and The Grey, Amyran, sighed.

"You're not wrong, Ayasha, but you are not right, either. You have no idea what she has done for us, and if you think this is the worst thing you will not be fast enough to stop, think again. I suspect you will find that by the end of this single turn, no amount of effort on the part of the White can stop everything that goes wrong in our world, especially with regard to the Netherspawn.

I highly suggest that you find a way to forgive The White. I have known her for seven thousand turns. I have never known her to attempt to manipulate a Speaker. I don't think she purposely tried to do so."

"You were not joking about me being the new leader of the Hearth, Honored Ancestor?"

The Grey shook his head.

"And you can call me Amyran the Speaker, or simply Amyran. Too many ta'el know me as only The Grey."

"How long can I put off the Hearth?"

"Not long. Long enough to teach you the basics of what you need to know about using the First Word so you don't accidentally put a hole in the world with Lightfire or level a mountain with a Stonewave."

Aya turned away, pulling from Ireana's arms. "Scales, do I really need power like that?"

Amyran nodded, then hesitated. "It's not likely you'll ever need to use power on that scale, but the First Word is absolute. Yes, you need to have access to this power. The Netherspawn are a power outside of our reality. Channeling will not always be enough to combat them."

"We can train together. But first, we need to find out where these cubs reside," Ireana offered.

"Some of the things I need to teach Aya will help you get these cubs back where they belong," Amyran said.

"We'll get started in the morning," Aya said, and then resumed her shamble towards the sliding doors.

Glossary

Ta'el	Ta'el is the term used to refer to the species of anthropomorphic humanoids placed on earth by the Dragons, gods of this universe, to investigate what wiped the humans off the face of the planet. Their species are based in the animals, and mythical creatures with each Ta'el choosing an animal or mythical creature to be born of. The creature chosen has various effects on the size, personality, and in many cases even the available life paths for each Ta'el. Note that the ta'el tend to be a small folk with even largest of species topping out at six(6) feet in height, but most are between four(4) feet and five(5) feet tall when standing on two legs.
Bit	English equivalent of a second.
Bout	English equivalent of a minute. There are 80 Bits in a Bout.
Shift	English equivalent of an hour. 50 Bouts in a Shift.
Round	A day. There are 25 Shifts in a Round
Spell	One week. There are 10 Rounds in a Spell
Turn	A turn is the English equivalent to a year. It is about the same length of time, but it is not calculated quite the same way as Ta'el are not as attached to the day/night cycle as human beings are. There are 10 Stints in a Turn.
Ni-	This is a prefix modifier for any term for time. Added to the front of any time term it means next though it is most commonly used with Rounds. Niround is equivalent to tomorrow.
Pre-	Prefix modifier for any time term, though most commonly used with rounds it means the previous term. Preturn would be last year.

Round Names	Like on our Earth there are names for the days of the week. Each round is named for one of the first ten ta'el placed on the planet. As follows Mawen Taien Saowen Taylen Wayen Lanen Felen Offen Naten Naven
Emta'el	The more feminine of the personality identifiers for ta'el. There are no physical genders among the ta'el. Only a single physical characteristic that allows for personality identification. This is not an unbreakable rule, but it is an accepted assumption that if one of the Ta'el has human-like hair usually kept at least shoulder length or longer they have more feminine leanings, and are referred to as Emta'el. Most Emta'el have higher softer voices, but this is not always the case. Note: There are no differences between emta'el and ehta'el in physical prowess.

Ehta'el	The more masculine of the personality identifiers among the ta'el. There are no physical genders among the ta'el. Only a single physical character allows for personality identification. This is not an unbreakable rule but is an accepted assumption that if one of the ta'el has no human-like hair only fur on their head they are referred to as Ehta'el. Most Ehta'el have lower bass registers in their voices, but this is not always the case. Note: There are no differences between emta'el and ehta'el in physical prowess.
Greatfather	The masculine leaned term for any ehta'el that is one generation removed in the family line of the ta'el using the term. Equivalent: Grandfather
Greatmother	The feminine leaned term for any emta'el that is one generation removed in the family line of the ta'el using the term. Equivalent: Grandmother.
Spirits	Spirit is a blanket term used for any being that does not reside on the physical plane of existence. It can be used for Ta'el Ancestors, Elementals, or Source Elementals.
Builtstone	This is the ta'el term for human made stonelike materials used in buildings. Most generally used to refer to concrete.
"Scales!"	General exclamation of displeasure equivalent to shit, or fuck among humans. Referring to the idea of fallen Dragon scales which would indicate one of the gods could possibly be injured.
"the Seven Sides"	This is used as an exclamation of disbelief. Usually used in the form of "How in the Seven Sides?!" referring to the idea that the universe has seven parts each part ruled by one of the Dragons, the gods of the Ta'el.

"Fire and Forge!"	Another exclamation of disbelief, though can also be used as an expletive for pain. Similar to "son of a bitch!"
Bardo	The Bardo is a reference to time a spirit spends in the Spiritlands directly after their death, but before they are free to roam across the Spiritlands. While not much is known about this time, it is known that it is during this time when the Ancestor Spirits are given their mystical abilities. This is sourced from the time when the Ta'el were beginning their studies in both human languages, and the nature of their magic. They discovered the concept of the Bardo in their studies of Buddhism and applied the concept to their own language.

C.M. Brown has been writing about fantastical worlds since he finished his degree in computer science, and realized that the voices in his head were far more interesting than writing code. It finally occurred to him to try to sell some of these delusional thoughts.

His lair squats somewhere in the wilds of Upstate New York where he is harassed by one family, is trailed about by one rubber chew toy destruction engine, and contends with as many imaginary friends as his mind can conjure.